P9-BYV-753

BLUE

NOVELS BY ABIGAIL PADGETT

Child of Silence
Strawgirl
Turtle Baby
Moonbird Boy
The Dollmaker's Daughters
Blue

BLUE

Abigail Padgett

THE MYSTERIOUS PRESS

Published by Warner Books

A Time Warner Company

This book is a work of fiction. Names, characters, places and incidents are either the product of the author's imagination or are used fictitiously, and any resemblance to actual persons, living or dead, events, or locales is entirely coincidental.

Mysterious Press books are published by Warner Books, Inc., 1271 Avenue of the Americas, New York, NY 10020.

Visit our Web site at http://warnerbooks.com

A Time Warner Company

Printed in the United States of America

ISBN 0-89296-671-8

To Johanna

"Make an effort to remember. Or, failing that, invent."
Monique Wittig, *Les Guérillères*

Acknowledgments

To Norman R. Brown, the Friends of Dorothy Book Group, and Janice Steinberg for wading through manuscripts and politely rescuing me from unspeakable gaffes.

To Professor Marilyn J. Ireland, California Western School of Law, for advice on criminal procedure and for tracking down feminist ephemera on obscure Web sites.

To my agent, Sandra Dijkstra, for her epic enthusiasm and advocacy.

And to my editor, Sara Ann Freed, for steadily encouraging the creation of this book, five others, and everything else I want to do.

Chapter One

When I was ten years old my godmother announced through clouds of Marlboro smoke that I was definitely not an old soul. It was clear, she explained, that I carried no baggage from previous incarnations and therefore should be encouraged to explore life without the usual annoying constraints. After all, I was starting at zero and had a lot to learn.

But for those long-ago remarks I might not have been here in the middle of the California desert when the body was found. I might have restrained my personal anarchy and conformed. I might have been a regular person, probably an insurance agent in the Midwest. State Farm. It's unlikely that I would have been anywhere near Wren's Gulch, California, less than three weeks ago when something large wrapped in a heavy-duty lawn and leaf bag began to thaw in a public freezer only ten minutes from my pool.

Not that I knew what was there and thawing, of course. But I think of that package now, the frozen blood melting, a pale hand moving sluggishly in the dark. Imperceptible movements. Lifeless but significant, nonetheless. Sometimes I think of these small motions as a last warning, a danger signal I would have ignored in any event. At other times I just wonder what it felt like, trussing an adult human body tightly in the fetal position with lengths of clothesline. Then tucking it into a plastic bag and rolling it into a public frozen food locker. Weird.

It's been twenty-five years since my godmother, Carter Upchurch, found temporary enlightenment with a New Age group and cheerfully defined the nature of my soul. But I haven't forgotten. When Carter arrived at my childhood home that day for one of her visits with my mother, I had just created and then arranged for the dramatic kidnapping of an imaginary set of parents whose sole function was to supplant the jolly tedium of the real set, Elizabeth and Jake. I was between the fictional scenarios with which I entertained myself. And I was thrilled to hear Carter's summation of me as a daring seeker who would never be bored. A New Age baby soul. Perhaps a bit of a flake.

The concept stuck. Without it I clearly would have been somewhere other than here when Beatrice "Muffin" Crandall, a sixty-one-year-old widow, confessed on the day the body was discovered to bashing a stranger in the head with a paperweight five years in the past. Then, she told police, she stored the stranger in a public freezer for half a decade. I read the San Diego newspaper account of her crime with interest but failed to imagine that I might have a role in its consequences. This perfectly ordinary oversight pales in comparison to the succession of dangerously erroneous assumptions I would soon make.

The body was found after a minor earthquake rumbled beneath the desert floor near San Diego. The quake disarmed the automatic timer on the generator at a public food locker called Roadrunner Ice and Food Storage outside the little desert town of Borrego Springs, where I live. Or at least where I reside. Roadrunner's proprietor, a retired high school chemistry teacher with a lust for blackjack, was in Las Vegas when the temblor occurred. The temperature in Borrego Springs that day hovered around a hundred and fifteen. Nowhere near a record for the last week of August. Nothing unusual. Except at the locker.

I'm convinced that Brontë and I were swimming in the motel pool when the timer failed and everything in the Roadrunner began to thaw. I like to troll images of things past for those moments in which cosmic inevitability becomes for the first time completely obvious. I'm a social psychologist, so this hobby isn't as weird as it sounds, although I am. I choose to believe that Brontë and I were swimming on that day less than two weeks ago when a man thawed inside a lawn and leaf bag and slumped against the locker door. We were undoubtedly still by the pool when the backcountry sheriff's department arrived in Borrego Springs to assign the body its fictitious name, "Jose Doe." The Spanish-American takeoff on "John Doe" never failed to make me think of square dancing.

I choose to remember that Brontë looked rather dashing then in the teal green life jacket that enables her to stay in the pool long after her lean Doberman legs have tired of dog-paddling. Human memory is quite selective, and I tend to select images in which things look dashing.

Certainly we were playing catch in the pool that day with a sodden orange tennis ball that might have been a small sun bursting through blue chlorine spray. Eventually I'll assign a title and music to this picture, a soundtrack. Sun/Woman/Dog. Mozart, probably. But for now there is only silence echoing brilliant light on water. That was the moment in which a process began that would force me to remember a woman named Misha Deland, even though I'd just spent two years successfully forgetting her.

Social psychology is the academic discipline in which I earned the dubious right to call myself "Dr.," but my business card says merely "B. McCarron, Consulting." The "B" stands for Blue, the only first name I've used since leaving Waterloo, Illinois, for college at eighteen. Names like "Blue" do not inspire confidence in businesspeople, however. Hence the more acceptable "B."

My increasingly adequate income is derived from advising retailers, mostly male, about the social psychology of women. The retailers are not aware that their wives and daughters could tell them exactly the same things that I tell them, without my exorbitant fees. They are also not aware that even shopping may be traced to its roots in primate behavior. To a man they have not read my book, an academic press release of my doctoral dissertation, which was roundly trashed as retro-Darwinian by postmodernists at the time of its publication. Postmodernists really hate the fact that males and females are innately different, and I agree that the concept is scarcely groundbreaking, merely supportable. Nevertheless, my book remains the answer to gangs, rape, drugs, teen pregnancy, and political imperialism, if only the right people would read it. Which is not to say that no one reads it. At least one man did.

My book, *Ape,* is responsible for my involvement in the Muffin Crandall case. Somebody read it. Then he showed up beside my pool on the first day in September, a Wednesday, two days after the body was found, displaying straight white teeth and hands that remind people of statues they saw when they were children. Big, out-of-proportion hands with no cuticles at the base of nails like shovels. I was, as usual, nude in the pool. And Brontë lost no time snarling her way up the net ladder I'd secured for her in a corner of the deep end.

Significantly, Brontë came to Misha and me four years ago after her owner, very drunk at his thirteenth birthday party, dressed the dog in his older sister's underwear and sprayed beer foam on her. Finally, she nipped him. That same night the boy's father, who had provided the lads with a case of brew and three of his milder porn videos as a birthday treat, drove the Doberman to a twenty-four-hour emergency animal clinic in San Diego. He explained that the dog had savagely attacked a child engaged in what he regarded as normal boyish hijinks. The father paid the euthanasia fee in cash.

But a clinic night attendant, an acquaintance of Misha's from one of the multitude of feminist groups invited to meet in our apartment, phoned at two in the morning begging that we drive into the city and rescue the Doberman before a lull in emergency room traffic permitted the on-duty vet enough time to load and discharge a syringe. That's how Brontë came to live with us, later with me. Not unreasonably, the scent of testosterone enrages her.

"Brontë, *stay!*" I bellowed as the man executed an impressive scramble to the top of the eight-foot chain link fence I installed around the pool to prevent its use as a watering hole by the larger desert fauna. The smaller fauna I net from the filter baffle each morning, waterlogged or dead. Limp mice, lizards, the occasional snake. These serve as a constant reminder that I don't really belong here any more than the pool does, but I love the solitude and the truth is, where else would I go? A tribute to careful training, Brontë froze at my command, forelegs flat on the pool decking, hindlegs paddling against the net ladder. But I could feel her ongoing snarl like a current that raised the invisible pelt of hair all over my body.

"I've read your goddamn book," the man yelled from atop my fence. "I want to hire you." Sullen, he said no more and looked away as I climbed the shallow-end steps and pulled on the shorts and T-shirt I'd tossed on a chaise loungue. Dressing while dripping wet in the presence of strange men is always awkward, and old habits die hard. I remembered the smoke-enshrouded Carter Upchurch as I stashed my panties and bra under a bright blue chaise cushion. In addition to the knowledge that I was a new soul, Carty impressed upon my juvenile brain the concept that men should never see female undergarments except those designed as erotic props. This injunction applied also, Carty noted, to the eyes of my twin brother, David, who is now called "Hammer" and won't see another brassiere until the Missouri State Parole Board releases him from a razor wire cage full of people noteworthy for their lack of breasts.

Any clinical psychologist would surmise correctly that David is the reason for my research into human behavior as it breaks down by gender. We're *twins* for God's sake. Same parents, same house, food, church, and school. But David is a public menace and I'm not. Who wouldn't be curious?

"Hire me to do what?" I inquired after helping Brontë from the pool and instructing her to sit. Competently, she managed the predictable canine flapping and spraying of water from a seated position. The electric snarl became a rumble of small tympanies, but her eyes never left the man on the fence.

"A job," he replied with an economy of presentation I would later understand was simply his style. At the moment it seemed insufficient.

"I guess you didn't notice the sequence of no trespassing signs, the locked gate across the only access to my property, and the Doberman in the pool," I pointed out. "If this were a hiring hall you'd have seen a coffee pot and a framed black-and-white glossy of Jimmy Hoffa. Either get the hell out of here or I say a word that frees this dog from the constraints of civilization while I dash inside to get into something more comfortable. Like the shoulder holster hanging on the other side of that door."

I tipped my head in the general direction of all twelve doors anonymously facing the pool. There was nothing behind nine of them but bare cement floor and unpainted drywall. "In the holster is a loaded Glock nine millimeter," I added. I didn't mention the old single-shot bolt-action .22 rifle that was also in there somewhere. It was one of a matched set given David and me on our ninth birthday by our father, Father Jake McCarron. An ordained priest in the Episcopal Church, dad nonetheless had and has a regrettable fondness for things that go bang.

David carried the concept a step further, beginning with convenience stores and ending with a St. Louis bank. The *St. Louis Post Dispatch* said that during the attempted robbery my brother shot holes in two Tiffany glass panels, a plaster frieze depicting scenes from St. Louis's early fur trade, and an enormous Made-in-Taiwan vase holding silk frangipani and bleached ostrich feathers. Men, for reasons explained in *Ape,* are sometimes made uneasy by large floral arrangements.

The man on my fence was being made uneasy by gravity. Baseball-sized biceps were straining to hold what looked like about a hundred and sixty-five pounds at the level of the horizon, while his heavy boots clanged uselessly against the chain link. Men in California, even the bikers and desert rats, do not wear boots like that. Their feet would rot off in a week, drowned in sweat. Men in California also don't wear wool plaid Pendleton shirts with the sleeves rolled up over waffle-weave long johns. Southern California's deserts still claim inferno status in late summer, at least during the day. It was becoming clear that Fenceman had dropped in from somewhere north of Seattle, at least. He reminded me of a poem dad adores and frequently struggles to work into sermons. It's about Alaska. "The Cremation of Sam McGee."

"There are strange things done in the midnight sun
By the men who moil for gold," I yelled at the man atop my fence.
"The Arctic trails have their secret tales
That would make your blood run cold . . ."

David and I could recite the entire thing from memory by the time we were five.

"If your name's Blue McCarron I've got to talk to you," he said, thin lips whitening beneath a handlebar mustache that draped his teeth.

"Who wrote the poem?" I demanded, expecting nothing.

"Robert W. Service. Will you hold that damn dog or not?"

"Get down," I answered. "Brontë, *stay.*"

Much nonsense can be made of coincidence that is merely coincidental. But there's another kind that feels like a typhoon in your bones and lets you imagine that the sky behind your right ear has just opened to reveal a hidden pattern. *The* hidden pattern. You jerk your head around and it's already gone. But it was *there,* and the certainty falls on and through you like a breath, like that first scent of autumn you feel in your soul. That happened to me when the man on my fence named an obscure poet he shouldn't have known. It was a message.

The improbable circumstances and eerie sense of connection created by his pronunciation of the poet's name provided a jolt I'd been waiting for. And the world may be divided into two camps—those who know precisely how this works and those for whom such a connection sounds like nonsense. You either get it or you don't.

"What's your name?" I asked as he dropped the last three feet from the fence and hit hard, dark blue eyes registering pain. He knew the poem's author and that meant I really was on the grid again. I was really alive and not just an entity marking time alone in a half-built, bankrupt desert motel until some poisonous snake, earthquake, or disease took my body to the great beige nothing I saw every night in an absence of dreams. I had feared for two years that "I," whatever that is, had already died. But after he answered my question I could feel again my own movement on the roaring, warp-speed grid of universal intention. And my first whole thought was to tell Misha. My second whole thought was that I couldn't. Misha was gone.

"Dan Crandall," he answered, wiping sweat with a thumb knuckle from bushy dark brown eyebrows that didn't match either his auburn mustache or the wiry mouse-tan hair he wore long and pulled back in a ponytail with one of those neon pink elastic bands little girls purchase at drugstores. He had left the pink plastic ball attached to the elastic band. "I'm Beatrice Crandall's brother. She's confessed to killing a man and freezing him like leftover pot roast. She didn't do it."

"The body in the freezer over on State Road Three," I said. He didn't look old enough to have a sixty-one-year-old sister, but these things happen. An aging couple with grown children discovers one day that the wife is barfing every morning. Plans for the Winnebago are canceled. Additional life insurance is taken out. My guess was that little Danny Crandall had been just such a golden-years surprise to parents whose daughter, Muffin, was already pushing thirty when he was born.

"Yeah, the body in the freezer."

"Why did she confess if she didn't do it?"

The sun had already dried my grown-out, top-bleached brown shag to the consistency of hay, and Brontë was panting. We don't just stand around in the heat out here, especially those of us covered with black fur. Or wool shirts.

"How would *I* know?" He sighed and gazed at the sky like a man who has just missed a plane. "Women."

In that single word was the entire thesis of my seven-hundred-and-thirty-two-page dissertation. An admission of boredom, hostility, and paralyzing despair. Like many men, Dan Crandall did not like or understand women, including a sister who had recently confessed to murder. But the dumb fascination with which he'd first observed my naked female body in the pool signaled the fact that he had not escaped the usual male primate wiring either. Still, it was clear that the gross biology of Dan Crandall had been socialized to acceptable lines. He had come to help this much older sister with whom he had not shared a childhood and probably barely knew, recognizing the bond of clan. The significance of this was not lost to me.

Until I quit teaching at San Gabriel University a year ago in order to consult with shopping mall designers, I insisted that my Intro to Social Psych 301 students understand this—that the clan bond was the first step out of preconscious, instinctual soup for every species. Including, I told them, that species which pulls weeds for twenty years in blazing hot strawberry fields so that its young may study social psychology at San Gabriel University. And the bond of clan is each individual's last defense against the slide back into brute muck. While it is primitive and flawed and not to be worshiped, it must at all costs be respected.

I was still searching for a way to respect my clan bond with David, whom I loathed as much as I loved Misha. And both were, for very different reasons, totally inaccessible. There was, as *The Book of Common Prayer* so bluntly puts it, no health in me. Nothing but black holes, head to toe. Until a short man who looked like Yosemite Sam climbed my fence, knew a poem, and hated his sister for being a woman but showed up anyway because she was family.

"Strip and get in the pool," I told Dan Crandall, observing a desert etiquette which demands the sharing of water. Any water. "It'll take me about ten minutes to make a pitcher of lemonade. Have your pants on when I get back."

In the kitchenette of the motel office I turned on the CD player to drown the air-conditioner whine, and squeezed lemons into a gallon plastic pitcher as Brontë lapped bottled water from a red ceramic mixing bowl. One of the several reasons I was able to buy an entire motel for the price of a single DKNY outfit is that the Wren's Gulch Inn has no piped-in water. That is, the pipes are there, but they're empty. And they'll stay that way until the settlement of a dispute initiated by the four remaining Indians on a tiny reservation everybody had forgotten existed until the Indians opposed a plan which would have extended water utilities to Wren's Gulch through a few feet of reservation property. The youngest of the Indians is seventy-eight, but his lawyer is only twenty-nine. In the desert, people understand the value of simply waiting.

Meanwhile, I had the water for the pool trucked in at enormous expense, and every week another truck arrives to refill my modest water tank, also at enormous expense. The Indians could do nothing about the buried power and phone lines the owner, Cameron Wrenner, ran two miles in here from the main line on the road before abandoning the motel project to whatever fate his attorneys could arrange. It could scarcely have mattered to Wrenner, whose empire of used-car dealerships had made him one of the richest men in Southern California. It isn't possible to live here without a car, and Wrenner's ruddy face, topped by a white cowboy hat, smiles down from billboard ads from here to the Nevada border. Anyway, Wren's Gulch, as the locals named this fiasco, has lights, music, and a state-of-the-art computer with a modem that allows me to chat with other weirdos all over the world whenever I feel like it, which isn't often.

"Coming out!" I yelled through the blue Mylar film I'd painstakingly glued to the office picture window after the sun ate leprous patches out of the original cheap carpet in less than three months. After that I installed a sand-colored indoor-outdoor nylon Berber in the office and the first unit, which serves as my bedroom. Then I plastered up this blue stuff which is supposed to filter ultraviolet rays and keep the sun from burning away the molecules which comprise carpets, drapes, and upholstery. The effect is like living in a furnished aquarium.

Dan Crandall was hopping around beside the pool, trying to pull gray knit boxer shorts over a penis that looked tired in its nest of jet black pubic hair. It occurred to me that nothing growing naturally on Dan Crandall matched.

There's an interesting study which suggests that women who have not been sexually assaulted score higher on tests of empathy for men after seeing pictures of naked men doing ordinary things like talking on the phone or grocery shopping. In interviews the women often admit to finding flaccid penises rather cute. Sort of like demitasse spoons or those little carved wooden fork sets from import stores that everybody gets as a wedding present from an aunt who wears jangling bracelets. Nobody ever knows what to do with these forks. And I'm one of those women who find penises cute despite the fact that the great love of my life is a woman. Or was. It had been two years since I had any definitive evidence that Misha Deland was still alive.

"I'm entirely tied up right now with a marketing research project, and I have no experience whatever in the legal-criminal field," I lied, setting the tray on a cable spool I found at a dump and painted bright blue to match the chaise cushions. "Your trip out here has been a waste of time."

Crandall failed one test when he poured himself a tumbler of lemonade while leaving mine empty, but passed the next with flair.

"The so-so lawyer I hired bills around a hundred-fifty an hour," he said while wringing water out of his ponytail onto my foot. "I can pay you the same up to ten, maybe fifteen thousand."

"Expenses?"

"Within reason. You'll have to clear with me first."

"What is it you think I can do?"

His dark blue eyes regarded me with the same interest people lavish on old movie tickets found in jacket pockets. "Save my damn sister's ass," he said.

Miles beyond the baking sky a black-silver grid flashed for a nanosecond and then wasn't there, had never been there. Its ten billion dillion bars and lines and filaments, each crossing each at curving right angles, was only a fairy tale. I had made it up myself.

"Call it God, call it Harriet," Dad told David and me in our backyard in Waterloo. "Doesn't matter what you call it. It's there and the only choice you have is to hang on for the ride or sit it out on the sidelines."

I was a kid at the time and decided to call it Snoopy. Now, at thirty-five, I just called it the grid because that's what it felt like. And I was tired of the sidelines.

"Deal," I told Dan Crandall. "You can leave a thousand-dollar retainer and fax me everything you've got tonight. I assume your sister's being held in Las Colinas?"

The women's prison in a suburb of San Diego had been named either "The Hills" or "The Cabbage Seeds," depending on translation. The notion of being confined in a cabbage seed struck me as mythical, even charming.

"Yes," Dan Crandall answered with distaste while pulling a slim checkbook out of the right pocket of his wool shirt.

"How am I supposed to get in to see her?"

"I'll tell the lawyer to fix it. Maybe you could analyze her and give him a report. He'll set it up."

"Crandall, my field is *social* psychology, not clinical. I don't analyze people. Are you sure you know what you're hiring here?"

"Talk to her," he insisted. "Just do that, okay?"

The check, drawn on a bank in Anchorage, Alaska, fluttered happily beside the lemonade.

"Okay," I answered, but the answer was more general than the question. I meant that I'd think about it while I wondered what it was he expected me to do.

In seconds he'd pulled on his socks and those platypus-foot boots, stuffed the rest of his clothes under an arm and walked away in the direction of the locked gate where I assumed he'd left whatever vehicle brought him out here.

"Misha," I whispered into yellow-gray afternoon light, "a man in his underwear is leaving, but I'm back."

It was the first time I'd spoken to her in two years.

Later I got on the Net to find out what you wear while visiting a women's prison. A retired cop in a Quaker chat room typed, "When visiting any prison you have to wear a bra, carry nothing that could be used as a weapon, and avoid dangling earrings in pierced ears. She might grab 'em and rip your lobes in half."

When the moon rose like the edge of a spoon over my bowl of broken rocks, I was pawing through storage boxes behind the third of my twelve doors, looking for the tiny lapis earrings that had been my mother's. They had gold posts. Muffin Crandall would have a hard time ripping them out of my ears.

Chapter Two

When the phone rang at five the next morning, Brontë snarled irritably from the foot of my bed. I knew that if I gave the attack signal she'd tear the phone out of the wall. It was tempting.

"Everything's set for you to visit my sister at nine-thirty, phone ten," Dan Crandall's voice announced. "It'll take them at least a half hour to bring her to the visiting area, so be there by eight-forty-five or it won't work. You'll be allowed ten or fifteen minutes this time, maybe more later, maybe not."

"Phone ten?" I pronounced thickly.

"Yeah. The lawyer told me there's a row of phones. You talk through plexiglass. They assign you a time and a phone. You'll talk to her on phone ten."

This set of instructions seemed unnecessarily concise for five A.M.

"Have you been to see your sister, Dan?"

"No."

"So why are you doing all this?"

His sigh was more resigned than hostile. Like the sigh of somebody who's been teaching introductory classes for too long. My kind of sigh.

"Just go talk to her. Incidentally, she won't want to talk to you. Have you read the stuff I faxed?"

"Oddly, I don't sleep with my fax machine," I said, trying for a confessional tone. "There are others like me."

"Ha," he answered. "Call me when you've got some ideas."

After leaving the number of a bayfront hotel in San Diego, Crandall hung up and I faced the rest of my life. At the moment it looked like one of those seventeenth-century Dutch paintings meant to emphasize the transitory nature of being. Wilted cabbage roses on a table with two dead birds and a snail. Except there are no snails in the desert, and my still life would be called *Rumpled Sheets with Black Dog and Large Human Foot.* Brontë had stretched happily across the width of my queen-size bed and was eyeing one outstretched paw as if contemplating a new shade of nail polish. The large foot was mine.

David and I are, for obvious reasons, fraternal rather than identical twins. He inherited dad's stocky frame and run-of-the-mill feet. I got our mother's gangly height, topaz eyes, and feet for which the term "extended sizes" was coined. Fortunately mom maintained a competent wardrobe. I was appropriately shod in her size ten double E black kid pumps for the all-stops-out funeral at St. Louis's Anglican bastion, Christ Church Cathedral. A drunk driver had plowed head-on into her car as she left a meeting of the Sierra Club. My brother and I were thirteen.

Misha theorized that David began his transformation into a sleazebag criminal named Hammer when our mother died. But then Misha never met mom *or* David, and for some reason couldn't envision the relentlessly pleasant childhood that David and I enjoyed. I did describe this childhood to her. Often I marveled at odd details which, I thought, pointed to the day I would meet her. But either Misha's own childhood, which had apparently been Faulknerian, or more likely her complete disinterest in narratives not involving the Flight of a Strong Woman from the Clutches of Patriarchy, rendered my stories meaningless. I remained strangely blind to Misha's complete lack of interest in the details of my life for two years. Love, as they say, is like that.

Only after she'd been gone an entire year did it dawn on me that Misha, whose feminist concern for the most insignificant forms of female life rivaled that of God for sparrows, probably couldn't have identified my hometown or remembered my mother's name on a bet. For a while that made me feel funny, as if for the years I spent with her my own history had been lost in the mail. Pieces of it were still drifting in as I went outside with Brontë for her morning run.

"David hasn't killed anybody," I announced to a lone cottonwood that was probably there when the first stagecoach stopped to water horses at Coyote Creek. "But there will be similarities between his story and this woman's. Criminology kinds of things. After all, they're both in prison."

As Brontë chased a black-tailed jackrabbit I recognized a certain flimsiness in this train of thought. I know a great deal about male primate proclivities, which, if not controlled, result in truly idiotic violence. But there was no precedent for what Muffin Crandall had done, or said she'd done, in the chemistry and subsequent social organization of female primates. Girl apes, as the song says, just wanna have fun. And babies. Although in the human ape the former urge usually dies almost overnight around thirty. That's when estrogen levels begin to drop and the brain looks around, wondering where it's been since fifth grade and where all these *children* came from. Females primates rarely kill except when defending their young or, more rarely, themselves. And the "self" being defended in the case of female humans is a more complicated entity than the mere physical body.

Muffin Crandall, I remembered, was sixty-one. Fifty-six when a man about whom I knew nothing was packed into a deep-freeze with sharks, tuna, doves, and mule deer. Muffin had been past prime for menopause with its rotten reputation at the time of the slaughter. Still, she might have been one of the late ones, one of the small, chagrined army of fifty-something women who secretly dread they'll have to be buried with a feminine hygiene product. I threw rocks at a spindly ocotillo shrub and thought about that until Brontë loped back over the low hill which forms the eastern boundary of the gulch.

To my knowledge, the female chemical transition away from fertility and into wisdom had not been used successfully as the defense strategy in a murder case. Despite the Victorian mystique it still wears in some quarters, I was sure menopause could not cause women to start killing random strangers with paperweights on their way to the freezer. In my experience all it caused them to do was have parties.

As Brontë snuffled and growled at a kangaroo rat hole under a creosote bush, I thought about one of those parties and about the feminist icon, Eden Snow. The mythic author Eden Snow, resplendent on the only occasion that I'd actually seen her. The occasion after which nobody saw her again, or at least that was the story. Eden Snow more than four years ago, already well past sixty but ageless in that way peculiar to celebrity.

She had come to San Diego to give a lecture, to be the big draw for a symposium on Contemporary Feminism sponsored by the Women's Studies Department of San Diego's largest university. After the lecture there was a party at somebody's house. Among Snow's credentials were an impressive array of degrees, ten increasingly radical books of feminist theory, fluency in five languages, and the respect of women the world over. Despite those credentials I didn't hear a single word Eden Snow said that night.

I had gone to the lecture and then the party with Misha, whom I knew in her capacity as program director for the Inter-Collegiate Women's Studies Consortium. That is, I knew she arranged meetings and seemed to be everywhere. She also knew everybody, including everybody on the faculty at San Gabriel University where I was teaching. With her wiry body and strangely compelling eyes, she always made me think of the Little Match Girl. That bathos. Put her in rags on a street corner, and within eight hours she could raise enough money to fund a respectable day care center for a year. Actually, she had been a fund-raiser for some now-defunct runaway kids' shelter before taking over the consortium directorship. I didn't trust her.

There was, despite my mistrust, a jittery attraction between us that in her company brought a taste of hot metal to my throat and made it impossible for me to be near common household objects without harming myself or them. That night I had already splintered a chair rung and tripped over a perfectly flat expanse of carpet. Misha had spilled white wine into a toaster. We seemed to be riding some foreordained conclusion about to happen with or without our complicity. And it would happen that night. I did remember that. I do remember that.

By two A.M. the party had thinned to drying wheels of cheese, sesame-seed cracker crumbs, and fifteen or twenty women in turtlenecks drinking chardonnay from plastic cups near a stereo. All night the background music had been foreign to me. Unfamiliar women's movement music Misha explained was from before my time. Misha, ten years my senior, suddenly the only thing I saw in the stale, winey air.

Most of the others made a circle around Eden Snow, who sat in a wingback chair looking exultant as they belted out "Song of the Soul" for the third time. Snow's wiry gray hair was tied back with a rumpled scarf, and she watched everything from lashless blue eyes that were at once brutally intelligent and too big. I remember that she was wearing beach thongs with a pair of baggy jeans and a silk kimono jacket so exquisitely designed most people would have framed it in an entry hall. From time to time she chewed thoughtfully on the kimono's sash.

The women surrounding her were tenured professors, authors, attorneys, directors of grant programs pulling eighty thousand a year in addition to whatever they picked up on the speakers' circuit. They were remembering dark childhoods in which little girls were forbidden such futures.

One of the lawyers strummed chords on a guitar, and two women I didn't know ran outside to their car to get balalaikas, they said. The tape ran out, and somebody found an oldies station on the radio in time for the opening "sho-dote-en-sho-be-doe" of the Five Satins' "In the Still of the Night." The song prompted the second most memorable event of the evening. A sing-along with the radio.

Teenagers in the fifties, they remembered, they stood, and they sang. Perfectly. They sang to Eden Snow in four-chord harmony of feminism, of a time beloved and lost, its ghost alive again in that moment among them. A bunch of drunk, middle-aged women singing old doo-wop, or a choir in transcendent celebration of an idea, you choose. I was in tears by the time Misha and I went outside alone. Into the backyard, in the dark.

By then there was nothing else to do, nothing left but the inevitable. I am certain that neither of us would have chosen anything quite as overwhelming if we'd been asked. But we weren't asked. We were simply drawn toward some huge intention whose purposes demanded a connection between us so deep and fierce that I realized even then, my mouth on Misha's hungrily on mine, that I might not survive it. I didn't care.

Later there was some stumbling, urgent progress to a shed. Bags of peat moss and potting soil. A sense of there being no time left to do this. No time at all. The suddenly pointless yet stubborn presence of clothes, buttons, zippers. The impossible necessity of touch, the pounding vortex of orgasm. And all the while, over Misha's ragged breathing and mine, the sound of balalaikas reaching out into the dark.

Much later, sometime the following morning, it would cross my mind that Misha was a woman and so this sexual cataclysm meant I could safely sneer at all further accusations of affectional ambivalence. I hadn't been sure what the fuss was about either way. Now I was sure. Totally.

Misha would scarcely make the A list of potential romantic partners, but I was unmoved by such distinctions. Prone to disguising a Southern accent under fake "Hahvahd" pronunciations and telling people she grew up in Wellesley, Misha was the object of more than one raised eyebrow. Deland wasn't her name, but that of a teenage husband long divorced, she said. Her real surname, she told various people at various times, was Carruthers. Or Hancock. Or McAdams. Names noteworthy for nothing so much as their presumed proximity to the *Mayflower.* Despite her ambiguous identity she wanted nothing so much as to be widely known, preferably admired. Misha never missed a meeting she could chair, and kept a Rolodex the size of the Manhattan Yellow Pages. She wasn't exactly a social climber, needing instead to be known by literally everybody. But none of it mattered to me. It would never matter.

What mattered was dad's response when I called to tell him I was really in love at last and with a woman. It had always been an option. Misha was not the first woman I'd made love with, just the first lover I'd been flung to infinity with. Dissolved with. Transformed with. All that. Dad didn't bat an eye until I told him about the balalaikas, about the unfathomable *intent* in me and Misha that seemed to come from somewhere else and have an agenda of its own. Then his voice broke and he whispered, "Oh, my God," in tones trailing history, and secrets. Because of Misha I would eventually hear the story of my own existence, and be shocked. Later I would begin to know two people named Jake and Elizabeth, who had dealt with balalaikas of their own.

Brontë interrupted this train of thought by getting a half

dozen fire ants up her nose, requiring my immediate attention. I was already hot even though I was wearing nothing but shorts and a pair of ratty tennis shoes. The Muffin Crandall investigation, I decided, would be a test of my ability to return to the real world. The World Before Misha. A world in which people do not run around racked by dead love affairs and inadequately clothed.

I was not brought up to walk dogs without first putting on a shirt. In fact, our two-story frame house in Waterloo was a veritable monument to those ordinary proprieties which make society possible. Dad was the rector at a little church called simply Grace, and our mother zealously cultivated at least the appearance of successful housewifery. David never noticed, but I'd often find mom poring over women's magazines, her high, tanned brow knit in concentration. Sometimes she jotted things in a small spiral notebook. Then, a few days later, we'd face the "Festive Ukrainian Borscht Compote" at dinner. Or we'd come home from school to find the front porch sagging under the weight of twenty-six pink geranium plants in wicker laundry baskets lined with calico. On these days there would be homemade cookies and dad would read aloud from old children's books about Abraham Lincoln or Clara Barton.

My parents sighed with relief at each successfully completed domestic vignette, each family outing and holiday. David and I were watched by glowing eyes that increased in wattage every time we succeeded, failed, or were merely average at anything. Our parents were terrified, but we didn't know it. What David and I learned from them was that every humdrum event unshattered by primal forces is cause for celebration. But we would find out about the primal forces later. Both of us. I pondered the fact that Muffin Crandall had obviously stumbled over them as well.

In my office/living room, actually the intended reception area for Wren's Gulch Inn, faxed documents lay in untidy loops of paper on the floor beneath the fax machine. After feeding Brontë I tore them into manageable segments and sat down to read.

Beatrice Crandall, I learned, had shortly after the earthquake confessed to assaulting the man in the Roadrunner freezer. In a prepared statement distributed by her attorney, she admitted to hitting an intruder in her garage over the head with a paper-weight on a Sunday night during July five years ago.

She awoke, she said, around eleven that night to the sound of her garage door opening. At first she thought it was an electronic glitch of some kind. Probably the door responding to a neighbor's battery-operated door-opener. After all, the garage of her condo opened into an alley shared with fifteen other units, which meant fifteen identical automatic garage doors with identical electronic openers. But after she heard the door close there was a sound of someone "mucking around down here." The garage, she said, was directly beneath her second-story bedroom. The windows were open because the night was warm. She could hear the intruder through both floor and windows.

Still, she wasn't overly alarmed. "I thought there was some reasonable explanation," she said. "Maybe a neighbor borrowing a ladder. I have a nice lightweight aluminum ladder that people are always borrowing. Of course nobody would do that, break into my garage in the middle of the night to get the ladder without asking me, but that's what I thought when I was walking down the stairs. What I really thought was maybe he'd had too much to drink. I have a neighbor who drinks a lot at night. Everybody knows. You can't hide much, living so close together. I really just thought it was probably him and that he'd be embarrassed and go away when he saw that he'd got me out of bed."

On her way through the darkened living room, Crandall had grabbed a paperweight from her desk "just in case." She hadn't really intended to use the object as a weapon, the narrative went on. There were plenty of knives in the kitchen if she'd been thinking about a weapon. She just wanted something in her hand when she opened the kitchen door to the garage. Something heavy. She didn't really know why.

But what she saw when she opened her kitchen door wasn't her tipsy neighbor. It was a stranger. "A dirty, evil-looking man with his back to me," she said, was pawing through some storage boxes containing items which had belonged to her deceased husband. "It didn't make any sense, it was horrible," she stated. "This disgusting *creature* touching Deck's things there in the dark. He was squatting on the floor like . . . like an animal, opening those boxes. He was sickening, somehow. And then his face turned toward me and in the light from the kitchen I saw his hand reach toward one of the rocks I'd been collecting for a little rock garden on my patio. The rocks were stacked along the wall. I saw this look in his eyes, saw what he was going to do with that rock. He was going to hit me. I could tell. He was going to kill me!"

According to Crandall's statement the subsequent events were a blur. "I hit him with the paperweight. I'm pretty sure I did that just as he turned back toward my little pile of rocks and started to stand up. It all happened so fast. I was so frightened. I knew he was going to kill me if I didn't stop him, but I didn't really have any idea of what I was doing."

Crandall went on to say that she did not own a gun. Her deceased husband, Roscoe "Deck" Decker, had told her that a gun is liable to be seized by an attacker and used against the victim. "In a surprise attack," he told her, "you won't be able to find and fire the gun before he sees what you're doing and grabs it." Prior to his death, Crandall's husband had disposed of his own gun collection for her protection. And even if there had been a gun in the house, she explained, she wouldn't have thought to get it before entering the garage. She hadn't expected any of this. It was just some kind of nightmare.

When the man toppled over and didn't get up, she thought he was faking. She thought that as soon as she moved, he'd spring up, roaring. She said she stopped breathing. She said she lost control of her bladder standing there, frozen with terror in the slice of light from her kitchen door. But the man didn't move. Finally she kicked his shoulder. When he didn't respond, she forced herself to feel his neck for a pulse. There was none. She knew he was dead.

I poured another cup of coffee and made a few notes. So far the woman's story seemed implausible yet very familiar. It was every woman's nightmare, the reason women fear noises in the dark. Rape, defilement, brutal death. This is the repetitive mantra bequeathed to us from hairy ancestors, cousins to chimps, gorillas, and humans. A glance at any chimp enclave, with the exception of the matriarchal bonobos, will reveal the source of the nightmare. Male chimps randomly batter females to ensure wholesale female subordination. And when she's in estrus a female who refuses sexual penetration by a male may be beaten to death by him as his companion males hoot and whistle and hop about. A glance at any newspaper will reveal that the nightmare has not been extinguished in human enclaves, either.

It's not hard to trace the primate archetype. It's there. But humans are different from other primates in numerous ways. One of them is that the human female, unlike her chimpanzee sister, is not statistically likely to be bludgeoned and raped by a gang of strangers creeping across the landscape beyond her dwelling. That popular terror is the shadow of our past, although it can and does still happen. More often now, the human female will be bludgeoned, raped, and possibly killed by a male who is no stranger. A male she knows and may even like. A male who believes that he must control her, that he owns her.

Muffin Crandall's story with its rock-wielding monkey ghost played to the old brain. I wondered whether she knew that. Then

I wondered how she'd explain the heavy-duty trash bag and the years that had elapsed since that night in her garage.

"I don't know why I did what I did then," Crandall's statement went on. "It was like I was in a trance or hypnotized. I don't remember thinking anything except 'Nobody can know. You've got to hide the body. Nobody can find out or you'll die!' "

The remark brought me up short. I dreamed once that I had killed a man and hidden his body in a little-used closet beneath the stairs of an old house I shared with four other graduate students. The man looked strangely like Beethoven. And the dream bore that certainty of *not* being a dream, of being an absolute reality somewhere other than the waking state. I sat up drenched in sweat and locked in such agonizing fear that ten digital minutes traveled through my bedside clock before I could move. And there was a slurred chirping in my head, like a distant siren. I knew the sound meant the body would be found and I would be killed.

Muffin's words echoed my dream, which I later learned is a common delusion in women at a certain stage in the progression of Alzheimer's and other dementias. A terror of being put to death for killing a man may lie encoded in every female brain. It may be released by the neural plaques and tangles of brain disease or the nightly neurological housecleaning which results in dreams. Muffin Crandall's narrative began to assume a particularly interesting framework. If it was the fabrication her brother believed it to be, it was brilliantly done.

"I tied him up with part of the clothesline I have in the garage for drying rugs and things I don't want to put in the dryer," her story went on. "I still wasn't really sure he was dead, but even if he was I wanted him tied up. Somehow I knew I had to get rid of the body right away or I'd die. Don't ask me how I knew that, or where the thought came from. I just knew that."

Crandall's story went on to describe her various approaches to removing the body. Getting it into the kitchen would be no problem, but cutting it up seemed too disgusting. Besides, the garbage disposal could not be employed out of fear that its excessive use at that hour would attract the attention of neighbors, or that "something would get stuck" and require a repairman.

Deck Decker had been a sportsman prior to his death at fifty-three from a massive heart attack two years before his widow's encounter with a stranger in her garage. He maintained the rented locker near Borrego Springs for game he killed and stored for home use. At the time of his death the locker was only partially stocked. Muffin Crandall said she kept up the rental fees and made regular trips to the locker, both using the game left by her husband and restocking the space with bulk-buy bargains and gifts of fish and meat from her husband's friends. She said she was used to making trips to the locker, and the idea of freezing the body "just seemed natural."

Long before sunset that day five years in the past, she had trussed the body in a fetal position, gotten it into a trash bag, and transported it to the Roadrunner cold storage facility. Muffin said she may have spoken to friends on the phone that day, but she didn't remember. She said that no one was present at Roadrunner when she used the freezer's hand cart to stash the new package behind boxes containing eighty pounds of chicken wings she'd purchased for a civic theater fund-raising picnic. She said the only thing she remembers from that day is terror, but after leaving the freezer, "it was as if none of it had really happened."

"When I'd try to think about it, think about taking that bag out and getting rid of it someplace, the fear would come back," she said. "It would just fill me up like black, cold ink in a bottle. My hands would shake and I'd want to throw up. I couldn't even walk, it would be so bad. So I just kept paying rent on the locker and going out there with stuff, taking stuff out to use. I knew someday I'd have to do something, but I just couldn't think about it."

Putting the rest of the faxed materials aside, I turned on the computer and opened a new file. "Crandall, Muffin—Initial Profile," I centered in fourteen-point type. Then I typed a list of factors which seemed, even at this point, potentially significant.

1. Subject a fifty-six-year-old widow at time of the assault, uses her own surname rather than her husband's.

2. Subject apparently living alone at time of assault, but maintains frozen food locker for bulk quantities of food. Why?

3. Subject does not mention children, friends, or family other than her deceased husband. Odd. Women typically refer to social cohorts in all narratives.

4. Subject displays a thorough comprehension of archetypal primate female fear in her narrative, leaving out no element but rape. Nowhere does she admit to fearing rape, only murder. This deletion from the usual fear profile is significant.

5. What was weight and physical condition of subject five years ago? Now?

6. What is estimated weight and physical condition of victim at time of assault?

7. Subject presents as self-sufficient and capable, yet permits herself to be called "Muffin." Check origin of this nickname.

8. Subject mentions that bulk chicken wings in her locker were for a civic theater fund-raiser. What civic theater? How was she connected to it? Who else was connected to it? Does it still exist?

9. Subject's deceased husband, Deck. Who was he, what did he do, what was the marriage like, and how did she cope with his death? Children of this marriage? Previous marriages?

10. What was/is her source of income? Education? Avocation?

After printing the list I took a cool bath, washed the woody, acorn-brown growth I call hair, and phoned for a haircut appointment near the prison at eight. My best gray linen suit with its long, straight skirt would make me look like an Edwardian nun, but that was okay. What wasn't okay was that the only matching shoes I could find were the same black kid pumps I'd worn to my mother's funeral twenty-two years in the past. Good shoes will last a lifetime if you take care of them, especially if you only wear them while in disguise. I wondered if Muffin Crandall would buy the act I was about to stage for her.

Chapter Three

As prisons go, Las Colinas is not unpleasant, at least from the outside. There are no coils of razor wire, no guard towers. There are no kennels of baying hounds waiting to track some hard-eyed woman in unflattering horizontal stripes through thickets and ravines. There are no thickets and ravines. Las Colinas is smack in the middle of a suburban San Diego community called Santee. The town is home to feed stores and barbecue restaurants where country and western bands play on weekends. And while my professional interests had skirted the field of penology, it wasn't difficult to draw a few conclusions about the prison from what I already knew.

Women are fond of enclosed spaces. A by-now-infamous study suggested that while boys are prone to build towers with toy blocks, girls build elaborate enclosures, giving special attention to the decoration and security of entrances. Indeed, a classic Renaissance motif symbolizing the Mother of God was a walled garden. And Las Colinas, while scarcely meeting the aesthetic requirements of the term "garden," looked to me less like a prison than a typical Southern California elementary school. Several single-story buildings, painted an institutional tan, clustered about a chain-linked central open area in which I could see a couple of picnic tables.

The few truly dangerous women confined here would be in

some special, high-security area, I guessed. But the preponderance of the women prisoners could be safely contained with minimal provisions for security. They would display here the same impoverished identities that had led them to the prostitution, drug dealing, or accessory status to a boyfriend's crime that had captured the attention of the police in the first place.

A very small statistical minority, the female criminal takes up less than five percent of the nation's cell space and almost none of its razor wire. With certain exceptions such as the rare sociopath and those with untreated psychiatric problems, women offenders are not difficult to control. Even as children female humans easily comprehend the larger social consequences of theft, battery, and murder, and as adults rarely engage in these activities. Those who do, know themselves to be compromised in a much more devastating sense than their male counterparts. The fall is different, farther, and has broken them long before they wind up in prison. As I completed my "Visitor's Request to See Prisoner" card I contemplated methodologies for learning the truth about the sequence of events that had landed Muffin Crandall in this sad and sterile place. Even then I suspected that the task might be over my head.

"Sit in there at phone ten," a blonde woman directed from the prison reception area. She wore a badge saying "Corrections Trainee," and was tucking a stray tail of her tan shirt into olive green wool-blend slacks that made me think of Boy Scout uniforms. I noticed that she carried a walkie-talkie but no sidearm, and looked as if she'd just arrived from a Junior League recruiting tea. That aura of cheerful wealth and privilege.

It seemed odd that she'd seek employment as a prison guard. I decided that she must be doing undercover research for some liberal foundation that would later publish a report decrying the poor prenatal care given pregnant prisoners or something. The fantasy explanation restored my sense of social congruence, as we social psych types are prone to say. It forced something puzzling to make sense.

"Your client's in B Unit, so it'll take a while," she explained, smiling. "More security there. You know."

I nodded, wondering in what sense Muffin Crandall was my "client" and why she needed more security. There had been nothing in the portion of paperwork I'd had time to read to suggest that in prison Crandall would do anything more dangerous than weave potholders out of cut-up socks. There had been no indication of prior criminal activity, not even a traffic ticket. So far, Muffin Crandall's profile was an epic of law-abiding conformity so devoid of suspicious behavior that I should immediately have been suspicious. Nobody who drives can go ten years without so much as a parking ticket unless there's a very good reason. Not wanting to come to the attention of police, for example. Unfortunately, this obvious concept had not yet crossed my mind.

The room with the phones was just off the reception area and a monument to sensory deprivation. Just a long, blah-colored room with a wall down the middle. In the wall were nineteen numbered plexiglass windows with phones on each side. Mismatched plastic chairs were fastened to the floor in rows facing the windows from both sides.

When the door to the reception area clicked shut behind me I felt something constrict in my chest. Walled gardens notwithstanding, I knew then why I've been so scrupulous about not robbing convenience stores at gunpoint. The reality that someone else was empowered to unlock or *not* to unlock that door tightened my ribs like a vise against my lungs. There wasn't a single picture on the wall, not even a months-old copy of *Good Housekeeping* to read. When a woman in blue pants and a blue shirt with "San Diego Jail" stenciled over the pocket was brought to the chair across from mine twenty minutes later, the hair on my neck was slick with sweat and I knocked the phone off its ledge when I grabbed for it.

"Christ in the foothills!" she rumbled in a gravelly voice. "You look like warmed-over swan shit. Don't tell me you've never been inside a prison before."

"Okay, I won't tell you," I said too loudly into the phone. "My name's Blue McCarron. Your brother thinks you're innocent."

The eyes watching me from behind bifocals in expensive alloy frames were the same dark blue as Dan Crandall's. Unlike Dan's, however, these eyes were circled with thick coverup that couldn't cover enough. Muffin Crandall looked twenty years older than I'd expected. The flesh over her facial bones seemed unable to support its own weight and hung in folds. Yellowish skin tones suggested a fading tan that had once been deep. Perched above her ears was a synthetic auburn wig, permanently set in tubular rows. I could see the cheesecloth wig cap between each auburn tube. The cap wasn't particularly clean. Wisps of dull gray hair jutted stiffly from its perimeter. Muffin Crandall looked like a poster for a very noir version of *Annie.*

"My brother doesn't know his ass from the Holy Grail," she growled. "And I don't care who you are or what he's paying you to do, it won't work. I have a lawyer who'll say I'm insane. That may work. I probably am insane. Nobody sane freezes people like stew meat."

She lowered pale orange lids over her brother's eyes and half smiled, revealing perfect teeth behind lipstick in a shade worn by peroxided exotic dancers in Germany at the beginning of the Cold War. A particularly ghastly purplish red. I knew this because I'd read an illustrated history of Barbie dolls and their origins in Teutonic pornography, not that the information was of any merit in deciphering Muffin Crandall. Then she opened her mouth again.

"Let's just say I've 'eaten on the insane root that takes the reason prisoner,' " she pronounced in rolling tones. I could see the tones vibrating in the plexiglass window between us.

And that's what did it. The line was from Shakespeare, I was sure. Probably *Macbeth.* And Muffin Crandall was acting. The wig, the grotesque makeup, the tough talk. All an act. I remembered that she'd had something to do with a civic theater.

"Great voice, but you can cut the act now," I said. "Your brother's not paying me to critique a performance."

"Cut the act?" she answered, a real smile animating the folds of her face. "If all the world's a stage, where do we go when we're *not* acting?"

In that moment, in an airless room built to obstruct all but the most superficial human interaction, I became Muffin Crandall's friend. I liked her. I recognized in her a kindred spirit, a person whose grip on the truly important questions remained unweakened by minor tribulations like dirty wigs and prison. Behind me the grid snapped and sizzled, leaving a scent of ozone in the air. It meant I was supposed to be there.

"We only have ten or fifteen minutes," I told her. "How did you get the prison authorities to let you keep that wig?"

"I told them it holds my brains in and that without it I forget where I'm supposed to go to the bathroom. Fear-of-potty is the great American phobia, you know."

"I know; I'm a social psychologist. But why do you want to wear a dirty Shirley Temple wig?"

"Because it holds my brains in and without it I forget—"

"Never mind," I interrupted. "Why are you called 'Muffin'?"

"I thought it sounded better with 'Crandall' than 'Cupcake.' " She sighed, managing to suggest that the decision had been a difficult one. I could feel the minutes ticking by inside my watch as I got nowhere.

"You're not used to interviewing people, are you?" she asked after a long silence.

"No," I answered. "Usually I just interview data."

"What have you learned?"

"Oh, you know," I hedged, wondering what gem of social science might push her off balance, "stuff about the effect of annual rainfall on Iowa voting patterns, ethnic demography among jockeys, profiles of murders committed by women, the usual."

"And?"

"And there are a lot more black and Latino jockeys than you'd think."

Muffin Crandall laughed. Actually it was a rumbling guffaw that made her eyes twinkle but seemed to tire her.

"So my brother wants you to say that the murder I committed five years ago isn't like the typical profile for murders committed by women five years ago? What is the typical profile?"

"Well—" I sighed as if reciting something everybody already knew—"for starters the victims of female murderers are typically husbands/boyfriends, or children, or least often strangers killed in the commission of felonies orchestrated by husbands/boyfriends."

"No lone women defending themselves from attacks by strangers?"

"Doesn't happen," I stated with authority because, in actuality, it doesn't happen.

"Never?"

"Never."

"Why not?"

"Because women are by nature passive and silly," I lied, expecting to be struck by lightning. "Despite all evidence to the contrary, we assume a sweet smile will defuse danger. We're simpering wimps. We don't defend ourselves."

Through Muffin's telephone I could hear a radio on the

guard's desk on her side of the plexiglass wall. An oldies station. I could swear the station was playing "In the Still of the Night," and in the music I imagined an army led by Eden Snow bearing down on me, shouting the names of a million women who fought bravely to the death. Misha would be in that army. *I* would be in that army despite the calculated stupidity of my most recent words. I had said them because I needed to know whether Muffin Crandall would be in that army.

Her sallow cheeks bloomed a dull cranberry color as she cocked her head and bellowed, "You fucking idiot! Get out of here!"

Muffin's outburst caused the guard to stand and scowl near her desk, but I had won.

Women tend to fall into three categories when exposed to demeaning remarks about women: those who start throwing the furniture around, those whose upper incisors draw blood as they bite their lower lips but say nothing, and those who seem not to have heard. Muffin Crandall's response was diminished only by the fact that all available furniture was bolted to the floor. And I had learned more about her than she wanted me to know.

"If you'd actually killed that man, you'd never admit it," I said as she stood to leave. "If you'd really killed him there would have been a good reason. You would have covered your tracks. You would *not* have stashed the body in a public freezer for five years. It's too stupid, and you're not stupid. Your story doesn't work."

I stood when she did so I could measure her against myself for height. I'm five six, and she was at least an inch and a half taller. Big-boned, although her hands weren't as overlarge as her brother's. She had a competent, self-assured posture even in prison denims. I concluded that Muffin probably could have killed a stranger in her garage five years ago, but that she probably didn't. Or if she did, the story she now told to account for her actions was not the truth. Not even remotely.

Slowly she sat down again and picked up her phone. I copied each move, my gaze locked on those dark blue retinas.

"Kid," she pronounced, "why don't you just go back to predicting the number of cow pies in Arkansas after a lunar eclipse? Stop wasting my brother's money. You don't know what you're doing, and that makes you an epic pain in the ass, *capisce?*"

"Capisce," I agreed. At thirty-five it's nice being called "kid."

"And you're right," I went on. "I don't know what I'm doing and only accepted Dan's offer because I've recently decided to make lots of money. God only knows why. There's nothing I want to buy. Nevertheless, I know enough to have concluded that your story about the body in the Roadrunner freezer isn't true. I have no idea what to do next."

"Jesus," Muffin Crandall said. It was not a prayer.

"Probably I'll prepare a report. On legal-sized paper, no staples."

"That will be nice," she murmured sweetly. "Then you can give it to your psychiatrist, who will know what to do."

The guard had looked at her watch and was moving toward Muffin.

"You've given me an idea," I said. "Very helpful."

"That was not my intent," Muffin Crandall mentioned over a sagging shoulder as she was led away.

The door to the reception area was opened by the same chipper guard-in-training who'd locked me in. She continued to strike me as a debutante who'd accidentally wandered into a Marine boot camp, again tucking her tan shirt into those ugly uniform pants. The tucking created a sense of déjà vu that made me question whether I'd actually talked to Muffin yet at all. The presence of another woman in the visiting area lobby confirmed the passage of time. I was sure she hadn't been there when I arrived. And I would have noticed.

I would have noticed because of the basket. She was an older woman with white curls framing a carefully made-up face. She wore a pastel blue shirtwaist dress accented by a flowered scarf used as a belt. And she carried a large basket lined with blue and white checked napkins. There was a blue ribbon on the basket's handle. Nestled within the napkins was a mound of cookies. They filled the prison lobby with a mouthwatering scent that immediately derailed my train of thought, whatever it had been. All that remained were two words—"chocolate chip." My trains of thought are easily derailed by any olfactory experience of chocolate chip cookies.

"Mrs. Tewalt," the guard said politely, "we've explained to you and your friends several times that you may not bring gifts to a prisoner. We cannot take these cookies to Mrs. Crandall as we could not take her the sandwiches, cake, and jug of lemonade you brought two days ago. You can bring her white socks and underwear, shoes that cost less than fifty dollars, and personal toiletries from the approved list. Would you like another copy of that list?"

"Oh, no, dear," the woman said. "But why don't I just leave these cookies for you and the other ladies who're looking after our Muffin. I assure you they're freshly baked and not one of them has a file in it!

"This sort of work must be very hard for you," she said to the guard as an afterthought, a sympathetic frown wrinkling her peaches-and-cream brow.

The debutante guard caved in. Anyone would.

"Here, have a cookie," she said to me after accepting a basket any American over twenty could immediately recognize as Red Riding Hood's.

"Um, I'll just take an extra one for my dog," I agreed. "She's out in my car.

"In the parking lot," I added as if there were some chance I'd left my car in a tree. Militaristic uniforms, even on toll booth operators and debutantes, cause me to attempt truly concise levels of explanation. I don't know why.

The woman named Tewalt gasped. "In your car! Oh dear, it's so hot out there. You know, leaving an animal in a closed car can be—"

"It's actually a truck with a camper shell," I explained, heading for the door with the Tewalt woman in fluttering pursuit. "And it isn't closed. The back is open, it's parked in shade, Brontë has water and a battery-powered fan covered in mesh screening so she can't stick her nose in it, and did I hear you say you brought these cookies for Muffin Crandall? I just saw her."

"Well, for heaven's sake!" Mrs. Tewalt said. "Are you with the police?"

"I'm a social psychologist. Mrs. Crandall's brother, Dan, has asked for my help."

As we reached the door the blonde guard called, "Please, Mrs. Tewalt, don't bother coming again except during official visiting hours, and please no more food."

"Of course, dear." The reply was not sincere.

"I'm Helen Tewalt, an old friend of Muffin's," she told me in the parking lot, averting her eyes to the ground for her second remark. "This has been terribly upsetting for her friends, you know. We're all afraid it could happen to us."

"You're all afraid you'll kill somebody and then store the body in a freezer?" I blurted.

"The, well . . . *mental* situation is what I meant," she said softly. "Muffin just fell apart after Deck died. That was her husband, you know. She never got over it, started doing such odd things. Now we're afraid it's Alzheimer's or something like that. If only we'd seen the signs long ago."

Her sigh joined the warm breeze blowing eucalyptus leaves across the paved parking lot. I could see Brontë's sleek head eagerly tracking my progress toward the camper. No doubt she'd already picked up the scent of the remaining chocolate chip cookie in my hand.

"What odd things did Muffin Crandall do?" I asked casually.

"Well, just lots of things, for heaven's sake. Keeping that food locker in the desert like Deck did when he was alive. We told her it was silly, but she wanted to keep everything just the way it was. She didn't even clean out his closet for months, just kept his clothes there instead of donating them to charity. That's the thing, you know, just donate to charity and try to get on with your life. That's what we do. But Muffin wouldn't let go. We should have seen there was a mental problem."

I should have seen that Helen Tewalt had just told me absolutely nothing, but I wasn't used to real people with their charming duplicity. Numbers, graphs, hard data—these I can deal with. Real people are so sweet and complicated that I'm almost always mesmerized by them. I forget to stand back and check to see if what they're telling me meshes with the big picture. Later I would realize that Helen Tewalt actually meshed way too well.

"Here's my card," I told her. "Would you mind if I called you at some point? There are so many things about this case that I can't quite grasp."

"Of course, dear." She smiled. "I'm in the book. In Rancho Almas. H. Tewalt. Any of Muffin's friends will be happy to talk to the psychologist who's trying to analyze this awful thing. Just call anytime."

"I'm not a clinical psychologist and I don't analyze . . ." I began. But Helen Tewalt had veered off toward a cream-colored Buick, snapping up the door lock with a little remote control on her key chain. She merely waved as she slipped inside and started the engine.

"Why do I feel as if I've just walked through the set for a Martha Stewart special?" I asked Brontë when I got to the camper and gave the command that she could run free. The cookie held more interest for her than my question. But I knew somebody else I could ask, even though I'd have to wait until seven that night when Auntie Buck's Country and Western Bistro cleared its hardwood floor for line-dancing lessons. I'd be there. I had a lot of questions.

Chapter Four

But first I had to make a living. It was, after all, Thursday. Tuesdays and Thursdays are devoted to accumulating wealth, although as I told Muffin Crandall, I don't know why I'm accumulating it. Nor is it wealth, exactly. More like what is meant when people say "comfortable." As in "Well, I wouldn't say the Kramers are rich, but they're comfortable." This comment is invariably accompanied by a meaningful look which suggests that the Kramers could buy and sell your grandmother if they wanted to. My wealth might be defined as a category of comfort several levels below that one. Many, many levels below, actually.

My truck is paid for and has four new tires. I own Wren's Gulch Inn outright, and can afford the hauled-in water necessary to live there. Brontë and I both have the best medical insurance coverage available in California, which isn't saying much, and except on Tuesdays and Thursdays neither of us really needs clothes. Still, when a year ago a Pakistani strip mall owner at a party bet me a semester's salary that I couldn't rescue his investment from bankruptcy, I jumped at the chance. The job would be fun, I thought. But the real draw was the lure of income derived from an application of my skill as a social psychologist. Income not requiring panty hose, faculty politics, or a cheery attitude.

The little mall was in a dicey, ethnically mixed area of San Diego. The owner assumed that nothing could be done about the sequential armed robberies, drug dealing, and shoplifting that were driving out his commercial tenants. Had he not downed too many margaritas by the time *I* had downed too many margaritas, he would not have responded as enthusiastically to my assertion that men do not, in fact cannot, understand shopping and its context.

I did tell him that with the exception of guns, automobile parts, and beer, between eighty and ninety percent of over-the-counter sales are to women. Women are the purchasers of goods and services. If you want a successful shopping mall, make sure women like to go there. That part is not complicated.

Where men lose it completely is in understanding the aesthetic, social, even spiritual dimensions of shopping. They think—you need an item, you buy it, you leave. A man who needs a plumber's wrench will buy the wrench from the back of a van, a dusty hardware store, or a mail-order catalogue. He doesn't care as long as he gets the wrench. He will make this transaction alone and will not discuss it with other men. Should another man later criticize the wrench, suggest that there are better wrenches, the first man will become defensive. There is no social context for the wrench, so an assault against it is an assault on the man. It is an assault on his competence, his status. In the presence of other variables such as alcohol consumption, this kind of thing can result in headlines the next day which read, "Local Man Murdered in Dispute Over Wrench."

What I didn't try to explain to the strip mall owner is that women are entirely different. Women nest, which is just a cute way of saying that women construct social reality. The sight, scent, sound, touch, and taste of life is the construction of women, and the work is never done. Variety is necessary to keep things interesting, has been since our hunter-gatherer days. Getting tired of leached acorns? Try these nettles boiled in salt water. Maddened by your bland little cubicle at work? I know this place where they have silk plants really cheap. Shopping is for women the sacrament of reality construction. And it is not done alone.

It is done in the company of other women so that all aspects of the construction may be performed at once. Fabric for bathroom curtains is selected as you discuss what to do about your brother-in-law's alcoholism. When somebody later suggests that the curtains don't quite pick up the blue in the floor tile, you know the curtains are just fine because that idiot Ben finally got himself into a treatment program like you suggested and hasn't had a drink in four months. When Ben falls off the wagon a year from now you'll change the curtains. And go on. It's an intricate tapestry, endlessly woven, ripped apart, altered, rewoven. Most men are completely oblivious to it. Certainly the Pakistani strip mall owner was.

But he gave me carte blanche to do anything I wanted, and I knew what to do. First I analyzed the demographics of the neighborhood and concluded that less than seven percent of the local women who might patronize the mall's remaining dry cleaner, convenience store, beauty salon, and Vietnamese take-out restaurant had access to cars. A twenty-four-hour surveillance of the parking lot revealed that it was rarely used except at night when local males bought beer at the convenience store and sat on their cars drinking it until they were ready to pass out or get in fights over whose wrench was the biggest. It was clear that the parking lot had to be reclaimed for the true purpose of the mall—shopping. Shopping in the sense of constructing life.

First I had a low cement block wall built around the lot, which claimed the space from the street. Then it and all the mall shop facades were painted a pale mauve, just pink enough to identify the structure's function as essentially feminine without deterring entrance by individual males on legitimate business. An extension of the wall into the parking lot created a small courtyard adjacent to the convenience store and beauty salon. A place for talking. This area was covered during the day by a roll-out awning for shade over conversational groupings of green plastic chairs around small tables. A number of flowering plants on casters completed the experiment. The plants, furniture, and awning were removed and stored in one of the empty shops at five o'clock each day.

There were a few disasters at first, involving trash left in the courtyard, competing music from the beauty salon (black) and the take-out restaurant (Asian) and several attempts by warring gangs of adolescent males to claim the courtyard for afternoon beer drinking and drug deals. The latter problem was addressed by a combination of classical music blasted alternately from the salon and restaurant, and some serious pressure on the convenience store owner to stop selling beer to minors. The alternative involved his explaining the practice to an Alcoholic Beverage Control agent whose name and number were taped to the window of each storefront, facing out. But it wasn't enough.

Incidentally, I don't know why adolescent males in gangs hate classical music, but they do. It actually seems to hurt them. My own research into primate behavior involves a time before there *was* music, so I can add nothing to the puzzle. Except that gangs are probably a regression to male primate social organization, and the complexity of the music reminds them that they're supposed to have evolved. I remember wondering at the time why David, who played French horn in our high school band, had become a criminal. David liked classical music. But then David was never in a gang. Until now.

That first mall conversion was eventually so successful that the owner began touting my services to his friends, all of whom seemed to own and lease retail property. I got gigs planning layouts for lingerie departments and security for sidewalk sales. A Japanese-run convenience store chain put me on retainer just to determine from store diagrams the optimal placement of feminine personal items. (Across from canned goods in an aisle which does not lead to the beer cooler.) I began to accumulate money. When I realized that the thousands in my savings account were at a number more than half my age, it felt sort of good. Nothing like holding Misha, feeling her birdlike heart, but good. We take what we can get.

Still, the project should never have worked. There were too many problems in the area. Charles Dickens named them—poverty, ignorance, disease. Even the life-building spirit of women is broken by these. But I found a secret weapon. When I tacked up an announcement for a part-time minimum wage job "managing" the mall at a community center up the street, the ad was answered by a large black woman in a conservative business suit. Her hair was in about a hundred and fifty looped braids woven with tortoiseshell beads. She wore cowboy boots. The beads made a pleasant clacking sound as she threw her substantial frame into a chair in the mall courtyard.

"Rox Bouchie," she introduced herself, carefully pronouncing her surname "Boo-she" so I'd get it. It would have helped if she'd given the same attention to her first name, which I thought was "Rocks" for the initial half hour of our acquaintance. I also thought she was either the director of the community center or a social worker as she questioned me about my work at the mall. When I explained that the part-time job I'd advertised would involve keeping the courtyard area clean and alerting the police about drug deals and illegal drinking, she lowered gold-shadowed lids over coffee-brown eyes and shook her head. The beads rattled. She just said, "Girl . . ."

The way black women say "girl" can be magical. Frankly, I have no solid beliefs about the survival of consciousness after physical death. But if it's going to happen I know what I want to see after my trek toward the light. I want to see a black woman who will smile and say, "Girl . . ."

The word's resonance is utterly female, the opening syllable of a story that will explain what's really going on. It says, "You don't have a clue, but I'm going to give you the inside scoop." The sound is hypnotic, like an audio version of that top-of-the-Ferris-wheel moment just before the downward rush. At that moment after my death I would like to be told exactly what the universe is, and why. I would like to see the *point.* And in my fantasy the story will begin with that word on the tongue of a black woman.

"Um, do you know of anyone, a woman from the neighborhood preferably, who might be interested in—"

"No," she interrupted. "Nobody in this neighborhood is that dumb. The job you're offering is suicide. But I like the way your mind works. I might be able to help."

A client of hers, she said, was looking for a small storefront in which to open a used-clothing boutique. Skilled with sewing machine and serger, he enjoyed redesigning clothes. He also created wall hangings and fabric art. For six months' free rent against a year's lease on one of the empty storefronts, he might be willing to clean the courtyard and police the mall.

"He sounds promising," I said. "Why don't you run the idea by him, and I'll talk to the mall's owner. But why would he want the job if it's so dangerous?"

"He learned to sew in prison and can handle anything that drifts in here," Rox Bouchie said, watching for my reaction. "Got a problem with hiring ex-cons?"

"My twin brother's in prison. In Missouri."

I felt that the response established my credentials as a savvy, street-wise person. The twin sister of an incarcerated felon. Way cool.

"How often do you get back to the Midwest to see your brother?" Rox asked while frowning at something stuck to the bottom of her left boot.

"Um, actually I haven't had a chance to visit him, uh, there," I answered, giving similar attention to the removal of a shipping label from the table leg.

"I see."

So much for cool. And the finesse with which Rox Bouchie unmasked my distance from David should have suggested that I was dealing with a pro in the unmasking field, but it didn't. I was too ashamed of what I'd just said to notice.

"What's this guy's name?" I asked, changing the subject.

"BB. BB the Punk."

"Uh, strange name."

Rox shook her head again, slowly. The beads made a sound like acorns falling on dry ground as I noticed a smattering of freckles over her broad nose.

"His real name is Bernard Berryman. Do you know what 'punk' means in prison?"

I sensed that I was already a million points behind. Why lie?

"Probably not," I said. "So just tell me."

"It means 'turned out,' as in 'whore.' It means being beaten close to death, repeatedly gang-raped, permitted to remain alive only in the role of slave to a group of predators or, if you're lucky, to one 'daddy' who protects you from the others. It's done to the young, the weak, the naive. BB has a flair for the dramatic. He saved his life by getting into the role. He got out of prison two months ago. He'll never get out of the role."

David had been twenty-eight when he went to prison. Was that young? And had he been weak and naive? I felt a crippling wave of nausea. A need to run away.

"Girl, you're turning green," Rox Bouchie pointed out. "Never seen anybody so homophobic."

"I'm not homophobic," I yelled at her and an additional hundred yards of mean street. "I'm ready to puke!" Anger was displacing the nausea, which felt better. Later it would occur to me that Rox had called me homophobic to make me angry. She had done it deliberately to distract me from my fears about my brother. She had been kind.

"Sorry," she said, rising and throwing a business card on the table. "Think about it and give me a call."

When she was gone I looked at the card. It said, "Roxanne D. Bouchie, M.D., Forensic Psychiatry, Donovan State Prison." I had been talking to a psychiatrist. A forensic psychiatrist. Now I can see the mark of the grid all over that encounter. I can see the shove at my shoulder blades. But I wasn't ready to hop back on the ride. Not yet. Because I'd be hopping back on alone. Thinking about David alone. And I would have to remember Misha. No way. I ignored it.

I did arrange for BB the Punk's management position at the mall, however. And his shop, Death Row, took off. When not creating stylish outfits for the mannequin in his shop window, he patrolled the mall in dreadlocks, missing nothing that went on. He wore a prison denim costume with "Needle Freak" stenciled across the back of his blue chambray workshirt. He kept an enormous, curved carpet needle hooked through a front pocket. And nobody messed with BB. Everybody assumed that he had nothing left to lose. My project, and my future, were secure.

So secure that close to a year later on the day of my first interview with Muffin Crandall, I had three jobs going at once. The first was the Crandall Case, and the second involved nothing more than picking up some data for analysis from a failing vegetarian restaurant in a mall where nothing else was failing but a shop specializing in silver gifts and tableware. I could have told the silver owner to give it up and move back east, if asked. No charge. Silver tableware just doesn't work in Southern California, probably because the region lacks both an entrenched aristocracy and cold nights. If a sterling compote can't point to seven generations who've lived in the manor, then it needs to reflect lots of candlelight. Even in winter, nights here are rarely cold enough to tolerate more than two tapers on a table for eight. And nobody knows which fork to use for the fish tacos, anyway.

My third job was the one I'd taken as backup in case more retail gigs failed to materialize. I also took it because I love teaching. Real teaching, where you get to see the lights go on as people start thinking. The third job is responsible for my Tuesday-Thursday wealth-mongering schedule. Those are the days in which I spend three hours, one to four, teaching a class called American Problems to girls at San Diego's juvenile detention center. The curriculum is vague to nonexistent, so I can teach the kids pretty much what I want as long as they glean a few standard concepts along the way. Like, there *are* social problems in the United States.

And of course my choice of a juvenile prison as venue may be traced to my ongoing conflict over David. At the time I thought it was just an interesting population on which to test the conclusion of my dissertation. I had concluded that understanding our primate behavior patterns enables us to reject them in favor of better things before we wind up with six kids or in prison doing twenty-five to life.

I wasn't going to talk high theory to the kids that Thursday less than three weeks ago, though. I wasn't going to talk any theory. On that day I was going to listen, because something was going on at juvy. Something weird.

Like all institutions, juvenile detention centers generate folklore. The traditional adolescent tales of prosthetic arms clawing at car doors and virgins who die of shock after finding mummified penises in their lockers are repeated, with jailhouse twists.

People in stressful transitional states lean on folklore to clarify fears and address them. Adolescence is nothing if not transition, and being in jail is major stress. Juvy produces a wealth of folklore.

For the girls it was a legendary former detainee named Frankie. Nobody currently in juvy had ever seen Frankie Lopez, who according to the story had been there and gone years ago. But Frankie hadn't just been released to her mother or the foster care system like everybody else. Frankie had (a) stabbed a guard and then starved to death while trying to complete a secret escape tunnel which was still there, complete with her bones, although nobody knew where, (b) romantically entranced a guard and been carried by him in a laundry bag to his car where she died of suffocation as he drove frantically toward the Mexican border and safety, or (c) been killed by a guard and buried late that night beneath the curbside flower bed of the gas station visible through the dorm windows facing the street.

And while the most obvious feature of the Frankie tales is conflict and confusion about authority figures as embodied in the guard, there is also the theme of death, which doesn't necessarily mean death. It can mean inexplicable change. It can mean absence. It always means fear.

Something had happened to Frankie Lopez, if indeed there had ever been such a person, which created enough fear for the story to become folklore. On the day of my interview with Muffin Crandall I walked Brontë in Balboa Park, picked up the data from the veggie restaurant, and arrived early at juvy. The kids were already in the classroom, which is unheard of. I'd changed into the slacks I usually wear so I can perch cross-legged on the desk to lecture. They were ordinary khakis with a nice-enough silk blouse. I'd worn them twenty-five times before.

"Hey, Dr. McCarron, you look pretty good today," one of them greeted me.

I insist on the use of honorifics in my classes, so the kids call me Dr. and I call them Ms. or in a few instances Mrs., which is unnerving when the person being addressed is fourteen.

"Yeah, pants are pretty cool, like that pretty top, too," said another.

"Gonna get me some tan pants like that, look like I'm in college."

"Yeah."

Female primates pick insects from the body hair of others in a grooming ritual which creates bonds and defuses tensions. Human females do this grooming verbally with compliments. I knew the kids were feeling tension about something and wanted to bond.

"Thanks," I said. "Who's read today's assignment, the chapter on patterns in marriage and divorce in the U.S. since World War II?"

Nobody had read it.

"I heard they found that tunnel Frankie Lopez dug," one of the girls said as though I'd never mentioned an assignment. "Did you hear that?"

"No, but then I just walked in the door and haven't talked to anybody."

"Well, somebody said they found it."

The room was silent but full of a twitchy energy even Brontë was picking up. She kept pricking her ears and looking around, puzzled. I knew nobody had discovered an escape tunnel because there had never been an escape tunnel. Nobody stays at juvy long enough to dig tunnels and there's no point in any event. It's easy enough just to climb out a window. The kids do it all the time and are almost always immediately recaptured at the 7-Eleven next to the gas station, stealing Coke Slurpees and cigarettes. But the discovered-tunnel story meant *something* had been discovered.

Something had changed. If I handled it right I might be enlightened.

"Wow," I said with forced neutrality, "that's interesting. Tell me about it."

The silence grew heavy as twenty pairs of clear young eyes looked grave.

"They didn't find Frankie's bones in there," somebody finally said.

"Weren't no bones in that tunnel."

"Nothin' there but mud, I heard. Just a buncha mud."

They all knew the other variants of the Frankie story, but were not mentioning them. It was as if everyone in the room had heard only the tunnel version, and had believed it. I knew this meant something, but what? It's always safe to punt.

"So it looks like that story about a character who died in an escape tunnel didn't exactly happen, huh?"

I used "character" in an attempt to set up a discussion about what's real and what are the uses of stories. I might as well have begun an explanation of the chi-square statistical analysis. They ignored the ploy. They wanted to talk about Frankie.

"Frankie was not in that tunnel," the oldest and brightest girl said with finality, nodding toward the north side of the building.

I vaguely remembered seeing some construction in that direction when I parked. It made no impression. There's always construction on government property. Campaign donors and relatives of elected officials have to make a living.

"There's a lot of mud over there because I heard they accidentally cut into a water pipe," another girl said.

It made perfect sense. But so what? What did somebody jackhammering through a buried water pipe do to get these kids worked up over an urban folktale? There had to be something else. I scrounged around for a thread in what they were saying.

"Frankie isn't in a secret escape tunnel," seemed to be it. Which left the question, "Then where is Frankie?" A question about the possible futures of young women already off to a bad start.

"Maybe this Frankie really did okay and has a job up in Sacramento repairing computers for the state legislature by now," I suggested. "What do you think?"

And it worked, sort of. One by one they advanced theories about where Frankie might be, doing what. The room has a pull-down map of the United States, which I pulled down so we could locate Frankie in cities all over the U.S. even though the map only has forty-eight states. We made a chart of jobs, job training, predicted income. At the break the kids went outside to smoke and play with Brontë as usual. I went to the office and asked for the record of a girl named Frankie Lopez. To my surprise, there was one.

Francesca Maria Elena Lopez had been in juvy several times, her last stay five years in the past, for prostitution. She was then fourteen. The ID photo clipped to her file showed a scrawny, big-eyed kid snarling at the camera. And failing to hide that hurt, lost look you invariably see in baby hookers. I can't stand that look. It makes me think about killing adults who use children for sex. And then about going to prison like David, breaking my father's heart. Unpleasant thoughts.

According to the record, Frankie Lopez served out her time and was released to the custody of juvenile court, which probably meant she was in foster care. The social worker, a Glenda Martin, had referred the girl to a family counseling center, but there was no follow-up on whether she ever went there. The juvenile probation officer had also contributed no paper to the file. Frankie Lopez, for all practical purposes, was just *gone.*

I didn't tell the kids any of this. Confidentiality rules prevent any discussion of cases, but that wasn't why. Something had happened to upset the girls, make them jittery as a herd rather than as individuals. Telling them about Frankie's file wasn't going to produce the explanation I wanted. Only their trust would do that.

After the break I talked about marriage and divorce rates even though nobody had read the chapter. They took notes as I drove home the fact that every woman must have a marketable skill, married or not. My mother and Carter Upchurch had told me the same thing. "You must be able to get a job and make money, just in case something happens to your husband." All little girls are told that. It made me wonder why I needed a Ph.D. to say the same thing.

When the class was over three of the girls somberly approached my desk. Two of them petted Brontë while the third handed me a postcard.

"I got a library book outta the library this morning," she said, watching me. "This book."

It was a copy of *Jane Eyre,* not a big seller at juvenile detention centers.

"An interesting book," I plugged. "About an orphan girl who has a rough childhood and later falls madly in love with a man who has a terrible secret. But she doesn't let him—"

"That was in it," she interrupted as the other two, and Brontë, looked at me expectantly.

I read the postcard, which had a photograph of tulips in a public park on the front. It had been mailed years ago, shortly after Frankie's discharge. It had been mailed from Albany, New York, to a Bugsy Sneller at the detention center's address. The message just said, "It's working out *great!* For *sure!* But you *can't* write to me or anything. Okay?" The bottom was a tangle of Xs and Os followed by "Frankie." The "I" was dotted with a heart.

"Frankie Lopez?" I asked.

They all nodded.

"So who is Bugsy Sneller?"

They all shrugged.

"I'd like to keep this until next Tuesday and think about it, if that's all right. It's so interesting, isn't it?"

Nods, big smiles of relief. They wanted me to take this voice from a past similar to their own. Take it away until they could revise their folktale. By next Tuesday it would be done. There would be new stories about Frankie Lopez, stories accepted as gospel, as if they had always been.

The clerical staff was gone when I left, so I couldn't check the file on Bugsy Sneller. But at least I knew what was spooking the kids. The postcard, no matter who really wrote it, meant to them that their legend hadn't died after all. And somehow that was scarier than starving to death in a tunnel. I realized how bad a real future could look to kids who didn't have any future. It made me sick.

And tired. After feeding Brontë in the truck and grabbing a curried tofu salad for myself at a health food grocery, I went to the beach. Brontë chased a tennis ball for fifteen minutes and then I stretched out on my beach towel for a nap. San Diego's beaches aren't crowded at dinnertime in September, and the summer lifeguards are gone. But it didn't matter. I could have been snoozing under a blanket of loose twenty dollar bills and no one would have come within six yards. Watchful Doberman eyes made sure of that.

An hour later I had more energy. A good thing, since I was about to hit Roxie Bouchie's Thursday night line-dancing class at Auntie Buck's Country and Western Bistro. I was going to ask Rox to do a psychiatric evaluation on Muffin Crandall. She'd do it; I already knew that. But I'd have to pay for the favor by learning the Tennessee Stomp or something. Rox had been at me to learn line-dancing since I discovered her secret two months after our first meeting. The secret is that on Thursday nights Roxie Bouchie assumes an alternate identity—The Only Black Woman in North America Who Knows All the Words to Every Song Recorded by Garth Brooks. I had resisted her suggestions about the line-dancing classes, but curiosity about Muffin Crandall was pushing me over the edge. I hoped Rox wouldn't expect me to have bought cowboy boots for my first lesson.

Chapter Five

As a rule, bars give me a headache. The music is usually little more than synthesized pounding, and I am always uncomfortable when total strangers sidle up to tell me they haven't seen me in here before. I mean, what do you say? "That's because I haven't *been* in here before"? The linguistic rules of bars are not rational. I can't cope.

But Auntie Buck's Country and Western Bistro, usually just called Auntie's, isn't like that. The music is recognizable as music and everybody assumes they've seen you before even if they haven't. A laid-back gay hangout, Auntie's still serves regular drinks although now practically everybody orders imported water. Noncarbonated, because nobody wants to burp while waltzing to Patsy Cline singing "I Fall to Pieces." And everybody dances at Auntie's. The two-step is everything. At Auntie's the only rule is that if you're not in a full-body cast you're expected to dance at least once with anybody who asks.

When Brontë and I arrived, Rox was out on the dance floor already, wearing a spectacular purple-fringed blouse with a vest in gold and white patchwork brocades. I recognized the brocades from a set of upholstery samples BB the Punk had scored from one of his many contacts in the decorating industry. BB could turn practically anything into haute couture, and Rox was his favorite model. A guy in a Stetson leaned over the dance floor rail to tell me proudly that BB was also designing the costumes for Auntie's competitive line-dance team. For a tournament the following weekend the team would be in sequined ecru peasant shirts with Levi's hand-dyed a particularly difficult shade of malachite green. A Celtic theme. Matching green Irish caps, also sequined, and homespun vests featuring lavish embroidery in Celtic motifs. But with Rox as trainer, Auntie's team could win wearing baggy boxer shorts, right?

I nodded agreement as Brontë stretched out against the railing to watch. Then with fake enthusiasm I hopped down the three steps to the waxed floor and Roxie Bouchie's suspicious smile.

"Ready to learn!" I pronounced weakly. Everybody else milling around on the floor was wearing cowboy boots and shirts with at least five mother-of-pearl snaps at the cuffs. I felt bland and underdressed.

"Girl, you must be lost," Rox said, grinning. "The Society for the Preservation of Boring Clothes meets across the street. To what do I owe the honor of your presence on my dance floor?"

"I need a psych eval," I admitted. "It's a woman at Las Colinas. She's confessed to killing a man. The body in the public freezer out by my place. Her lawyer says she's crazy."

"Whoa!" Rox replied, interested. "How did you get involved . . . ? Never mind. You're gonna have to dance *real nice* for this, hear?"

"I hear," I said, taking my place in a row of people whose thumbs were already hooked in the waistbands of their jeans. We were going to learn the Tush-Push, Rox announced as a spotlight clicked on, highlighting her in gold.

"Misha, I have a good reason for doing this," I thought into the haze around the yellow light. I pushed the thought on through the ceiling and out into a dark sky beneath which Misha Deland probably was, somewhere.

Misha hated country and western music, although the hillbilly accent she tried to bury under her contrived Bostonese suggested that she might have had some familiarity with it in the past. She said country music reinforced the subservient role of women, who in its lyrics did nothing but sob over abusive husbands who'd run off with other women. The other women, she pointed out, would later sing about empty beer cans and foreclosures on double-wide trailers when the same men ran off with yet other women. Misha would have preferred a classic two-step urging housewives to shoot their husbands and live communally, growing their own food and hammering out social policy at night. I never bothered explaining to her why that two-step wouldn't work.

Although I know why. It's one of my favorite notions that the universe is essentially music, and that we came from there. Psychoneurologists document cases in which people with brain deficits who can't talk or read or understand words at all can nevertheless *sing* entire arias after one or two exposures to the music. Mute and autistic *idiots savants* have surprised their caregivers by sitting down at a piano and playing the themes from every commercial on television in the dayroom that morning. Even the ancient reptile brains of certain snakes respond dramatically to music.

I think music is the original language of life, half buried in the crumpled map of the brain. I think verbal discourse is an evolutionary newcomer, like opposable thumbs and politics. Music about communal utility bills would be like a mountain wearing a sweater. Beyond incongruous. Music has to be, and always is, about joy and despair, illumination and darkness, life and death. Even reptiles know this. But Misha wouldn't have gotten it.

That is, she wouldn't have gotten the theory. The practice she had down pat. Everyone said that on a good day Misha could seduce furniture, and it was true. She didn't mean to be seductive, certainly didn't cultivate an image suggesting steamy nights in heroin-chic hotel rooms. Scrawny little Misha in a leather bra and crotchless net tights would arouse guffaws from the dead. It wasn't that kind of seduction.

It was more like an old hunger, deep and lonely and mean. Misha could touch people just by pronouncing their names and then staring at them with those huge gray eyes. Men, women, animals. Everything seemed stunned by some coded message she conveyed. It made her extremely good at her work, which involved organizing, getting people to show up and do things. I have seen the most rampantly macho throwbacks—cops, drywallers, tow truck operators—paralyzed with fascination for this butchy little middle-aged woman in designer clothes that never quite fit. Misha's blouses were always buttoned wrong, the cuffs of her slacks coming untacked at the seams. She never cut the pocket threads of her jackets, but her pockets sagged anyway. She was everybody's favorite waif, with an attitude.

And, she was music. Minor chord darkness, chaos, something from before even the idea of order. And then a nearly beatific sense of light I could almost see trailing from her fingers. I did see it once, when she touched Brontë's head that first night at the Emergency Animal Clinic. Misha didn't either like or dislike animals, and would later forget to feed Brontë half the time. It was something about hurt that made Misha into music. Hurt in others and a scrambled hurt that permeated the woman herself. I never knew what it was about. I did know that I was supposed to make the very strength of my soul available to her, stand with her in some battle raging just beyond my comprehension. I still know that.

"Blue!" Rox yelled over Garth slipping on down to the OH-ay-sis, "that's slide, step-step, slide, honey. Not step, stop, and stand there."

"Yes'm," I shucked back. It was already clear that I wasn't going to make the line-dance team, but then I look dead in green, anyway.

After an hour I could boast a beginner's proficiency with three different line dances, although my hair was matted with sweat and I'd have to bury my blouse as soon as I got home.

"Where's my minnow badge?" I asked Rox when we settled at a table in the back. I ordered an Evian for Brontë and a hazelnut-flavored Italian fizzy thing for me. Rox ordered tap water and took a baggie of soda crackers out of her purse. I thought it was strange, since Rox is usually one of the few who still order drinks with names like Cuba Libre and Singapore Sling.

"No minnow badge," she said, letting most of her hundred and fifty beaded braids clatter against the tabletop as she leaned into a cracker. "And don't drink out of my glass. Stupid stomach flu's just about shut down the prison and me, too. You don't want it, trust me. I've been barfing for a week."

"What makes you think I'd drink tap water?" I replied.

"Oh, that's right. Out at your place you squeeze water out of barrel cactus."

"Actually, the liquid from barrel cactus pulp is poisonous when it's milky," I noted. "It's just one of the reasons I drink the stuff that comes in bottles. So when can you do the psych eval?"

"She's at Las Colinas?"

"Yeah."

"Saturday, but only if her attorney or the court requests it. Have the attorney call me tomorrow at Donovan. How did you get messed up in this thing?"

Sixty people were two-stepping around the dance floor now, some in routines so polished that the rest applauded after a tricky turn or bit of footwork. The best dancers were two gray-haired guys in Wranglers and button-down dress shirts. The president of a small bank and his boyfriend of thirty years, a TV actor easily recognizable for his ongoing role as the bishop-sleuth in a religious detective series. My dad loves the show.

"Her brother showed up at my pool yesterday and hired me to help her," I told Rox. "How outrageous would it be if I asked Bishop Brannigan to autograph a napkin for my father?"

"Tacky. Most people buy an Auntie's T-shirt and he autographs that. I didn't know you *had* a father. And why would this brother hire you? Hire you to do what?"

"To use my great skills as a social psychologist in proving his sister innocent," I answered after paying fifteen dollars for a T-shirt. It featured the Wicked Witch of the West in cowgirl drag right down to her ruby-red boots. Beneath was the message, "It's the *shoes,* stupid!" The actor signed his name across the back in red laundry marker. Dad would be overjoyed.

"And why would you think I'm the product of an immaculate conception?"

Rox let her head loll to one side and regarded me from tired brown eyes beneath sparkly purple lids. A real, no bullshit look. "You know what I mean."

I did. She meant we'd known each other casually for almost a year since my first mall job. We'd seen each other around, talked on the phone about BB, had lunch a few times. Once I'd gone to Auntie's with some of the old crowd from my years with Misha, and seen Roxie dancing provocatively with a woman who looked like Diana Ross. It was safe to say Rox and I were comfortably, if dimly, acquainted.

Now she meant it was time either to open up and acknowledge that we might be friends or else draw the line squarely at our safer acquaintanceship. A dicey decision demanding navigational precision at least equal to that required for brain surgery. I knew she probably wouldn't have even brought it up if she hadn't had stomach flu for a week. Sometimes being sick makes people maudlin. The proximity of death and all that. Still, I was flattered.

"My dad's an Episcopal priest named Jake. He lives in St. Louis," I offered. "My mother, Elizabeth, was killed in an automobile accident twenty-two years ago. I grew up in a really little town in southern Illinois just across the Missouri state line. Waterloo."

"Never heard of Waterloo, but we're homies," she said with a grin. "Sort of, anyhow. I was born in Chicago, brought up over on the Indiana side in Gary. My mother died when I was young, too. Twenty. God only knows about my peckerwood father."

"Peckerwood?"

"*White,* honey, as in good old redheaded Scots-Irish stock. You know, four-chord harmony, plaintive ballads about lakes, ten thousand years of stomp-dancing just like you see on that floor out there. It's genetic. Inherited. As it happens, I inherited it. Had to hide it from my friends, growing up. They'd have kicked my butt right into Lake Michigan."

"You think tastes in music are genetic?" I asked, intrigued. It fit right in with my universe theory.

"Girl," she replied, drawing out the word on purpose, "look at me. Do you see Reba McEntire? No you don't. What you see is an African-American woman whose DNA helix has a few codes that didn't come from Africa. God, I *love* this music!"

"And you're a psychiatrist," I ventured, risking accusations of racism for suggesting that all little black girls in blighted Gary, Indiana, don't grow up dreaming of the day they'll prescribe their first antidepressant. "Is your father a doctor, too?"

"I have a picture of him and my mother," she said, taking her wallet from her purse and showing me an enlargement of one of those photos that come in strips from a booth. The photo had captured a black woman with Rox's eyes and broad nose, and a white man with Rox's freckles and big ears. They both looked too young to be anybody's parents. "I don't think he was a doctor," she added. "Probably a steelworker. Mama got a lot of those before the mills shut down."

"A lot of steelworkers?"

The beads rattled conversationally as she turned her head. "I was a trick baby. This man was the trick. She said she knew she was pregnant that very night, and kept the picture so I'd know what my daddy looked like. She never remembered his name, probably never even knew it. And maybe she made the whole thing up. That's very possible, but this dude sure as hell looks like do-si-do to me."

"And the ears, too," I agreed, ducking the issue of mothers and prostitution entirely. "But why psychiatry?"

"All kinds of genetics," Roxie mumbled through a soda cracker, curbing further inquiry. "So what about this woman you want me to evaluate? Do you think she's faking it for an insanity plea? Is that why she confessed, so she'd appear incompetent?"

"I don't know, Rox. Part of what I saw was a scam, some kind of act. I'm sure of that. On the other hand, there is something wrong with her. She looks like she's been living on the street for years even though she hasn't. And the prison has her in a high-security unit despite the fact that this is a first offense and there's no record of any violent behavior subsequent to her arrest. Why would they do that?"

"Suicide precaution maybe," Rox suggested. "If they think she's crazy that's standard practice. A stripped cell, no sharp objects, belts, cords, or shoelaces. A guard will check on her every twenty minutes."

"But they let her wear this grungy old Shirley Temple wig . . ."

"I can't think of any way to commit suicide with a wig, can you?"

Wig suicide was not a concept I had ever entertained. Suicide itself was not a concept I had ever entertained, even on the night I came home to the beach apartment Misha and I shared for two years, and she was gone. Misha, her clothes, books, and complete collection of *Ms.* magazines in Mylar slipcases, gone. There was a note taped to the refrigerator. "I'm sorry that . . ." had been scratched out in favor of "We'll always be together. I know you and Brontë will be okay." It was signed merely, "M," as was Misha's habit.

There was never any question of Brontë and me not being okay. Brontë is a dog and I'm not exactly unfamiliar with surviving the loss of loved ones, as they say. You just go on. Mothers die, brothers become felons, soul mates vanish without warning. I was in shock, but knew I wouldn't die. Explanations were necessary, however. Some sort of accounting for the roaring in my ears and a sense that the only thing keeping me from a fall that would never end was my personal belief in the floor. The kitchen floor, in the kitchen, where there was a phone. It was ringing.

"Misha met someone at a conference several months ago," I was told minutes later by the ex-nun editor of a feminist journal that published mostly translations of foreign articles about the role of women in the banking industry. The journal was so boring it was unreadable, and the editor, a nondescript woman in wire-frame glasses whose name I could never remember, was a friend of Misha's.

Elaine Dennis. Or Denise Edsel. Something like that. She never came to our apartment and I assumed Misha saw her for lunch during the week occasionally. Now she was telling me that Misha had fallen head-over-heels for a multilingual grant writer who had just left the country for some project in New Zealand. She was telling me that Misha had gone, too.

No one among our mutual friends knew about the grant writer, but no one was surprised, either. In the following days they brought me pasta salads and sighed. Misha had always been so intense, they said. So odd. A bird of passage. Remember that time she couldn't remember her maiden name when somebody asked her and then burst into tears at the English Department reception? Later she'd been seen defacing Republican bumper stickers in the Business School parking lot. Misha was, well, not always entirely *appropriate,* although God knew she could charm the socks off the pope when she wanted to. And she'd done such a great job with the Women's Studies Consortium, and how difficult this must be for me, and blah, blah, blah.

I was numb. Then unbearably hurt. Then homicidally angry. Then numb again. I did take Brontë that weekend and drive as far as Mesquite, Nevada, before turning back. The plan had been to lose myself in some desert ghost town where no one has lived since the borax mine played out in 1947. I would waitress in a derelict truck stop with a flyblown picture of Willie Nelson on the wall. My only customers would be escaped convicts and local Native Americans exuding wordless understanding. Eventually I would publish a series of stark but transcendent essays about getting drunk and lying in ditches beside roads traversed only by tumbleweeds. Readers would be brought to their knees by my uncompromising metaphors of loss.

But people raised in the Midwest do not lie drunk in ditches writing about tumbleweeds. It just doesn't happen. I had classes to teach on Monday. So I turned around and drove home, sick and sobbing and scared. Then I called dad, who flew out the following weekend and helped me move to Wren's Gulch. When he'd left and I was alone in the desert, I decided to kill Misha in my mind. I instructed everyone never to mention her name. I would not think of her beyond the most superficial level. The sort of level required by the fact that she'd forgotten to take her gallon bottle of windshield cleaner refill and about three hundred knee-high nylons I found on the floor of her closet. Suicide with or without hairpieces was never an option for me, but a sort of murder was. Somehow it didn't seem like a good time to explain this to my pal, the psychiatrist.

"Muffin might die if she *ate* the wig," I suggested as Rox scowled into her tap water.

"Nah." She sighed. "You wouldn't believe the stuff people swallow and don't die. The stomach is an amazing organ. At least most stomachs are. Mine is just whining to go home."

Brontë seemed reluctant to leave in the middle of Mary Chapin Carpenter, but I suspected that had more to do with the popcorn people kept slipping her than the song. Like most dogs, she prefers opera.

"So I'll have the lawyer call you at work tomorrow," I reminded Rox as we hit the cool night air of the street.

"Yeah, sure." She seemed thoughtful.

"Blue?"

"Yeah?"

"What's your brother in for?"

"Armed robbery," I answered, veering off toward my truck. "He held up a bank. Shot a vase. I don't know why."

"Poor bastard," she said, smiling over her shoulder before vanishing into the shadow of a potted oleander by the curb.

An hour and a half later I was home and there were three messages on the machine. One from Dan Crandall saying he'd be by at ten tomorrow to talk about Muffin's case. One from the owner of the vegetarian restaurant wanting to know if I'd had a chance to look at the declining sales data he'd given me. And one from Father Jake, who sounded like he'd just had drinks with the Holy Ghost. I was too interested in his message to wonder why Brontë was dashing back and forth across the carpet, sniffing and growling. A field mouse had been there, probably.

"Betsy Blue," my father's voice announced, using a childhood endearment, "it's good news. Your brother has found someone to love, and I think it's going to make a difference. A big difference. Call you tomorrow with details. Love you. Bye now."

"Oh, God," I said to the answering machine as Brontë barked at my filing cabinet, which I thought in all likelihood contained the field mouse. Then I went for a quick swim and fell in bed trying not to think about what had happened to BB the Punk. About the sort of "love" my brother might find in a prison. I was pretty sure it wouldn't be like the banker and the actor at Auntie's.

Brontë was still sniffing and casting concerned looks in my direction when I fell asleep and into what would become a recurrent dream. Misha hurrying up the steps of an old stone house on a residential street, agitated, maybe scared. Looking over her shoulder but not seeing me as I tried to call out to her but couldn't. I had no voice. It was like I wasn't really there. In that first dream I wanted to cry with disappointment.

I did cry, actually. Although it was dawn when I woke up sniffling. Dreams, like the grid, have a sort of funky disdain for linear time. But I wondered where I'd been in that flatland between an image of Misha dredged from my own brain for the first time in two years, and what should have been an immediate response to that image—grief. I was pondering the question when I realized Brontë had not come to bed.

She was still in the office/living room. I could see her through my open bedroom door, her nose resting on outstretched paws and pointing to something lodged in the carpet against the side of my filing cabinet.

First light in the desert is more felt than seen, even inside bankrupt motels. An abrupt shift from the otherworld of shadows and skittering silence to a real world at once comforting and banal. Then things come into focus with jarring speed.

What came into my focus was a small bright blue capsule being watched by a Doberman. Cerulean blue, I decided as gooseflesh crept up my arms. Nobody had been in my living room in two weeks and I hadn't been sick since I moved. There was nothing in my medicine cabinet but generic aspirin substitute, natural vitamins I rarely remembered to take, and some worm pills from the vet that Brontë hadn't needed in years. None of these was bright blue. I knew I had never seen, anywhere, a pill like the one nestled unaccountably in my carpet.

Still, it seemed ludicrous to be shivering in fear at the presence of a toy-colored pill, so I picked it up. "Inderal LA 160," was etched in a wide light blue stripe around the overcap. The smaller half of the capsule sported three narrower light blue stripes.

There is no television at Wren's Gulch Inn because I prefer books. But Misha loved CNN, so our apartment had cable and we sometimes watched killer dramas because she liked to cheer when the bad guy finally fell into a vat of boiling molasses or was run over by an armored car full of zany manicurists. From these dramas I had learned what to do with striped blue capsules found in my carpet. I dropped it into a zip-lock sandwich bag.

Brontë seemed relieved and immediately headed for bed. I joined her after checking my files and finding nothing amiss, but I didn't go back to sleep. I was listing the phone calls I had to make as soon as the hour was decent. One of them would involve finding out what Inderal was, because the information might be useful in determining who had been in my living room without my knowledge. I didn't like that. I didn't like that at all.

Chapter Six

Dad gets up early, so after coffee and a run with Brontë I called him first. The voice that answered was not his but female, and familiar.

"Baby Blue!" Carter Upchurch greeted me with another of the color-oriented endearments favored by significant adults in my childhood. Elizabeth and Jake had named me Emily Elizabeth at the same time they chose Henry David for David. The idea had been to honor both Emily Dickinson and Thoreau as well as my mother. I was to be called Emily. But as it turned out nobody liked the name. At least not on me.

Baby Emilys are supposed to be demure and show great interest in capitalized abstractions such as Truth. I blasted that hope when I tore down a mimeographed copy of Dickinson's "Much Madness is divinest Sense" mom had taped to the teething rail of my crib so she could read it aloud to me while changing my diapers. I was only four months old but apparently I managed to wad the purple letters into my mouth. The result was a foamy blue drool that would bring the only scream anyone can remember my mother producing, and a lifetime of nicknames involving a color that does not exist in nature.

David's adjacent crib, I'm told, was adorned with a similar mimeograph of Robert Frost's "The Road Not Taken," which David left intact. It makes you wonder.

"Jake called me in Boston yesterday about the wedding. Of course I flew in immediately!" Carty went on happily. "Let me get him so he can fill you in. God, I have no idea what to do about gifts, do you?"

I heard the phone drop against a hard surface as David's and my godmother dashed off to get dad. Carter took her godmother role very seriously despite being Buddhist at the time of our infant baptisms. Thirteen years later when mom died, Carter was living in an ashram in India studying some esoteric branch of Yoga. Nevertheless, a month after the funeral she bought a duplex in St. Louis and moved back so she could take the role even more seriously. Carter Upchurch, through sequential boyfriends, hair colors, and affinity groups, was there for me and for David. In the next five years she never missed a school play, band concert, or Episcopal Youth car wash. She chaperoned field trips. Our friends called her Aunt Carty like we did, and she remembered all their birthdays. Carty and I often went shopping in St. Louis, and over strawberry crêpe luncheons she dropped reams of information about boys and sex.

"Your mother would have told you to wait for your one great love no matter how long it takes," she confided when I was sixteen. "But I'm telling you not everybody gets a love like that. You could die of old age waiting. The rest of us take a more practical approach."

Here she dropped a box of condoms into my shoulder bag.

"Boys will be pressuring you to have sex," she went on. "Sooner or later, you'll try it. Just make sure to pick somebody you actually like for the trial run, and practice slipping one of those on a carrot. The boy will tend to get careless at that point. Remember, your attention to the correct use of these things can determine your future. Protect yourself, Betsy Blue."

As I waited for dad to pick up the phone I remembered the slumber party at which my friends and I practiced with the box of condoms and an entire bag of carrots, roaring with laughter but shaky inside. Most of us had never liked carrots much to begin with.

"Blue!" Jake bellowed seconds later. "Isn't it wonderful? David has fallen in love!"

"Dad," I began diplomatically, "are you and Carty on drugs? She said something about a *wedding?*"

"They've asked me to perform the ceremony," my father said proudly.

Now, nobody is more pleased by open-mindedness than I am. However, prisons are the last places to look for this quality. I was sure that in his excitement over David's heretofore questionable ability to bond with another human being, dad had overlooked that fact. I didn't want to think about the warden's probable response when Father Jake McCarron phoned to make arrangements for a same-sex marriage in the prison visiting room.

"Dad, slow down," I said. "Start at the beginning. Who's the guy, for example? Have you met him? Is this an, um, *healthy* relationship?" I couldn't bear to think of David as either the macho "daddy" or caricatured pseudowoman Rox had described as typical in these situations.

"Who's what guy?" dad responded, puzzled.

"The guy David has gotten involved with in prison, who else?"

There was a long silence followed by an "aaahhh" signaling sudden comprehension.

"Of course," he said, "you would assume that. Quite reasonably under the circumstances. And I hasten to add that such a relationship might have been equal cause for rejoicing. If, as you point out, it had been a healthy one," he added. "But David's transformation must be credited to feminine agency. The person he wants to marry is a woman."

The long silence this time was mine. In it I could feel my

brain deleting files and opening new ones. I could also feel an enormous sense of politically incorrect relief.

"What woman?" I asked. "How could he find a woman in an all-male prison? You've met her, right? Is she nice?" I managed to stop just before adding, "And what in God's name does she see in David?"

Carty had apparently picked up the extension in dad's home office where he writes sermons for his visiting-minister gigs. At sixty-seven he's semiretired, but between his prison ministry and filling pulpits for vacationing clergy all over St. Louis, he works as hard as ever.

"You'll meet her at the wedding next Saturday," Carty answered. "And Blue, she's just fantastic! Her name's Lonni Briscoe, and—"

"And she met David eight months ago when her church began a Bible study program at the prison," dad interrupted.

I couldn't envision David going to a Bible study group. For that matter I couldn't imagine dad going to a Bible study group. Episcopalians are not big on Bible thumping. Not even Episcopalian felons.

"David was rearranging chairs after his Western Civilization class when this Bible group came in," Carty went on dreamily. "He was supposed to go back to his dorm, but then he noticed Lonni."

"She looks a little like your mother," dad mentioned. "I think that's what got him at first. Anyway, he got permission to stay for the Bible class just to be near her, and afterward they talked a bit. Lonni says she knew she loved him right then, but she didn't trust her feelings until she really got to know him. She started visiting him on Sundays when I'm working and can't be there, and they wrote to each other daily. I noticed the change in David, but I didn't know why it was happening. Then two weeks ago he just broke down with me, Blue. He let me hold him, cried against my shoulder, right there in the visiting room. He told me about Lonni, how he wanted to marry her now, not wait until after his parole hearing next year. But he said he couldn't ask her because he had nothing to offer except the shame and humiliation he'd brought on all of us."

I found this logic hard to debate. But then I hadn't quite gotten over the mild heart attack dad had seven years ago working three jobs to pay for David's legal defense. I was still in graduate school at the time, and sent dad my whole stipend. A hollow gesture, and I knew it. David had responded by defacing his forearms with blurry jailhouse tattoos of knives and butcher's mallets, earning himself the coveted criminal moniker Hammer. He'd told dad to fuck off, leave him alone. Dad hadn't. I had.

"So what happened then?" I asked, feeling ambivalent about prodigal sons.

"You will recall a concept of love that 'desireth not the death of a sinner,'" my father said in his booming pulpit voice.

The line was from the Anglican Declaration of Absolution recited by priests to kneeling congregations the world over. Of course I would recall it. I'd heard it a trillion times during my first eighteen years, and in that voice.

"'. . . but rather that he should turn from his wickedness and live.'" I recited the rest of it while holding my nose in order to achieve that singing chipmunk effect. "So you gave him absolution, right?"

"It felt as though that moment was the reason I became a priest, Blue," dad went on, ignoring my characteristic nastiness where David was concerned. "If I couldn't offer forgiveness and a new life to my own son, what was the point?"

Buried in that mini-sermon was a shadow version I heard loud and clear. "When will you shape up and forgive your brother for wrecking his own life?" it whispered. "Everybody *else* has, for crying out loud."

"So he asked Lonni and she said *yes!*" Carty went on. "The wedding will be next Saturday, at the prison, of course. Lonni and I are shopping tomorrow for her dress, and although we're not allowed to have a photographer, we've got permission to bring in our own camera. Catering is out of the question, too, alas. But the warden has said we can buy ice cream and soft drinks from the prison canteen for the reception. He said the canteen also occasionally has Twinkies. So call your travel agent now for tickets, and we'll pick you up at the airport. And get something nice to wear, Blue. My treat. Something sisterly but not too formal. Something blousy in silk, maybe a pastel. And *what* are we going to do about gifts—?"

"Twinkies?" I broke in rudely. Carter Upchurch sets her table with tiny Waterford crystal salt bowls at each plate. And each bowl has its own miniature silver spoon. She won't drink domestic champagne or any champagne not served in a correct, hollow-stemmed glass.

"Yes," she agreed over Jake's chuckling. "This reception is quite a challenge. I thought we might slice the Twinkies diagonally against a dark background—maroon paper napkins, say—and just hope the prison canteen has cherries jubilee ice cream to pick up the napkin color. I'm wearing neutrals, of course, but now that I think of it, if you could find something in a pink—"

"I may not be able to leave next week," I interrupted tentatively. "See, I'm working on something unusual. A murder case."

"Unless I've missed something, your field is social psychology," dad said thoughtfully. "In what way are your skills useful to the police in this case?"

"It's not the police, it's the accused woman's brother. Her name is Muffin Crandall, and her brother, Dan—"

"Oh . . . my . . . God," Carty gasped in the background. My first thought was that she'd once been married to Dan Crandall.

Carty has once been married to a number of men, and it was that kind of gasp. But then I remembered their age difference. Carty's sixty-three now, and Dan's about my age. Surely that wasn't it.

"What, Carty?" I said. "Do you know Dan Crandall?"

"No!" she answered too vehemently. "I don't know anybody named Crandall. It's just that I can't believe you'd let anything interfere with this once-in-a-lifetime chance to witness your brother's happiness."

It was a nice save, but I wasn't buying it. Nobody can live to sixty-three, be married more times than Henry the Eighth, and live in countless U.S. cities without knowing somebody named Crandall. Carter's reaction didn't make any sense.

We eventually determined that I'd make the plane reservations and be there unless something drastic prohibited it. Dad knew I needed some time to get used to the idea of seeing David, changed or not. Even fraternal twins often bond uncannily as children. David had broken that bond when he chose to live as a chimpanzee rather than as a human being. It hurt.

When I'd hung up I immediately phoned my travel agent and discovered that the only reasonably priced flight I could get would involve departing on the following Wednesday. I'd have to miss my Thursday class, but the kids would be thrilled.

"Book it," I told the travel agent. There was no way around it. I had to go.

Just thinking about my brother always makes me feel like cleaning something, so I stripped the bed and then drove six miles into Borrego Springs. The Laundromat there is air-conditioned and never empty. That morning I was greeted by a neighbor whose aloe farm fronts the only road to my turnoff.

"Lot of traffic up to Wren's Gulch lately," she observed as I stuffed sheets and towels into the big-load washer. "Must be hard on your friends from the city, driving way out here to see you."

"They don't, usually," I said. "By the way, did you see anybody heading up to my place yesterday? I was gone all day, but I think maybe the pool cleaner got his schedule confused and showed up. He's supposed to come on Mondays, not Thursdays."

It could have happened. Borrego's only pool service is owned and operated by a twenty-year-old community college student who wants to be a Park Service ranger. He might have come out to my place on the wrong day, found the gate locked, and walked in to see if I was okay. He might then have slipped the lock on my front door with a penknife and come in to use the phone or something. I wouldn't mind if he had. I know him. We all know each other out here. And maybe a blue pill from his jeans pocket got stuck on his watchband and then fell to the floor as he reached for my phone. Except my phone is at least five feet from my filing cabinet. I wondered how far a gelatin capsule could roll in nylon Berber carpet.

"Nope, didn't see Carlos at all yesterday," my neighbor replied. "Pretty sure he has classes on Thursdays. Did see somebody, though, at about one o'clock. In a pretty new car, light-colored. Had those tinted windows so I couldn't say who was in it. Did think it was funny when they didn't turn around and come right back like most people do when the pavement runs out just past your turnoff. Not the kind of car to be driving off road."

"But they did come back?"

"Yeah, or I would've called the rangers. People like that come out here from San Diego and don't realize how easy they can get stuck in a wash somewhere and die from dehydration. I would've called, but about an hour later I saw that same car heading back into town, so I didn't."

"Dirty?" I asked. Going off road involves stirring up a lot of dust. Vehicles returning from forays into the desert are always filmed with the dust of long-vanished seas and the creatures who lived beside them. Mammoths, giant vultures who preyed on giant pigs, and an ancestor of Brontë's called by anthropologists the "Bone-crushing Dog." I often think about this Triassic dog, who existed before there were any humans. It must have been lonely, but at least it didn't have to worry about being captured for use in cosmetics experiments.

"No, the car was clean," my neighbor answered.

So either somebody in a regular car drove to the end of a paved road and sat there for an hour in the heat of the day, or quite possibly parked, hiked to my Shangri-la, broke in, and dropped a pill in my carpet. I thought about that as I watched my linens tumbling in suds. I wondered why front-loading washers always have windows and top-loading ones don't. It was one of several things that were making no sense.

The desert, however, does make sense. After loading my wet laundry into the truck I went home to experience it. After stretching my retractable clothesline to its metal hook set in a rock partway up the dry wash behind the motel, I hung out my linens. The smooth wooden clothespins gave me a sense of continuity and peace. My mother had done this. Women had always done this.

For me watching sheets billowing in a desert breeze is perfect Zen. The center. After sheets-in-the-desert I can usually think calmly and clearly. And everything's dry in ten minutes, including towels. After a while I realized that David's marriage would bring me a sister-in-law named Lonni, and that might be fun. A fresh personality in our ravaged little clan would be good.

I decided on a set of those red ceramic plates with the white Christmas trees marching around the borders as my wedding gift. Matching coffee mugs, too. We had those plates in Waterloo, and mom made much ceremony of their annual emergence from the previous year's crumpled newspaper. They marked the beginning of the season. David was invariably overjoyed at the sight of them. Maybe he could be overjoyed again.

Then I phoned Roxie Bouchie at her office.

"Have you ever heard of a drug called Inderal?" I asked.

"Sure. It's not something I routinely prescribe, but then most people with high blood pressure don't flock to psychiatrists for treatment. Let me grab my *PDR.*"

"Your what?"

"Physicians' Desk Reference," she muttered. "Big, fat book with everything you ever wanted to know about every drug produced in the U.S. Pictures, too. Which Inderal do you want to know about?"

I described the capsule in its zip-lock bag on my kitchen counter.

"The big blue one. Ah. A hundred and sixty milligrams, propranolol hydrochloride. Your patient probably suffers from hypertension at a fairly serious level, and probably also takes diuretics to aid in keeping the blood pressure down. Of course, Inderal is also prescribed for the prevention of migraines, and for an inherited kind of hand tremor and a bunch of other stuff. Why?"

"I found this pill in my carpet, or rather Brontë did. I don't have high blood pressure. I think somebody was in my house yesterday."

"I never misuse medical terms," Rox snorted, "so I won't tell you you're getting paranoid out there among the iguanas and sidewinders. In all likelihood it fell out of your cleaning lady's purse. How old is she? The typical Inderal patient is probably sixty-plus, give or take a few years. Unless she's black, in which case the average age goes down because—"

"I don't have a cleaning lady," I told her. "Why would I need a cleaning lady for two rooms? And there are no iguanas this far north."

"Sidewinders?"

"Yeah, a few. I keep four vials of pit viper antivenin, sterile water, and a syringe in my pack just in case, but rattlers aren't always as lethal as you think. Twenty percent of the time when they bite they don't even inject venom. And unless the bite is near your heart you've got up to four hours to get medical treatment before things get nasty, anyway. I'd say the odds are better out here than on the street in front of BB's boutique, wouldn't you?"

"I'm sorry I mentioned paranoia," she said. "You're not paranoid, you're plain crazy! By the way, I haven't heard from your client's lawyer yet."

"Dan, the brother, will be here in a few minutes. I'll have him call the lawyer and set it up from here. And I'd like to sit in on the psych eval tomorrow. I've never seen one."

"It's not like seeing Old Faithful, but no problem if the gal and her lawyer say okay."

I'd left the gate open for Dan Crandall, and an approaching dust cloud suggested his impending arrival.

"Thanks, Rox," I signed off as a small rental car stopped and disgorged Dan Crandall into stark white sunlight. He was wearing new tennis shoes, swim trunks, and a polo shirt. From the car he pulled two large grocery bags.

"Guacamole," he said as I opened the door and remembered how sparse was his enjoyment of language.

"I assume that means you're going to *make* guacamole, right? And you've brought chips and a gallon of Mountain Dew. Let me get you a bowl. And Dan, there's something I'd like to ask before we discuss your sister."

"Yeah?" he said, crushing the juice from a lemon with one

large hand into the bowl without slicing the lemon. "What's that?"

"My book, *Ape*, is a rather tedious academic analysis of several contemporary social problems posited on the notion of primate behavior as both inherent and normative in humans absent external social conditioning."

"So?"

"So it might be described as polysyllabic, pretentious, and pedantic. Unless you're in my field, why did you read it?"

"My field's construction," he said, sighing. "Missing out on some work to be here. Season's short in Alaska. Another month and it wouldn't have mattered, you know?"

"What do you construct?"

"Buildings," he said. "And I read your book because my wife . . . or my ex-wife, I guess . . . uses it for a class she teaches at U. of Anchorage. It was lying around the house. I thought it was pretty good."

Another lemon, three tomatoes, and five avocados were sacrificed as I pondered what "good" might mean in this context.

"And you thought its author could help your sister. Why?"

Dan Crandall appeared to consider the question deeply while hacking with a knife at a gigantic red onion on my cutting board.

"Do you have any cumin?" he finally replied. "It's my secret ingredient."

Misha must have bought cumin for something because I found a little plastic jar of it in a box of spices still unpacked from the move. The fact that I couldn't remember the precise moment in two years of domestic bliss at which Misha bought less than an ounce of a common spice seemed significant. Had she made some special dish requiring cumin? What was cumin? Misha never cooked. I added cumin to the growing list of things I wasn't comprehending, and waited for Dan Crandall to tell me what he thought I could do for his sister.

It may just have been the onion, but he suddenly looked miserable.

"I want my wife back," he mumbled. "I thought, you know, maybe while you're figuring out Bea, or Muffin she calls herself, you could give me a few pointers."

It occurred to me that soon I would need a scroll of butcher paper and felt-tip pen to record the list of completely senseless things comprising my life. I would tape the scroll to my wall and conduct a focus group of one.

"What does primate behavior have to do with your marriage?" I had to ask.

"A lot, according to my wife."

"And your sister?"

"Same thing."

The room was starting to spin. Non sequiturs really make me dizzy.

"*What* same thing?" I bellowed, wild-eyed.

"They're women," Dan Crandall replied as if that were the answer to everything from garage homicides to Alaskan divorce.

I should have taken this remark seriously, but my attention was waylaid by what he said next.

"Oh yeah," he went on, "the sheriff's office has identified the guy bagged up in the freezer."

I couldn't wait to hear.

Chapter Seven

"Name was Victor Camacho," Crandall continued after we'd moved out to the pool with the guacamole packed in ice at my insistence. What can happen to unchilled guacamole after fifteen minutes in desert sun doesn't bear discussion.

"Apparently they got a couple of good prints off the fingers, and matched them up with local files."

"So this Camacho had a record?"

"Been busted in San Diego over and over. Two convictions. He's done some time."

"For what?" I watched a glob of smashed green vegetable fall from a corn chip to Dan Crandall's bare chest as he stretched amiably on my chaise. He scooped it up with an index finger and plopped it in his mouth. I was beginning to get a glimmer of what his wife had meant when she mentioned primate behavior in regard to their marital problems.

"Drug dealing, sexual assault, pandering. Small potatoes, just your basic street-scum loser. Cops think he probably had it in mind to skim garages in my sister's condo complex for whatever he could pawn for drug money. Rancho Almas has a lot of well-off older people, especially in the condo developments. They keep golf clubs, fishing and scuba equipment, even guns in their garages. The cops think he just meant to scare her when he started to grab that rock. With the three strikes law he was looking at some serious time, maybe life, if she could identify him. And she was just this old lady up against a five-foot-eleven, hundred-and-seventy-pound man. Guess the asshole thought it'd be easy to intimidate her, make her run back inside before she got a good look at his face. He sure as hell didn't know my sister!"

There was still an ounce of guacamole stuck in his mustache as he stood, tossed off his shoes and shirt, and then jumped into the pool. Oily substances are hard on the filter and tend to disperse in a film across the water's surface, but I stifled the urge to point this out. Neither did I point out that a rock seemed an unlikely choice of weapon for a seasoned criminal who'd just jimmied a garage door for the explicit purpose of committing a crime. The rock belonged to ape memories, I thought. Victor Camacho would have carried a knife or a gun or both.

"The initial sheriff's department report said he appeared to be Hispanic," I yelled as Crandall paddled around, creating diamond flashes on the water. "That's why they called him Jose Doe. So was he Hispanic?"

"Could be, but he was born in Texas." Crandall whooped just before executing a surface dive to the bottom and a long underwater swim to the shallow end. Swooping up near the ladder, he swung his head in an arc that threw a trail of water from his ponytail. He made me think of boys at Waterloo's municipal pool when I was a kid, squishing water from their cupped hands and snorting. And he made me think of Eden Snow's most popular and controversial book, entitled *Frog Latitudes.* It was a narrative of sad and furious poesy on the origins of the male.

"Brownsville," Crandall concluded and then began a series of butterfly-stroke laps. I watched the churning water and remembered Snow's tale. I often tell an abridged version to the girls at juvy, who love it.

A story about the very, very beginning when there was just Life, nothing more. Simple, one-syllable Life replicating in hot carbon seas, still agasp at the brand-new fact of its own existence. But already there was a hunger, the genetic hallmark of Life's origin. The hunger was simply to *know.*

Eve, Snow pointed out, has taken a lot of flak for the apple business. But metaphorically she's just a sort of preconscious amoeba extruding pseudopods in a mime of the curiosity there was as yet no brain to experience. She's just Life, propelled by this hunger toward the cataclysmic change that would make a real brain and knowing possible. And the change involved being thrown out of that original, female garden we would never really forget. It involved the evolution of males, who of course later turned the story upside down in order to come out on top. As she reached for that apple, Eve was losing a rib that would eventually turn and beat her bloody, but what choice was there, really? We have to know at any cost, Snow said. We just have to.

In order for consciousness to evolve, in order to know, and know that we know, and all that, there apparently had to be sex differentiation. At least that's how I interpreted the story, which, like all of Snow's work, is prone to moments of impenetrable brilliance. I had intended to ask Eden Snow if I'd got it right on the one occasion I would be in the same room with her. But the question was forgotten between Misha in my arms and the balalaikas. Now I'll never be able to ask. Word was that shortly after that night Eden Snow suffered the mental collapse everybody had expected for years. Then she either died or was discreetly installed at an expensive private clinic by those among her legions of admirers who could afford the clinic's fees. Misha heard rumors from time to time. The last was that Snow perhaps hadn't died but was in Iceland, or Finland, or someplace cold ending in "land," and was either hopelessly mad or orchestrating a feminist coup in a small Arab nation.

Whatever had happened, Eden Snow's tale of Life slogging eagerly on through swampy millennia, now accompanied in many of its forms by a mutant copy with breasts that don't work and ovaries carried awkwardly between its legs, remained wildly popular. Every Women's Studies Department in the civilized world still has on a wall of its graduate student lounge a poster of the *Frog Latitudes* dust jacket—a cartoon of a transparent frog couple in bracelets and a muscle-T respectively. Their reproductive organs are highlighted to demonstrate that the male's are just a distorted copy of the original female's. In the cartoon the T-shirted male frog is red-faced with outrage.

What Snow didn't discuss in that or any of her books was the cell-deep fondness felt by the original form for its bungled clone. A fondness tinged with longing. "Come back, come home," the original sings to her metaphoric lost rib. And in spite of his chronic self-absorption, he wants to go home. Wants to and does, and for a brief moment they are one again, only to be torn apart by their permanent difference, which is *his* permanent difference and only source of identity. The price paid for being able to think. I am continually amazed that my semiliterate and criminally inclined teenage girls understand this with the absolute clarity that they do.

Dan Crandall hoisted himself from the pol, unaware that he represented several hundred million years of a botched evolution which instead of seeking knowledge was killing everything in sight, including the basic model from which it was reassembled. I didn't think now was the time to tell him.

"So," he went on happily, "it was self-defense and all we need to spring my sister is somebody to explain why she left the body in that freezer for five years. Somebody to say she's crazy. You know, when it happened she was at that age when women get, you know . . ."

"Wise?" I suggested, remembering Misha and the party of over-fifty women, officially "crones" in feminist terms. Mothers of Time, Wise Ones seasoned by long experience, their elevated stature celebrated in feminist rituals held at the waning of the moon. Even women who would never call themselves feminists were performing crone rituals now, reclaiming the word and the final third of their lives for themselves. I'd just seen an article about it in a women's magazine in my dentist's waiting room.

"You're saying that now you think Muffin really did kill this man?" I said, puzzled.

"Hell, who knows?" He shrugged. "I don't know; it doesn't matter. The dead bozo had a record and the cops have a theory. It'll fly. We just need somebody to say she's crazy and get her out of there. Can you do it?"

"No, as I've explained several times. I analyze social data and make hedged predictions. I don't analyze people. But I've got a psychiatrist who's already employed by the prison system set up to evaluate Muffin tomorrow. The lawyer needs to get the court to order the evaluation. Her diagnosis, if there is one, will carry weight in court because she hasn't been hired by the defense and can arguably be seen as neutral. I left her name and number by the phone. All you have to do is call the lawyer and have him call Dr. Bouchie."

"Dr. Bushy?" Crandall chortled, heading toward my door to make the call.

"Boo-she. She's a statuesque and extremely fit black woman who outweighs you by ten pounds," I yelled across the pool. "You probably won't ever meet her, but if you do, don't pronounce her name Bushy. She feels that white people have grown linguistically lazy and are in danger of losing their edge. She's been known to make this point rather strongly."

"I'll tell the lawyer," he said and vanished into the blue pond of my office.

I gave Brontë a single chip with guacamole, which she licked from her whiskers before jumping into the pool with me. At times even canine women deplore messes.

"Look," I said when he returned, nodding that the lawyer had agreed to call Rox, "there isn't much more I can do with your sister's case. Why don't I just deduct my expenses so far and return the rest of your retainer?"

"I want your help with this other situation," he replied, slipping into the water and resting his elbows on the side of the pool. "You know . . . my wife." The dark blue eyes were hooded with a misery I recognized from seeing it in mirrors.

"I can't do marriage counseling, Dan. No license."

Something a cut above nudity had seemed appropriate for Crandall's second visit to my pool, but dog-paddling around with Brontë I realized that there is no such thing as a comfortable swimsuit. Wet cloth is wet cloth, spandex or not.

"Maybe you could just sort of explain a few things, tell me what to do," he went on somberly. "I love her. I just don't know what she wants."

Brontë climbed the shallow-end steps and then walked all the way around to where Crandall was lounging before she shook the water from her fur.

"Your dog hates me," he said with some irritation.

"She doesn't like men. She has her reasons."

"Like what?"

"Let's leave my dog out of it and start at square one," I said, resigning myself to several more minutes trapped in spandex. "Are you sure you want to do this? What I have to say is going to be insulting, condescending, and simplistic, and in the end won't make any difference anyway."

"Shoot," he muttered.

"Okay. Some, though by no means all, men are so insecure about what they are that they hurt everything around them more or less constantly. Harming things, nature, animals, and other people, especially women, gives them a transitory sense of identity. Women don't like this. The concept is basic. If you don't get it, then it's scarcely surprising that your wife is cruising the bar association for a good divorce lawyer. You're a hopeless dimwit. A gorilla."

"Yeah, okay," he replied, stretching to raise his toes above the water's surface. "That's the kind of stuff I mean. I don't run around beating up women or anybody else, but when I ask my wife what's the problem, she just gives up, starts crying. She doesn't explain whatever she's so pissed about."

He stared at his toes in the bright sun and then glanced at me. I sensed that he wanted some acknowledgment of the fact that they were relatively hairless, with the big toes lined up beside the others rather than splayed sideways, ape-style. It was hard to know where to begin.

"Dan, bottom line," I said, wishing I were standing fully clothed behind a lectern instead of half naked beside a bowl of now-liquid guacamole, "we're all apes who happen to have an ability to consider our own behavior. We get to *choose* what we think and what we do. If we choose *not* to choose, then we default to the ape setting. In your case a promising first step might be taking a look at male primate behavior to see where you're defaulting and driving your wife up the wall. I can suggest some books . . ."

"You've got to be kidding," he hooted, kicking with sufficient force to splatter water all over me, Brontë, and four feet of decking. A masterful display of territorial marking, it pretty much defined the problem. Which appeared hopeless.

"Splashing fluids around will not change the fact that you are in my pool and on my property." I sighed. "You cannot claim this territory as yours despite an old message your brain is sending, telling you that you can. By contemporary standards your marking behavior seems merely juvenile, like boys spraying graffiti. But both derive from the male proclivity to define territorial boundaries with messy substances. Since you haven't consciously chosen to eradicate or control this proclivity, you've defaulted to it. Understand?"

I have a series of slides I show the girls. Chimpanzee females grooming each other, human females in a beauty shop posed in identical postures. A gang of chimp males threatening a female; an identically posed gang of teenage boys threatening a lone girl. The kids easily get the message about choosing more productive behaviors, but I didn't think Dan Crandall would.

"Come on!" he guffawed. "I was just playing around. You're so uptight."

"Whatever," I replied, longing for an end to my confinement in spandex. "I have some work to do now, Dan. It's time for you to go. Tomorrow I'll see your sister one additional time, make sure her lawyer arranges for the psychiatric evaluation as quickly as possible, and that's it. I'll return the unused portion of the retainer to the address that was on your check. I really can't help with your marital situation."

"So you're just blowing me off?" he grumbled after hauling himself from the pool and drying off with a towel he then threw on the chaise. The end of the towel landed in the disintegrating guacamole.

"Did your mother ever mention anything to you about manners, courtesy, things like that?" I asked after letting Brontë lick the green gunk off the towel. Crandall's level of boorishness, I thought, could not be attributed solely to primate brain-wiring.

"Our folks were both killed in a small-plane crash when I was eight months old," he said into the shoe he was cramming angrily on a foot. "Dad was a pilot, operated a crop-dusting business in southern Illinois. That day they were flying to Indiana for the Indy 500. Never made it. Bea raised me, did the best she could. Sent me to a military academy in Indiana for high school. Culver. Ever hear of it?"

"Your sister raised you?"

"Yeah. I came along pretty late. The surprise kid, you know. Bea was twenty-eight, married, had her own kid already, but she just took me right in and brought me up with Susan. That was her kid, her daughter."

"Was?" I said, struggling to keep up with the sudden avalanche of information.

"Susan died. She was three years older than me and I was still pretty little when it happened, six I think. She had some serious disease, was always in the hospital, I don't remember what it was. But Bea and her husband split up over it when Susan died. He just took off, got a divorce and married somebody else. So did Bea, later. After I'd graduated from Culver and gone into the Air Force. That's when she hooked up with Decker. Nice guy.

"I don't want you to think Bea didn't try to teach me manners," he added as we walked to his car. "She had a lot of stuff to deal with in those days. She worked full-time as a high school English teacher and coached school plays for extra money. In the summer she was always taking classes so she could get her master's degree. She had to get it or lose her job. Things were tight sometimes, but me and Bea, we did okay."

After he threw himself into the baking rental car I leaned on the driver's side door and asked why he hadn't gone to Las Colinas to visit the woman who was for all practical purposes his mother.

"The lawyer told me not to go," he answered evenly. "Said Bea didn't want me to see her there. We always respected each other, even when I was a kid giving her trouble. She always sat me down and explained the reasons for what she did, all the rules and shit. Did it over and over until it made sense. My sister always makes sense. If Bea says don't come to the prison, I don't come to the prison. No questions."

I watched Dan Crandall drive away and wondered what kind of sense a woman named Muffin in a Shirley Temple wig had made when I talked to her. There was something in her brother's conviction about her that made me suspect the sense was there, but I'd missed it by a mile. Rox Bouchie wouldn't miss it. And even though I'd pretty much decided to bow out of the case and get myself back to Missouri for Twinkies and soda pop behind bars at my brother's wedding, I was anxious to see what Rox would turn up in the psych eval on Saturday. There was still time, I told myself, to do a little more work on Muffin Crandall.

If Muffin was crazy, maybe that's why she didn't want her brother to see her. But the rationality necessary to imagine another's feelings and to structure protection for those feelings wasn't consistent with what I knew about psychotic states. I didn't think Muffin Crandall was mentally ill at all. But then why wouldn't she want to see the brother she had raised as her own child? Because she was guilty of homicide? Neither sibling seemed the sort to swoon or wax judgmental about much of anything. Not even murder and freezer burn.

Back in my office I brought up Muffin's file on the computer, typed in the new information Dan had provided, and stared at the screen. What flickered back at me was shaping up as a good twin/bad twin story. Beatrice Crandall as a competent, responsible woman who had survived the loss of her only child and divorce, then gone on to raise her orphaned brother alone. Or Muffin Crandall as an eccentric killer in bad makeup who'd preserved her victim's remains in a public freezer for no apparent reason. The two profiles couldn't possibly be the same woman, but they were, and there had to be an explanation.

"Subject the mother of a daughter, Susan, who died at age nine about twenty-eight years ago," I wrote in answer to my own question about Muffin's marital and family history. "Divorced from first husband after Susan's death, took in infant brother, Dan, after deaths of their parents about five years before Susan died. Subject supported herself and Dan as a high school English teacher, and has a master's degree. She moonlighted as a drama coach."

Of course, I thought. The drama coaching dovetailed with Muffin's involvement in a community theater. In her official statement she said she'd bought eighty pounds of chicken wings for a community theater fund-raiser, and stored them in the freezer beside the packaged Victor Camacho. I figured I could locate information on community theaters in Rancho Almas five years ago by combing old newspaper files, but microfiche viewers give me motion sickness. Muffin's friend, Helen Tewalt, would not have the same effect.

After an hour's perusal of the vegetarian restaurant data, which showed nothing significant except that the place had enjoyed almost no business since its first week, I pulled on a knit dress and sandals. Then Brontë and I drove west through Yaqui Pass, over a hump of the Laguna Mountains, which stand between San Diego and the Sonoran Desert, and back down I-8 into the city. Only after I'd hit the outskirts of the inland suburban community called Rancho Almas did I phone Helen Tewalt.

"I happened to be in your area and wondered if I could drop by for a few minutes," I said cheerfully. "I have just a few questions about Muffin Crandall. It'll only take a minute."

Helen Tewalt would be delighted to chat, she said. She provided directions to her condo and offered to contact a few of Muffin's other friends.

"That's awfully nice of you," I answered, "but—"

"Oh, it's no problem!" she insisted.

I assumed my no-warning arrival would leave scant time for preparations. The theory, I realized after walking at least a quarter mile from the condo parking lot to her door, was only partially adequate.

Helen Tewalt's two-bedroom condo in an over-landscaped

setting, which included a pump-powered stream, was very prepared. It seemed to have been prepared for a long time. On the limestone entryway floor stood a hatrack laden with a collection of straw bonnets. Four or five were adorned with ribbons and scarves in colors complementary to Helen Tewalt's pastel artwork and upholstery. On a marbled coffee table a profusion of pink floribunda roses and eucalyptus branches spilled from a wicker basket. The place smelled like Camelot, I thought. A fragrance of dreams, drying herbs, and noble purpose.

"Please sit down." She smiled as I took out a small notebook. "I'm just making iced tea. And oh, if you've brought your dog, she's welcome to come in. It's still so hot outside."

How to win friends and influence dog lovers.

"She's fine in the truck, but thank you," I answered, trying not to be reduced to mush. I'm a sucker for people who are kind to animals, especially Brontë.

When Helen went to get our tea I looked around. The morning paper and a rhubarb cookbook had been hastily stuffed under the coffee table, but there was no sign of a massive scramble to tidy the place. Helen Tewalt's living room had been tidy already. While waiting I flipped through the rhubarb book and learned that the plant's ruffled leaves contain a toxic acid; they're poisonous. Mom grew rhubarb in our backyard in Waterloo, and served it cold in the sweet syrup it made while cooking. I loved the pink, chewy stuff as a kid, and was disturbed to learn that its leaves could have killed me. So many things are like that.

Behind a color photo of sliced rhubarb bread on an antique plate I saw the black-silver grid flash and then vanish. And while in hindsight it's tempting to interpret this as another warning, it was more of a chuckle. Irony is the grid's thing and these elusive blips are just teensy eye-contact moments between some uproariously amused system of which we are only dimly if at all aware, and us. Or maybe just me. The reminder that I was alive again felt good, though. Even after Helen Tewalt brought out frosted tumblers of herbed raspberry iced tea and told me she'd created the recipe herself. There was no reason for me to wonder if the recipe had included rhubarb leaves, but the thought did cross my mind.

"The authorities have identified the, uh, body from the Roadrunner cold storage facility," I mentioned. "A man named Victor Camacho. Is the name familiar to you?"

She considered the question for a solid second and then said, "No, dear. And I don't think Muffin knew of him, either. It's just one of those terrible . . . things."

A downward cast of her eyes at "things" was an acknowledgment of Muffin's presumed dementia at the time of Camacho's dismemberment, I assumed.

"I'd like to know a little about the community theater," I said, smiling appreciation for my possibly poisoned tea.

"Oh," Helen answered with some surprise, "we're doing a retrospective on *The Fantasticks* right now. It's very exciting. Each act begins with one set of characters in fifties-style costumes, and then for the big numbers like 'Soon It's Gonna Rain' and 'Try to Remember' they're replaced on stage by other actors in sixties, then seventies, et cetera costumes. It's quite effective."

I hadn't known whether Helen Tewalt was involved in the community theater or whether it was still in existence. Her answer made me feel lucky and shrewd, like a cop on one of Misha's TV thrillers.

"Was Muffin working on *The Fantasticks*?" I went on, shrewdly.

"She did props, some ticket sales, worked the concession at intermission a few nights, the usual. Why?"

"How long have you and Muffin been connected to the community theater?" I said, ignoring her question. Shrewd cops always did that.

"Oh, the Rancho Almas Community Theater's been around

for twenty, thirty years," she replied, also ignoring my question with a disregard for protocol never seen in people being interviewed by cops on TV shows. Unless the people are the bad guys.

"But you and Muffin. When did you begin working with the theater?"

"You mean when did we meet? I think it was *Arsenic and Old Lace.* Muffin auditioned for the part of—"

"What year did the community theater do *Arsenic and Old Lace?*" I insisted, trying to suggest by ostentatiously jotting "A. and Old L." in my notebook that I could easily look up the date of its opening. Somewhere.

"I think that was about ten years ago," she said brightly, as if we hadn't just been in mortal combat over this shred of information. "Oh, that must be Nanna! She's one of Muffin's friends from the theater. Just excuse me for a second while I get the door."

"Nanna," I wrote in my notebook. So far Helen Tewalt was the only member of this strange little group with a real name. I assumed "Nanna" would be grandmotherly, probably in an apron. As was becoming my pattern, I was wrong.

"I'd like to introduce Nanna Foy," Helen said. "This is Dr. Blue McCarron, a social psychologist who's been hired by Muffin's brother, Dan. Dr. McCarron has some questions about poor Muffin's history."

As Helen dashed off to get more tea, Nanna Foy took a seat on the edge of an upholstered chair facing me. For several minutes we raved politely about the convenience and general attractiveness of Helen's condo. I agreed that the sound of the fake stream outside was pleasant. Nanna Foy regretted a certain sterility inherent in her own high-rise apartment, apparently a unit in a large and gated suburban San Diego retirement community.

Nanna, rather than appearing grandmotherly, had the look of a madam whose unlisted and deeply exclusive escort service only accepts clients whose pedigrees can be traced to legitimate royalty. I sensed that she was dying to talk about stock options.

"We're so grateful for any help you can give Muffin," Nanna said in a husky voice that managed to suggest hauntingly erotic interludes over candlelit champagne which will never be drunk because Something Tragic is about to befall. Her enormous maple-sugar-colored eyes were dramatically lashed beneath frosted salt-and-pepper hair looped casually atop her head and falling in seductive tendrils. For several seconds, maybe thirty, I forgot why I was wherever I was, and muttered random syllables in response. Things like, "Umm, yes, well." I did not imagine the transitory flicker of amusement I saw deep in Nanna Foy's eyes.

"What can we do to help?" Helen called from the kitchen in the voice of that woman you meet in grocery stores everywhere. The one who keeps asking if you know where the Italian bread crumbs are.

"I'm not sure," I answered honestly.

For an hour Helen dashed in and out of the bathroom between servings of tea and little imported cookies. I asked questions and learned that Muffin Crandall had hunted game with her husband, Deck, in Alaska on visits to Dan. Presumably she'd learned skills related to the moving of large carcasses during these hunting trips, although she hadn't mentioned it because, Nanna pointed out, who would? The nickname Muffin had arisen from her habit of baking exotic muffins to sell at community theater intermissions. Nobody knew anything about the night of Victor Camacho's death.

"We only heard about the body a few days ago, after the earthquake and all that," Helen told me sadly. "We should have known something was wrong. Well, we *did* know something was wrong, with Muffin, I mean. She just fell apart after Deck died, although he left her very well off. Insurance, you know. She was well provided for. This is just so terrible."

What they told me was another recitation of Muffin Crandall's activities since the death of her husband. Acting, theater management, fund-raising, constant participation in community events as well as solitary trips from time to time in order to "get away and think." None of it was consistent with the profile of a woman in depression and decline, spiraling into isolation and delusional thinking. And yet that picture would be accepted by most people, especially by men. Middle-aged women are expected by men to disintegrate when their childbearing years are over. Poor things, they're useless.

And so was my interview, in which I had discovered nothing except that my presumed dead response to attractive women flirting with me wasn't dead after all. Nanna Foy's husky voice had been a reminder. I'd forgotten that flying around on the grid involves that, too. It seemed overwhelming.

Helen Tewalt hadn't offered much, but then she'd been busy hostessing and excusing herself to go to the "little girls' room" what seemed an excessive number of times despite the tea. Prior to leaving I asked to use the facility, and was not surprised to see a reproduction Fantin-Latour floral print on the wall above a white wicker basket of lace-trimmed hand towels. In the hall I glanced into Helen's bedroom, done in whitewashed antiques. Very nice.

The other bedroom door was closed, but I opened it and ducked into a combination library and office. Built-in bookcases on all four walls, desk, computer, filing cabinets, phone. The computer was on, showing a photo screen saver of an impish teenage girl in a nose ring, too much makeup, and a black T-shirt printed with greenish beaked insects. On the desk beside the computer was a huge rectangular paperweight. The masks of comedy and tragedy imbedded in Lucite over a plastic text plate which read, "Happy Retirement, Ms. Crandall!"

"Oh, boy," I whispered. It had obviously been a gift to Muffin Crandall at her retirement from high school teaching, but what was it doing here? And was this *the* paperweight?

I could hear Helen moving in my direction, and ducked back out into the hall just as she showed up to ask if she'd remembered to put hand lotion in the bathroom. But my glance had also grazed the titles visible in the bookcase beside Helen's desk. I was sure I saw the green binder's cloth and gold title of an unjacketed *Frog Latitudes,* Eden Snow's feminist tour-de-force.

"Just looking for a full-length mirror. Knits," I concluded as if the drape of my clothing was deeply important, and smoothed my skirt while straining to inspect its back.

"Always a problem," Helen Tewalt agreed as we headed for the door.

After a long beach run for Brontë, I had an early dinner at the vegetarian restaurant and discovered the reason for its disastrous sales performance. The food was inedible. On Monday I'd offer to help the owner find a decent chef. At outrageous fees, of course.

On the drive home I tried to imagine why a sweet sixty-something widow in a sweet widow's condo would have read Eden Snow's radically feminist book at all, much less enough times to wear out the dust cover. There wasn't any reason. It didn't make sense. And why was Muffin's paperweight on Helen Tewalt's desk? Had Muffin made a gift to her friend of the weapon she used to kill Victor Camacho? The sentiment seemed strange, at best.

On my answering machine was a message from Nanna Foy. "I know a few things Helen may not have mentioned," she said huskily. "They may be of interest to you. Give me a call. Ciao."

I fell asleep smiling. I couldn't help it.

Chapter Eight

Rox phoned Saturday morning when the sky was still cool, telling me to be at Las Colinas by eight if I wanted to observe Muffin's psychiatric evaluation.

"I read the sheriff's department report and everything from both attorneys last night," she said thoughtfully. "There's something new, something I don't think you know."

"What?" I muttered while trying to smash half an orange over the rotating top of the electric juicer with one hand. I succeeded only in overturning the juicer, which went right on rotating as Brontë lapped orange juice off the floor.

"I'd rather wait until after I see the client to discuss it. Over lunch, okay?"

"Sounds serious."

"It is," she said. "And it complicates the evaluation."

"Either tell me or stop talking about it, Rox. You're driving me crazy."

"Hmm," was all she said before hanging up. I could tell she was deep in psychiatrist-type thought. I was about to find out what that was like.

Rox's interview with Muffin was to take place in a small room with a table, chairs, and a dead-obvious two-way mirror through which I would observe from an adjacent dark room equipped with speakers. Muffin was already there when Rox and I arrived simultaneously. She still wore her grimy wig and looked a year older than when I'd first seen her only two days earlier.

"My God, it's Aunt Jemima!" she greeted Rox. "In cowboy boots. I thought they were sending a shrink."

"When's the last time you looked at a pancake box?" Rox countered, flipping on a tape recorder. "Aunt Jemima, she practically *white* now. Lost that bandanna and a hundred pounds, too."

"So many of our cherished cultural icons have been sacrificed to demonic forces," Muffin noted sadly. "Little Black Sambo, lawn jockeys . . . where will it end?"

Rox segued into a bland, professional smile. She stated her name and the date, and then explained that while she was a physician and a psychiatrist, Muffin should in no way regard her in the role of a helping professional.

"I am in the employ of a court charged with determining your competence to stand trial, participate in decisions regarding your defense, and waive rights. In particular, I am here to determine insofar as possible your mental status at the time of the alleged offense and your mental status now. Everything you say to me will be evaluated from a psychiatric perspective and my evaluation will be made available to the court. There is no confidentiality in this evaluation. I'm not here to help you, but to help the court. Do you understand what I'm here to do?"

"I do, but do *you?*" Muffin answered, cracking her knuckles. "Who's behind the mirror?"

"Blue McCarron. Your attorney told me you'd given permission for her to observe."

Muffin nodded and waved at me. I waved back even though she couldn't see me.

"You could save us all a lot of time by just explaining what happened," Rox began.

"I have explained what happened," Muffin answered, and they were off.

I watched and listened as Rox elicited an exhaustive re-creation of Victor Camacho's last moments on earth. Muffin produced essentially the same narrative I'd read. She was sleeping and heard an intruder in her garage. She absentmindedly grabbed a paperweight on her way to investigate, and wound up killing a man with it. She had never seen Victor Camacho before in her life, and in fact didn't really see him that night. It was dark. She was afraid. Later, during the tying and packaging of his body, she hadn't really looked at him. She was in some kind of trance. If she saw a picture of him right now, she wouldn't recognize him.

"Tell me a few ways in which Presidents George Washington and John F. Kennedy look alike," Rox suggested.

"Both white males." Muffin grinned, locking eyes with her interrogator. "You could have mentioned *any* two presidents."

"Which sedentary games do you like best?"

"Sedentary? As in 'games that sit'?"

"Like Monopoly, cards, word games," Rox answered.

"Haven't played Monopoly in twenty-five years. Used to play with my kid brother, though."

I couldn't imagine what Rox might be getting out of all this, but she seemed content.

"Tell me about your brother," she went on.

Muffin provided a quite motherly recitation of Dan's childhood illnesses, grades, activities, and successes. I was interested to learn that he'd been a model kid until halfway through seventh grade, when he'd begun to act up. It sounded just like David.

"And how old was your brother when your daughter, Susan, died?" Rox asked, looking pointedly at her notebook.

"Four and a half, five. He was close to five."

I distinctly remembered Dan saying he was six, but I assumed the mother's memory would be more reliable than a small child's.

Rox moved the evaluation impassively forward, showing Muffin Rorschach cards and listening to descriptions of butterflies and Siamese twin coneheads playing alphorns. I wished I could see the inkblots. They remind me of the big cumulus clouds back in Illinois that you never see here.

Rox had Muffin assemble colorless puzzle pieces and copy geometric designs with colored blocks. Then she asked a series of questions that sounded spontaneous, but weren't. I'd had to take a course in standardized testing as an undergraduate. The questions were from something called the Wechsler Adult Intelligence Scale.

"What is the thing to do if you find a stamped and addressed envelope on the ground?" Rox asked as if people routinely strewed their mail around to be found by strangers.

"Drop it in a mailbox," Muffin answered, eliciting a loud cheerleader's "Yea!" from me that was apparently audible on the other side of the mirror. It was the desired "best" answer, indicating social conformity, lack of criminal intent, and a willingness to help others. I couldn't remember whether the "best" answers on this subtest got three or four points, but I was glad Muffin would get points. Rox turned to roll her eyes menacingly at the mirror, and Muffin Crandall laughed out loud. I hadn't realized that I wanted Muffin to win. I hadn't even realized there was a battle. But there was.

A battle at the ramparts of Muffin's interior life, her mythology and symbol system, her reason for being. And Roxie Bouchie was the intruder, armed with measures both concrete and subtle that could dredge secrets from Muffin like a seine in a pond. "Don't let her do it!" I thought toward Muffin through the glass, forgetting that I'd been the one who asked for this in the first place. Suddenly I felt like a traitor.

They took a bathroom break, got Cokes, and came back. Muffin seemed exhausted but when Rox asked her if she'd like to quit, she just said, "Hell, no."

"Okay, why did you pack Victor Camacho's body in a heavy-duty trash bag, and store it in a public freezer?"

Muffin told the same story I'd read. She just "knew" she had to do it, get the body out of sight before the sun set. Anything else would have resulted in a terrifying capture and punishment. The freezer business was secondary, an afterthought, merely practical.

"I couldn't think of anything else to do with it," Muffin said.

By "it" she meant the dead Victor Camacho. I found it interesting that she didn't say "him."

"And then you just left the frozen body in the Roadrunner freezer for five years?" Rox went on.

"Yes."

"What would you have done if the public storage facility had gone out of business?"

"I don't know," Muffin answered, and I believed her.

Rox wound up with a long series of biographical questions, mostly about Muffin's health. "Were you ever treated for a head injury as a child? An adult?" That sort of thing. I found my attention drifting and then realized it was over. Rox smiled, tucked her equipment and notes into a woven leather briefcase, and stood. Muffin stood as well and then grabbed the chair back as she almost fell. The guard and I dashed in at the same time, but Rox already had Muffin seated with her head between her knees.

"This woman is ill," Rox told the guard. "She must have immediate bed rest and medical attention."

"How'd I do, kid?" Muffin asked from beneath the now-crooked wig. Her skin was chamois-colored and her eyes shot through with threads of mustard.

"Bravo!" I answered. "You were stunning."

Her smile suggested satisfaction with a job well done.

"Give Dan a shove in the right direction if you can," she said as the guard helped her stand and move toward an interior door. "You know how they are."

I had no idea that was the last time I would see Muffin Crandall.

Later I imagined a shadow of finality in her remarks to me, but at the time I just thought, "I know how *what* are?" as the guard slammed the door and left me and Rox alone in the little room.

"So?" I asked.

"Damnedest thing," Rox answered, frowning. "There's no evidence whatever of psychiatric disorder although there easily could be, given her condition, but there isn't, and yet she's clearly deceitful."

"Deceitful?"

"She's lying to create an impression of psychiatric illness. Problem is, she's malingering to be seen as guilty, not to evade trial and punishment."

"You mean the confession?"

"No," Rox replied as we hit the welcome freedom of the parking lot. "Parts of the confession may actually be true, although the form in which she recites it is not. I'm talking about her responses to less stress-producing questions. Too many were just off the mark even when you factor in . . ."

We had reached Rox's shiny blue Oldsmobile as she trailed off and opened her trunk. After tossing her briefcase in it, she turned to me.

"You like that old coot, don't you?" she said as a breeze rattled her beads.

"Yeah," I answered. "There's just something about her."

"Come over here." She took my arm and pulled me into the

shade of a coral tree near the front of her car and motioned for me to sit on the hood.

"Muffin Crandall is dying," she said quietly, brown eyes looking straight into mine. "She refused to sign a release, so her attorney only got copies of her medical files late yesterday after getting a court order. There'll be a bail reduction hearing on Monday, based on Muffin's medical condition, and she'll be out on bond. The trial can be postponed indefinitely, which is to say there will never be a trial. It's cancer, Blue. She was diagnosed six years ago with breast cancer, underwent treatment, partial mastectomy. But it had got to the lymphatic system, cropped up again in the stomach. More surgery, chemo. Her oncologist says it's everywhere now, but what's gonna take her out is the liver. That's what the jaundice is about, why she looks yellow. Her serum bilirubin count is sky-high. She won't be around much longer."

"Does Dan know?" I asked, upset and angry for Muffin and Dan and for myself. Why did people I liked keep *leaving?*

"Couldn't say. That's between the two of them, Blue. People handle these things in different ways."

"So Muffin deliberately withheld her medical history from her lawyer after her arrest, even though it would have kept her out of jail?"

"Looks that way."

"Why?"

"Why is she trying to convince me she doesn't *quite* remember significant life events and can't *quite* compute simple mathematical formulas? She wants to be in jail, and she wants to die an accused murderer of questionable sanity. I'll explain over lunch, if it's safe for us Aunt Jemima types to sit at lunch counters out here in God's country."

The remark was meant to cheer me up.

"No problem," I answered. "I have to run Brontë for a few

minutes, then you can follow me to a barbecue place on the main drag. It's owned by a Syrian family with no connections to the Klan. You're safe."

My choice of restaurants turned out to be another mistake. I don't eat mammals for what are probably sentimental rather than political reasons. I mean, I *am* a mammal. Everyone I love is a mammal. It's just too close. But I thought Rox would go for some baby-back ribs after a grueling three hours locked in a prison. The menu suggested several preparations of two mammals—cow and pig—and little else. We wound up splitting large orders of potato salad and cole slaw.

"Still got this stomach flu," she explained. "Last thing I need is a pound and a half of greasy ribs. White folks can't barbecue, anyway."

I could see the turbanned owner scowling at her remark. Rox might be the queen of savvy in psych evals, I realized. But in terms of social change she was lost in the sixties, or at least the seventies.

"So what made you think Muffin was lying?" I asked after we polished off our plates of pale vegetables and settled back with coffee.

"Forensic psychiatry isn't really complicated," she said, removing the bright green linen jacket she'd worn over a matching silk blouse throughout the interview and stretching both arms to rest her elbows on the back of the booth. "It has to do with predictable patterns and erroneous assumptions."

"My business is predictable patterns," I reminded her. "And I'm constantly making erroneous assumptions. So I'll get it. Tell me."

The big smile lighting her face was real. The kind of smile people get when someone is genuinely interested in what they do, which is to some extent who they are. It occurred to me that as a black woman in a white man's profession, Rox probably didn't have a lot of close friends among her peers. I couldn't see her playing golf with other shrinks at the country club. She'd fit in about like Bessie Smith at a sailing regatta. And while she had scores of friends at Auntie's, I didn't think any of them would have had occasion to ask her how she can tell when an accused murderer is lying. Most people want to believe that their own fabrications have a ring of truth.

"I'm really interested," I said, and was.

"Well, the bottom line is that people don't know anything about psychiatric disorders, although they think they do. After all, they've seen movies and read thrillers. They're sure violence and bizarre behavior are constant features of every disorder. But where we catch 'em is in something more subtle. See, they always link mental illness with mental retardation. Guess it's because both involve the brain. So in interviews they produce what's called the Ganser syndrome."

"Ganser?" I said, thinking of male geese in cute bow ties.

"German doctor at the turn of the twentieth century. He noticed that criminals faking mental illness to avoid prosecution or execution tended to give approximate answers to ordinary mental-status questions like 'Do you know where you are?' "

"San Diego," I answered promptly. "More specifically, Santee."

"Goot, ze patient iss oriented to place," Rox growled in a Freud-impersonation that made me choke on my coffee. "But if you were faking a psychiatric disorder to avoid prosecution, you'd pretend not to know quite where you are. You'd say something approximate, though, like 'Los Angeles.' You'd think you were supposed to get answers to everything a little bit wrong because a mentally retarded person might get them wrong, and in your mind there's this nonexistent overlap between mental illness and mental retardation. That's Ganser."

"So did Muffin do that?"

"Over and over. Remember when I asked her what games she liked? That's not a typical question, but my way of suggesting she *was* playing games. She knew what I meant, and ducked answering by producing an approximation. I'd suggested Monopoly, so she latched on to that, saying she'd played Monopoly in the past. And when I asked her how old Dan was when her daughter died, she said he was four and a half or five."

"And Dan was six, right? He told me that."

"Right. She did it consistently, but the approximations were only slight. The sort of thing you'd expect to see in early Alzheimer's or one of the presenile patterns when people are aware of their forgetfulness and still trying to save face. Nothing flamboyant, like the 'I'm from the planet Mars' stuff we hear from guys at county jail."

"But Muffin's sixty-one and terminally ill," I said, wanting to defend her. "Maybe she really does have some mental problem because of her illness, something like the beginning of senility."

Rox's eyes widened with glee.

"That's exactly what she wanted me to think!" she bellowed. "And it was a damn good act. A researched and coached act, I might add."

"How can you tell?"

"She can remember every detail of the night Camacho died, even her reasons for not cutting him up and using the garbage disposal in her kitchen to get rid of him. But she can't do serial sevens beyond ninety-three, puts the trunk of an elephant puzzle on the elephant's back, and wants me to think she's so embarrassed about her inability to remember what games she likes that she seizes one I've mentioned and relates it to her brother. Then when I ask about the brother, she has perfect recall. You can't have it both ways."

"But you don't know that everything she said about Dan was true. Maybe she was being approximate there, too."

Rox sighed. "Approximation is hard to expand, Blue. Almost impossible. It gets obvious and ridiculous. One-word responses are easily approximated, but not whole narratives. For example, tell me about the town you grew up in, only approximate the town. Make it someplace close, but incorrect."

"Okay, St. Louis. I grew up in St. Louis. That's near Waterloo where I really grew up."

"Tell me more. Where'd you go to school, shopping with your friends, swimming in the summer?"

"Um, Baker Elementary School, and shopping downtown, and swimming . . . I didn't go swimming. I have this phobia about water."

"Lame," Rox snorted. " 'Baker' is one of the first fictitious names Americans come up with for practically everything, and children in large urban areas hang out in neighborhood shopping malls, not the more dangerous and inaccessible downtown commercial districts. And even if I didn't know you swim every day, it's obvious from your tan and musculature. More to the point, as your anxiety about producing a credible story rose, you went further afield, got more dramatic, even chose a psychiatric term, 'phobia,' in hopes of convincing me. What you did was typical."

"So I failed?"

"Girl . . . " Her beads rattled mockingly as she shook her head.

"What's off-the-wall about Muffin Crandall," she went on, "is that she's lying in order to be seen as guilty, not to evade the consequences of her behavior, which she has already described as subject to legal scrutiny and possibly criminal. She's perfectly competent in psychiatric terms now and probably always has been. She may actually have killed Victor Camacho in precisely the way she describes, although I doubt it. There were no witnesses. It could have happened."

"So why the body in the freezer for five years?" I finished the train of thought. "That's what's crazy."

"No, it only seems crazy to us because we've been excluded from the rationale behind it." Rox sighed, frowning. "It was done deliberately and for some purpose, but what?"

"She would have to assume the body would be found, Rox. The point was to preserve the body until it was found. Otherwise she could have disposed of it a thousand ways. Rented a boat and dumped it in the ocean, buried it in the desert, the possibilities are endless. I agree that the whole setup was deliberate, including the story she gives to explain what happened and how she felt. What interests me is a gap she left in the framework of the story, the assumed structure of the event."

"What gap?" Rox asked.

"The strange male predator in the dark is a female archetype," I began after declining a third cup of coffee from the restaurant's proprietor, who was clearly fascinated by our conversation and kept lurking around with the coffee pot. "It's the premise, the backbone, of Muffin's story about what happened that night. Every woman immediately recognizes it, and men recognize it as something they've heard from their mothers, sisters, girlfriends, and wives. Nobody questions the likelihood of its actually happening because it's so familiar. But statistically it's very unlikely. Not only that, but the archetypal story involves a fear of rape, of violation, not just a fear of murder. Yet the dramatic framework supporting Muffin's narrative *only* involves murder. She says he was going to kill her. She doesn't mention any fear of rape."

"Rape wouldn't immediately come to my mind if somebody was about to whomp me over the head with a rock," Rox replied. "Death is what I'd think. Bastard's gonna kill me."

"It's like your Ganser thing," I explained as we paid the bill. "Only instead of looking close-up at every word, every response, you look at the panoramic view, the whole history of people with this particular story. Nothing happens only once. There are patterns, and the patterns get made into stories that are told over and over until they're perceived as reality whether they are or not. This is one of those stories, but with a piece missing. Fear of rape is what's missing, and in a narrative told by a woman that's significant."

"You mean if Muffin's whole night-in-the-garage thing isn't true, then this missing piece tells us something about what *is* true?"

"That's my best guess at the moment," I said. "Maybe Camacho did rape Muffin at some point, or one of her friends, who knows? It would be interesting to see the police reports on his arrests. Might be something there."

When I asked for a big cup of water for Brontë, the restaurant's proprietor smiled and brought out a large, cooked beef rib wrapped in tinfoil as well. "At least your dog may want to visit us again," he said politely.

Rox and I stood in the parking lot and watched Brontë in ecstasy with the rib.

"This Crandall thing is weird," she said. "Never seen anything like it."

"Yeah."

"Seems like together we might be able to sort it out, though. Might be fun."

"Think so?"

Brontë was gnawing the bone in some dead grass beside the pavement, and bits of grass were getting stuck all over it. The scene was less than attractive. Rox opened her car door and turned to watch my dog chew bloody plant stems.

"We work pretty well together," she said, capturing my attention abruptly and completely with a particular thrum in her voice. Thoughtful, it said.

I liked Rox, a lot. In the back of my mind there'd always been a vague notion that someday when I stopped talking to Misha's ghost, well, maybe I'd feel Roxie Bouchie's beaded braids falling around my ears, hear her call me "girl" close-up. Maybe. But not now. Or was I just too cowardly to face my own loneliness and do something about it? The air outside the restaurant was dusty and smelled like hay from the feed store across the street.

"Yeah, we do," I answered, panicked. In the hay-smell I recognized the fact that I didn't want Roxie Bouchie out of my life. But if I handled this wrong she might be just that. One of those awkward moments. You never know when they're going to turn up.

"If we put our heads together we could probably figure this thing out," she said as Brontë tried to scrape an ant from her teeth with a forepaw. I would have killed for a lighthearted soundtrack and a less disgusting dog.

"You're right," I mumbled, staring at her left front tire. Then I straightened to my full height and thrust my shoulders back.

"I'm totally snarled in an old relationship that doesn't even exist anymore, but the truth is I like you a lot," I pronounced bravely, ready to take the hit. "It would be fun to work together."

For a split second she looked a little baffled, but then wrapped me in those big arms. I hugged her back, hard.

"Honey, you need to get out more," she crooned over a chuckle that was making her breasts bounce. "But what I meant right at the moment was maybe we could have some fun figuring out your Crandall job. I spend my time with felons and line-dancers; I don't have a lot of people I can *think* with, you know? No strings. I didn't mean strings. I've had enough of that mess to last a while, too."

"The woman who looks like Diana Ross you were dancing with that night at Auntie's?" I had to ask.

"Uh-huh," she answered, seeming to ponder some amusing

and delicious memory that made her smile and made me want to go home and bake all my Motown CDs to a crisp in the desert sun. It had never occurred to me that I could feel anything other than admiration for Diana Ross.

"Okay," I agreed, tossing the offending bone into the truck so Brontë would follow. "I'll give you a call tomorrow when I've checked out a few other things."

She just nodded and drove off. I wasn't sure whether I'd just made a complete idiot of myself while wrecking what might have been a great love affair, or had consented rationally to an alteration in our relationship which would now involve working together. I was sure that whatever had happened, it was going to be more interesting than skimming lizards out of my pool for two more years.

Chapter Nine

On the long drive home I thought about murder, starting with Cain and Abel and ending with Muffin Crandall. The allegorical Judeo-Christian first murder, Eden Snow had pointed out in one of her early works entitled *Wonder Bread of Heaven,* was a revisionist mess. Originally it involved conflict over growing plants to sustain human life as opposed to butchering animals for the same purpose. When the patriarchal deity rather predictably snubbed Cain's offering of grain but was thrilled with Abel's dead infant cow, Cain murdered his brother in a rage over the unfairness of it all. I sang a few bars of "The Farmer and the Cowman" from *Oklahoma!* until Brontë gave me a baleful look and draped one foreleg over her head.

"You can listen to Verdi highlights when we get home," I told her. One of the perks of living in the middle of nowhere is that there are no neighbors to complain when dogs listen to opera. Or when reclusive social psychologists blast Fauré's *Requiem* into the lavender dusk in order to wallow in sadness echoing back from marble-streaked Paleozoic hills much older than Genesis.

Since agriculture was the invention and practice of women, Snow had insisted in *Wonder Bread,* the allegorical Cain should have been Abel's firstborn *sister* and would have had no interest in macho comparisons between her grain and his dead calves. She would just have gone on planting and harvesting. After all, there was bread to bake, people to feed. The whole Cain and Abel tale, Snow said, was yet another patriarchal usurpation of female expertise with the usual regrettable ending. Murder.

A male-tale of murder with envy as motive. "You think your (fill-in-the-blank) is better than mine? Well, I'll show *you!*" Biff, pow, blam. Another allegory bites the dust. Yawn. Cain and Abel would never explain Muffin and Victor. I would have to look elsewhere.

Unable to think of any biblical stories involving murders committed by women, I remembered Lizzie Borden. On August 4, 1892, thirty-two-year-old Lizzie either did or didn't take an axe and give her (step)mother forty whacks, followed by forty-one directed to her father. The evidence was scant. Lizzie was acquitted and lived out her days in Fall River, Massachusetts, with an older sister, Emma, believed by some Borden scholars to have been the axewoman.

Lizzie Borden died in 1927. Her story did not. Murders committed by women are rare, unsolved Victorian ones rarer and interminably fascinating. Since Lizzie's death three quarters of a century ago there has been unrelenting interest in her. Three well-researched biographies, one one-act and two full-length plays, two celebrated novels, countless ballads and folk songs, and a complete ballet have spun from the bloody events of a single afternoon in a small Massachusetts town. A double murder in which the perpetrator was, whether Lizzie or Emma, a woman. A violent, dramatic, gore-splattered murder still unsolved more than a century later. Mother's milk to the American psyche. I wondered if I'd stumbled into something similar.

"Muffin Crandall took an axe," I sang to Brontë, "and gave Camacho forty whacks . . ." It did scan nicely, although Muffin had said she used a paperweight. Additionally, I thought, the century separating Lizzie and Muffin had wrought such enormous changes in female self-perception that the two women might be from different planets. Lizzie Borden had seen few options for her life through the heavily draped windows of that Fall River parlor. Muffin Crandall had not only seen options, she'd grabbed them.

And murder is, typically, not a function of option. People who kill do so in a perceived *absence* of options. For whatever reasons, whether to establish status, protect themselves or others, or to wreak vengeance, those who murder are unable to imagine other methods for achieving those goals. Yet Muffin had a life history which suggested no impulsivity and great facility with options. If Victor Camacho had harmed her or someone close to her, I was sure she could have come up with numerous methods for redressing the wrong. These methods would not have involved killing and then freezing him. And yet that was the story Muffin held out to the world in yellowed, dying hands.

A story about a pathetic, half-crazy old woman in a dark garage. A woman who in a crisis could only remember those primitive, bloody skills learned from her husband. Why, the poor dear must have seen countless fish and small animals bashed over the head in her role as companion to a sportsman. It's sort of understandable, isn't it, that when this stranger attacked her, and with her mind getting fuzzy, she just did what she knew how to do?

As Brontë and I left cool mountain air for our descent into the desert, I acknowledged again the brilliance of the story. Especially given Muffin's terminal medical condition. At her death the case would be closed. No further inquiry. Just a yarn told by sheriff's deputies from time to time and then forgotten. The intelligence behind it took my breath away. Muffin Crandall, or somebody she was protecting, might just have committed the perfect murder. But why?

After getting home and putting *Rigoletto* on the stereo for Brontë, I phoned Nanna Foy.

"I'm aware that Muffin is terminally ill," I told her. "Is that what you called about last night?"

"Yes, Blue," she said in what I was beginning to think of as her Baudelaire voice. "But there's more to it than that."

"Well . . . ?"

"It's not something I want to discuss over the phone. Perhaps we could get together for a drink somewhere?"

I remembered translating Baudelaire in an undergraduate poetry seminar. At nineteen I imagined myself deeply sophisticated because I could recite Anne Sexton's "Her Kind" while smoking a cigarette and tossing my hair in the curious way Sexton did. But in Baudelaire I discovered the real scaffolding of sophistication—an ability to understand the forbidden without being brought to the poet's *"Pluviôse,"* a January bitter and drenched with ruin. Except for my wild love of Misha I had escaped ruinous passions, and thus escaped dying from debauchery in a Parisian gutter. In Nanna Foy's voice I heard rain falling on cobbled French streets.

"Someplace 'where your flames still bite my thigh . . . '?" I quoted from Sexton's poem, skirting disaster for the second time that day, but staying in the game. I was flushed with pride at my brazen display of worldliness.

"I had thought we might have dinner first." Nanna laughed, winning the round.

She would win all of them, I suspected. Nanna Foy was at least twenty years older than I and had been around the block more times than I'd been around my living room. She was also stunningly attractive and bold. I felt like a hamster under the hypnotic spell of a hooded cobra.

"I'd like to hear about the history of your little group with Victor Camacho," I said, blasting my way out of hamsterhood. "Dinner would be fine."

"Tonight then?" she suggested as if I'd never mentioned Camacho. "Why don't I make reservations at La Fève. Have you been there? Of course Saturdays are impossible, but I know the owner. Say eight or nine?"

I'd heard of the restaurant named in French "The Bean" but I'd never been there, principally because it's not in San Diego where I hang out when I'm not at home, but in Palm Springs.

"You want to drive all the way to Palm Springs for dinner?" I gasped, losing my tenuous cool entirely. "I really don't think—"

"Of course not, Blue," she interrupted efficiently. "We'll fly. I lease a small plane for business trips and what-have-you, and I'm sure I can get a pilot. There's a private airport in Borrego. Can you meet me there at six-thirty?"

"Fly?" I repeated as if attempting to name a rare insect.

"I'll have a limo meet us at the airport near Palm Springs," she went on. "The restaurant is very nice."

I was sure it was. Its drop-dead gorgeous owner was a local legend. Rumored to be a retired Marine colonel, she had parlayed the annual lipstick-lesbian migration to Palm Springs for the Dinah Shore Golf Classic into a string of highly successful businesses. She'd started with Jeep tours to catered midnight picnics in the desert, then bought up a few rattletrap motels, refurbished them in thick carpets and indirect lighting, and advertised heavily in gay publications all over the world.

But the flagship was her restaurant, La Fève. Its three chefs did incredible things with Portobello mushrooms, caramelized garlic, and a rare pink basmati rice that, I'd heard, smelled like bananas and could only be purchased once a year from a handful of vendors in Calcutta. And that was only the first item on the appetizer menu. La Fève was the place to be seen when you were ostensibly away from L.A. or San Diego in order not to be seen. All the right people were said to fawn on the owner with her dashing crew cut, tux, and military posture. Lesbian chic with your radicchio miso.

"I'm afraid I have plans for this evening," I said without mentioning that my plans involved a long walk with a dog among spiny plants, followed by ten games of computer solitaire before checking my carpets for the presence of unusual medications. I wondered how to ask subtly if Nanna Foy had high blood pressure.

"Oh, but I was looking forward to seeing you," she replied in tones which hinted that she might fling herself from a balcony out of disappointment. Not a high balcony, but something with enough pizzazz to wrench an ankle. I loved it.

Nobody, I realized, had ever pursued me with dramatic fervor. Not the boys I dated in high school and not the boys and girls I dated in college and grad school after it dawned on me that my pool of potential soul mates was slightly more than twice as big as I'd been led to believe. Even Misha hadn't strewn my bed with rose petals or begged me to fly with her to pretentious restaurants.

"I'm free tomorrow night, though," I capitulated while managing to remember that Nanna Foy might not be what she seemed. "Why don't you drop by my place for a swim and dinner? I'll make something salt-free."

The ensuing silence was just a half second too long either due to my turf grabbing or to something about salt. Maybe I'd snagged the culprit who for unknown reasons broke and entered my home. Or else Nanna Foy thought I was one of those people who remove one food item from their diets yearly until there's nothing left to eat but grits and they die.

"Mmm," she finally murmured, overdoing it suggestively, "but I love salt, don't you? Should I bring a suit?"

"Whatever you like," I chirped, my voice cracking as Luciano Pavarotti sang to Brontë that *"la donna e mobile,"* the woman is fickle. "Brontë and I usually don't wear them."

"Brontë?"

"Oh, that's right, you haven't met her. She was out in my truck when I spoke with you at Mrs. Tewalt's condo. She's black, you know."

Rox would have crushed my instep under a cowboy boot for the racial innuendo, but I couldn't resist using every underhanded ploy available in this fencing match with Nanna. It was fun.

"I look forward to meeting her," Nanna parried. "But I'm afraid our conversation about Muffin must remain private. You understand."

"Of course. But Brontë is the soul of discretion. She doesn't talk."

"I think it would be better if we met somewhere privately," Nanna insisted. "Everyone talks."

"Perhaps you're right." I sighed, stretching the phone cord to the kitchen where I grabbed a desiccated liver treat and waved it near a wet Doberman nose, drawing a polite "woof" of interest. "She's talking now."

"Blue, you're adorable," Nanna Foy told me with that undercurrent of irritation you sense in losers at Wimbledon. "I'll drive out. Shall we say six?"

"Six," I repeated. "We have said six."

"Ciao, then."

"Chow."

After hanging up I dived to the floor and rolled around with Brontë, celebrating my temporary triumph in a game at which I've never been any good. An education centered on demographic analyses and the history of social science since 1902 when Max Weber wrote *The Protestant Ethic and the Spirit of Capitalism* has not proven useful to me in conducting flirtations. Or evading them, either. No one wants to hear about Durkheim's notion that fluctuations in national suicide rates may be indicators of social problems while flirting. Or at least most people don't. Misha did.

Misha wanted to hear everything involving impersonal data, and she listened. She even read my dissertation and asked questions about the footnotes, an exercise not even my committee had bothered with. Often in the sweaty, still-enmeshed moments after lovemaking she'd prop her head on a bony fist and whisper questions like, "Do you think Marxist women make love like we do, or is it sort of political?" Then she'd blush and pull on a T-shirt and go wash her car or comb Brontë for fleas. Misha was perennially skittish about our ongoing hunger for each other, as if it were an embarrassing and dangerous relative best hidden in the attic.

Alone in cooling sheets I'd ponder a different perspective. One that accepted a mystery that could throw two people together with such force that the collision threatened sanity. Make them crave that moment, its echo and spiraling light, forever. I had learned how it was from my parents, Elizabeth and Jake, although I didn't know what I'd learned until Jake told me the story two years ago, after Misha was gone. I have wanted to tell her the story ever since then. Needed to tell her. The impossibility of telling her felt like a Volkswagen dropped suddenly on my chest and made the carpet itch against my cheek. That impossibility and another one that had slipped into my brain unnoticed.

"Wait a minute," I said to Brontë. "How does Nanna Foy know where I live? How does she know where to show up tomorrow night at shall-we-say-six?"

Dan Crandall, he'd told me, had learned from my publisher that I taught at San Gabriel University, even though I didn't anymore. The switchboard operator at San Gabriel had forwarded his call to the Social Sciences Department office, where somebody had asked around and finally informed him that I supposedly lived in Borrego Springs, a hermit. My name is not listed in the wafer-thin Borrego Springs phone directory, and my business cards list only a Post Office box address. Dan had rented a car, driven out here, and asked at two gas stations, the Dairy Queen, and a real estate office before locating somebody who told him how to find me. I couldn't see Nanna Foy going through that hassle. And besides, she seemed to know already. Had Dan talked to Muffin's friends, mentioned the precise location of my nearly unfindable digs? Why would he? Or had Nanna Foy been here before? For all its pleasant nuance, there was something about Nanna Foy's interest that was beginning to give me the creeps.

Everything was giving me the creeps. Victor Camacho in heavy frost, Muffin Crandall already the faded page of an old book you can't quite read. Dan, Roxie, Nanna Foy. Helen Tewalt's too-perfect country design condo with a cute, punked-out kid on her screen saver next to a paperweight that wasn't hers, and a book that shouldn't have been in her bookcase. Everything obscure and just out of reach. Like my life.

Late afternoon is silent in the desert, baking hot and shimmering with emptiness. It's the worst time to be out there. No moisture remains from the previous night's condensation. It's all been drawn to the sun and burned to black, voiceless specks that look like floating pinholes in the air. Boulders and rocks are hot and exude auras that touch you, brush you with feathers of deadly warmth as you walk over J-shaped tracks left by sidewinders. Nothing moves but swarms of shining, ebony-colored ants on their mounds of sand. In the heat they're like robots—tiny, alien machines going about business you couldn't comprehend and wouldn't want to. I knew it was time to go out there, alone.

Like me, Brontë has a white visor with a flip-down polarized eyeshade to protect her from sun blindness. Hers is like a little cloth helmet with ear holes and a chin strap, and she'll wear it. But she won't wear the four padded boots I got to protect her paws from the heat of the desert floor. That day she would have to stay behind.

After pulling on white shorts and a huge white T-shirt, I slowly drank two quarts of water and then put two more quarts in my pack before jumping into the pool in my clothes. Then socks, shoes, and visor, and I was off to search for the secret passage back to my other life. The one I'd had before Dan Crandall showed up and I flung myself into a universal pattern that was moving too fast. I couldn't keep up. In two years I'd forgotten how fast it moves, how elusive and perplexing it is. I wanted out, off, away. Wanted to go back. The sidelines had been fine. Now where was the path that would take me there?

Behind Wren's Gulch is the northern quadrant of the Anza-Borrego Desert State Park, named for Juan Bautista de Anza, Spanish captain of a 1776 colonial expedition, and for the reclusive bighorn sheep who still live here, called *borrego* in Spanish. I had never seen one of the bighorns, who are like ghosts. But I knew my way to Coyote Canyon where they sometimes come down from the mountains for water. That's where I'd go, I decided. At least as far as Lower Willows along Coyote Creek. An eight-mile round trip. It wasn't the most intelligent decision I'd made in thirty-five years or even that day. But it seemed right.

It wasn't. I had hoped for a doorway to my earlier disconnected complacency, but the desert was locked. Behind a yellow-white sky I knew the grid pulsed with intention and the song of vast equations. If not exactly joyful in the human sense, it was wild with delight at its own design. And it was inaccessible. Oblivious. Nonexistent. Having rejoined it, I couldn't detach. It just doesn't work like that. I was stuck in its strobing pattern, alive and shuddering.

"Grid!" I yelled up into blinding hot stillness a mile from the creek, "I want to go back! I was happy out here eating brown rice and reading obscure novels. People just dazzle me. I screw everything up. My brother's getting married and Misha's gone. I feel like a pinball machine. I want darkness. Okay?"

Nothing happened. Not even a tiny sandslide triggered by the feet of ants. Nothing moved, everything just baked as it had done since the evaporation of ancient seas. I was walking on the crust of time, whining.

Or something was. I could hear a sound wending through the iron and marble rocks, the sandstone and shale and schist of those moist, lizard-filled days when the brain I would inherit lacked frontal lobes, hadn't split into hemispheres. When things were automatic, simple.

I sighed for the good old days and drank some water. The sound stopped, then started again. A sort of "oo" lost in the heat. It was weird, but then the desert is weird. Light swims by, fills the empty eye socket of a prospector who fell and broke his ankle in 1870, and then draws a shadow behind it, a wake of blindness. There is nothing to see. Just rock, rubble, cholla cactus, ironwood, and smoke tree. Everything seems dead. But it isn't.

The sound snaked over my head again. "Oo." Its register was low, not that mosquito whine you sometimes get from dehydration. And I wasn't dehydrated, anyway. Three miles on nearly three quarts of water is more than acceptable. When I got to Coyote Creek I'd purify two more quarts and then walk back.

"Oo," the thing said again, closer now, irritating the silence with its urgency.

I carry the Glock, loaded, in my pack despite the park's rule about no guns. I don't like or dislike guns. I just had one with me. Taking it from the side pocket of my waist pack, I checked the clip, snapped it back in, but left the safety on. From a narrow slot-canyon which afforded good cover I held the gun in both hands, left supporting right, and waited. The "oo" could mean anything. A rabid coyote, practicing tenor, wind in a rock formation. Except there wasn't any wind.

And it wasn't saying "oo," it was saying "Blue." It was calling my name.

The rattle of dislodged gravel from a wash signaled the direction of its approach, and I lowered the gun. In seconds Dan Crandall rounded an outcropping of iron-riddled granite, flushed and stumbling in shorts and a navy blue polo shirt. He had no hat and no water.

"Dan, are you out of your mind?" I yelled, emerging from behind my rock.

"Why do you have a gun?" he said, squinting.

"You might have been a crazed mastodon. What in hell are you doing out here with nothing to drink?"

"Tracking you," he said as I handed him my last quart of water. He looked as though somebody had kicked his ribs in, and it wasn't just the heat.

"It's Bea," he said, weaving in the dry, hot air. "She's dead. She died. Bea's gone. It happened this afternoon after you and the shrink saw her. They'd taken her to the infirmary, and . . ."

I tucked the Glock back into my pack, and held out my arms to him. "I'm so sorry, Dan. The cancer. I'm so sorry it happened now. Rox said the lawyer was going to ask for a bail reduction and get her out on Monday. I'm just so sorry."

His eyes bore a puzzled look like a skin over the grief he hadn't yet begun to feel.

"But it wasn't the cancer, Blue," he whispered. "She was murdered."

Chapter Ten

"Murdered?" I repeated. "Murdered in a prison infirmary? How? By whom? Why?"

I was having trouble with context. This conversation didn't belong in my solitary inferno. It didn't belong anywhere.

"I don't know," he answered, shaking his head too hard, whipping his ponytail violently. "There's an investigation. There will be an investigation. It looks like poison, they said. I had to authorize an autopsy. They said it might be suicide, too, except . . ."

"Muffin would not commit suicide."

The comment seemed appropriate, but I had more to do. Dan Crandall had apparently come to my place because he had nowhere else to go, no other friend to talk to. But when I wasn't there and my truck was, he must have correctly assumed I was out hiking and launched himself after me. Into baking, hundred-degree heat and glare. In a dark, heat-absorbing shirt and with no water. At the moment, I realized, my first job was to keep him alive.

"They said maybe somebody brought her something, sneaked something to her," he said. "A pill or something. There were visiting hours this afternoon. Her friends came. The prison authorities think maybe, you know, she was in the infirmary, maybe somebody brought . . . something."

He was repeating himself and kept squinting as if his eyes were burning, which they were. I could easily walk to Coyote Creek from where we were in fifteen minutes, but with Dan it would take longer. Still, there was no other option. A waterless three-mile forced march back to my place with a man already half sunblind and in shock would be asking for trouble. At the creek we could get water, cool down, and wait for dusk to start back.

From my pack I took a large square of white percale cut from an old sheet and sawed two slits in it with the little Swiss Army knife on my belt. This I draped over his head to his nose and secured it with a length of the fifty-pound-test fishing line I also carry along with plastic bags and antivenin.

"Adjust it until you can see through the slits and keep your head down so that your brow ridges shade your eyes," I told him. "That's what they're for. You'll eventually get a headache and may temporarily lose your vision. If that happens, don't worry. I'll get you to the creek, leave you with drinkable water, hike back, and call the rangers to pick you up. I can do it in well under an hour once the sun goes down. You'll be fine."

"What's going on, Blue?" he said, ignoring reassurances that I would prevent his transformation to a brittle corpse. "My sister didn't kill anybody and should never have been in jail and now somebody's killed her. Everything's crazy. I don't understand what's going on. I know she wouldn't kill herself. She wouldn't. I know her. Nobody's telling me what's going on."

Through the slits in a piece of old sheet I'd never expected to need, I could see Muffin Crandall's dark blue eyes. The brother and sister had inherited the same eyes. Twin eyes. Except the sister had taken the role of mother, been the only parent Dan Crandall would ever have. Now she was gone and nothing stood anymore between the child he'd been and the mystery religions are created to explain. I knew a little about how that felt. So did my brother. The comparisons were making me dizzy.

"Don't talk anymore," I explained quietly. "I mean that literally. Breathe through your nose, keep your mouth closed. Too much moisture is lost by drawing hot, dry air across the mucous membranes of your mouth and throat and then exhaling. You're really in minimal danger and I'm overdoing the precautions because you're in a little shock over the news of your sister's death. Just follow me and don't think about anything except putting one foot in front of the other. We'll talk later. Do you understand?"

"Okay," he agreed, "but it seems silly."

"It isn't," I said, and headed east toward Coyote Creek.

After twenty minutes or so I could smell the signature of water in the air. Tendrils of oxygen molecules promising life. We all spend our first nine months underwater, breathing that scent. No wonder it smells like home.

"We're almost there," I told Dan while pointing to the grove of tamarisks, desert willows, mesquite, and wild grape growing beside Coyote Creek. The area is called Lower Willows because there are three patches along spring-fed Coyote Creek where sufficient sand and plant debris has accumulated to provide footing for tree roots. The earliest English-speaking travelers through Coyote Canyon, probably Mormons, named these with a singular lack of imagination. Lower, Middle, and Upper Willows. Boring. I had my own names for the three oases, gleaned from Emily Dickinson. "Route of Evanescence, Resonance of Emerald, and Rush of Cochineal." Dickinson had been describing a hummingbird, but desert creeks are like that, too.

"Wow," Dan said when he saw water spilling through troughs of rock, "this is heaven."

"It may well be," I agreed, filling the two wide-mouthed quart containers and dropping a water purification tablet in each. In a half hour we could drink it. "There's a shallow pool upstream about fifty yards. Go up there, take your clothes off and lie in the water for about ten minutes. Then air-dry before you put your clothes back on. When the sun goes down the temperature can drop as much as fifty degrees, although not usually at this time of year. More like twenty now, but enough to cause a problem with hypothermia if your clothes are wet."

"Blue, I can see town from here. Nobody could die from anything this close to a town."

"You don't understand the desert. It's different. Distances are deceptive and the danger is invisible. It's all chemistry and physics out here. Keep as much of your brain as possible in the water for the full ten minutes and fold the white cloth over your eyes."

"My wife would love this," he said, heading upstream. "She thrives in sun."

I sat on a shady rock with my feet in the water until he came back.

"If she thrives in sun, why is she living in Alaska?" I asked, avoiding the topic of Muffin's death until he brought it up.

"She married me, I got a job there," he said as if no further explanation were necessary. "I was still in the Air Force when we got married, but this friend of mine—he's a bush pilot—had left the service already and moved up there. He loved it, knew I would, too. So he told me there was plenty of work building hangars on lakes for the pontoon planes everybody has in Alaska, and he'd help me get started. Kathy, that's my wife, was game to try it when I mustered out, so we went. That was eleven years ago. She started taking classes at U. of Anchorage and got a degree. She teaches there now. Bea and Deck came up to visit a lot. I thought it was okay."

"But it wasn't?"

"I guess not."

"Dan, Muffin said something about you yesterday just as the psychiatrist and I were leaving. She said I should give you a shove in the right direction if I could."

"No shit?" he said, tears filming his eyes. "She said that?"

"Yeah."

He was so pleased I had to look away. My mother had told me how proud she was that I'd made a Jell-O salad with celery and crushed pineapple for dinner that night before her Sierra Club meeting. The last night of her life. You remember these things. She'd told me how good the salad was. And she made sure dad and David would wash the dishes so I could work on my science report for school the next day, which was about bird skeletons. I hadn't cared how birds achieve flight with hollow-boned "hands" attached to their shoulders and didn't want to do the report. Her last words to me were ordinary and compelling. They said that my Jell-O salad was good, that I was a good person, but that I would still have to write my report. A report on wings.

Muffin's last words about Dan seemed to have risen from a similar love.

"Blue," he said after a while, "where is she now? Where do you think she is?"

I had expected the question. Dad has said a hundred times it's the one people always ask after a death, and the one for which there really is no answer. We'd been at the creek for a while, maybe forty-five minutes, and the sun was low in the west, layering the last corrugated waves of heat over granite hills that would soon swallow the day. In the desert this moment is holy, a fleeting blend of things sensed but unprovable. I laid my hand on the ground and told Dan to do the same.

"I think it's like this," I said. "Feel the ground but look up. There are no birds. The sky is empty."

"But my sister . . ." he said.

"I know. Keep your hand on the ground. Wait."

Then in the silence it happened, just a soft snap you feel in your eyes. The beginning of dusk. An edge of dimness that suddenly floods the sky. And then birds. From nests in the ground beneath our hands, from under creosote bushes and inside beavertail cactus they soared. Swallows, cactus wrens, elf owls, and phoebes. Far away, swooping forms that were not there before became ravens, a hawk. The sky was not quiet, but laced with chirrs and pipings.

"Oh, my God, Blue," Dan wept, "do you really think it happens like that, after we die?"

I was thinking of my mother and crying with him, wishing I had cried with Misha, wondering if David ever cried when he thought about mom. "I hope so," I said. "I think so."

We were sitting close together, touching. It didn't seem strange when he turned to kiss me. The scratchiness of him, the mustache and sandpaper cheeks, were surprising after so many years of a softer face, but it was all right. I wanted not to be alone. So did he. As a thousand desert birds rose and cartwheeled above Coyote Creek, he moved above me and then stopped.

"Is it okay?" he asked.

"Yes," I said, pulling him close. It had nothing to do with love and little to do with sex. What it had to do with was loneliness and grief. And the birds.

He seemed like one of them, more graceful and aware than any of the men I'd slept with in the days before Misha. He was slow, tantalizing, adept, like a woman.

"Where," I asked later, "did you learn . . . ?"

"From Kathy," he answered, brushing my white shorts carefully before handing them to me and then turning away as I pulled them on. "From my wife."

We had made love to Kathy, then, and Misha, and a desert sky laced with birds. So bemused was I with that trinity that I failed to remember my godmother, Carter Upchurch. I would remember her later, though, a lot.

"I thought about what you said yesterday," he began, avoiding the issue of our recent intimacy as I also avoided it by dramatically capping the now-pure water and securing it with much flourish in my pack. "About how I revert to acting like an ape when I haven't decided to do something else."

"And . . . ?"

"Like right now," he said, nodding. "I want to take that gun out of your pack and shoot it. Shoot at that rock over there or maybe set up a target, maybe set up those plastic water bottles and blow 'em away. It's because I'm upset about Bea and want to even the score by claiming some territory, right? Make a bunch of noise and blow something to bits, then I'll feel better?"

"It wouldn't work because there are no other males nearby to reinforce you by cheering and jumping around, joining you in the racket and destruction. All that would happen is you'd drive the birds away, destroy the water bottle that kept you from dehydration this afternoon, and probably get arrested when somebody irrigating the nearest orange grove hears the shots and calls the rangers. The goal is to think of other behaviors to supplant the stupid ones. You're at a disadvantage because you were in the military, which is based on the primate model, but you're intelligent enough to overcome it. What are you going to do?"

"How about throwing some rocks? That's quiet and nothing would be hurt."

"Try this," I suggested. "Envision a gorilla throwing rocks in a desert. How does he look?"

"Stupid."

"Is that how you want to look?"

"No."

"So how do you want to look?"

"Like me, Dan Crandall, Bea's brother and Kathy's husband, a guy who's good with his hands, who builds things. This sharp, cool, competent guy who can build anything."

"So what does a sharp, cool, competent guy who can build anything do when he's out in a desert and upset because the sister who raised him has just died?"

Dan eyed the terrain thoughtfully. "Build something," he answered softly. "A monument to remember Bea."

"Can you envision the gorilla doing that?" I prodded the concept home.

"No. A gorilla wouldn't . . ."

"Then good," I concluded it. He was doing even better than the kids at juvy. I hoped Muffin Crandall knew I was trying.

For an hour I watched birds as Dan selected rocks and carried them to a spot on the sandy floodplain stretching east from the creek. When he was finished, he stood back, hands on hips, and beckoned to me. It was an impressive cairn, well constructed to withstand the spring floods that would wash over it year after year.

"This is for you, Bea," he said simply. "Thanks for being my mom."

For once, I didn't say anything.

After drinking half the water we started back. It wasn't dark yet, but already a few pale stars were visible. In the chemical aftermath of sex my body was sending messages to which my brain was responding by dredging up buried images. Misha wide-eyed and giggling after we'd made love in her office with seventeen host families for a student-exchange program drinking coffee in the conference room next door. Misha on a moonless beach. On our apartment balcony in the rain. In the back seat of her car under parking lot lights after a movie in which we'd held hands so tightly I could feel her fingers laced to mine for a week.

"Um, I'm sorry I . . . the sex I mean," Dan mentioned tentatively. "Guess that was gorilla, huh?"

"No," I hedged. "Not gorilla, exactly. Well maybe. We both wanted to do that. It happens."

"I want Kathy to see the rocks, the monument I built for Bea," he said after a silence. "Then if she and I get back together and I talk about it, she'll be able to picture it in her mind."

"But she's in Alaska."

I didn't want to talk. I wanted to stomp over rocks in silence until my brain had finished flipping through its sexually explicit photo album. Far overhead a jet flashed soundlessly, catching the last orange of the sun. Its passengers, looking down, could not see me or Dan, could see nothing but rumpled grayness. The plane itself was dollhouse-sized, a toy lost in the sky. Misha, wherever she was, was equally far, equally out of all reach.

"Kathy's flying down Monday for the funeral," Dan went on. "The autopsy will be done on Monday and they'll release the body. My sister's friends are setting up the funeral for that afternoon, and they've got a plot in a cemetery for her. She'll be buried here, in San Diego. Kathy said she wanted to come, and I want her to. And I want her to see the stones I built, if that's okay with you."

Carter Upchurch had never mentioned this particular awkward situation.

"It's a wonderful idea, Dan." I nodded, flinging tender pictures of Misha Deland from my head like feathers into desert dusk. I needed the space to cope with the prospect of meeting the estranged but nonetheless still-married wife of a man with whom I'd unaccountably just had sex. Was I now an "other woman?" I wondered. If so, what should I wear?

"But I wouldn't feel comfortable tagging along," I concluded. "Can you find your way out here by yourself?"

"I think so. Just wanted to clear it with you."

"Cleared," I said.

Back at the Gulch we ate salty canned soup and Dan took aspirin for his predictable headache. Then we played catch with Brontë until she was tired, and sat by the pool in the dark. Already Dan Crandall with his ponytail and mustache seemed the stranger to me that he actually was. A transitory shadow cast across my life by a pattern humming gleefully out of sight. The damn grid.

"There isn't much time and I'm tired," I said, "but I want to honor Muffin's request. You're figuring out how to avoid the lowest-common-denominator primate behaviors that bring your wife to despair. But there are a couple more things. More superficial things."

"Okay. What are they?" he rumbled, interested.

"First is Alaska. If she doesn't want to be there, can't feel at home there, she'll leave. No one should stay in an incompatible place just because someone else finds it compatible. Have you ever thought of living with her in some locale that you *both* like?"

"No," he said, "I haven't thought about that, but I can."

"The other thing is a kindergarten basic involving messiness, bodily wastes, intestinal gas, belching, references to private body parts, general grossness. For reasons which are unclear, some human males seem to tolerate messiness very well, and actually enjoy endless jokes and references to unpleasant body functions. Most women find all this repugnant. If you want to live with a woman it's absolutely essential that you pick up after yourself, don't leave messes for her to clean up, and confine the bodily-waste and sex jokes to all-male contexts. It may seem manipulative and unauthentic, but it wouldn't be a bad idea if you bought an ordinary etiquette book tomorrow and studied it. On Monday she's coming to a strange place, away from the web of her daily life. As the only familiar figure here, you will by default be the center of her attention. You will have an opportunity to convince her that you love her by convincing her that you're *aware* of her. Her feelings and needs."

"She says I'm, you know, pretty good in the sack," he muttered, looking at the pool decking as I felt a flush creep up my neck. She was right.

"It's not enough," I said, wishing I were somewhere else. Anywhere. Tibet, maybe. Or South America. The Falkland Islands would do.

"You really think reading an etiquette book will help?"

"It's a start," I sighed. "A gesture."

"I'll do it," he said with a military squaring-of-shoulders. "I'm going to win this. I'm not going to lose her."

"Good luck." I smiled as he stood to leave. "And let me know about the funeral arrangements, okay? Just leave a message on my machine."

"Roger," he answered, not looking back as he loped up the road toward my gate two miles away. Toward his rented car parked there. Toward his future.

I watched him turn to pewter in the light of a half-moon, his ponytail like a metronome as he jogged. In minutes he was just a moving distortion on the horizon, then gone.

Only then did it come back to me, a picture of rhubarb bread on an antique pewter plate. An article about rhubarb in a magazine at Helen Tewalt's condo. About the plant's deadly, poisonous leaves. Had one of her friends, maybe Helen Tewalt, taken Muffin a rhubarb dish this afternoon? In the prison infirmary security would be lax. Everybody knew Muffin was dying, anyway. Had one of the guards looked the other way as a nice old lady friend of the prisoner brought yet another basket of goodies? Were there such things as rhubarb cookies, and would the medical examiner think to check for rhubarb poisoning? I imagined a glossy magazine cover with lots of calico tablecloths artfully spilling from an antique Pennsylvania Dutch coffin. *Last Desserts,* it would be called. Subscribe now.

"I'm losing it," I told Brontë a few minutes later as I splashed in the tub and selected an herbal bath gel. "Women rarely kill, and when they do they don't kill their friends. There was no point, anyway. So who poisoned Muffin Crandall?"

Outside a barn owl repeated the question, "Who, whooo?" But nothing else said anything.

Chapter Eleven

That night I dreamed of Misha again. It was the same stone house in a residential neighborhood usually described as "transitional." Meaning a little run-down with a few boardinghouses, a lot of unkempt yards, and shrubbery that went to woody stem during the Reagan administration. A gray neighborhood of leaning wrought iron fences and cheap lawn furniture on a sagging porch where somebody has dismantled a motorcycle. The occasional gentrified property is obvious for its new gas lamp, cleaned and tuck-pointed bricks, and border of marigolds. There are no neighborhoods like this in California, where there are no bricks to tuck-point. The dream had taken me somewhere else.

Somewhere east of the Mountain Time Zone, I thought in sleep as I pushed against the decorative window of a warped exterior door. The window sported peacocks etched like frost in the glass. The doorknob was loose and blackened with age, but I could see that it had been crafted of brass in the shape of a rose. The frozen peacocks and forgotten rose were terrifying, but then in dreams anything can be terrifying. Q-Tips, foreign cars, lint. It was one of those dreams where you know you're dreaming and feel snobby and condescending about the scare tactics. I remember that the house smelled faintly of Doberman, and remember thinking that was because I wasn't in the house at all but in my own bed with a Doberman. The Dobie scent is like warm crackers. Like Wheat Thins.

Misha wasn't visible, but I knew she was in the house. Some other people were there, mostly women, moving around with great purpose. One of them talked on a phone, looking worried. Another pulled a bulging trash bag into the hallway where I stood. I couldn't hear and I couldn't speak. I couldn't move past the dingy, oak-paneled hallway. Then it was over.

I awoke some hours later, fully aware of the dream and vaguely disappointed. Surely something racier was in order after my sad dalliance with a dead woman's brother, I thought. At least something reminding me of patriarchal evils. A scene in which the Washington Monument falls on Elizabeth Cady Stanton seemed appropriate. This dream was so devoid of symbolism that it was boring. And it felt real. Padding my way to the chemical toilet in my bathroom, I wondered for the first time in two years where Misha was. Where she was now.

The dream had kicked up a dim but spreading awareness that I actually knew nothing except that she was gone. A single syllable of pre–Anglo-Saxon origin comprised the entire canon of my knowledge about Misha Deland for the last two years. Gone. As in absent, not here. The point of view was heinously singular. Mine. It was arrogant. And it no longer felt righteous. I had murdered Misha in my head and created a vacuum around which my life flowed with shallow ease. It was, I realized, the coping strategy of a world-class wimp.

After feeding Brontë I phoned one of the old crowd, a casual friend who was still on the faculty at San Gabriel.

"Do you remember the name of that ex-nun who published the boring feminist periodical?" I asked. "All the articles were about banking. She was Misha's friend. Elaine Dennis or Denise Edsel. Something with Es and Ds."

"You mean Deirdre Eckels," she said. "Haven't seen that magazine in a long time. Years. Not that anyone misses it. I think I heard she left town a while back, too, right after Misha left. Deirdre, I mean. Something about Bosnia. She was going to work for Amnesty International, editing something about the atrocities against women, the rapes. Why?"

"I . . . I've been having this dream," I stammered. "It's about Misha. I want to know where she is. This Deirdre Eckels would know."

"Nobody's heard from Misha since she left, and nobody really knew Deirdre well enough to keep in touch with her, either. People come and go, Blue. Sorry I can't help you, but it's probably best if you just forget it. I mean, my God, how long has it been now?"

"Two years," I answered. "Listen, thanks."

Next I called Amnesty in San Diego. They always have an answering machine that gives a bunch of numbers to call depending on which set of political prisoners you want to help. I picked Bosnia and caught an unbelievably well-organized radical lawyer at home.

"There's nobody named Deirdre Eckels writing for us on Bosnia, never has been," he said. "I don't recognize the name, haven't seen it on any of the stuff coming out on Bosnian war crimes, not just our stuff. She might be writing for somebody else under another name, but I doubt it. I'd have heard. Sorry."

It took me an hour to unearth an old copy of Deirdre Eckels's periodical from one of the dusty boxes in Room No. 3 of Wren's Gulch Inn. I had bought it in the early weeks of my love affair with Misha because it had something to do with Misha. Its editor was her friend. Of course I would read it. But not even that hunger to incorporate, overnight, every nuance of the beloved's history could get me past page three of a twenty-seven-page article entitled "Barter in Beirut: The Usurpation of Female Economic Tradition Under the Turkish Ottoman Empire."

I had put the thing in a bookcase and later dumped it into a box for the move.

The magazine's text had obviously been printed with a desktop publishing program, and no name but Deirdre's appeared in the front with a Post Office box address. My copy was Issue No. 3, Volume I, which meant that only two issues had been printed before this one. I wondered why a former nun would develop an obsessive interest in feminist analyses of foreign banking practices. Then my cheeks flamed as I wondered if Deirdre Eckels was the "multilingual grant writer" with whom Misha had presumably eloped to New Zealand. It occurred to me that one would scarcely need to be multilingual in order to write grants in New Zealand.

I had no proof that the story Deirdre told me was true, and now that I considered it closely it didn't *feel* true. Something was wrong with the story, had been wrong for two years. So why had I believed it?

Back in my office cum living room I edged the air-conditioning up a notch, closed the Venetian blinds I practically never use, and tugged my handmade drapes over the window. A Federal blue houndstooth design on an ecru background, I'd lined the fabric with that silver Teflon stuff ironing board covers are made of. My drapes could probably withstand the burning crash of an asteroid two feet outside the window. It occurred to me that what I'd done out here in the desert was to build an impenetrable fort. Against losing Misha, against confusion, against everything.

Sitting professionally at my desk, I tapped a thumb against my copy of *The Chicago Manual of Style,* then opened it to a random page. Other people do this with the Bible, the *I Ching,* or Tarot cards, but I find random contemplation of the Franco-Joycean dash or the rules for mathematical punctuation just as meaningful.

"Indonesians of Javan origin use only a personal name, family names being nonexistent in Java," the *Manual* informed me. Although some Muslin Indonesians might take Arabic names, it said, and Indonesians living in Western cultures might just fake surnames in order not to look odd in phone directories. A problem for indexers of Indonesian names, but not for me. *The Chicago Manual of Style* never lets me down. Like a good therapist, it had pointed out that the issue at hand was one of identity. Mine.

Why had I accepted, whole-hog, Deirdre Eckels's explanation of Misha's absence? Well, because Misha *was* absent, I told myself. There were no signs of foul play. And she'd left a note. What more did I need to know?

Only everything. In the cool gloom of my lost motel I considered Misha carefully. Yes, she was odd, told conflicting stories about her past, manipulated all sentient life constantly and often for no apparent reason, craved attention. I suspected that Rox might handily diagnose Misha as one sick puppy. But she was also intelligent, driven, and at times possessed of an otherworldly aura that enveloped me like myth. Within the aura I had always sensed an enormous danger, had believed that I might be called upon to fight for Misha, perhaps to the death. And I would. I was supposed to. I loved her.

And despite the ten million pop psychology books on this subject currently in print, most of them using "co-dependent" in the title, I had almost no choice in the matter. Dad had explained it to me when he came out to help me move. When he told me the truth about what had happened between him and my mother. Pop psychology is a prissy little joke compared to real life, a fact everybody in my family has learned the hard way.

I have ponderous academic credentials and a supposed expertise in the interpretation of social data. Yet I had allowed a total stranger to convince me in one phone call that an extremely unlikely event had just occurred without a hitch. Now, twenty-four months later, my behavior suddenly seemed inexplicable.

People do not vanish. Mates, lovers, relatives, friends do not simply vaporize, even when they've run off in the throes of passion. Usually they're thirty miles away at a Red Carpet Inn, realizing how much they hate motel salad bars but afraid to mention it for fear of shattering the romantic illusion. They buy gas with credit cards and call relatives on cell phones. A Brownie Scout with enough money to throw around could find them anywhere in two days flat.

The few who cannot be found are likely to be seriously mentally ill, dead, or deliberately in hiding. I didn't think Misha was any of these. I didn't know *what* Misha was except gone. That was enough. I had loved her and she was gone. What I hadn't factored into my reaction was that she had loved me and she was gone. That, I realized in a sluggish flash of insight, made it interesting.

And she had loved me in her strange way. I knew it when she called me at work to tell me some woman politician in Ohio had won an off-year election. When she brought me armloads of orange birds of paradise she'd bought from a vendor at a freeway on-ramp even though I detest orange. When she clawed at her neck in sleep and then butted her head against me until I woke up enough to hold her. These gestures were messages, and I ignored them. I ignored hundreds of them for two years because I'd bought the lesbian myth of permanent transcendence, which is every woman's myth only squared because there's no male around to diminish its power. The myth that love is bliss and everything that's not bliss is not love.

Coming home and finding Misha gone was not bliss, therefore I had concluded that Misha did not love me. Deirdre's story of a grant writer met at a conference had just enough romantic drama to seem credible. These things happen all the time in lesbian romance novels, which like romance novels involving men conveniently end at the moment of maximum bliss. Chance meeting, undeniable attraction which surmounts insurmountable obstacles, soul-moving sex scene, and fade to black. Well, hell, I thought in my darkened office, this must be the black.

I ran Brontë and then devoted several hours to tracking Misha Deland and/or Deirdre Eckels all over the Internet to no avail. I left cryptic messages on feminist and lesbian bulletin boards. "Misha Deland—Brontë critical. Call Blue." It was not inaccurate. Brontë is always critical when I sit at my desk for hours instead of swimming, hiking, playing ball, or putting food in her bowl. Once several months ago she quite critically placed a paw on my computer keyboard, inserting several hundred "less than" symbols into a report on book marketing at gasoline pumps. Car-care manuals, that sort of thing. But the Internet messages were just shots in the dark. Misha had no interest in computers when she was still around. There was no reason to assume she'd be cruising bulletin boards now, wherever she was.

Only at three in the afternoon did I remember that Nanna Foy was scheduled to arrive for dinner at six. It seemed inappropriate, given Muffin's death the previous afternoon, but there were no messages on the machine declining dinner. There were no messages at all. Whatever information Nanna had wanted to tell me about Muffin was now moot, I assumed. Wrongly, as usual.

"If anything, I need to talk with you more than ever," Nanna whispered urgently when I phoned to offer a postponement of our tête-à-tête. "This may be quite serious, Blue. Perhaps dangerous. I'll leave in an hour."

She sounded less seductive than before, but scarcely straightforward. I didn't know what to make of her remarks. Was she suggesting that Muffin's death represented some further danger? And to me? I doubted it.

My guess was that the prison authorities were correct in their assumption that one of Muffin's friends had smuggled a suicide pill to her either yesterday or earlier. I didn't think anyone had murdered Muffin, but that Muffin might very well have chosen to end her own life, and done so. The thing was odd, but perhaps it fit with whatever scheme had linked a dying woman to a frozen man. A scheme that was now a concern only of the sheriff's department, not of mine. I had something else to do. A vanished love to find.

Mom and Carty had trained me well, however, so I turned off the computer and went into high domestic gear. I steamed vegetables and brown rice, then tossed them with sulfur-free raisins in a curry sauce. Certain that Nanna Foy would cringe at the sight of iceberg lettuce, I cut three presentable summer squashes paper thin and soaked them in the pepper vodka I keep in the freezer for just such nonexistent occasions. Overlapped atop fresh spinach and sprinkled with toasted pine nuts, they would do for a first course. Exotic breads are unknown in Borrego Springs, but Carter Upchurch had prepared me for that crisis as well.

"Just trim the crusts from bag bread," she'd explained, "then roll the pieces flat with a can or something, stab them with a fork, brush them with egg and bake them for a few minutes. At the last minute dump on some grated cheese or *herbes de Provence*." I found some Parmesan in the refrigerator. Fine. But there was nothing for dessert.

Ten minutes later I was hovering over a freezer case at the grocery in Borrego, wondering what Carty would do to transform Popsicles into elegant little sorbets. I chose a tub of lime sherbert instead, took it home, and beat the air out of it with a big spoon, shaved some semisweet chocolate into it and froze two servings in fluted champagne glasses I hoped wouldn't crack in the freezer.

By the time I'd straightened up my office and set the blue cable spool for dinner, I saw an approaching cloud of dust that would be Nanna Foy. I changed into my best khaki shorts and flip-flops, and chose a clean T-shirt with a daringly stretched-out neck. Très chic.

Nanna stepped from her classic black Mercedes convertible in a white jumpsuit that set off her tan, and a white pith helmet wound in a black scarf that drifted behind her. No jewelry but something gold fastened close about her neck. She held a bottle of wine, the setting sun bathing the scene in amber. I was looking at an ad for an investment program, I thought. "Secure Your Retirement Income Now!" Gorgeous older woman, status car, obscure-looking wine bottle, and lush sunset symbolizing well-endowed golden years.

"Hello, Blue," she said in the Baudelaire voice.

"Where do I sign?" I answered, shaking my head.

To her credit she just grinned and handed me the wine. "Needs to be chilled, I imagine," she said. "Did you mention a swim?"

I introduced her to Brontë, showed her to the pool, and went inside to stash what appeared to be a Portuguese white table wine in the refrigerator. The price tag, of course, had been removed. But not the film of dust hinting that the bottle had been waiting a while for just the right occasion. When I went back outside, the white jumpsuit was folded neatly under the pith helmet on a chaise, and Nanna was playing with Brontë in the pool. Beneath the flashing surface of the water I could see pale swimsuit lines on lean, muscular flesh. I hoped I'd look like that at Nanna's age. For that matter, I hoped I'd look like that now. Gracelessly I pulled off the clothes I'd just put on and dived into the pool.

"I was sorry to hear about Muffin," I said with characteristically bad timing as I surfaced from the dive. Carty had not taught me to extend condolences nude in swimming pools. Still, the acknowledgment of Nanna's recent loss was a social priority and offered momentary distraction from the effect of her sinewy progression around my pool. Occasionally I bumped into her, or she bumped into me, as we played catch with Brontë. Just a smooth kneecap or shoulder touching underwater, slick and cool. She was wearing nothing but the gold necklace, which seemed to be a string of tiny, linked axes. I was having trouble breathing. I would have to do better.

"Muffin's death has been a terrible shock for all of us," she said after a while. "We knew she was very ill, but the way it happened . . . that's what I've come to talk to you about."

"Okay," I said, helping Brontë climb from the water and then reluctantly climbing out myself. "Why don't I get the wine and our salads, and we can talk." I tried to sound distant and professional, a near-impossibility under the circumstances. I hoped she'd assume my gooseflesh was the result of contact with cold air even though the temperature was still in the nineties.

After toweling off I carried my clothes inside to dress, then poured wine as regular splashing told me she was swimming laps. A silence as I loaded the wine and our vodka-squash salads on a tray suggested that she was dressing. I waited a few minutes in feverish courtesy, allowing her privacy before sweeping outside like a contestant in the waiter olympics. Nanna Foy was sitting on a chaise in white silk panties with a towel around her neck, smoking a cigarette.

"I hope you don't mind," she said, exhaling, her head tipped back, eyes closed.

"Mind what?" I replied, lost. Somehow I managed to put the tray down without taking my eyes from her.

"The cigarette," she said pointedly without opening her eyes.

"Um, no, of course not. Let me get an ashtray."

I didn't have an ashtray, but I could improvise. There was an old soap dish somewhere, I thought. An old Baccarat crystal candy dish. My bare hands.

"I have one, Blue. I always carry my own."

She reached for a wine glass.

"Shall we toast something?" she asked, her voice dropping again to the French poet register.

"To Muffin, who knew it's all an act," I said, lifting my glass to touch hers.

"Is it?" she asked after a thoughtful sip, her long lashes rising dramatically as the maple sugar eyes regarded me, up close.

"Not always," I answered, matching the intensity of her gaze. I was being measured, I knew. But I could measure right back. "And those are the scenes you want to watch out for."

"Touché," she whispered, stubbing out her cigarette and stabbing a slice of squash with one of my mother's sterling silver salad forks.

"Are you trying to get me drunk?" she asked after tasting the squash. "This is delicious."

"Local native people gathered pine nuts in the mountains between here and San Diego for thousands of years," I reported idiotically, as though the pine nuts atop our salads were the last of a pine nut reservoir left by once-proud but now vanquished Indians. In truth, the local Indians had survived a century of abuse and now ran reservation casinos earning more per week than most midsized corporations. None of them dealt in pine nut commodities, and who cared, anyway? The gold necklace at Nanna's throat flashed as she laughed. I could see that the links weren't regular axes, but the double-headed kind called labryses.

It was curious. Misha had a gold labrys on a chain, although she never wore it. Some of the women at Eden Snow's party wore labrys-shaped earrings, lapel pins, and rings. The ancient ceremonial axe wielded by the goddess in many of her names, it had been at one time the favored symbol of radical feminism. I couldn't imagine a context in which Nanna Foy would come into possession of such a politically charged piece of jewelry.

"What an unusual necklace," I mentioned, forcing myself to chew two pieces of peppery, vodka-soaked squash. It was horrible, but then I don't like cheeseless pizzas slathered with vegetable pâté and cilantro, either. The corn-belt palate runs to fried chicken and berry cobblers under crusts so butter-laden they flake like mica at the mere brush of a stainless steel fork. Where I come from, a vodka-squash salad would lead to social ostracism and rumors involving the ongoing threat of communism.

"Thank you," Nanna said politely. "I hope you won't find me too forward, Blue, but I would very much like to get to know you better. As it happens a friend has offered me the use of her yacht and crew for a two-day cruise down Baja to Cabo San Lucas. I'll be leaving from San Diego immediately after Muffin's memorial service Monday and would be delighted if you could join me."

This does not happen. The gorgeous and tastefully wealthy older woman-with-a-yacht who invites you to join her for a wee cruise to someplace fun just for the hell of it is a classic fantasy. Depending on context, the wealthy older woman also offers to fund a day-care center for the children of migrant workers. Or to underwrite a bed-of-nails tour to the birthplace of the Marquis de Sade. Or to assassinate at least five petrochemical company executives. In the fantasy she invariably has a tragic, if shady, past. Frequently she's dying of something which might easily have been treated if the male medical establishment spent less time improving penile implants and more researching women's health issues. Nanna Foy did not appear to be dying of anything.

"What a delightful idea, but I'm afraid I just can't," I said, staying in character. "Let's finish eating and then you can tell me whatever it was you wanted to tell me about Muffin Crandall.

I'll confine Brontë inside so she can't hear. You've led me to believe that we can't be too careful."

As I carried the salad plates inside I could hear Nanna exhaling dramatically through her nose. A sigh of irritation. So far I was holding my own.

When I returned with a tray bearing the rest of our repast, she was again fully clothed and tight-lipped with an emotion I couldn't quite identify. A sort of thoughtful peevishness. Or maybe a somber fear.

"I suppose you think one of us provided Muffin with a poison or dangerous medication, and that she then used it to take her own life," Nanna began. "That's what the prison authorities suspect. It isn't true."

"Try your rice," I suggested. "It's organic."

"Blue, *dammit!*" she snapped. "Stop playing this puerile game and listen. Muffin Crandall was murdered in that prison. Poisoned. I suspect that her death may have been contracted by someone connected to Victor Camacho. There has been no mention of her deteriorating medical condition in the papers, no way anyone outside her circle of intimates could have known that she was dying. It's possible that there will be further . . . reprisals. Camacho may have been involved in organized crime. They might . . ."

I could see an artery throbbing in the hollow of her neck, and the fork with which she prodded a bit of broccoli was trembling. It would have been easy to nod in astonished agreement. Easy to remove the fork from her hand and then kneel beside her to kiss that artery while murmuring, "Of course. This pathetic loser robbing suburban garages was really a Mafia kingpin. Everyone connected to Muffin may be in danger. Let's flee this mysterious threat from unknown but vengeful criminals by sailing to an exotic Mexican tourist trap."

What I actually said was, "Nanna, you can't possibly expect

me to buy this. It's ridiculous. Unless there's a lot you're not telling me, which I suspect to be the case. What's important is that you understand how much I don't care. I don't care what actually happened to Victor Camacho or how Muffin Crandall was connected to it. It's irrelevant to me. It doesn't matter. So you don't have to continue this charade or lure me across azure seas on yachts. I have something else to do now. I'm out of the whole Crandall thing."

The sun had vanished behind a western mountain, the yellow-lavender sky cascading promises of darkness across my face. Nanna seemed to feel the change, and her eyes grew darker.

"What do you have to do now, Blue?" she asked, reaching to touch my cheek with long, tanned fingers.

"I have to know what happened to somebody, to my lover Misha," I answered. "It has nothing to do with you and Muffin Crandall."

Then somehow she was on her knees in the space between us, her arms around my neck. I could smell a vestige of perfume beneath the damp chlorine scent of her hair as my arms found their way around her. My hands felt ribs, vertebrae, the warmth of her skin beneath her clothes.

"Oh, Blue, you're wrong," Nanna breathed into my breastbone. "You don't understand. It's not what you think. You must be protected. Please . . ."

I did understand one thing, spelled out in tropical storms moving through my body. I understood that Nanna was irresistible and that I was well on my way to becoming a cartoon character called Simba, Sex Queen of the Sahara. Two years of contented celibacy and then blam, back on the grid, electricity everywhere. First a man out of sympathy and loneliness, now a woman out of something much deeper. What next? I could feel my own pulse match hers perfectly as I kissed the artery in her neck, then her jawbone, then the edge of her mouth, already soft in that way only women have. A roaring, terrible softness revealed to be a path, a journey, a way to somewhere else. Somewhere I was dying to go.

"No, Blue," Nanna whispered, burying her head in my chest but not letting go of me.

"Why?"

"It . . . it's not supposed to be like this. I'm just so tired, so scared. I'm sorry, Blue. There's someone that I love, someone who loves me. She's . . . somewhere else. I didn't mean to let it go this far. Please forgive me."

Sighing, I helped her off her knees and back onto my chaise before asking the obvious series of questions.

"You've been flirting with me for days," I pointed out, "and you're good at it. Why? And what is it I'm wrong about? What don't I understand, and what makes you think I have to be protected? From what?"

"Blue, I'm asking you to trust me," Nanna said while stirring her cooling rice nervously with yet another of my mother's forks. "Dan Crandall has inadvertently involved you in a situation which has become dangerous. You must trust me. I can't explain, but the danger is real and may affect you. It would be best if you were away for a while. Later, when you return, it will be taken care of. You'll be out of danger."

From the iron rigidity of her backbone I could tell she meant business. There would be no more information, no explanation, no denouement. The sky slipped to gauzy gray and revealed several hundred flickering stars as we sat in silence.

"Well, I'll be out of town next weekend," I said, finally. "Will that do?"

"Be very careful between now and the time you leave, Blue. Be watchful. What I said about Victor Camacho's associates is in a sense true. They haven't known for five years what happened to him; now they do. They have unquestionably arranged for Muffin's murder as a payback. There's no way to know what else they may do or if they'll do anything. Your involvement in this has been peripheral, but they don't know that. Just don't ask questions, don't discuss this with anybody, and be extremely careful. Will you do that?"

She had stood to leave, and I could feel her gaze on the top of my skull.

"Okay," I answered, rising to walk with her to her car. "But there's still dessert."

"Rain check." She smiled at a distant mountain. "Blue, what are you doing out here with your Midwestern manners and sterling silver? You don't fit."

"What are you doing out here with your black Mercedes and sexy voice? I tend to assume that whatever's here, fits."

"Touché," she said as she opened her car door.

"Nanna?"

"Yes?"

"Why did you say I was wrong when I said finding out what happened to Misha had nothing to do with you and Muffin Crandall?"

In the twilight I saw her face turn ashen and brittle, a thousand papery crevasses showing her age. The huge brown eyes were wet.

"Oh, Blue, Betsy Blue." Nanna Foy sighed, hugging me now as an aunt might. "Don't ask any more questions."

Something had just driven a wedge between my eyes. The space there felt like sky, star-filled and dizzy. Nanna was already driving away when I realized what it was.

"How do you know my name?" I yelled at her retreating taillights. Nobody but my parents, Carty, and David ever called me Betsy Blue. Nobody in my adult life had ever heard the nickname. Not even Misha.

Nanna waved and I thought I heard "Ciao," drifting back on the clean desert breeze. Then she was gone.

I took Brontë for a walk, remembering the people who called me Betsy Blue. Mom, David, dad, Carter Upchurch. Remembered Carter dropping a box of condoms into my purse, saying, "Protect yourself, Betsy Blue," when I was a teenager. Remembered what I was supposed to protect myself from. Stopped dead two feet from a cholla cactus.

"Oh, shit," I told the cactus, shivering. "Dan is a . . . I should have thought . . . oh, damn, shit!"

Above me thousands of stars became little tadpoles of light, squiggling happily in a navy blue firmament. I knew what the firmament felt like. It felt like exhaustion, from all that squiggly potential. I couldn't remember when my last period was, but then until the day before I had no reason to. Had an errant tadpole contributed by Dan made its gleeful way to some red moon of an egg waiting avidly in the bordello corridors of my abdomen? Had tadpole-moon already transformed, erupting in a choreographed symphony of replicating cells that would soon have Dan Crandall's big hands and my big feet? I'd be fifty-three, I calculated, when the cells were ready for college. I'd have to do something about investments, savings bonds, sanity. And I'd never be able to look Carter Upchurch in the face again. She'd told me exactly what I needed to know. I'd just forgotten.

"Come on," I called to Brontë, and stomped toward my now-ruined illusion of safety to call Roxie.

I wanted to hear her say "Girl," in just the way I knew she'd say it. Like the grid chuckling in pleasure at its own *vastly* dumb joke.

Chapter Twelve

"Rox, I may be pregnant," I blubbered into the phone minutes later. "And Muffin Crandall is dead, poisoned, maybe murdered. Her friends think it was murder because Victor Camacho may have been involved in organized crime. And I don't know why, but I just almost seduced Nanna Foy, and—"

"I, um, can't really talk right now," Rox said in a voice like warm cocoa. "I have someone here."

"Oh," I said glumly, feeling a stab of something uncomfortable. I'm always dismayed when the entire world continues to function as if my personal crises were just that, but this was more than dismay. This made my throat constrict and bathed my face in sticky warmth. "It's the Diana Ross clone, right?"

"Right."

"But I thought you were . . . I believe the phrase was, 'tired of that mess.' "

"Not quite tired enough. Old times' sake. You know how it is. I'll call you tomorrow."

"Too late. I'll be a mother by then, adrift on a haze of hormones," I replied, trying not to whine. "That dreamy, bovine attitude. You won't recognize me."

"I'll know it's you because nobody else ever answers your phone." She chuckled, exhibiting a total absence of concern. "Bye, Blue."

It was clear that Rox had not heard a word I said, which left the words piled up on the mouthpiece of my phone. I believe that unheard words do that, just hang around in ghostly clumps, unsure about what to do next. The only way to get rid of them is to listen to them yourself.

"Okay, I'm probably not pregnant," I told Brontë. "I'm just appalled at my behavior with Dan and have selected Puritan Pariah from the identity menu in my head. I might have chosen Traditional Victim or Sexually Ambiguous Slut. That I went straight for the scarlet A suggests a healthy identification with mainstream American values, a response not particularly interesting in Americans. Tomorrow I'll drive down to the city and get one of those pregnancy test kits and a strapless chiffon sheath dress like the Supremes wore in the sixties."

Black Doberman eyes gazing upward from the level of my knee suggested interest in other things. Walks, for example. I had curtailed our nightly hike to call Rox. Brontë easily conveyed dissatisfaction with those arrangements by wagging her docked tail and pointing toward the door with her nose. It made me wonder for the millionth time why we attach so much significance to words.

"Okay," I agreed, continuing to use them out of habit. "Let me get my pack and we'll go." I could listen to my own words outside, I thought. And dispel the tantalizing images in my head of Roxie Bouchie holding someone close, saying "girl" in a way I'd never heard but, I was forced to acknowledge, probably wanted to. What that might mean was too ominous, too scary. I pushed the thought into conceptual limbo and concentrated on manageable things like dogs and walks.

Loaded with two quarts of water and the Glock, my waist pack was heavy. Hefting it, I almost removed the twenty-six-ounce gun, which tends to drag the pack down on my right hip after the water bottles are empty. Then I remembered the multitude of reasons I might need it, and didn't. Among those reasons was not the one which would shortly bring the Muffin Crandall case into more personal focus for me, as well as produce the seven pure white hairs I found growing in a cluster from the crown of my head the next day. That "white in a single night" business is supposed to be a myth, but it isn't.

The Indians who roamed the barren landscape I would later call home were part of the Shoshonean linguistic group, and called themselves *wiwaiistam,* the coyote people. And not for no reason. Coyotes, who cannot contract syphilis and smallpox from invading missionaries, were and still are the inheritors of this desert. I hear their howled music every night, although the *wiwaiistam* are silent. All traces of their long-deserted village washed away in a flood that swept Coyote Canyon in 1916. But I thought of the coyote people as Brontë and I moved silently beneath a shadow of the San Ysidro mountain range. A lost tribe. One of ten thousand little lights that flicker on the grid and then are gone. Things vanished in time. Civilizations, understandings, people. The *wiwaiistam* made me think of Misha, who also was gone.

In the tattered patterns of light and shadow cast by broken rocks that seem to breathe at night I looked for a morphology, a shape-of-events which might account for the abrupt and complete departure of a woman from place and social context. Delusions, I thought in the spindly tracery of a paloverde shrub. Mental images of horrific threat could drive a woman from place to place in unending search of a safety that only dissolves again and again as the brain-generated threat distorts each new locale. Drugs and illnesses of the brain can cause delusions, as can starvation, dehydration, sensory deprivation, physical and psychological torture. But Misha never used drugs, hated swallowing so much as an aspirin. And while she was strange, I was fairly sure that strangeness derived from a social history I didn't know rather than from a psychiatric illness she couldn't have hidden for very long. Misha hadn't been driven from my arms by delusional demons. Neither was there any evidence of starvation or torture the day before she left. I would have noticed. It had to be something else.

After about four miles Brontë and I paused for a drink beneath an ocotillo that looked like a huge, emaciated squid upended against the night sky. Women with children sometimes ran from child-molester husbands, I remembered as Brontë lapped water from a plastic sandwich bag. There was a network of safe houses between which these women could move in secrecy until either some private detective caught up with them or the molested child grew old enough to demand protection in court. But Misha was childless and hadn't seen the adolescent husband who gave her the name Deland in twenty-five years. Or so she said. Had that been a lie? Was there a vengeful husband somewhere, tracking Misha through a sequence of identities? That would account for her legendary inability to remember her own name as well as for the badly constructed East Coast accent that routinely failed to mask the Southern lilt beneath.

And maybe the tracker wasn't a husband but somebody else. The law? Maybe Misha had committed a crime and jumped bail. Maybe she was an escaped convict. I pondered these unlikely options as snarls erupted from a blind canyon two hundred yards away, followed by a bloodcurdling shriek that lasted only seconds.

"Brontë, *stay,*" I commanded, halting her dash toward the darkened canyon. Domestic dogs are cousins to the wolf and coyote, and thus understand the language of wild canines, or at least the spirit of the communication. From the snarls I could tell that two coyotes, probably a mated pair out hunting, had just made a kill. No doubt a rabbit. And Brontë was twitching with some vaguely remembered blood lust despite the reality that her food comes in bags and cans from large corporations whose administrative offices are not strewn with tufts of fur and bloody bones, although their processing plants are.

As a distraction I veered west toward Collins Valley north of Santa Catarina Spring, where more small mammals were unquestionably being eaten by larger mammals as well as by larger birds. I'd double back down the Lower Willows bypass after the coyotes had left, I decided. There is nothing to be gained by hanging around fresh kill unless you happen to want some, although I could tell Brontë hated leaving the party. I wondered why what we call instinct so often leads straight into truly disastrous situations, and why we follow it anyway. The frequently uncomfortable results of instinctive behavior are not a convincing argument for social Darwinism, I concluded, again.

Was it instinct, for example, that led Muffin Crandall to her curious death behind prison bars? And was it instinct that popped Misha like the lost spring from a ballpoint pen into oblivion? For that matter, did some old-brain proclivity lay beneath my headlong full-gainer into a love affair that would in the end bequeath me only eccentric solitude in a city of nocturnal beasts? Instinct is supposedly innate and adaptive. We don't learn it, we just follow it automatically and it promotes our survival, or so the theory goes. But Muffin hadn't survived. Maybe Misha hadn't, either. I arguably had, but the argument was inverse and feeble. Survival *despite* instinct is not survival *as a result of* instinct. In the desert dark I remembered that my own parents had survived it the way you're supposed to, by riding it out of danger.

David and I didn't know that Jake and Elizabeth had both been married to other people when the two-egg and two-sperm event that would become boy and girl twins happened. Dad told me the story only two years ago, after Misha was gone. I remember that at the time of this storytelling he was perched on a rock wearing his Desert Father costume. One of his lady friends had whipped up the tan, all-cotton monk's robe complete with cowl on her Singer in the week between my phone call announcing Misha's departure and dad's arrival to provide solace as well as to help me move. I'd found my waterless desert motel in the "Desert Property for Sale" section of the paper minutes after that call, and arranged for the sale in two days. Cameron Wrenner's lawyer had been happy to unload the place. And dad had waxed eloquent about an unfulfilled dream of desert asceticism he could now indulge. But despite the rope-belted robe and sandals, the tale he recounted from that rock was far from ascetic.

"Love and hate are both terrible forces, both God," my father said, doing his best Thomas Merton impersonation. "Their antithesis is indifference, which is evil. Your mother and I fell terribly in love, and terrible things happened because of that, but not evil things."

"What things?" I asked, stunned. Why had I never suspected the existence of a passionate drama behind my own birth? How could I have lived with these people for eighteen years and not known?

"People were hurt," he replied. "The woman I had married was hurt. So was the man your mother had married. The parishioners of the little church I was serving were hurt. Your mother and I were altered in ways from which we would never recover. I believe it is safe to say that we lived in a paralysis of awe from that point until your mother's death. I still live within it, as you must now, with or without Misha."

"I don't want to live in awe," I told him. "I intend to live aweless. So what happened to your wife and my mother's husband? And what about your career?"

"I would never become a bishop, if that's what you mean by career, not that it mattered anymore. When we knew that your mother was pregnant, there were quick, grotesque divorces followed by a somber wedding. No one attended but Carter and my best friend from seminary, another priest who died in an Alaskan avalanche when you and David were still toddlers. He used to write me about how much he hated the cold, so I called him Sam McGee. I taught you and David the poem as a sort of memorial for him.

"My wife and your mother's husband," he went on, "suffered, were angry and outraged. Fortunately there were as yet no children in either of our marriages. After a time they built new lives. My former wife remarried and is the mother of five grown children. One of her daughters is an Episcopal priest and a damn good preacher. I was a guest at her ordination. Your mother's first husband married two more times but ultimately found that his path led to a successful entrepreneurship that left no time for domestic pleasures. He died three years ago. His estate was worth over twenty million."

"Gee, mom could have worn diamonds if she'd stayed with him," I said in a burst of inane shock that dad merely absorbed.

"No, she couldn't. There are fewer options than we think, Betsy Blue. Really, only two. Hang on or jump off. What are you going to do?"

"I don't know," I told my father two years ago. "I just want not to be hurt anymore."

"That's jumping off," he said without judgment. "It's always an option."

So I had, jumped that is, although I didn't think of it that way. I just thought of it as peace and was perfectly happy until a man from Alaska knew the author of a poem dad loved because it reminded him of a friend. Then I was back on. The grid works in elegant, underhanded ways.

A distant howl and its descant reminded me that I'd been thinking about instinct. The term wasn't operative, I realized. Not exactly. Not unless the yearning toward invisible music, the hum of the grid, is the only real human instinct, which it may be. If so, the keys to both Muffin Crandall's peculiar death and Misha's evaporation into thin air would lie in understanding their instinctive lives. The keys would lie in whatever captivated their souls, whatever they loved or feared most deeply.

I felt wise as Brontë and I looped back east toward Lower Willows bypass and our five-mile trek home. At Muffin's funeral I would outline this wisdom for Nanna Foy, demonstrating how easily a thoughtful person can figure out anything. Nanna, I thought, would be impressed. Then I would put theory into practice by following the tracks of Misha's soul backward in time. I would find her, and all would be right with the world. A familiar growl alerted me to the fact that, presently, all wasn't.

Brontë was sniffing the breeze eddying from Coyote Creek across Lower Willows bypass, her sleek body tense. I followed her gaze and saw rising dust. Guttural curses could be heard. The groans and expletives of male physical exertion. Instructing Brontë to heel, I moved closer but kept out of sight. From a hundred yards away I could see two men attempting to dig a Jeep out of Lower Willows bypass, a treacherous, rock-strewn gully with forty-five-degree pitches on both sides. The Jeep's lights were off and the men were doing everything wrong. In particular, they were trying to gun the Jeep forward from its nosedive position in the gully. I could smell burning rubber as the front tires threw arcs of sand and the Jeep's front bumper sank another three inches.

I knew how to get them out of their predicament; I've done the bypass fifty times in my truck, which doesn't even have four-wheel drive. The trick is to get out, plan the route, move any large rocks out of the way, and then just do it. No hesitation. Momentum is everything in sand. The slightest loss of momentum, regardless of fishtailing, screaming fan belts, and banging oil pans, will result in getting hopelessly stuck.

The thing to do, I calculated, was to dig out the rear wheels and then jam the floor mats under them for enough traction to get the Jeep backward up to the lip of the gully, from where I could take it down and up, fast and clean. But I didn't leap into their dust cloud to volunteer my services immediately. Instead I gripped Brontë's collar and crept to within fifteen yards of them, where I crouched behind a flat-topped chunk of granite rubble in the side of the gully. My caution may have sprung from the fact that their lights were off. It didn't make any sense to attempt the bypass, hands down the worst quarter mile of Jeep trail in Anza-Borrego, blind. There was just something *wrong* about that.

"Fuck, you asshole, it's just dug in worse," yelled the man who'd been trying to push the Jeep from behind. He was about six feet tall, dark-haired, around forty, and wearing jeans and a black T-shirt. Although he was coated with dust I could see smudged discolorations on the pale skin of his arms, an observation which did not increase my willingness to help. Tattoos may be all the rage in the corporate biker set, but not tattoos that cover both arms all the way to T-shirt sleeves. Those tend to suggest an unwholesome familarity with iron bars, seatless toilets, and starchy prison food.

"Look, it's not far," he told the driver, his words carrying audibly along the gully walls. "Let's back the fucker up and leave it, walk in and do McCarron's place, walk back and get outta here. She'll be asleep, make it easier than that last one throwin' books and crap around until she had herself a fit and dropped dead. Shoulda got there later when she was asleep. Old broads sleep like the fuckin' dead, prob'ly tires 'em out haulin' them damn saggy tits around."

The driver chortled appreciatively and then slammed the Jeep into reverse, throwing another seventy pounds of sand skyward as I pondered what might have been meant by "doing" my place. I realized that I was grinning, which seemed inappropriate. Then

I noticed that my skin felt clammy and my heart was pounding. I hadn't known you could grin in response to fear.

They'd come in the long, back way, off road from the end of the blacktop outside the little town of Anza west-northwest of my place and outside the park boundary. After that they'd had to navigate the Jeep trail through Nance Canyon and then the entirety of Coyote Canyon, only to get stuck four miles from their destination. They didn't want to be seen, I assumed. That's why they'd inched through the desert with no lights rather than driving through Borrego Springs where many pairs of eyes might have taken note. The determination reflected by such a journey made my fingertips feel numb. And who was "that last one"? Last one what? "Had herself a fit and dropped dead," he'd said. Had somebody died? Who? And what did it have to do with me?

I was presumed to be sleeping because "old broads sleep like the fuckin' dead." Did that mean they thought I was old and that they'd already done something to an old woman? I remembered Nanna Foy's warning that danger suddenly lay near everyone connected to Muffin Crandall. Something about Victor Camacho and organized crime. It had seemed silly when she said it. Now I wondered if Nanna were still alive as I gripped Brontë's collar with both shaking hands.

The situation was manageable, I told myself. I could easily slip away into the desert and stay there all night as they did whatever they were going to do to my quarters. Even if they noticed the tracks I'd left on the trip out, they could never find me now. The desert is a maze of rubble and blind canyons. I'd pick a sheltered niche near the top of a canyon and just sit there until morning, when I'd head into Borrego to the east of my place and call the sheriff. No problem.

The driver gunned the Jeep backward up the wash without looking, propelling the left rear tire straight up a jagged boulder and dragging the right rocker panel against the ground. When the wheel came off the boulder I heard the scree of ripping metal as the left rocker slid down the boulder's surface, but the Jeep kept moving. After hitting three more rocks and, I was sure, cracking the differential housing, the Jeep was out of the gulch. In the air was that burnt-metal scent even egg beaters and wind-up toys produce under extreme stress.

Whispering "Stay," I released Brontë's collar and duck-waddled into the deeper shadow of our protective boulder, a vantage point from which I could see the entire gulch and from which Brontë and I could head upward and west into bigger rocks. The driver, a shorter man with stringy, colorless hair, hunched shoulders, and a sagging paunch over his hipless pelvis, joined his companion at the bottom of the gulch.

"You sure you know the way?" he growled, hitching a chrome-studded belt to a more comfortable position under his stomach.

"That way," the first man said, pointing to the gray haze of light over Borrego. "It's the last place in the northwest corner. A fuckin' motel."

"The old broad lives in a motel? What the hell are we doin'? There could be fifty people at a motel."

"Not this one," Tattoo replied ominously. "Baggy tits number two lives out here alone. Must be some kinda nut. Too many fuckin' nuts in the world already. All we're s'posed to do is trash the place, put the fear a God into her. But if she fights like that other one, well, it's a mercy killing."

"Yeah," Paunch agreed happily. "A mercy killing. Old bag with her dried-up pussy be glad to get it over. That's fuckin' mercy all right. Fuckin' mercy for sure!"

They didn't know the referenced old bag was less than twenty yards away and armed. That was fine. I wasn't about to do anything stupid. In the darkness Brontë and I were safe. Once they were out of earshot I'd deflate the Jeep's tires and drain the gas tank. Then I could circle east into Borrego and alert the sheriff to meet them at the disabled Jeep. Plan B.

And it would have worked had a desert cottontail not chosen that moment to hop out of the shadows and nibble at a seed pod dangling from a large honey mesquite shrub. The shrub was growing from the ridge of the gulch about thirty yards east of the men, fully illuminated by a waxing half-moon. And Brontë had seen the cottontail.

Before I could stop her she was barking and running, no doubt inspired by our earlier encounter with her cousins, the coyotes. She was going to have her own rabbit. And she was going to get killed.

In the slow motion of panic I saw the cottontail climb to safety ten feet up in the mesquite. At the same time the short man yelled, "What the fuck!" and pulled a .38 from the waist of his pants. He aimed it at Brontë and fired. I must have pulled the Glock from my pack already, although I don't remember doing it. All I remember is Brontë in motion and then falling as her screams filled the gulch. She had collapsed in a spill of beach-ball-sized rocks and cholla cactus, which provided some cover, but her thrashing forelegs were still visible. Brontë, the companion of my heart, my truest friend, screaming in pain, maybe dying. The sound was like shrapnel in my head. Intolerable.

I remember sliding the safety off the Glock with my right thumb and standing to brace my arms atop the flat rock. I wasn't going to miss. I was going to kill the man who'd shot Brontë, and then the other one if necessary. I didn't care about anything else. Brontë's shrieks were everything.

"It's a wolf or something," Tattoo said, spitting on the ground as if to document his assessment of the situation. "Kill the fucker and shut it up."

Paunch moved forward a few steps, took aim. His back was to me, a winged skull across the shoulders of his dark T-shirt useful as a target. When I had the skull in both sights I began to squeeze the trigger softly, but then dropped the barrel sight to his hip and then his thigh as the flash and report of my gun stunned me. I don't know why I didn't kill him. I'll never know.

After breathing cordite for ten seconds I regained enough vision to see that he was down, writhing and gripping his left thigh near the knee. Tattoo was also holding a gun now, trying to get Paunch on his feet and staring narrow-eyed at the nimbus of smoke rising above my rock. He knew where I was, but now seemed a bad time to attempt a move. Neither did I think yelling would accomplish much except to alert them to the fact that I was a woman, a guarantee of further violence. Brontë's cries had assumed a regular pattern, the painful sounds seeming to accompany the scrabbling movement of her front legs. This was followed by a brief silence, then more movement and crying. I had to get to her, but couldn't.

Tattoo had raised his arms in the traditional gesture of surrender, but had not dropped his gun. He seemed puzzled, looked in Brontë's direction and then in mine. Slowly he pointed the gun at Brontë, although his face was turned toward my rock. I got the message and fired again from around the side of the rock without standing to aim. The round tore into gravel two yards from his feet and he lowered his gun, then yelled something I couldn't hear over the ringing in my ears. Apparently it involved a decision to get the hell out of my desert.

Tattoo hauled Paunch up the side of the gorge to the Jeep, leaving a trail of blood that looked black in the moonlight. I wondered if Victor Camacho's skull had bled when Muffin hit him. She hadn't said anything about blood. Muffin had killed Victor Camacho, or said she had. But unless he bled to death from his wound, I had not killed Paunch despite more than adequate provocation. In the ringing overstimulation of my brain I felt a certain curiosity about this, an oddly remote interest. I filed it as I watched the two men regain their Jeep and then heard the gear shifting as they drove away. First, second, then after a long time, third. Tattoo had turned the lights on and was hauling ass in full retreat.

In seconds I'd reached Brontë, grabbed a sharp-edged rock and begun hacking away the roots of the fuzzy, tentacled cholla cacti in which she was painfully snared. There was congealing blood on her right croup about four inches from the base of her tail. Gently I touched the wound, eliciting a yelp. Had the bullet struck her spinal cord? Was it lodged there now? Was that why she couldn't stand up? What would happen if I moved her? For a moment I just bent over her, my forehead against hers, and cried.

"It's all right, girl," I wept. "Let's just take it easy, take it slow. Let's figure this out. Don't try to move. Just *stay.*"

A heartfelt lick on my cheek was all it took to get me back in gear. This was my dog. She deserved my best, which at the moment did not involve emotional swampiness. Taking the little penlight I always carry from my pack, I cursed myself for not checking its batteries. The light was dim, but enough to see the wound clearly as well as to see the reason she wasn't moving her hind legs, which were buried in chollas. Any movement would cause excruciating pain from the thousands of barbed spikes imbedded in her flesh.

"Stay, stay," I whispered as with the rock I dug the vicious little plants out of the ground and kicked them away, revealing her right thigh and another bullet wound. The sight made my heart soar. Paunch had fired only one shot at Brontë, which meant that the bullet had entered her right thigh and exited at her croup on the same side. A flesh wound. It hadn't hit her spinal cord.

"Thank you," I breathed at a completely oblivious grid of electrical impulses humming and snapping everywhere. "Just thank you."

It took at least an hour for me to remove enough of the cholla spines from her legs for Brontë to stand. Still, there were too many left in her hind paw pads to permit walking even if the pain of the bullet wound would permit it.

"This is going to hurt," I said firmly and then gathered her in my arms, carefully supporting shoulders and rump while holding her against my chest, wound-side out. The movement brought fresh blood that I could feel trickling between the fingers of my left hand, but Brontë didn't yelp.

"Brave dog," I told her over and over as I stumbled the four miles home, my back registering increasing pain at the extra weight. "Brave, brave dog."

In the three A.M. dark surrounding my motel I left Brontë on the ground and checked the place out, the Glock ready in my right hand. No one was there. No one had been there. And no one was going to be there. I was pretty sure they wouldn't come back. Too much trouble. Armed desert rats with dogs. A hassle they couldn't afford.

After settling Brontë in the truck I went inside to phone a vet I knew outside Palm Springs. She was on Rox's line-dance team at Auntie's. She'd meet me at her office in an hour, she said. No mention that it was the middle of the night. No referrals to twenty-four-hour animal clinics over the mountains in San Diego. I was grateful.

Next I phoned the San Diego County Back-Country Sheriff's Department and reported that an altercation with two men at the Lower Willows bypass had resulted in shots being fired, and that I would not be staying at home for the remainder of the night. There was no point, I decided, in mentioning that I'd inflicted a gunshot wound on one of them. The paperwork on gunshot wounds to humans is voluminous. And in this case it would not be in my interests, a viewpoint unquestionably shared by the two men in the Jeep. I told the sheriff's deputy I thought one of the men was an old boyfriend who'd gotten drunk and decided to come after me, and asked for a patrol of my property for the rest of the night. The dispatcher said he'd send somebody out every hour until daybreak and that I shouldn't worry. Right.

Less than an hour later we were in Palm Springs, where the vet irrigated and dressed Brontë's wound, dug the rest of the cholla spines from her foot pads, and gave her antibiotic and pain-reducing injections.

"She'll sleep now," the vet said. "Might as well leave her here until tomorrow afternoon when she'll start to perk up. I'm assuming you've reported this gunshot wound to the authorities?"

"I have," I lied. "But if it's safe to move her again, I'd like to take her with me."

"Suit yourself, Blue, but I'll need to see her again in three or four days."

"I appreciate this," I said while writing a check for Brontë's treatment. The amount didn't seem like enough for getting out of bed in the middle of the night.

"Family," she said with a shrug as she turned out the office lights.

Then I headed for one of the motels operated by the lesbian entrepreneur and got a room. The desk clerk looked like Keanu Reeves, wore a rainbow flag earring, and asked no questions about the hour, no questions about the drugged dog in my arms.

After settling Brontë in the bed I called Nanna Foy. Her answering machine suggested that callers phone her office in Santa Barbara, as she was out of town for an extended period. Next I called Helen Tewalt's number in Rancho Almas.

"This is Detective Sergeant Phillips," a male voice answered, clamping icy fingers around my heart. "Who is calling please?"

"Um, this is Helen's cousin," I improvised as the cold seeped outward along my arms. "Who are you? Why are you answering Helen's telephone?"

"I'm afraid there's been a fatality, but I can't give information over the phone," he said solemnly. "I would suggest that you contact our office in person."

I listened as he gave an address, then made the requisite, "But what's happened, is Helen all right?" noises, although I already knew. Helen Tewalt had been "that last one" who had apparently put up a fight when two strange men arrived. Helen Tewalt had thrown things at the invaders. She'd been angry, livid with rage. Then something had happened, some kind of "fit," Tattoo had said. And she'd "dropped dead." The police were there because Helen Tewalt was the fatality. Helen Tewalt was dead.

Falling into bed with Brontë I felt a sour tingling at the crown of my scalp that I identified as fear, but I was too exhausted to care. For the moment nobody knew where we were. Nobody could find us. We were safe. Although, I realized, only for the moment.

Chapter Thirteen

Brontë and I slept until noon, grabbed lunch, and then headed back to Borrego Springs. At the motel I'd had a shower and used all the complimentary toiletries except the shoe mitt, so I felt better, although not much. It's difficult to feel really good while embroiled in life-threatening situations no one has bothered to explain. From the passenger's seat Brontë exuded a sense of doglike shame, as if her momentary lapse over the rabbit were responsible for our plight.

"Look at it this way," I told her. "If you hadn't insisted on another walk last night we would have been home when Paunch and Tattoo showed up. With any warning I would have fought back, just as Helen Tewalt apparently did. They might have killed me; I might have killed them. As it is, you and I are still alive and I'm not facing arraignment. Despite the rabbit incident, you saved us. Okay?"

She merely licked a paw thoughtfully, but seemed less chagrined. Next I had to get a handle on what was going on.

At home I found a note on the door from the San Diego County Back-Country Sheriff's Department saying that foot patrols of my property at four and five-thirty A.M. had revealed nothing out of the ordinary, but that I should come to the office and file a written report of the shooting incident and then repeat the process at the ranger station, since the incident had occurred within park boundaries.

"Not a chance," I told the note. Official reports have a half-life similar to that of carbon and can be dug up long after their original purpose has passed. They're paper land mines with the potential for blowing your feet off years in the future. I didn't want to file a report admitting that I'd shot a man in the leg, and I didn't want to file a report neglecting to mention that. I wasn't going to file a report at all.

My answering machine was blinking with an urgency no doubt appropriate to the messages within it, but I didn't push the play button right away. First I rolled an antibiotic tablet in a bit of cheese for Brontë and put out her favorite canned dog food and fresh water. Then I turned on my computer and opened the Muffin Crandall file. Nothing in it made any sense.

For all practical purposes it seemed to indicate that a nice older lady, a widow connected to a suburban community theater group, had killed and frozen a stranger who only incidentally turned out to have a criminal record. Then somebody had managed to poison the nice old lady murderer inside a prison, even though the nice old lady murderer was already terminally ill and wouldn't have survived much longer in any event. To these completely nonsensical data I added the death of Helen Tewalt, another nice old lady, and my unpleasant encounter with Paunch and Tattoo in the desert last night. Despite Nanna Foy's warnings about Victor Camacho's possible connections to "organized crime," I might as well have been reading a recipe for eggs Benedict written in Sanskrit.

Drawing both knees up under my chin as I sat in my desk chair, I wrapped my arms around my bent legs and tried to make sense of it. Paunch and Tattoo, I realized, did make sense. Unsocialized and feral, their behavior had conformed precisely to guidelines established by our primate ancestors millennia in the past and widely reinforced all day every day since then. Reinforced in governments based on subjugation to alpha males. Reinforced in patterns of human interaction characterized by territoriality and notions of ownership. All determined by nothing more than the exchange of threats. The gun talk I had learned to speak last night.

Blam! ("That's my dog you shot, you idiot!")

Aim. ("So? What will you do if we shoot your dog again?")

Blam! ("Kill you.")

Retreat. ("Understood. We're outta here.")

Paunch and Tattoo, whatever the origins of their mission in the desert darkness, were comprehensible. Paunch and Tattoo, I thought while gnawing softly on my left knee, were actually *trite.* There was nothing unusual about anything they'd said or done. What was unusual was the rest of it. Muffin Crandall and her friends. Suburban clubwomen, community volunteers. Just those little ladies you see at fashion luncheons everywhere, holding chaos at bay. Without them we'd still be sleeping in caves and there would be no schools, hospitals, or red petunias in white window planters. But luncheon ladies don't kill or get killed. Not usually.

I noticed that my thoughtful knee-gnawing had left teeth marks in my skin. Three pale indentations from the edges of upper incisors pressed against the thin flesh over a round bone called the patella. "Muffin, Nanna, and Helen," I named the little marks. Then with my thumb I smoothed out the first and third. Muffin and Helen. Dead. These weren't your run-of-the-mill suburban matrons, I acknowledged. These were something else entirely—women involved in a violent world where the obliteration of life is nothing beside the need to maintain territorial supremacy.

The women didn't belong there. They had stepped into that world, violated its boundaries. Now at least two of them were dead. Underling couriers, fourth-class deltas at best, had been dispatched to make a show of defiling Helen Tewalt's and then my property. The usual pissing tactics. But why?

Male primates, I remembered, including the human variety, usually prefer posturing, melodramatic threats, and public skirmishes to actual murder. But then that's only true when all the players are male. This game involved female encroachment. Taboo. Traditionally, girls are never allowed in the real game.

So what was the real game? I could see no clues on my computer screen. But then, it occurred to me, I wasn't supposed to. Nobody was supposed to. Slowly, very slowly, like a photograph just emerging on paper in its bath of developing fluid, I saw what Muffin and her dear little lady friends wanted to be seen. A show. A comedy of manners so impeccably performed that it was unnoticeable. Who pays attention to weeds growing in vacant lots? They're just there. They've always been there. Like the army of graying women in sensible shoes and pastel microfiber jackets who eat Waldorf salad from the buffet at the Holiday Inn out by the interstate and speak freely only to each other, in whispers. They've been through it all. They know everything. And they're invisible. The perfect cover. But for what?

I ran the computer through its exit program and turned it off. There was nothing in Muffin Crandall's official story that would explain what had really happened, or why. Which didn't mean the information wasn't available, just that unearthing it was going to require the exercise of some intelligence. As Brontë stirred uncomfortably atop a blanket on the floor I felt that "thunk" of gears engaging inside my head. Brontë would heal, would run again, but it might have been otherwise. If my renegade priest father hadn't taught me the unpleasant value of bearing arms in situations of potential danger, Brontë and I might well be dead. I had a personal stake in this now. Very personal.

The day was overcast and cool, so I opened all the doors and windows and then paced barefoot across my carpet. Pacing helps me think. Something about the relationship between feet and the brain.

"I don't really know anything about Muffin Crandall, Nanna Foy, or Helen Tewalt," I told Brontë. "But the one I know least about is Helen. They're all caricatures to some extent—Muffin the pathetic, incompetent widow, Nanna the gay sophisticate, and Helen the anal-retentive homemaker."

The carpet spoke to the soles of my feet about ancient connections between walking and brain stimulation as I focused my thoughts on Helen Tewalt. I had been inside her home, usually a good way to get a sense of what people are like, although not this time. Helen Tewalt's condo had been a stage set, too tidy and pale, too precisely the quarters of a retired primary school teacher whose greeting cards all feature watercolors of cats sleeping in baskets. And Helen had even brought one of those baskets to the prison, I remembered. A ribboned basket full of chocolate chip cookies. All part of an act.

But I'd had a glimpse of the backstage, too. I'd ducked out of the bathroom Helen had used so frequently and into an office crammed with books including at least one very radically feminist classic. And a computer showing a screen saver photo of a teenage girl in a black T-shirt decorated in beaked insects. Beside the computer was Muffin Crandall's paperweight. Why did Helen have it? And who was the girl on the screen saver? Helen's granddaughter? Niece? It was a cute picture even with the nose ring, but most doting grandmas would quietly shred such a photo in favor of the nice one from prom night or that family trip to the lake last summer.

And for that matter, I thought as a queasy sensation in my stomach made me think of my own bathroom, why had Helen spent so much time using that facility while Nanna and I were there? Even after factoring in copious amounts of herbed raspberry tea, most adults do not use bathrooms three times in an hour. Was Helen ill? Were all these women ill, a doomsday club devoted to nefarious activities for which they would never pay the price because they'd all be dead soon anyway? Muffin Crandall had looked sick, was sick. But the others appeared robustly healthy. I didn't think they were into slaughtering minor criminals as a gesture toward leaving the world a better, cleaner place when they were gone. With the exception of Muffin, they weren't planning to be gone yet.

That backwash feeling in my upper abdomen was getting worse, making my breath taste rancid and metallic. Nausea is not something I like to think about, but I know it when I taste it. Two things crossed my mind as I jogged reluctantly toward the chemical toilet in my waterless bathroom.

The first was something Rox had said about the blue pill in my carpet, the Inderal. Something about how people taking medication for high blood pressure usually also take diuretics. From her frequent trips to the bathroom during my visit, it seemed likely that Helen Tewalt was taking a diuretic, which might mean that she was taking Inderal as well. Which would mean that Helen Tewalt might have broken into my house, accidentally leaving a calling card on my floor.

Hadn't my neighbor at the Laundromat said she'd seen a light-colored car go out toward my place on the day the blue capsule was lost and then seen the car return an hour later? I remembered Helen Tewalt in the prison parking lot, unlocking the doors of a cream-colored Buick with a battery-powered remote on her key chain. The pieces were beginning to fit, although I couldn't imagine what Helen might have been looking for in my filing cabinet. Then I remembered again the computer in her office and wondered if she'd gone into mine. I don't code anything, and my initial series of questions about Muffin was in a standard seven-letter file labeled, "Crandal." Helen could have found the file in less than a minute. No wonder she and Nanna had so efficiently provided answers to every question in that file. They'd rehearsed!

The second thing crossing my mind was that nausea is not uncommon in the first trimester of pregnancy.

After a disagreeable bout of retching I grabbed a Coke from the fridge and drank it slowly while rehearsing my conversations with Muffin Crandall. I couldn't see any point in thinking about pregnancy. The events of the night before had been traumatic, I reasoned. It's not every day you shoot people who've just shot your dog. Probably a lot of people would be upset the next day, maybe even upchuck a little. I didn't need to start worrying about the environmental impact of disposable diapers yet. I needed to sift the available data on Muffin for clues to what was going on.

The available data were that Muffin had lied to Rox during the forensic evaluation in an attempt to establish both her guilt for the crime and her nonexistent senile dementia. And that she was in actuality smart and engaging. I had liked Muffin Crandall, I remembered sadly. She was gutsy and funny and in only a few hours I'd be wearing my mother's shoes again at her funeral. Possibly cradling in my pelvis a by-now suspiciously familiar clump of cells which would become her niece or nephew. Muffin would have gotten a kick out of that, but it wasn't what I wanted to think about.

I wanted to think about why Muffin had been hell-bent on confessing to the murder and then seeming to be mentally incompetent. Why she had refused her attorney permission to see the medical records which could have sprung her from prison hours after she got there. Muffin had wanted to die in prison, play her part to its finale like a trouper. And she had. But what was her part a part *of?*

There was an aura of fanaticism about her behavior that puzzled me. The grandstanding was unnecessary. She was going to die soon anyway, and she knew it. Why choose to go out in misery when comfort is available at the drop of a signature on a medical release form? In the desert before my encounter with Paunch and Tattoo, I'd concluded that the way to find Misha was to follow the track of her soul. Now I wondered about a similar track left by Muffin Crandall. What had she loved? What had moved her to such depths that she would make her very death available to its service?

I had read about saints in dad's library on rainy afternoons in Waterloo. David and I played out the martyred Saint Sebastian story using shish kebab skewers for arrows one day, flinging them at the cute scarecrow mom had made for the vegetable garden from a pattern in a women's magazine. The skewers kept bouncing off, so finally we just jammed them through the scarecrow's newspaper-stuffed chest. Then we used Prang watercolor paint for the requisite streams of blood arrow-filled Saint Sebastian always gushed in his pictures. We were about nine at the time. Dad took the scarecrow down and mom made the first of many attempts to explain visual allegories for passion. Something about Muffin's behavior reminded me of Saint Sebastian, of that passion. But passion about what?

Nanna Foy exuded passion as well, if of a different sort, I recalled. Nanna with her expressive eyes and chain of golden axes seemed to have been assigned responsibility for me. She'd flirted with me, driven miles to bring me Portuguese wine and invite me to join her on a sudden cruise, then admitted it was all an act. She was involved with someone, she'd said. The invitation had been a ruse to get me out of town and out of danger.

The assumption had apparently been that I'd follow her, hypnotized, out of harm's way. And I might have. Anyone might have, man or woman. Nanna Foy is just one of those people who exude erotic promise even with head colds and bad hair. But I'd pushed the illusion over the edge into reality, which was a verbal warning of danger I didn't take seriously.

Victor Camacho had ties to organized crime, she'd said. "They" hadn't known for five years what happened to him, but now they did and had arranged for Muffin's death in prison as retribution. So far so good. But why would these mavens of organized crime bother to harass somebody like Helen Tewalt, or me? We were peripheral noncombatants who had nothing to do with Victor Camacho's death. It didn't scan. Now I wondered if another set of deltas had been sent to put Nanna in her place, and if they'd found her.

I also wondered who'd sent them. In male primate social hierarchies these types are the drones. The not-too-bright fourth-class males who have no chance of defeating the alpha and so never try. They just hang out on the edges of the group, fighting among themselves and earning their right to be there by doing the bidding of their superiors. Beneath them in the ape pecking order are only injured or handicapped males who can't fight, females, and the very young. On these the deltas vent their frustration incessantly.

Human deltas would welcome an order to terrorize or even harm women, I acknowledged. It's their only source of status. But they would never initiate an attack on women outside their immediate frame of reference. Impulse-driven and devoid of long-term planning skills, it wouldn't occur to them. The order had to come from somewhere above. But where? Who was the alpha who gave the order? And what could three suburban clubwomen have done to result in his orchestrating this wholesale retaliation?

The answer seemed obvious. One of them had outraged the alpha by killing one of his deltas. Victor Camacho had been a delta, interchangeable with Paunch or Tattoo or a thousand others. Dan Crandall had defined him as such. "Just your basic street-scum loser," he'd said. Camacho's criminal record supported the thesis. A minor criminal, a loser's loser. But what did Camacho have to do with Muffin, Nanna, and Helen? More significantly, I thought as Brontë licked at the wounds in her side, what did the alpha controlling Camacho have to do with them? Who was behind all this? What *was* all this?

Mentally I drew a picture of a scene five years in the past. A middle-aged woman and a man with whom, under normal circumstances, she would never have contact. A drone predator. He does something, threatens her in some way that results in his death. She kills him. Then she packs him in a freezer.

I thought about that. Dan Crandall had said Victor Camacho was a large man. Five feet eleven inches tall and a hundred and seventy pounds even after considerable evaporation of fluid from frozen tissue. In my bathroom is a cheap but fairly accurate scale Misha bought years ago when she was afraid that three days of inactivity after a bout of oral surgery had caused her to get fat. I took the scale and a trash bag outside and began weighing rocks.

There is no shortage of rocks outside my front door, and in minutes I'd learned to estimate the ten-pounders by sight. I filled the bag with seventeen ten-pound rocks. Victor Camacho's weight. The distance from the ground to the edge of a standard automobile trunk was about two and a half feet, I guessed. Maybe less in a small car, and I had no idea what kind of car Muffin had driven. Not that it mattered.

At the time of Camacho's death Muffin Crandall had been fifty-six and the recent survivor of a mastectomy and chemotherapy. Not a woman in peak physical condition. I am thirty-five and in shape from constant swimming and hiking, and I could not lift that bag of rocks two feet off the ground. Which meant that Muffin Crandall couldn't have done it, either.

Not alone. But then, I realized as the bag ripped open, she hadn't been alone.

She'd had help in this endeavor as she'd had help managing a theater, help dealing with widowhood, and help with terminal illness. They were a team. Muffin, Helen, and Nanna. It was not unlikely that her friends had helped Muffin in this situation as well. Possibly they had helped her commit murder. Maybe in her garage as Muffin described, maybe somewhere else. Probably just as she'd said, at her condo, since the access to her kitchen through a ground-floor garage suggested a reasoned approach to the problem of getting a body into a car trunk.

Certainly they couldn't have used Helen's place, with its quarter-mile landscaped trek from parking lot to door. And Nanna had said she lived in a secured high-rise apartment building. A place like that would have a doorman. It would have a brightly lit lobby through which hundreds of tenants might come and go. Elevators. Impossible to haul a corpse through all that. They'd bagged Camacho at Muffin's, just as she said. Except there had been six arms to lift the weight, not two.

"Assuming that the three of them did it," I told Brontë, "certain questions remain. Did he really die in Muffin's garage? Who actually killed him, why was he killed, and why was the body preserved?" It was time to listen to my messages, I decided. Now that I had a framework into which I might fit the barrage of new information they were sure to contain.

"Blue, you must get out of there now!" Nanna Foy's voice had told me about an hour after Brontë and I left for our hike the night before. "Helen Tewalt is dead. Someone broke into her home, threw things around. It appears that she had a fatal stroke. You won't be able to reach me, so don't try, and don't leave any messages at the forwarding number announced by my answering machine. They may not come after you since you aren't really involved in this situation, but they may think you are. Don't take the chance. Leave and stay gone for at least a week. I'll try to contact you then. And Blue, don't do any further investigation. You would never have been involved in this except for Dan hiring you, which could not possibly have been foreseen. The situation is very dangerous and not your concern. Stay away!"

I pushed the pause button on my answering machine and watched as Brontë painfully stood and limped to her water bowl. Dangerous or not, the "situation" was definitely my concern. And arguably that of the San Diego Police Department. Helen Tewalt had died at her home in Rancho Almas, a suburb of San Diego. My call last night had been answered by a detective sergeant, a representative of an agency which might be happy to hear what I knew, which was a description of two men I had heard discussing their role in the death of a woman. But something told me to hold off on calling the SDPD.

It was pointless, I decided. The descriptions I could give of Paunch and Tattoo—medium height, stringy tan hair with a beer gut, and tall, dark hair with tattoos—wouldn't go far toward helping the police find two delta males virtually indistinguishable from the multitude of counterparts readily available in the nation's seventh largest city. And why would the law want to find them, anyway? There was no provable connection between their overheard remarks and Helen Tewalt's death. Besides, Paunch and Tattoo were no doubt already in Vegas or Phoenix or L.A., drinking up the proceeds of their night's work in a bar where somebody rips the pay phone off the wall every night and throws it across the room.

More important, I sensed that whatever Muffin, Helen, and Nanna were involved in had been structured to avoid the involvement of police. They had been careful about that. Muffin Crandall, I remembered, had not so much as a parking ticket on her record. Clean as Clorox. I was willing to bet the other two were just as spotless, and I was willing to leave it that way. At least for the time being.

The second call had come in about ten minutes after Nanna's. It was dad, and his opening remark unquestionably added a couple more white hairs to the odd patch of them now growing from my cowlick.

"Betsy Blue, I'm going to be a grandfather!" he announced. There was more but I couldn't hear it over my own voice screeching. "You're *what?*" Father Jake is predictably prone to things mystical, but he's not psychic. When my heart slowed to a rate approximating that of high-altitude clog dancers, I ran the tape back and listened closely. Lonni, he said, was expecting David's baby. The blessed event would occur in about eight months, just about the time of David's parole hearing. They hadn't wanted to wait, or certainly Lonni hadn't, and so had opted for a low-tech insemination devoid of romance but just as effective as a cold night beside a fire. Something about smuggled-in condoms and separate, sequential trips to the men's and then the ladies' room in the prison visiting area. My niece or nephew had been conceived, dad pointed out, in love and a minimum-security correctional facility. Of course now the wedding carried even deeper significance for everybody, and he'd call again later to confirm my arrival time in St. Louis on Wednesday.

"For God's sake," I said to Brontë, "babies."

She merely wagged her tail a bit and seemed to smile. The whole world appeared to be knitting booties while I stumbled around in a desert failing to kill people who deserved it. There was some kind of parallel there, but I wasn't interested. I was going to be an aunt.

"Let us pray," I intoned while kneeling to nuzzle my face against Brontë's neck, "that David isn't going to be an uncle."

Dad's church supports the right of women to terminate unwanted pregnancies and so do I. But, I thought as Brontë played her biting game with my right hand, if somebody was taking shape inside me I had no grudge with her or him. That person was welcome to the use of my blood nutrients for a few months. No big deal. What was unwanted was my own motherhood, an overwhelming lifelong responsibility for which I knew I was not designed. The answering machine light suggested I table the question for a later, less pressing moment.

"Blue, where the hell are you?" Rox's voice boomed from ten o'clock that morning when I'd still been asleep in Palm Springs as several hairs atop my head completed their fade to white. "I've got Camacho's complete police jacket, but your damn fax isn't working. Also, Muffin Crandall officially died from strychnine poisoning. Rat poison, to be exact. The prison keeps crates of the stuff in a locked storage room on which the lock happens to have been broken sometime between Friday night and Saturday morning. An opened container of this poison was found in the kitchen trash Saturday night. No more than a tablespoon was missing and there were no fingerprints on the container. None of the prison staff or inmate workers in the kitchen was anywhere near the infirmary where Muffin sipped a Dr Pepper laced with rat poison at about one-thirty P.M., which doesn't really say anything. That small amount of poison could have changed hands several times during the day and never been noticed.

"The prison infirmary is staffed on weekends entirely by inmate trusties in three shifts. The four on duty at the time of Muffin's poisoning all claim not to have provided the Dr Pepper, but also confirm that the vending machines hadn't been serviced on Saturday morning as they usually are, so there was nothing left in any of them but Dr Pepper and some off-brand strawberry soda that everybody hates, so there were half-full cans of Dr Pepper lying all over the place all day Saturday. Anybody could have grabbed one from anywhere. There were various fingerprints on all of the Dr Pepper cans found in or near the infirmary, but none except Muffin's on the Styrofoam cup from which she had her last drink. A dead end.

"Muffin had two visitors that afternoon—N. Foy and H. Tewalt. The five inmates besides Muffin in the infirmary Saturday had nine visitors, six of whom were children. Of the remaining three adult visitors, two visited one inmate and one another. All three adult visitors were accompanied by children and none was there for the first time. Three inmates in the infirmary had no visitors. If you exclude the six children, Muffin's angel-of-death will turn out to be one of these fourteen adults—her two friends, the three visitors of the other women in the infirmary, five sick inmates, and four inmate trusties. But unless somebody talks there'll be no way to prove anything.

"Fix your damn fax machine and call me ASAP."

So it wasn't rhubarb leaves after all, I thought as I checked my fax machine and discovered that it was out of paper. After making a trip to the storage room for a roll of fax paper I installed it and listened to the next message. Dan giving me the time and place of Muffin's funeral. Next I phoned Rox, who wasn't in her office but out at Donovan. Three more calls got me through the web of prison bureaucracy.

"This phone isn't secure," she interrupted as I began last night's tale of Paunch and Tattoo. "Let me call you back."

I took Brontë outside and then dressed for Muffin's funeral while waiting for the callback and wondering what a secure phone was.

"Other lines running in, people maybe listening, not a secure phone," Rox explained minutes later. "Why put your business in the street? And this business you're talking sounds nasty. Now tell me the who-shot-john again."

"It's the who-shot-Brontë," I began, and narrated the whole thing, including Nanna's warning message with its confirmation of Helen Tewalt's unpleasant death.

"Girl, you are in deep sewage," Rox noted professionally. "Foy's right. Get your ass outta Dodge and don't come back till whatever this is, isn't."

"I'm not leaving until Wednesday," I said. "I can't miss that many classes."

"How you gonna teach while dead?"

"The kids won't notice. I put a new roll of paper in my fax, so you can send me Camacho's police file. If you do it now I'll get it before I leave for Muffin's funeral."

Rox's sigh was more despairing than impatient.

"Do not go to that funeral," she said.

"Why not?"

"The idea is to distance yourself from this mess. You show up there, you're seen there. Any reasonable person might think, 'Blue McCarron must have some connection to Muffin Crandall, the wacko who killed some guy in her garage, froze him, and then got poisoned in Las Colinas.' So far whoever is doing your society ladies isn't really sure how deep you're in whatever this game is. Keep it that way. If you can't get out of town, then go check into a hotel and watch pay-per-view movies until Wednesday. Do not show your face anywhere near anything connected to Muffin Crandall."

"I liked Muffin, and I want to be there for Dan," I hedged. "Call me reckless, but I'm going." I didn't tell her that new souls like me are driven by curiosity and cannot be deterred by common sense.

"What I'm calling you is a stupid dimwit who can't stay away from trouble," Rox spat with a crankiness I suspected was the result of being up all night with someone who sings "Love Child" in the shower. "This funeral is trouble. You think you're going to learn something there, but all you're going to do is *be* learned by somebody else. What time is this thing and where?"

"St. Hilda's in Poway, five-forty-five. Why? Do you want to join me?" Unreasonably, I found I wanted to see her, even at a funeral. The awareness had come out of nowhere like one of those roaring columns of dust you see in the desert, and I hated it.

"I have work to do," Rox answered. "It's important that I stay alive to do it. I'll fax the Camacho file as soon as you hang up and then I'm out of this. Bye, Blue."

The hand that replaced my phone in its cradle was shaking, but I wasn't sure whether the cause was anger or hurt feelings. I hate being told what to do, but then we new souls are like that. Rox was probably right about the funeral, I decided, but she was also a control freak. The last thing I needed. Diana Ross was welcome to her.

I felt headachy and alone as I watched the fax coming in, but that was better than what I'd been feeling earlier, I thought. Dust storms, wild, irrational events—these were the images I associated with love. And I didn't want to love Roxie Bouchie. I only wanted to love Misha. Find her. Hold her close. And I would. Just as soon as I'd made sure no more delta males would be hanging around my desert shooting my dog. Or shooting me. Then I'd track Misha. It was a plan, and I didn't ask myself why it felt as faded and dusty as an old photo stuck in the back of a drawer.

The answering machine was still blinking as I helped Brontë into the truck, wadded Rox's fax into my arms, and headed out for Muffin's funeral. There was only one message remaining on the tape. I'd listen to it when I got home, I decided. Everybody significant had already called anyway. Later I would recognize in that assumption a personal record for bad judgment. The final message waiting behind my blinking red light was the last thing I expected.

Chapter Fourteen

An uninspired organist was halfway through "Jesu, Joy of Man's Desiring" as I walked into the little church. Muffin Crandall's body lay in a casket amid an ocean of flowers at the front. The pews were packed, but I didn't recognize anyone as I found a seat behind a pillar at the back and pulled down the kneeler with my mother's right shoe. That is, I didn't recognize anyone until a pair of folded brown hands joined mine on the back of the pew.

"Worst spot you coulda picked," noted the man who was now sharing my kneeler. "Can't see jack shit from here and your back's to every damn door. Easy to just stick you and leave on out. Let you bleed to death on your knees, everybody thinkin' how fuckin' holy is that bitch in the back row, prayed through the whole fuckin' funeral!"

The man wore dreadlocks now fastened neatly in a ponytail, a three-piece pin-striped suit, and a blinding white shirt accented by a gold collar pin beneath his rep tie. A Rastafarian banker. You don't see them every day. It was BB the Punk.

"I don't believe this," I whispered. "Let me guess who sent you."

"No guesses today, dildo," he whispered back, piously making the sign of the cross before taking a seat in the pew beside me, his head bowed in a show of grief. With his left hand he tugged up a pants cuff, displaying the six-inch stiletto secured to his leg.

Then he turned to the right, ostensibly reaching for a prayer book. At the small of his back was a bulge I was sure contained at least fifteen rounds, just like the Glock 9mm now locked in a metal case welded to the floor of my truck.

"Isn't carrying weapons a violation of your parole?" I mentioned into my clasped hands.

"Get real," BB answered, smiling as if at a shared memory of the deceased. "Roxie say you too dumb to know shit from fudge, walk into this mess like Goldilocks in a bear house. Ain't nothin' gonna happen, but if it do, little parole violation don't mean bubba when it go down.

"I will be *here*," he stressed, indicating the back of the church with a toss of his head as he stood. "At the door, keep an eye in and eye out to your truck. Your dog bark, I'm there. You see anything funny, drop that hymn book, lean down, stay down. At the end I will escort you to your truck and you will leave by the route I tell you to leave. You will not go to the cemetery for the burial."

"I will do as I damn well please," I hissed through clenched teeth, but BB was already out of earshot and positioned next to a rear door.

The organist was winding up and the woman priest already standing before the casket as Dan Crandall and the woman I assumed to be his wife, Kathy, hurried to take seats in front. Dan was resplendent in a new suit similar to BB's, and conducted himself with elaborate courtesy toward the attractive woman at his side. I was sure he'd taken my advice, bought himself a book on manners and read it before his wife's arrival. If he could keep it up, I might have saved a marriage. The thought was bizarre.

"I am the resurrection and the life, saith the Lord," said the priest in a good, clear voice that reminded me of dad. Maybe she was the daughter of dad's ex-wife, I imagined proudly. A sort of sister.

As the usual stuff was said and sung I looked around. No deltas in sight, nobody watching me except BB at the rear door. The mostly older crowd seemed affluent and at ease. A typical retirement community bunch, I assumed they were accustomed to attending funerals. And they had liked Muffin Crandall, if the masses of flowers were any indication. Probably she had hit up most of them for tax-deductible contributions to the community theater and then charged them two dollars for instant coffee at intermission. I doubted that any of them had a clue about her mysterious connection to Victor Camacho. Of course, I was wrong. At least one mourner at St. Hilda's that Monday afternoon less than two weeks ago knew the connection better than I. And that mourner, I would soon realize, was permanently outraged about it.

At the time I was oblivious to this, and noticed nothing except the conspicuous absence of Nanna Foy. I was willing to bet that the dramatic spray of white roses atop Muffin's bier was from her and Helen, though. Waxy white roses in full bloom punctuated here and there with tiny blood-red buds, all secured by a wide black velvet bow. It was an odd combination even though white is the proper liturgical color for funerals. But red isn't, and the wired black ribbon trailing over the foot of the casket seemed jarringly Victorian. You just don't see black ribbons at funerals in Southern California, where death is less a mystery than the inevitable result of not finding a good nutritionist. Something about the floral arrangement bothered me.

"Into paradise may the angels lead thee," chanted the priest. "And at thy coming may the martyrs receive thee."

"Martyrs" would include shot-full-of-arrows Saint Sebastian, I remembered. Bleeding copiously but single-minded in his passion. Like Muffin. In that confluence of imagery the flowers adorning Muffin's casket began to make sense. I'd heard about those colors from another passionate group years ago. A group led by the woman who phoned Misha in the middle of the night to come rescue Brontë. White, red, and black. The colors of an ancient trinity.

The woman who phoned that night from the emergency animal clinic had been the leader of a feminist religious group. Misha had invited them, like many others, to meet at our apartment before realizing that the group's purpose failed her standards. Intolerant of feminist inquiry into anything more abstract than anti-pornography legislation, Misha had quickly found them another meeting place. But not before I'd picked up a few things.

Like the colors on Muffin's casket. "White is the girl, the breath and spirit of life. Red is the woman, in the sea of whose blood-lined womb life begins. Black is the crone, whose wisdom after much living is dreadful." I had heard the goddess worshipers recite this litany of colors at their meetings. Now the colors of that trinity lay before me on the casket of a woman who had confessed to murder, feigned insanity, and been poisoned in prison. A woman who was a crone, whose wisdom was dreadful.

I had no idea what it all meant, but something about the wisdom now silenced in that casket made me shiver. Muffin's wisdom, and Nanna's and Helen Tewalt's. All crones, these women. All well into black. And they knew something, were involved in something that was getting them killed.

My mother would have been like them now, I realized. If her life hadn't been obliterated by a man who'd drunk sixteen beers in less than two hours while watching a football game at a bar. He'd walked away from the wreckage after running a light and ramming his pickup at seventy miles per hour into mom's VW station wagon. It occurred to me, sitting behind a pillar at yet another funeral, that I still wanted to break every bone in that lout's body. Some angers just don't go away, although they quickly become mere transitory fantasies.

In the first hours after learning of my mother's death I really would have taken a hammer to her killer if I could have. But the instinct toward violent retribution is swiftly eroded by the passage of time with its ten thousand demanding details. Usually. I wondered how much time had passed between whatever Victor Camacho had done and a reaction of rage sufficient to keep three women up all night preparing him for storage.

"In the midst of life we are in death," said the priest as Dan Crandall and five other pallbearers lifted Muffin's casket by the brass rails attached to it for that purpose. I ducked out of the pew and stood beside the aisle, causing BB to glower menacingly. I had to see the card attached to that spray of flowers as they carried Muffin out. I had to be certain I was right.

"Brava!" said the message on the card. "Nanna and Helen."

I was right. The flowers would have been ordered before Helen's death the night before, I concluded. And at Helen's service later there would be an identical spray of flowers with a card from Nanna. They would be consistent. It was important. No one would know the significance of the white and blood-red roses, the wide black ribbons, but the significance would be there. I could hear Dan Crandall singing the last line of the recessional hymn's refrain as he passed. "Leave we now thy servant sleeping." Muffin might have been the "servant" of an idea, I thought. But it probably wasn't the one the hymnist had in mind.

I could also hear BB the Punk muttering something unpleasant about my racial heritage as he slipped an arm about my waist and propelled me through the exiting crowd. His arm felt like steel beneath the pin-striped wool of his suit jacket.

"You're overdoing it," I mentioned as I stumbled to keep up.

"Overdoing it was pressing my luscious body into this pimp suit," he replied, smiling vacantly at a young woman in a green silk dress who was fumbling in her purse for something. It was the green dress that did it, that gave me the clue to why I thought I recognized her. It was the same Boy Scout green of the wool-blend uniform pants in which I'd last seen her. She appeared to be with an older man who was also vaguely familiar, although I couldn't place him. He was working the crowd outside the church, shaking hands and glancing at his Rolex as if he were late for dinner with Donald Trump. I couldn't shake the idea that I'd seen him before, many times. I knew I'd seen the woman in green.

"BB, that woman is a guard at Las Colinas," I whispered. "What's she doing here?"

"Right now she lookin' at you, which is why D-U-M-B stamped all over your face. Get in your truck and take surface streets down to Auntie's. Streets don't nobody use. Stay off the freeway. Roxie gonna meet you there. Now go. I got a little somethin' to do here."

I will never know how he did it, but by the time I got in the truck and began the maneuvering necessary to exit the church parking lot as everybody else was trying to do the same, a small crowd had gathered at a shiny black Lexus. The guard in the green dress tossed her purse into the car and then stood back as her irritated companion rolled up his designer shirt sleeves and wrestled a spare tire and jack from the trunk. A flat tire, it seemed. BB was nowhere to be seen.

In no rush to hear Roxie's plummeting opinion of my common sense, I stopped to walk Brontë in the weedy parking lot of a defunct grocery store. As she stretched and then hobbled off to sniff out information concerning recent events on the expanse of cracked cement, I looked at the fax of Victor Camacho's criminal record.

Victor Wayne Camacho had been born in Brownsville, Texas, thirty-six years before, I calculated, his fatal run-in with anywhere from one to three women past childbearing age. He'd earned a GED in a Texas juvenile correctional facility and later received training as a welder while imprisoned for grand theft auto in Arizona. His usual occupation, however, was listed as "salesman." Ten years in the past he'd arrived in San Diego and immediately been arrested for dealing drugs to children at five different inner-city junior high schools. He'd done two years in Donovan for that, no doubt the reason Rox had been able to get his file so quickly. After all, she worked there. And even though Victor Camacho was long gone, his paper "self" was still around. In his mug shots he looked like a Mexican gang member, but that had probably been a disguise to mislead police at the time of his arrests. He wasn't Mexican at all. He wasn't much of anything.

As Brontë sniffed a flattened gardening glove next to several fragmented plastic spoons lying on the pavement, I looked closely at the record of Camacho's final three years on earth. Suspicion of burglary, vagrancy, public intoxication, suspicion of drug sales to minors, driving under the influence of a controlled substance, suspicion of aggravated assault, suspicion of pandering, suspicion of sexual assault on a minor. He was coming down in the world, his crimes reflecting a descent to the lowest even among criminal behaviors. Probably feeding a habit, I thought. Or just plain lazy.

The file went on and on, a tedious compilation of criminal code numbers documenting behaviors I didn't want to read about as well as names of accomplices and victims, names of arresting officers, dates and times. Muffin Crandall's name did not appear as a victim, nor did Nanna's or Helen's. No Crandalls, Foys, or Tewalts anywhere in the file. Which pretty much blew my feeble theory that Camacho might have attacked one of them. I hadn't really expected to see that, anyway. It was too simple.

Doggedly I continued to scan the file, looking for nothing in particular. I read names. Hundreds of them. Victor Camacho had been arrested or interrogated by thirty-seven different police officers, I noted. At these times he had been in the company of crime partners named everything from Ackerman to Zeebar, that last one almost certainly an alias. A little over a year before the end of his unsavory career there was a cluster of pandering arrests in connection with a woman named Anna Lopez. Somebody had handwritten a note in the document's margin to the effect that Anna Lopez, a prostitute, had died from a drug overdose while detained at the San Diego County Jail after her arrest in Camacho's company.

"Lopez dead so unavailable as witness," the note's author had concluded matter-of-factly.

Camacho had been pimping for somebody named Anna Lopez, I assumed. Taking her money and feeding the habit that had killed her. There was nothing unusual about the scenario, but there was something familiar about the name. Lopez.

"Nah," I told myself while sitting in my truck in the middle of an abandoned parking lot as bleak as Anna Lopez's life had been. It couldn't be. There were probably six hundred people named Lopez in the San Diego telephone directory and twice that many who did not have phones. Mexican illegals, I knew, frequently assumed the name because it was both common and pronounceable by the American tongue.

There could be no connection, I reasoned, with an urban folktale spun from the fears of jailed teenage girls. It was ridiculous to think that Anna Lopez might have been related to a girl named Frankie Lopez, whose bones had only four days earlier not been found in a nonexistent escape tunnel beneath the juvenile detention center. A girl who was believed by my students to have sent, six years in the past, somebody named Bugsy Sneller a postcard from Albany, New York. The name Lopez was just a coincidence, I lectured myself. And not much of one at that.

At six-forty-five Auntie's dance floor was empty but for Rox and the TV actor, who'd seized the moment to enjoy their passion for elaborate footwork. The music was a Cajun waltz, one of Beausoleil's called "*Valse de grande Mèche,*" a traditional accordion foot-stomper laced with fiddles, field hollers, and rippling country guitar. Rox and the actor moved around the floor with athletic grace, her head thrown back in pure enjoyment. I was sure her childhood friends would *still* kick her butt into Lake Michigan if they could see her now. But her freckle-faced father with his big ears would understand perfectly. After all, he'd brought Rox's love of these particular harmonies all the way from Western European campfires gone to ash centuries before Chaucer. I wondered if he even knew he had a daughter.

"So," Rox greeted me when the waltz was over, "how was the funeral?"

"BB was stunning in banker drag, and one of the guards from Las Colinas was there with a man I'm sure I've seen somewhere before but I can't remember where. He drives a black Lexus. But what's interesting is the flowers—"

"I don't suppose you bothered to notice the license plate on the Lexus," she interrupted.

"Um, no."

"BB did. I'll run the plate numbers tomorrow, see who this dude is. Meanwhile, have I told you lately that you lack sufficient sense to stay off rooftops during lightning storms? You, you run up there barefoot, stand in a puddle and wave golf clubs at the sky. There's no reason you're not dead."

"I'm not dead," I insisted as we found a table and ordered a couple of grilled cheese sandwiches brought in from the restaurant next door, "because I have a gun. Actually it's Brontë who's not dead because I have a gun. I didn't know they could serve food in here."

"They can't, but nobody's around so it doesn't matter. Is Brontë going to be okay?"

Auntie's has one of those revolving balls covered with pieces of mirror over the dance floor. In its flashes I could see that Rox's hair had been rebraided, this time with beads of carved soapstone and ebony. She looked gorgeous, but my appreciation was dimmed by a suspicion that the cosmetic effort had been in preparation for her date last night.

"Brontë's recovering rapidly. She's sleeping in the truck right now," I answered politely, forcing myself not to mention how terrific she looked. "Do prison guards usually go to the funerals of prisoners?"

"Not usually," Rox explained as our sandwiches arrived. "But it happens. No rule against it. Sometimes over the years a guard and a prisoner get to know each other, become friends. No problem as long as the guard doesn't go soft and start bringing things into the prison for his buddy. Cigarettes, a couple pair of socks, a lid of weed—it's all the same. Guard finds himself at an employment office two days later. But Muffin wasn't in prison anywhere near long enough to form that kind of attachment. That the guard was at her funeral is probably significant, but let's do a little catch-up before getting into that. For example, when's the baby due?"

"Agghh," I groaned over a bread-and-butter pickle in its bed of carrot curls on my plate. "I, um, don't know that I'm really pregnant, but I could be."

Roxie Bouchie smiled at an identical pickle on her plate and then took a bite of her sandwich. A scent of sharp cheddar and toasted sourdough bread wafted around us. She said nothing, but continued an ostentatious enjoyment of her meal while I squirmed.

"Dan Crandall showed up at my place Saturday afternoon," I began. "Actually it wasn't my place, but out in the desert. I'd gone for a walk and he followed my tracks. He was upset. He'd just heard about Muffin's death."

"Uh-huh," Rox said with equal emphasis on both syllables.

"Oh, hell, I don't know. I was thinking about my mother; he wanted to know where Muffin *was*; it was dusk and the birds came out of the ground. We had sex. I forgot about the stupid *sperm,* for God's sake. Then later I lost my breakfast. Can we talk about something else?"

"Uh-UH." Emphasis on second syllable.

"Well, what more is there to say?" I said. "It was stupid. My godmother, Carter Upchurch, explained the whole thing to me when I was sixteen. Every detail. My friends and I practiced with carrots. Later I had plenty of practice with the real thing before I figured out why it was so boring. There's just no excuse."

Rox dipped her head to one side, the ebony and soapstone beads making a softer sound than the tortoiseshells. A sound like leaves blowing on snow.

"I'm not gonna ask about those carrots," she pronounced quietly as a smile, probably a laugh, tugged at the corners of her mouth. "No, I'm not, much as I'm dying to. You should, however, be reminded that you've probably got my stomach flu rather than Crandall's tax deduction. So what's this about almost seducing Nanna Foy?"

I'd forgotten about the stomach flu, but it made sense. Or at least I hoped it made sense. If not, I was afraid dad would insist on raising the baby rather than helping me find a nice set of Episcopalian adoptive parents. They would have to be Episcopalian, I'd decided. No English-speaking child should grow up without exposure to the language of *The Book of Common Prayer.*

"Who knows? Nanna's gorgeous and an outrageous flirt, although it was all an act meant to lure me away from the danger that showed up anyway," I told Rox. "I blame the grid."

"The what?" A carrot curl arrested halfway to her mouth looked like an orange question mark in the dim light.

"You know," I answered, "whatever it is that slams you around like a roller coaster with ninety-degree turns. My dad always says there are no choices but to hang on or get off and sit it out on the sidelines. After two years of blissful peace, I'm afraid I got back on."

Roxie chomped the carrot curl, stared at the pale half-moon of a thumbnail for over a minute, then looked at me.

"Girl, I hear what you're saying," she agreed, nodding. "Never thought about it like that, but your daddy's right. You're lucky, Blue. Do you know that?"

"Yeah," I agreed. "Rox?"

"Hmm?"

"How in God's name did you wind up being a psychiatrist?"

From the snotty grin on her face I could tell she was about to relate some deft story, the same line of bull with which she probably handled anybody intruding on her personal turf.

"You can tell me to mind my own business, but I'm too tired for bullshit," I said into my cooling grilled cheese, which was making me sick.

"Fair," she said thoughtfully. "Okay. My mother died in a state mental hospital. She had schizophrenia. I barely knew her when I was a kid. I was . . . afraid of her. I lived with my grandmother and sometimes my mother would be out of the hospital and on the streets and she'd come to the door begging. She'd be all raggedy and hungry. She smelled. When I was little I'd hide while my gran tried to clean her up, feed her a little before she took off and vanished again for months. Sometimes my mother thought the food gran gave her was poisoned and wouldn't eat it. She was always terrified. A thought disorder, voices in your head, they're terrifying. Then when I was about twelve—"

"Rox, I'm so sorry," I interrupted. "You don't have to do this. I didn't mean to—"

"When I was about twelve gran went to court and signed the papers to have my mother committed. We'd go to the hospital to see her every Sunday. It was better. I guess it was better. In those days the medications were as bad as the illness. She got fat. She was like a zombie and her arms and legs shook all the time. But she was clean and had food and a bed at night, crafts and stuff. She liked that. She liked to make God's eyes . . ."

Rox trailed off and glared at the flashing mirror chips revolving above the empty dance floor. I didn't say anything, just waited.

"Colored yarn wrapped around crossed popsicle sticks," she finally sighed. "I figured God's eyes must be dead blind to see her misery and do nothing. Figured I'd have to do it myself, find some way to fix it. By the time I was fourteen I was determined to be a doctor like the ones trying to help my mother, only I'd actually *help*. I got a scholarship for my undergraduate work and finished in three years.

"Gran and I brought my mother out of the hospital to the graduation ceremony. She wore an electric blue muumuu with one of her God's eyes for a necklace. I could see her when I went up to get my diploma, see her blue dress and that diamond of colored yarn wrapped around popsicle sticks. I couldn't see anything else. Two weeks later she died in the hospital. Her heart just stopped. Gran's church scraped together enough money to fill in after student loans and what I made working part-time, so I could go to med school. Any more questions?"

"Just one," I answered, reaching to clasp her right hand. "How about a dance?"

"You can't dance." She grinned and shrugged her shoulders as if throwing off an invisible weight.

"I'll fake it," I agreed over k.d. lang singing something not really meant for dancing, exactly.

A few other people drifted onto the floor, but they might have been ghosts. Roxie filled my entire frame of reference, made my breath shallow. It wasn't the story she'd just told me as much as the fact that the story was flat-out real. It stood alone and so did she. My reaction to the story was irrelevant, as everything external to her own convictions was irrelevant. I was dancing with one tough, magnificent woman.

"So, what's next on the Crandall agenda?" she asked while leading me easily in a simple four-step.

"You run the license plate BB noted on the Lexus at Muffin's funeral, I teach my class at juvy, do some research on Nanna and Helen, and find something to wear at my brother's wedding on Saturday. There isn't much else we can do right now."

A significant warmth palpable in the space between us signaled that there was, in fact, something else we could do. In my escalating heart rate I identified the warmth as desire, but a desire anchored in something so solid it felt like home. Roxie Bouchie, nothing like me in any way, a stranger with a history I could never truly understand, was nonetheless home. My home. I'd never felt that before, a person suddenly revealed to be a place where you've always belonged.

The awareness was more compelling than the more familiar one drawing my face to hers as we danced. I touched her cheek with the corner of my mouth and then turned to kiss her again. Cheekbone, jaw, the downy skin at the edge of her ear. With each touch of my lips she held me tighter until we were barely moving to the music, her beads whispering against my hair. I could feel her heart pounding, her breasts urgent against mine as the corner of my mouth found the corner of hers.

"Honey, don't," she whispered raggedly. "I want you so much I won't be able to stop. Why don't we just get out of here."

"Okay," I concurred. Every synapse in my entire nervous system concurred. I needed Roxie so deeply my bones were dissolving. I stumbled from the dance floor on rubbery legs and then something slid sideways deep inside my skull. Waves of metallic taste flowed in my throat.

"Rox, I'm . . ."

"Sick," she completed the thought while half carrying me toward the ladies' room. "I don't usually have this effect on women, but then maybe it's just my cologne, huh? Midnight in Fresno. Picked it up at a swap meet along with a Michael Jackson glove and two quarts of Mexican vanilla I'll use to get the oil stains off my garage floor. Go, girl, before you upchuck in my cleavage."

I vaguely remembered having other intentions regarding her cleavage, but my immediate concerns were more pressing.

"I *told* you you had my damn stomach flu, hon," Rox mentioned through a stall door behind which I was hanging over a toilet. "I'll be at the table when you can tear yourself away."

Ten minutes later I felt like the inside of a popped balloon, but I was better. BB was sitting with Rox when I wobbled back to the table. He was wearing a lime green T-shirt with a huge, beaked insect printed on the front. The insect looked familiar.

"Well, well, here come the great white hope," he snickered, shaking his dreadlocks over lime green shoulders. "You look like the tube after the toothpaste run off with the spoon," he noted in a metaphor I was sure had something to do with drugs and was terribly hip.

"What is that bug?" I asked him after slumping into a chair.

"What bug?" he said, managing to draw the word out to two syllables. Buu-uuug. It sounded like the way my evening was going.

"On your shirt."

"You ain't heard of the Weev?"

"Weave?" I said. "As in warp and woof, mohair scarves, Irish tweed?"

"Weev-IL," he explained. "As in the sweetest electric bass you ever heard, the juicetest keyboard and synthesizer, the *mutha* of all skin, the—"

"It's a heavy metal rock group called Hell's Weevil," Rox interrupted. "I think they're in town. Here, I got you a Coke, settle that stomach a little."

"A rock group," I said into my glass. "Rox, I saw a picture of a girl on Helen Tewalt's screen saver last week when I was at her condo. The girl had on a T-shirt with those bugs all over it. Lots of them and smaller than the one on BB's."

"Black T-shirt with the bugs sorta metallic green?" BB asked.

"Yeah."

"That was Weevil's concert shirt from, let's see, five years back," he said. "I was twitchin' my bootie up and down the big yard about then, listening to that concert tape on a fine Walkman one of my big ole daddies scored for me. Knew some guys who woulda killed for one of those shirts. Shit, maybe one of 'em did!"

"So where do you get these shirts?" I asked.

"Get 'em at Weevil concerts, get 'em from the promoter by the boxload if you a rock DJ or a writer for one of the 'zines. Get 'em at music stores later if any left after the tour. But the Weev, there wouldn't be any left, 'specially from that tour. That was their Dead Larvae tour. Fuckin' album sold millions. That shirt was an instant collector's item."

"BB, you're a gold mine," I said, dragging myself into a semblance of alertness. "So how long after the end of the concert tour would a kid wear the T shirt?"

"A truly righteous kid? No time. As soon as the last concert ended that kid would hang the shirt on a wall and never wear it again, but keep it, see? It's like a way of bein' tight with the band, bein' on that tour. But when it's over, it's over. The shirt, it be retired."

I wondered if the girl in Helen Tewalt's screen saver had been "righteous," a serious fan who knew the T-shirt rules. If so, the photo on Helen's monitor had been taken five years ago before the end of Hell's Weevil's Dead Larvae tour. Something, I thought, had gone on five years ago. And it had culminated in a secret frozen in a desert food locker until a minor earthquake revealed it in a soggy plastic trash bag. A secret that might have died with Muffin Crandall, was *supposed* to die with Muffin Crandall, but didn't.

"Girl, I think you'd better head on home," Rox said. "Eat some clear soup when you get there, sleep. I'll walk you out to your truck."

I watched her wrap the remains of my grilled cheese sandwich in a napkin for Brontë. Going home was not what I'd had in mind for the remainder of the evening, but I could tell she was feeling skittish about our earlier eruption of lust. I felt skittish, too. Also weak and queasy and scarcely the passionate lover I'd be just as soon as my stomach got out of the picture.

"Blue," she said in the darkness beside my truck as Brontë growled happily over the grilled cheese, "I don't think we should, you know, get involved. It's too complicated. It's not a good idea."

"Is it the Diana Ross look-alike?" I asked. "Does she make it a bad idea?"

"She *is* a bad idea, completely superficial." Rox sighed. "And that's all I have time for. My work is everything to me, Blue. I work twelve-hour days and I love it. It's what I want to do. Nothing else really matters to me. You know why."

"Yes," I agreed, not arguing.

"I don't want anything serious, don't want to be tied down. You're the real thing, Blue. God knows you're the real thing, but I don't want a real thing. So let's just end this before it starts, before anybody gets hurt."

"So sensible, so rational," I said in that voice actresses use while doing commercials for floor cleaner. "I might even agree with you, Rox, except for one thing."

"What's that?" she asked as Brontë sighed over the last bit of sharp cheddar and I slid into the driver's seat of my truck.

"It doesn't work that way."

I drove off without looking back.

When I got home there were no new messages on the machine, just the flashing red light and a digital 1 on the display. That last call from yesterday, I remembered. Probably Carty with a flurry of ideas for wedding presents. That's what I thought as I hit the play button.

But it wasn't Carter Upchurch who'd called me.

It was Misha Deland.

Chapter Fifteen

"Blue, it's Misha. I'm . . . um, I going to be in San Diego in a few days," she'd said. "I'd . . . I'd like to see you. Can I call you?" After the closing question there was a nervous sigh and then the sound of a phone hanging up.

I pushed replay and listened to the message again as Brontë's ears perked at the familiar voice. I flashed on an image of my life as a half-completed jigsaw puzzle falling through space. There were, I thought, too many dimensions involved ever to get the thing put together. There also seemed to be colored tinsel drifting around inside my arms. At least it felt like that.

Misha's question was rhetorical. Of course she could call me. She'd already called me. Yesterday. So what did "in a few days" mean? In a few days I'd be in Missouri swilling canned soda pop under armed guard at the wedding of a man named Hammer. I wouldn't be home.

On the other hand, what sort of person hangs around two years waiting for a phone call? The answer wasn't flattering, but I wanted to see Misha. Seeing her would bring order to my life, I thought. Things would make sense again. But seeing her would mean staying in California, missing my brother's wedding. I remembered the lecture I used to give my social psych students at San Gabriel. The lecture about respecting the bond of clan.

"I hate my brother," I told Brontë. "He turned his back on all of us, flipped us off, and became something people cross the street to avoid. I don't care that now he's suddenly decided to rejoin the human race, get married, and have a baby. It's too late. I'm not impressed. What does it have to do with me?"

Brontë said nothing, but I could hear the answer in my head. "He's your brother," it said flatly. "You have to be there."

I had known that, all along. It wasn't just David, it was dad and Carty and the memory of my mother. It was a woman named Lonni Briscoe who for some incomprehensible reason loved my brother and was willing to join her future to his, which meant joining her future to the rest of ours as well. The traditional entanglements felt like a straitjacket, but hadn't I told impressionable college students these entanglements were the last defense against a slide back into brute muck? What had I meant by "brute muck"? Of course, I'd meant David. Now he was attempting a climb out of the sewer. I was obliged to honor that, show up for it, no matter what.

Misha had left no number where she could be reached, no clue as to where she was or why she would be in San Diego. I listened to the message five more times, my ear pressed to the tinny speaker for background noise, context. There was nothing, just a clean connection. No crackling static or ghost voices conversing in foreign languages. From this I deduced that the call was probably domestic. It had been placed from somewhere in North America. So helpful to know that. I wondered how she'd found my number.

"Misha is alive and on this continent," I told Brontë as she wagged her stubby tail to document her interest in the chicken broth heating on the stovetop. The news was jarring. Misha, vanished into thin air for two years and murdered in my head for as long, was back. She would be where I lived in a matter of days, although I wouldn't be. The whole mess bore the stamp of the grid. That nasty, distant irony. I was mentally framing a snide rejoinder when the phone rang.

"Misha?" I gasped eagerly on the first ring. "Where are you?"

"Who's Misha?" Roxie Bouchie's deep voice answered.

The grid again, close-up. I threw a finger at the sky beyond my picture window, pointlessly.

"My ex," I said, embarrassed. "She vaporized two years ago, supposedly ran off to New Zealand with a multilingual grant writer. Apparently she called yesterday. I just heard the message tonight."

"Hmm. New Zealand was a British protectorate until very recently, Blue," Roxie lectured coolly. "Grants there are almost certainly written in English. So is this the old affair you told me still has you tied in knots?"

"Yeah, it did, I guess. I don't know anymore. And I'm pretty sure that story about the grant writer wasn't true. I don't know what happened to Misha, Rox. One day I came home and she was gone, all her stuff, everything. I didn't exactly cope with it, just moved out here, went into a coma and decided to get rich. Then Dan Crandall showed up and knew who wrote 'The Cremation of Sam McGee,' and I said I'd try to help Muffin. Everything started moving too fast. Am I making any sense?"

"I like the rich part, but the answer is no, you're not. You will soon, though. That's why I called. First, BB saw two dudes hanging around outside Auntie's after you left. Tall guy with wall-to-wall tattoos and a shorter one with a bad limp and a beer gut."

"Paunch and Tattoo," I breathed. It seemed that Paunch hadn't bled to death from his leg wound after all.

"Sounds like it," Rox went on. "BB made the usual noises about castration and death, and they took off, but you're not safe out there, Blue. They're trailing you. I wasn't thinking clearly when I told you to go home. You need to get out of there."

"I didn't come home because you told me to," I pointed out.

"I came home because I live here. You said 'first,' what's the second thing?"

"The research you mentioned on the ladies of Rancho Almas. Write this number down. It's, let's just say someone I know professionally. He runs a perfectly legal business procuring information. For a couple hundred bucks or so he can probably run down anything you need to know about Nanna Foy and Helen Tewalt. Income, investments, past names and addresses, credit card purchases. Medical records cost considerably more but I don't think they're necessary, do you? And he works at night. You can call him right now, before you leave to go sleep in a secured hotel. He'll have the data by tomorrow."

"I assume this is one of your patients?"

"Assume anything you want. We agreed to work together on this thing. He'll get some work done that needs to be done."

"Rox?" I said tentatively, hesitating to change the subject.

"Hmm?"

"When we were dancing tonight, you felt like home to me."

There was a long silence in which I could hear Brontë lapping water from her bowl in the kitchen.

"Honey, sounds like that one and only girlfriend's headed straight back into those stringbean arms of yours," Rox said quietly. "And as I told you, I don't do relationships, I do work."

"Still, I wanted you to know," I said.

"I do know, Blue. You felt like that to me, too, but let's don't turn it into a musical. Just one of those things. Now get out of there and go to some fancy desert resort place in Borrego where they have security guards. Don't stay there and get killed waiting for your lady to call, okay?"

"Okay," I agreed and said good-bye. I meant both that I wouldn't get killed and I wouldn't stay waiting for Misha to call. I didn't mean that I wouldn't stay, exactly. Language is fundamentally misleading, I thought as I hung up the phone. Quite possibly this duplicity is what sets us apart from animals, rather than our highly touted skill with verbal symbols whose function is inevitably to obscure. It was depressing.

"I dissemble, therefore I am," I told Brontë.

Then I phoned Rox's anonymous procurer of information, who with only the names and addresses I provided said he could answer all my questions by tomorrow and would fax the information to Rox. He also said he stayed up all night because his medication made him sleep all day, but it was better than hearing voices that seemed to come from the walls. I told him I wasn't planning to sleep much that night either, that we all have our reasons for wakefulness and to hang in there. Deirdre Eckels's boring periodical on feminist banking was still lying on my desk by the phone, so I added her name and old PO box number to the list for him to investigate. Admittedly, at that point I was thinking more of ways to find Misha after I got back from Missouri and she was gone again than about Nanna and Helen. On a whim I threw Misha's name into the mix as well, using our beach apartment as her last known address.

Next I went out to the truck, took the Glock from its metal box and put it in my pack. Then I dug two sleeping bags and the old .22 bolt-action out of the storage room and stashed a box of shells next to the Glock. When I'd lashed the sleeping bags to my back I slung the rifle strap over my shoulder and called Brontë.

"We're going camping, girl," I explained as I slipped a rarely used dog harness over her head and fastened it under her chest.

On the way out I tied the end of the spool of fishing line in my pack to the door handle of my truck and ran the line through the metal clothesline ring set in a rock several feet up the wash behind Wren's Gulch. The line stretched invisibly across the front of the motel. Anything approaching my front door from either side would run into it. When Brontë and I had scrambled to the top of the wash I cut the line and tied the end to a limb of saltbush. I tugged at it and the limb's dry foliage made a satisfactory rasping sound. When I'd snapped a leash to Brontë's harness and tied the end to my belt, I settled her on one of the sleeping bags and slid into the other. But I didn't go to sleep.

Instead I lay on the ground and felt crabby, fat, and put upon by everything. A pebble beneath my shoulder seemed consciously determined to make me miserable. And little convulsions of pain were surfing my lower abdomen. I was angry at David for scheduling his redemption contrary to my convenience. I was angry at Misha for inviting me to Eden Snow's party, making love with me in a potting shed, and then vanishing two years later. I was angry at Rox for eroding my devotion to a ghost, and angry at three women old enough to be my mother because they'd done something which was keeping me from sleeping in my own bed. I ran a finger along the cool barrel of the .22 and hoped Paunch and Tattoo would show up. It would be nice to have an excuse to shoot at something, I thought, since I didn't seem to be going to sleep.

An hour later, when the sky had darkened to a texture like black wool, I realized what was behind my wholesale crabbiness. The cramps brought the point home. Not stomach cramps, which I might have expected with Roxie's flu. These cramps were lower, specific and familiar. I'd had them occasionally since I was twelve. Most women do.

"I'm premenstrual!" I gleefully told a wet nose peeking from the sleeping bag beside mine. Brontë had crawled inside her bag to avoid the light dew which was condensing on me as I sat, a damp ogre in the dark. "That means I'm not pregnant!"

My relief was expansive. I was jubilant. David and Lonni would provide dad and Carty a new little soul on which to lavish their attention, and that was enough. I would be an aunt but not a mother, free of that relentless tie to the future. Free to be myself in my own time, completely. For somebody else's offspring I could occasionally be Auntie Blue zipping in and out with fabulous gifts. Accompanied by the soundtrack from *Bladerunner.* Then gone. Perfect. I hadn't realized how much I needed that freedom, how essential it was. Sighing happily, I fell asleep in seconds, my head directly beneath the saltbush limb.

I slept for hours. It was close to four A.M. on my phosphorus-faced watch when the limb jerked violently, only once. But I'd heard it, been expecting it. Brontë was already on her haunches, growling.

"Shh, quiet girl," I whispered as I cut the fishing line so it wouldn't provide a path directly to us in the predawn dark. Then I jammed the Glock into the waist of my jeans, slipped a shell into my childhood rifle, and rammed the bolt home. The gun oil smell of the .22 was comforting. It reminded me of a time when I still had a mother, a human brother, and no delta males tracking me around deserts. A nice smell. We can fixate on anything, I guess.

From the top of the wash I had a three-hundred-sixty-degree view of the road, the motel, and the boulder-strewn desert stretching in every direction. Rising slowly to my knees, I released the safety on the .22, braced my arms on a rock, and aimed at the front door of my own home. From two hundred yards I knew I'd be lucky to ding the door, much less do any damage to something smaller and moving, but I wanted to launch this skirmish with a little girl's rifle. Call me sentimental.

There was nothing in the rifle's sights, but on the periphery I could just see the rear bumper and trunk release of a dark car parked on the other side of my truck. An Oldsmobile, I thought. Maybe Roxie's car? I almost stood up and yelled to her before I realized there was nobody there. Nobody kicking at my door with elaborately stitched boots. Nobody yelling, "Blue!"

Just silence as the loose end of fishing line suddenly snaked through the rocky soil beside me and vanished. Somebody hidden in shadows below was pulling on it. And that somebody was not Roxie Bouchie.

"So if that's her car, why is it here?" I whispered to Brontë as I took the leash from my belt and tied it to the saltbush. My injured dog was going to stay out of this. "Did they steal Roxie's car to come out here? Did they do something to her? Who in hell *are* these people and why don't they just get over it? Victor Camacho's been dead for five years, Muffin's dead, they managed to kill Helen Tewalt, too. What do they want? To kill everybody who in any way appeared to help Muffin Crandall?" Brontë strained at the leash as it occurred to me that's just what "they" might have in mind. Except "they" would ultimately be "he," an alpha male so humiliated at being bested by a coven of crones that he would lay waste to every imagined witness.

It still made no sense, but I didn't have time to think about it. Shouldering the rifle, I crept halfway down the wash, then climbed out and belly-crawled over the eastern slope of the hill to a protected spot about thirty feet from something moving in shadows where I'd strung the fishing line. Somebody skulking in darkness, on my property. I was fed up and premenstrual. Not a fun combination.

From thirty feet even a .22 can inflict a mortal wound, so when I pulled the rifle off my shoulder I aimed it nowhere, straight up. Oddly, I still didn't want to kill anybody.

"I'm *sick* of this shit!" I yelled at the shadowy figure before I pulled the trigger and discharged a single shot into nothing but the grid, snapping and humming behind a wool sky. I had the Glock halfway to firing position when the figure yelled back.

"Blue? What the fuck you shootin' at? Them ugly little dark birds? 'Cause you sure as shit ain't hit nuthin' on earth."

BB.

"They're bats, BB," I answered, shaking. "Don't ever sneak up on me again! And tell Rox I don't need a bodyguard. This is getting ridiculous."

"Rox don't have nuthin' to do with it," he said as he emerged from rumpled shadows with a sturdy garrote of braided fishing line dangling from one hand. "I jus' took her car, come on out. Woulda been here a hundred years ago if I coulda *foun'* this place. Had to drive around that gate of yours, too. Hard on the car. You pretty sharp with this fish line!"

"BB, why are you here?"

With both hands he pushed back his long, wild hair in a classic gesture. Mortals confronted by varieties of the intolerable. That hair-tearing gesture usually performed by naked statues who are also wrapped in large snakes. BB did have a certain flair.

"Roxie, she know the score a little," he said as his hair fell dramatically back over his face. "You, you dumb as dirt. But don't neither of you know how bad this thing gonna get. Those dudes outside Auntie's tonight? I done time with dudes like that. They like robots. Do what*ever* somebody tell 'em. They dead men already. Don' matter what they do, they ain't here anyway. Ain't nobody more dangerous, Blue. I oughtta know."

"So you came all the way out here, on your own, to protect me?"

"Look that way, don't it?"

"Shit," I said, hugging him as weapons stuffed in the waists of our jeans clunked together. "Thanks, BB. I hope my brother is anything at all like you."

"Well, I hope he ain't like *you,* dildo, or he be a corpse by now. Where your dog?"

"Tied up in the wash," I answered. "I didn't want her to get killed. I'll go get her."

By the time we got back inside it was four-thirty, still dark, and there was an additional message on my machine. It was from Rox.

"Blue, BB has stolen my car and will no doubt show up at your place even though I told him you were going to spend the night in a hotel. He didn't believe it. Don't shoot him when you get home."

" 'Fraid I bent an axle gettin' around that gate," BB told Rox's voice on the machine. "Your lady live on the fuckin' moon."

"BB, I'm not . . . Rox and I don't have that kind of relationship," I said, sounding thin-blooded and prissy. "I'm not her lady."

"Get fuckin' real," he sneered sweetly. "And go to bed. Dog and I, we keep an eye out."

An axle had been sacrificed, I reasoned. Why waste it? I went to bed.

In the morning I found BB drinking coffee with his shirt off, his jeans rolled up, and his feet in the pool.

"BB, you said men like the two outside Auntie's last night will do whatever they're told," I thought out loud. "So who's telling them what to do?"

"Hard to say. Somebody tell somebody what he want done, that second somebody put the word out down the line, it get to the street."

"Do Paunch and Tattoo know who's paying them?"

BB flexed and admired the bricklike contours of his abdominal muscles.

"Sure, they know who pay 'em, but that ain't where the money come from. Prob'ly only one dude know the man, and that dude be invisible. Work from a phone, drop his payments off with some ho, she turn it over like she told, and the dude, he come 'roun later with some nice blow, keep her happy, you hear what I'm sayin'?"

"That whoever's behind all this has a low-profile lieutenant who does the dirty work, tells the scumbags what they're supposed to do, and pays off prostitutes in cocaine to provide a payroll service. How do we find out who the alpha is, the man?"

"We don't," he said. "We jus' lay low till the whole mess fade. Roxie keep tellin' you, now I tellin' you. Best thing is be *gone* for a while. This hoo-ha ain't none of your affair anyhow. Don't know why they still on yo' ass."

The comment seemed to give him pause, and he cocked his head to give me a penetrating look.

"You been straight with Roxie?" he asked, showing a lot of very white teeth in a smile that suddenly wasn't friendly.

"What do you mean?"

"I mean is there somethin' you ain't said, somethin' tyin' you to this dude in a freezer?"

"No," I answered. "It's all just like I told Rox."

The death's-head smile relaxed as he knit his brow.

"Somethin' not right, then," he observed. "Got to be some connection between you and freezerman or they'd of forgot you already. Somethin' *off* about this, Blue."

"It hasn't made any sense from the beginning," I agreed. "But right now we need to get Rox's car towed to a garage. Then I'll drive you to your shop. I need to find a dress for a wedding before my class at juvy this afternoon. I don't have time . . ."

"What kinda dress?" BB asked, batting his curly long eyelashes.

"Pink," I answered. "My brother's getting married in prison Saturday and our godmother thinks I should dress to match the ice cream. Compared to the rest of my life, this could be construed as refreshingly rational."

"Hey, that's great about your brother." He beamed. "But pink?"

He surveyed me thoughtfully, then nodded. "Got jus' the thing. Some drapes a friend scored at an estate sale, just back from the cleaner's. To-die-for antique watered silk in a chamois color, pick up your eyes. A-line skirt, little boxy jacket, maybe rhinestone buttons. Very Jackie O. You got a tape measure?"

I phoned Rox's office and left a message about her car as BB measured every inch of my body and made arcane-looking notes. I was glad Rox was with a patient. Her probable response to the boxy little jacket with rhinestone buttons was something I wanted to avoid.

After driving back over the mountains and down into San Diego, I dropped BB at his shop with ten twenty-dollar bills I'd just gotten from an ATM. He wouldn't take more despite the fact that I'd have paid three times that amount for the first pink dress I found at Nordstrom. Then I drove straight to juvy, two hours before my class.

"I'd like to see that file on Frankie Lopez again," I told an office clerk. "And one on a girl named Bugsy Sneller."

I opened Frankie's folder immediately and glanced at the face sheet. And there it was.

"Mother: Anna Lopez."

"Okay," I whispered to myself, "Anna's a common name. Don't jump to conclusions. This Anna Lopez probably isn't the woman who died in jail six years ago of a drug overdose after being arrested along with her pimp, Victor Camacho. Go slow. Check it out."

From the pay phone outside juvy's office I called juvenile probation and learned that after three years all inactive records were microfilmed and stored. There was no file for a Francesca Lopez in the computer, I was told, so either there had never been one or it had become inactive and stored at least three years in the past. Frankie Lopez would have been seventeen three years ago, I calculated. Still legally a minor until eighteen. That meant she hadn't been arrested again after her release from juvy five years back, or the record would still have been in the computer. So what happened to her?

Frankie's social worker had been somebody named Glenda Martin. I wondered if she were still around.

"Took early retirement a couple of years ago," the juvy office clerk informed me. "But I think she still lives in San Diego. Her husband owned a restaurant-supply business, maybe still does. Sorry I don't have a number for her."

The clerk was lying, but then she was supposed to. Names, addresses, phone numbers, and license plate data for all corrections employees, past and present, are zealously guarded. Still, she'd given me enough. In the Yellow Pages I found "Martin Restaurant Supply" and dialed the number.

"Mrs. Martin, please," I said. "Glenda Martin. This is Dr. Emily McCarron."

The "Dr." bit works every time. And, it's true.

"Let me give you the Martins' home number, Dr. McCarron. This is her husband's business."

"Fine."

Glenda Martin was home, and no dummy.

"I'm sure you understand that I can't discuss any juvenile case," she explained tersely. "That information is protected by law. It's confidential. Who did you say you were?"

It took fifteen minutes of my best persuasion to convince Glenda Martin to meet me for coffee after my class. What drew her was the dangling carrot of Frankie Lopez.

"There's an outside chance that I may find Frankie," I told Glenda Martin, "but I need your help."

"I'll be there," she agreed after I named a popular coffee bar in a shopping center five minutes away.

Next I walked Brontë in the residential neighborhood surrounding the juvenile courts and detention facility, Bugsy Sneller's slim file open in my hand. Her real name was Lisa, the file told me, and she'd only been in juvy for about a week awaiting trial on a minor vandalism charge. The only reason she was there at all was that she'd refused to give police her name at the time of her arrest, and it had taken her frantic grandmother that long to learn where she was. She'd been released a day after Frankie Lopez had been released. The two girls had been together less than a week. Yet Frankie, if indeed the postcard the kids found was from Frankie Lopez and not some other Frankie, had wanted to reassure Bugsy that things were just great.

"What things?" I wondered aloud as Brontë watched an orange cat dash across the street. "And how did Frankie get to Albany, New York?"

Probably she'd been sent to relatives there, I reasoned, perhaps after the death of her mother, Anna. The social worker, Glenda Martin, might remember. Bugsy Sneller hadn't been in juvy long enough for a picture to be taken, so the rectangle in the upper right-hand corner of the face sheet was blank. The file seemed like a dead-end until I absentmindedly shook the front page away to glance at the second, the disposition sheet.

Bugsy Sneller's trial had been scheduled for three weeks after her release, but there had never been a trial. Like Muffin Crandall, Bugsy hadn't lived long enough to see the inside of a courtroom. "DECEASED" was stamped across the disposition sheet. In the lower margin another stamp said "CLOSED."

Septembers in Southern California are hot and sunny, even in coastal regions. I'm sure it was hot and sunny as Brontë and I strolled that residential street. But what I remember is a shadow spilling from two pieces of paper stapled to a manila folder in my hand, a sickening chill. Bugsy Sneller had been fifteen years old.

I copied both sides of the Frankie postcard before my class, but it wasn't necessary. The kids didn't want it back.

"Oh, yeah," one of them said, "Frankie Lopez, my sister told me she escaped and ran off with this guard to New York City."

"I heard that," somebody else said. "Heard he got her pregnant and got her out so they could get married. Ran away with her to New York City to get married."

The mythical Frankie had been assigned a life of domesticity. She was no longer interesting. I tucked the postcard back into my purse and wondered what had happened to the real Frankie. And to her pal, Bugsy. The two teenagers seemed to haunt my classroom, their bond still alive in the hazy sunlight and a tangle of Xs and Os over a signature in which the I was dotted with a heart.

"How many have read the chapter on drug and alcohol abuse?" I asked.

Eleven out of twenty hands went up. A record, but then the topic was not unfamiliar to most of them.

"Let's start by talking about why people drink and do drugs," I began, drawing a passable brain on the blackboard and labeling the salient parts. "Which substance anesthetizes the frontal lobes?"

"Alcohol!" young voices yelled in response.

"And what goes on in the frontal lobes?"

"Judgment," the oldest girl read from her book. Then she looked up and grinned.

"That's the part of our brain where we get to decide not to act like chimpanzees, right?" she said.

These moments are what keep people standing behind chipped lecterns at low pay for entire lifetimes. I was so thrilled I forgot about Frankie Lopez and Bugsy Sneller and the retired social worker who was about to hand me another piece of the puzzle. A big piece that would begin to make sense of the picture on Helen Tewalt's screen saver. And a piece that would escalate my fear for the remaining crone, Nanna Foy, off the scale.

Chapter Sixteen

Glenda Martin had ordered a plain coffee and was glowering into it as I hurried to join her at a little table outside the coffee bar. People who order plain coffee when hazelnut-mocha latte is available do so, I assume, in order to establish themselves as no-nonsense types. Down-to-earth, all business. The former social worker had reinforced that image by having short gray hair and wearing oversized bifocals perched on a sunburned nose. I could tell she had a heart the size of South America and was determined that I not take advantage of it.

"I'm Blue McCarron," I said. "Brontë, sit."

A wounded dog is a plus when dealing with people who've spent their lives guiding wounded people.

"Jesus, what happened to your dog?" Glenda Martin asked, glancing at Brontë's shaved side and scabby wounds.

"She was shot, Mrs. Martin," I said dramatically. "The man who shot her was looking for me. I have reason to believe he and another man were sent to avenge the death of a lower-echelon criminal named Victor Camacho, who among other accomplishments was the pimp of a woman named Anna Lopez. Does the name ring a bell? Anna died in jail over five years ago on the night she was arrested. She may have been the mother of Frankie Lopez, who was on your caseload at juvy, as was Frankie's buddy, a girl named Bugsy Sneller. Bugsy died within weeks of her release from juvy. Frankie apparently vanished. Since the discovery of Camacho's body in a freezer less than two weeks ago, and the confession of a woman named Muffin Crandall to his murder, hired thugs have been terrorizing everyone connected to the case. Muffin Crandall was poisoned in prison and died. Another woman with dangerously high blood pressure apparently had a massive stroke and died after these men broke into her home. To date, the only solid information I have is this link between Victor Camacho and a woman who I suspect was Frankie Lopez's mother. I'm aware of the confidentiality surrounding juvenile court files, and I respect your professionalism. But please . . ."

I trailed off and stared somberly at Brontë.

"Anna Lopez was Frankie's mother," Glenda Martin confirmed. "I don't know anything about this Camacho. What did you mean when you said you might be able to locate Frankie? In what capacity are you investigating these events?"

"I was hired by Muffin Crandall's brother," I answered. It wasn't a lie.

"And Frankie?"

"Frankie may have sent Bugsy Sneller a postcard at juvy within a week or two of her release. Bugsy was no longer there, but the card was mailed from Albany, New York. There's no way to verify that this postcard was mailed by Frankie Lopez, but I have it with me."

Ace in the hole.

Glenda Martin's wide-set blue eyes registered an eagerness she couldn't hide.

"May I see it?" she asked.

I dug the card from my purse and handed it to her, then said nothing as she read it several times. After a while she handed it back to me and nodded.

"Okay," she agreed. "I'm going to tell you what I know, which isn't much. First, my guess is that Frankie Lopez sent this card.

Not that the handwriting's recognizable or anything, but those two were close, Frankie and Bugsy. Kids do that in jail, you know. They bond ferociously, trying to create something they can hold on to. But these two, well, it was more like one of those Victorian girls' school attachments. Nothing sexual, I don't mean that, but very intense. Frankie had been on the streets for years and Bugsy was just this wild, innocent kid from a very protected background, lived with a well-to-do grandmother out in the suburbs. The parents were dead. She had private schools, riding lessons on weekends, the whole nine yards. Bugsy was in trouble for the first time in her life and intrigued by it all. She worshiped Frankie from the minute she laid eyes on her, thought Frankie was sophisticated and tough. Frankie basked in the attention, seemed awed by everything Bugsy told her. Things about her fancy school, speaking French, trips to foreign countries. Frankie just ate it up. To her Bugsy was like something from another planet."

"So what happened to Frankie when she was released?" I pushed. "You recommended follow-up at a family counseling center, but there's nothing in the file after that. There's certainly nothing about a transfer to New York State."

Glenda Martin raised her coffee to her lips, grimaced, and put it back down.

"You know I don't know what happened to Frankie," she whispered. "You knew it when you phoned me. Nobody had a clue then and nobody has a clue now. These things aren't supposed to happen. There are safeguards. But it happened."

I could feel her dismay from across the table, a drifting clot of professional shame.

"*What* happened?"

"The mother had died," she began, eyes closed as if visually reconstructing the event. "There was no other family, so Frankie was to be released to a worker from Child Protective Services.

The worker would transfer Frankie to a foster home. That's what was supposed to happen, but it didn't."

Here she looked at me curiously, shaking her head.

"Oh, somebody showed up and took Frankie all right. Four people saw this woman. Two clerks from the office, a guard, and an attorney who happened to be interviewing another girl in the atrium because the interview room was being painted. I remember that. They all saw this woman who looked like every other CPS social worker, maybe a little older than most, had white hair, but typical. One of the clerks said she thought the woman was a CPS supervisor filling in as a caseworker because there was a flu thing going around and a lot of the caseworkers were out sick.

"She had an ID badge, they said, and wore nice slacks, a cotton sweater, a scarf, Rockports, carried a briefcase, the usual. The attorney even said he thought he'd seen her before in juvenile court, although of course he hadn't. It never even *occurred* to anybody that this woman was lying. She signed Frankie out with the name Hope Theobald, and they were gone. Problem is, an hour later a CPS worker showed up to transport Frankie to foster care. The *real* CPS worker. Nobody named Hope Theobald worked for CPS. Nobody named Hope Theobald had *ever* worked for CPS.

"Frankie Lopez was kidnapped in full view of the entire juvenile corrections system. A massive investigation turned up nothing, and despite bulletins circulated to CPS, the police, every social service agency, drop-in center, and teen counseling program in San Diego County, Frankie was never seen again."

No wonder the kids were frightened enough to turn Frankie Lopez into a folktale, I thought. What had happened to her meant they weren't safe even in jail!

"But with all that," I pointed out, "when this postcard showed up somebody would have noticed the name, wouldn't they? They would have checked it out."

"Two things," the woman went on, frustration coloring her cheeks. "Then and now mail distribution is handled by volunteers. Social work students, women from church groups and juvenile court advocacy programs. None of these volunteers would have been likely to know about the friendship between Frankie and Bugsy, and none of us thought to have them monitor the mail. But they would have known about Bugsy Sneller. It was all over the papers. My guess is one of them just tucked the postcard away somewhere to avoid sending it on to the grandmother, causing her more pain. Who knows?"

"What happened to Bugsy?" I asked. "I wouldn't have seen the newspaper accounts because I wasn't in San Diego yet. I think it was July five years ago, wasn't it, when she died? That's just before I started teaching at San Gabriel. I wouldn't get here until August."

Glenda Martin reached down to pet Brontë and didn't answer for a few minutes.

"Yes, it was July," she said. "Bugsy was raped and beaten to death in an alley behind one of those drop-in centers for street kids downtown," she finally said. "The man was never apprehended."

"But you said Bugsy was from a protected background, had a family. Her file said she was only in juvy because she refused to tell anybody her real name, and that her grandmother was frantic until she turned up. She had a home, a good one. Why would she be hanging around a drop-in center for homeless street kids?"

"Here's my theory," Glenda Martin said, rapping the knuckles of her clenched fists together softly. "It's only a theory and it's as far as I'm going with this. Bugsy was arrested with some boys spraying graffiti on a freeway overpass. I doubt that she was more than an observer in this, but she thought it was all very exciting and dangerous, getting picked up, riding in a patrol car, being a *criminal* for crying out loud. She was an adventurous kid, but green from the scalp down. Being in jail was just a lark for her, and the thrill would've worn off after one night if she hadn't met Frankie.

"But she did, and she wanted to stay around Frankie for as long as she could, so she continued to hide her identity. Frankie was being released in a week, anyway. I think Bugsy knew something about Frankie's plans, whatever they were. But here's the key. That drop-in center where Bugsy was killed? That was Frankie's hang-out when she was on the street. They knew her there. I think Frankie asked Bugsy to go down there and tell somebody, probably one of her pals from the street, where she was going, that she was okay. I think Bugsy went there to carry the message—she would have done *anything* for Frankie—and wandered into the situation that resulted in her death."

"My God," I breathed. "But surely the staff at this place saw something. Surely the police—"

"The police interviewed everybody," Glenda Martin interrupted. "These centers are staffed pretty much by volunteers, lots of church types, students, academics doing research, the usual. Short-term dedication to a long-term problem, high turnover, no permanent, trained staff. Nobody knew anything. Nobody remembered even seeing Bugsy at the center. I told you, my theory is just a theory. Now, I really have to go. If you find Frankie, you'll call me, right?"

"I will," I said. "Just one more thing. Her file said Bugsy's real name was Lisa. Why did she call herself Bugsy?"

"Oh, you know kids. She was obsessed by some rock band, the name had something to do with insects. The band was in town for a concert, in fact I think the boys with Bugsy were spray-painting the band's symbol—these insect shapes—on the overpass when they were arrested. She wore a T-shirt with these bugs on it, so the kids called her Bugsy. She loved it."

"Was the band called Hell's Weevil?" I blurted as that enormous puzzle piece began its slow fall into place. "Was that the rock band?"

"Yeah, that was it," Glenda Martin said as she rose and carefully placed her cold coffee in a trash can. "Why?"

"I'm not sure," I answered. "Mrs. Martin, do you remember who came to get Bugsy when she was released from juvy?"

"The grandmother. I remember because of course we were policing every discharge after the fiasco with Frankie. I met her, a woman named Helen something-or-other, seemed nice. She had a copy of Bugsy's birth certificate, ample identification. I'm sure she was really the grandmother. Call me if you find out anything about Frankie. That's the deal. I've told you everything I know. Good-bye."

With that she smiled at Brontë and then was gone. I sat staring at the plastic tabletop wondering if Bugsy's grandma Helen's last name might just be Tewalt.

"That photo on Helen Tewalt's screen saver may well have been her granddaughter," I told Brontë. "Bugsy Sneller may have been Helen's granddaughter, and she was raped and killed behind a drop-in center for street kids where Anna Lopez's daughter hung out. Anna Lopez, whose pimp was Victor Camacho."

Brontë's sleek ears raised slowly at the tone in my voice. The look in her dark eyes was one of interest. "So what do we do next?" she seemed to ask.

"We don't jump to conclusions," I told my dog. But it was difficult not to. Victor Camacho, I thought, might well have been involved in Bugsy Sneller's death. Victor Camacho might well have raped and killed her in a downtown alley. The absence of rape from Muffin's tale of archetypal female fear now made sense. They'd left out fear of rape to avoid drawing attention to the real story behind Camacho's death. But what was the real story?

If Camacho had raped and killed Bugsy, in a frenzy of rage and grief the child's grandmother might just have tracked him down and killed him, or more likely had him killed. After all, the murder had occurred while the teenager was under her care. Hadn't Glenda Martin said the girl's parents were dead? Helen Tewalt might just have killed Victor Camacho somewhere, and managed to stuff his body into a car trunk, but then what? I could see her calling her friends, frantic. I could see them framing the plan.

"Drive to Muffin's and back the car into her garage," they would have said. "We'll be there."

But how would Helen, a suburban matron, have found a piece of street slime like Camacho and managed to kill him without being seen? Or how would she have located a hired killer? It didn't scan. The validity was zero. I was sure Helen wouldn't have been able to pull it off, no matter how heartbroken and enraged she was. But maybe the three of them together could.

Muffin Crandall, whose own daughter had died so many years ago, would have felt Helen's loss deeply, personally. And she already knew her days were numbered. I was willing to bet that Muffin had been the first to volunteer, maybe had masterminded the whole thing, maybe killed Victor Camacho alone, just as she'd said. Nanna would have planned the logistics, provided whatever financial backing was needed.

Maybe they'd concocted a way to lure Camacho to Muffin's condo in the middle of the night. And maybe he'd been met by one or possibly two of the strongest people on earth—women who have survived the death of a child. In Helen's case a child *and* grandchild. Deep in my heart I hoped the hand holding that paperweight had been Helen's.

I was sure neither Muffin, Nanna, nor Helen would have entertained the slightest qualm about removing Victor Camacho from the earth. It made sense. But then why would they leave his body in a public freezer for five years? That didn't make sense. I kept juggling the options as I drove away from the coffee bar and across town to a less trendy locale.

BB was adjusting a split cuff of my ensemble for David's wedding when Brontë and I arrived at Death Row.

"That A-line skirt just *too* sixties," he said from behind a steamer. "Woulda gave you a knobby look, y'know?"

"Knobby?"

"Knees, ankles. A-line jus' make 'em look knobby. So I went for sleek. A modified bijou look—long skirt with hip darts and side slits, little metallic overstitching to pick up the gold buttons with the rhinestones at the cuff, see, not down the front, which actually has hook-and-eyes under this three-inch placket, give the bust a smooth line. So try it on!"

The suit was stunning. Even I knew that, and I couldn't define "placket" if you paid me. From its padded hanger it whispered things about impeccable taste coupled with a certain flair for the outrageous.

"Wait!" BB said as I reached for his creation. "Face. Let's find those cheekbones first."

After sitting me in a chair, BB did things to my face with about fifteen brushes ranging from hair-fine to stencil, and then agonized over lipstick.

"Don't have no bronze light enough for you, honey," he said, sighing. "So let's just outline in bronze over this dusky pomegranate, see how it meld. Ah . . ."

After massaging something that smelled like tangerines into my stubby hair, he allowed me to don the outfit and step onto a large Rubbermaid lazy Susan under a bright light and three full-length mirrors. What looked back at me from three directions would make Carter Upchurch glow with pleasure, I thought. It was me, only polished in a way I'd never bothered to learn.

"Gold earrings," BB was muttering as he spun me around, tugging at hems and seams. "Little, simple, solid gold. You got those? No hoops, nothing big. You wear one big thing, you gonna look like the Mayflower Madam, y'know?"

"I've got all my mother's jewelry at home," I told BB. "There are some gold disks, very small . . ."

"Good." He grinned as I heard the front door open. "Roxie, come on an' check this out!"

At that moment I realized I'd been set up, that he'd planned this, but it was okay. I liked the way Roxie Bouchie's jaw dropped as she wended her way through BB's shop to the cul-de-sac of mirrors where I rotated like a prize cabbage at a county fair.

"Hey, Rox!" I said, giving her my best smile, putting everything I had into the eye contact. "So what do you think?" Flirting. I felt that my practice run with Nanna Foy had improved my skill.

"Girl," she pronounced breathily, taking the challenge by not hiding her attraction but letting it smolder in a knowing smile. "You look good enough to—"

"Hey, I'm outta cigarettes," BB interjected gleefully, heading for the door. "Jus' run out an' get some . . ."

"BB, you don't smoke," Rox said with a laugh, never taking her eyes from mine.

"Didn't say I smoked," he yelled over a shoulder. "Said I was outta smokes. Be right back."

Roxie was winning, I acknowledged as I stepped from the lazy Susan. Flirting was never going to be my sport, so the hell with it. I'd cut to the chase.

"I have some important new information on Victor Camacho," I said, moving close to her and draping both watered-silk arms around her neck. She smelled like ballpoint pens.

"And I've got a half mile of faxes on your ladies, as well as the name of the owner of the Lexus at Muffin's funeral," she countered, letting her hands slide around my waist and pulling my hips tight against hers. "How far do you want to go with this game, Blue? I keep telling you . . ."

"Just this far," I answered. "One kiss . . ."

But we were both already into it, briefly tentative and then with that fierce softness that becomes a road, a map to someplace forgotten, suddenly revealed. And beneath the searching hunger of mouths and tongues I felt that same sense of bone-deep welcome I'd felt in her arms before. Inside our desire like the refrain of a song I'd never heard but nonetheless knew, was *home.*

"Roxie," I whispered against her mouth, wanting to tell her, "you feel like—"

"Honey, we need to talk," she interrupted, pushing me away and turning to stretch her arms against a rack of malachite green Levi's and vests embroidered in Celtic motifs. Her dance team's costumes. She was shaking and I wanted to wrap my arms around her and press my face to her broad back, but I didn't. In a few seconds she turned to face me, her brown eyes troubled.

"Blue, I'm asking you to quit playing now," she said quietly. "You win, but this thing can't. Do you understand?"

"No," I answered, unnerved by that look in her eyes. "Tell me."

"Girl, you're lonely and scared and you're in a hell of a mess at the moment," she explained what I already knew. "You'll let BB help you. You think you want me. But we're just shadows of your real life, Blue. Two black people with histories you can never share or even understand, but similar enough to fill some empty forms for a while. Brother and lover. A brother you hate because he turned his back on you, a lover you fear because she did the same. Now you're going to have to deal with both of them. And as if that weren't enough, you've been dragged into a very dangerous situation which, if you're not careful, may just get you killed. It's serious and I want to help you, but I don't want to be used. There's just too much distance between us for a love affair, Blue. And when the lights go on in your life, as they will soon, you'll see that."

What I saw instead as I stood there was my own years of education in a discipline which acknowledges the meanings in social differences, the care that must be taken when attempting to understand those meanings. Training I had managed to forget entirely because I needed not to be alone, just as I needed not to be alone when Dan Crandall reached out to me in his grief. Mistakes. But Roxie hadn't forgotten her training, earned at an expense I could only dimly imagine. A psychiatrist, she'd stood back and analyzed what she saw. And her analysis was apt, except for the one thing neither of us had learned in graduate school. I loved her. I hadn't known it until then, standing in BB's shop still dressed in silk for my brother's wedding. I loved Roxie Bouchie for a strength and kindness I wished I had. A strength and kindness I *would* have.

"You may be right, Rox," I replied carefully. "You probably are right, to some extent. I'm not going to argue with you. And there won't be any more games. You told me your work comes before everything else and I ignored you. I also ignored the obvious differences between us because I needed you. You're right, I'm scared. I acknowledge our differences and will respect them, Rox, but that doesn't mean I don't still need your help, and BB's, if you're willing."

The speech had been a masterpiece of rationality, I thought. Full of maturity and insight, not qualities for which I'm known or even care to be, usually. Not the qualities of a new soul at all. I wondered what it was going to be like, living up to them.

"No problem," she said too brightly.

"Um, I'll just change," I mumbled, slipping into BB's little dressing room. The silence falling between us was so intense I could hear it rolling around in the air beyond the brocade curtain of the dressing room. That sound that comes in the minutes after a door has been closed. I hated it so much my hands shook, but nothing, I decided, on earth or in the roaring grid above the sky could make me break it. I hadn't realized that loving someone might entail deliberately *not* loving them, but I was sure the grid understood it perfectly. It was a grid kind of thing.

"She-it!" BB pronounced as he returned. "What goin' on here? I thought you two were gettin' *friendly*, and now this place feel like a fuckin' morgue. Who died?"

"I love the suit, BB," I said, stepping from the little cubicle and smoothing the jacket on its hanger. "It's the most spectacular thing I've ever owned, and my godmother is going to want one just like it. Thanks. You're very talented."

"Rox, how you turn this lady into *dead* so fast?" BB snarled. "She soun' like tin where 'sposed to be gold. This ain't right."

"BB, I need to take my *rented* thanks-to-you car and go home now," Roxie said pointedly. "There are some documents for Blue on the front seat. Will you get them?

"I guess we aren't going to be able to work on this tonight," she said, not looking at me. "But here's the scoop. The Lexus you and BB saw at Muffin's funeral, the one used by the Las Colinas guard and her male companion?"

"Yeah."

"I ran the plates. The car is leased to a business called Wrenner Enterprises. Hard to learn anything from that. But I think you'll have a field day with the stuff our info man turned up. By the way, he needs a check for two hundred and fifty dollars."

"Wrenner," I said as I dug out my wallet and wrote the check. "I bought my place from a man named Wrenner. Cameron Wrenner. Big deal around here. Used cars. You see his face on billboards everywhere . . . Rox! That's the man I saw outside Muffin's funeral. The older man with the young woman guard. I knew I'd seen his face somewhere, but I didn't remember the billboards. That was Cameron Wrenner!"

"Hmm," she replied. "So what's the news you learned about Camacho today?"

BB returned with an armload of faxes as I told the story of Anna Lopez and Frankie and Bugsy and Victor Camacho.

"If you hadn't known about Hell's Weevil I never would have made the connection," I told BB. "That's what made it all fall together."

"So you think the old ladies did the pimp," he concluded thoughtfully.

"It's possible, BB," Rox said. "This is an unusual collection of women."

"Did him and iced him like a grocery store pizza."

I could see BB's bright eyes beaming toward a conclusion as the narrative assumed a rhythm.

"So the old ladies did the pimp an' pissed off the man the pimp work for, but nuthin' happen for five years till the pimp body turn up like the missing ingredient for a fricassee, you hear me?"

"We hear you," Rox responded in what I suddenly recognized as the elegant speech pattern brought from Africa on slave ships and preserved in every black church from Watts to Harlem. I had studied it in an undergraduate linguistics class, along with border Spanglish and the less accessible verbal conventions of Asian immigrant populations. I had studied it, recognized its origins, appreciated its elegance, and still stood completely outside it. Rox had been right, I acknowledged. Even without the personal complications of my life at the moment, we were irredeemably different. I felt sad and wise as BB continued his sermon.

"The man read the paper, find out the pimp been froze in the desert for five years, he want some catch-back. He been *had,* don'tcha see? Been had by a buncha old women!"

"Oo, honey!" Rox supplied the response as BB paced across the floor of his shop, his dreadlocks backlit by the neon lights of the Asian take-out restaurant across the little mall.

"So he hire a hit on the prison lady, get his catch-back, but it ain't enough. Got to show the whole worl' he still the boss, ain't that right?"

"Got that right," Rox said.

"So he hire some zombies, do the work on *all* the old ladies."

Here BB's voice dropped an octave as he pointed a long finger at me.

"What we *do not* know," he intoned ominously, "is who the man and why he think *you* got some part in this, ain't that so?"

"Right," I answered, breaking the rhythm, my voice sounding thin. "We don't know who's behind this or why he thinks I'm a part of it, but Rox did find out one thing, BB. Maybe it'll help. The man with the Las Colinas guard at Muffin's funeral? That was a man named Cameron Wrenner. He's a big-deal car dealer, invests in local developments. He built my place before it turned out to be impossible to get piped water out there."

"Dude in Wrenner's position wouldn't usually choose his lady friends from among prison guards," Rox observed. "And didn't you say she was considerably younger?"

"An ole man, he like his sweet young *thang,*" BB pointed out. "Ain't nuthin' strange about that."

"But he wouldn't attend a funeral accompanied by a girlfriend," I noted. "Funerals are important community social rituals and one of their functions is to reinforce community norms. He would only attend a funeral with his wife or a family member."

"And this wife just happens to work as a women's prison guard," Rox completed the statement.

"Guard trainee," I said, remembering my first visit with Muffin Crandall. "That means she'd just started to work there."

"Jus' started when Muffin Crandall show up," BB said. "This ain't no coincidence."

The little shop seemed stuffy as we stood staring at the floor and pondering it all. Nothing quite fit.

"What would a man like Cameron Wrenner have to do with any of this, and why would his young wife take a job in a prison?" I said. "The man's wealthy, a mover and shaker. This is sad little street stuff—prisons, pimps and prostitutes, drugs and runaway kids. Not Wrenner's world."

"You so dumb you make mud look smart," BB observed thoughtfully. "I can check this out on the street tomorrow, see if Wrenner turn up in any wrong places. Meanwhile, Miss Dumb-Ass Blue, you an' me on our way to the OK Corral."

"I'll be all right, BB," I insisted. "You don't need to stay out there with me every night, although I appreciate your—"

"I will be there tonight, you leavin' tomorrow," he said, glaring at Roxie. "No other way."

Rox was at the door and not looking back. I wished I hadn't made that remark about prostitutes being "little street stuff." Her mentally ill mother had been on the streets. The problem for Roxie and her grandmother had been anything but little. BB was right, compared to me, mud was a pinnacle of brilliance. There wasn't a chance of redeeming myself, but I had to try.

"By the way," I whispered girl-to-girl in the parking lot as BB locked his shop, "I'm not pregnant. The blessed event arrived today. Thought you'd be impressed that there's at least one thing I haven't managed to screw up."

It brought a smile, which was all I'd hoped for.

BB and I stopped for a carry-out pizza, which he and Brontë ate in the truck as I drove up I-8 and through the curving mountain roads that would soon feed us through Yaqui Pass and down to the desert floor.

"What went down back there, you and Roxie?" he asked through the scent of pepperoni as we started the descent. There was nobody else on the road ahead, and I could see the lights of Borrego twinkling far below.

"She thinks I'm using both of you, and she's right," I told him. "You as a stand-in for my brother and her as, uh . . ."

"Don' have to spell it out," he said, grinning. "Blue, you love that lady?"

"Yeah," I answered, feeling strangely calm about it. "I didn't really know until tonight, but yeah. And so I'm going to respect her feelings and—"

" 'Gonna *ree-spect* her feelings,' " he mocked. "Fancy book words, not from the heart, Blue. Truth is, Roxie need somebody like you, keep her from workin' herself to death. Don' listen to her put you off, Blue, tell you black and white be *insurmountable* an' all that. They ain't. Nuthin' ain't. And Blue?"

"Yeah?"

"Don' turn your head, don' look in the mirror, but those headlights way back there? They the same since we left the shop. They been with us all the way. It's our boys."

Chapter Seventeen

"Are you sure it's the same car?" I asked as a chill fell across the empty road. "How can you tell?"

"One of the fog lights burned out. Take a look when they come roun' the switchback. See? Little yellow light next to the driver's side headlight but no yellow on the other side. Bulb out, prob'ly. Loose wire. That light been out the whole trip."

Against the eastern sky mountains loomed beyond my little town, marking the badlands boundaries. The Santa Rosas, Toro Peak, Font's Point, the Borregos. In the dark they and Coyote Mountain to the north made a vast and silent bowl cradling the town lights at its center. Beyond that there were only shifting patterns of moonlight. I had been safe here, I remembered. This desert had absorbed the little frenzies of my life without a sound. Old beyond comprehension, it had simply been there. Now some violent, diseased thread of consciousness was trailing me into that peace. And I couldn't stop it.

"BB, what do they want?" I said, sighing. "What's this about?"

"Don't know," he answered simply. "Prob'ly gonna find out, though."

The car stayed well behind and didn't follow as I turned north off Palm Canyon Road in Borrego along the narrow asphalt feeder Cameron Wrenner had built to access his doomed investment. It didn't matter. They could park anywhere and walk to my place in secrecy through desert rubble.

I locked the gate to my property anyway, recognizing the futility of the gesture. BB and I walked Brontë for a few minutes close to the motel and then went inside. There were no messages on my answering machine. Nothing from Nanna Foy, who could be anywhere or could be dead. Not a word from Misha. BB had taken a flashlight and my set of keys and gone to check out the nine empty, unfinished rooms facing the pool beside my living quarters. In a few minutes he was back, carrying what looked like a tape recorder.

"Shit," he said. "Look at this!"

"It's a tape recorder, BB. Where did you find . . . ?"

"What do this look like?" he interrupted, waving a phone cord in my face. At the end of the cord was the usual little plastic clip that snaps into a wall phone jack.

"A phone cord?"

"Right, dildo. Why didn't you think of this, what with bein' so smart?"

"Think of what?"

"That your phone be tapped maybe? An' this ain't even a real tap, you made it so easy. All these rooms run off the same phone line, right?"

"Well, yeah, I guess so," I answered. "This is a motel. I guess the room phone lines were set up to run through a switchboard that would've been in here, in the office. I never paid any attention to any of that after I moved in and got phone service, the modem hooked up. Why would I? I never go in any of those rooms."

"Well, somebody did." He sighed in disgust. "Easy enough with you gone all day, pick one of these cheap little door locks and jus' go on in. This here's a multi-extension recorder, plugs right into a phone jack and records everything off the phone line. Everything you hear, everything you say, they know."

He pushed the recorder's play button and we listened to a recording of my answering machine's computer-generated voice saying, "You have . . . no . . . messages."

"This just from today," BB noted. "Mean they checkin' it every day, maybe changin' the tapes. No way to tell how long this been goin' on."

Probably since I first saw Muffin Crandall, I thought. Certainly since my encounter with Paunch and Tattoo. But why? What did they think they could learn, and more to the point, who was it that wanted to know? Not the hireling deltas who were mere puppets. No, there was somebody else behind all this. But who?

BB closed all the blinds and drapes and then played with Brontë on the floor while I heated a bowl of noodle soup and ate it. My stomach had settled to something approximating an armed truce, but I wasn't taking any chances.

"What you gonna do with all that mess?" BB asked, indicating the pile of faxed data he'd brought in and stacked on my desk.

"Analyze it," I said. "Analyzing data is what I do. And it's going to take hours. Feel free to go sleep in the bed. I'll wake you up when I'm ready to collapse. There's no point in both of us staying up at the same time, and you didn't get much sleep last night."

"Yeah," he agreed, pulling off his shoes and heading for the bedroom door. "I sleep light, hear everything. Your gun there?"

I took the Glock from my waist pack and laid it on my desk beside the computer keyboard. It looked out of place beside the tidy technical gadgetry, brutal and primitive. Even the mouse seemed to quiver and recoil from it.

"Right here," I replied as I began a cursory first read of the faxes.

There was no information on Misha Deland. Rox's info man had tried twelve different spellings of Deland in combination with five versions of Misha. He'd turned up nothing except Social Security Administration deposits under the number of a Claudette M. Deland who'd died in Calcasieu Parish, Louisiana, six months before I arrived in San Diego. The dates of the deposits conformed almost exactly to the two years during which I lived with Misha. Years during which she received standard payroll checks for her job as director of the Women's Studies Consortium. Standard payroll checks from which standard deductions were being taken for a dead woman whose surname and Social Security number Misha had apparently been using. I wasn't really surprised, but couldn't help wondering whom it was I kept so close to my heart, then. What was her name, this woman I had loved and with whom I still felt a frightening and unfinished destiny?

"I don't care, Misha," I whispered sappily into thin air. "What you call yourself doesn't matter. It never did." Sappy or not, it's what I felt.

Next I glanced at the data on Deirdre Eckels, the ex-nun who'd supposedly been an old friend of Misha's and who'd apparently been around for the sole purpose of grinding out a feminist periodical nobody read. It seemed she really was an ex-nun, a former member of the Society of the Sacred Heart, which kept her name on its list of associates. But so what?

Data is useless unless it tells you what you want to know, which means you have to know what you want to know. Since I didn't, I booted up the computer and opened a marketing program I use to tease out commonalities in diverse sets of data. The program makes easy work of, say, cross-referencing mail-order lists for the purpose of generating a new list composed only of Jewish soccer fans between eighteen and thirty-five who live in Michigan.

Since I didn't know what I was looking for beyond a connection among these women which might explain what was threatening my life, I went the long route. History. Trails of data back through time. Even with a scanner it was going to take forever and still might not provide anything pertinent. For a moment I considered abandoning the project. Hadn't I already patched together a framework of events with the information from Glenda Martin? What else could I learn from cross-referencing a ton of data on three late-middle-aged women, two of whom were dead? But, I told myself, I'd paid for the data. The Midwestern soul cannot abide waste. Besides, you never know what these statistical exercises will turn up. I selected variables and started scanning.

Two hours later I knew that all three women had been married at least once, and that Nanna and Muffin had been divorced. Muffin and Helen had also been widowed. Of the three, Nanna's monthly credit card charges were by far the highest, but then they included the business expenses for her company, which analyzed federal securities regulations as they applied to the investment strategies of certain mid-sized financial institutions. Yawn.

Muffin and Nanna flew on commercial airlines often, Helen rarely. Muffin's most frequent purchase in the last five years besides gas and groceries was books, Helen's was craft supplies. Nanna had several purchasing spikes—restaurants, theater and symphony tickets, home decorating, and high-end women's fashions. No surprises there.

All the women had lived in other cities before converging in San Diego, and Nanna and Helen had once lived in the same place. In the early fifties they'd both spent four years in Newton, Massachusetts, their stays overlapping by one year. I stopped and thought about that. Four-year spans typically indicate schooling, high school or college. Nanna and Helen had been teenagers then, which would mean high school. But for them to have addresses under their own names they would have to have been away from home, probably at boarding schools. Had Nanna and Helen been at some Massachusetts boarding school together? It was a match, but it didn't seem to lead anywhere.

Another hour went by as I reconfigured the program for increasingly arcane matches, and came up with no pattern. My office felt stuffy with the windows sealed and my left eyelid twitched uncontrollably. Brontë lay on the carpet at my feet, her paws paddling as she ran in some dog dreamscape I wished I could share. The pulsing light of my computer seemed to be hiding what I wanted, that connection between discrete variables from which a pattern grows.

"Damn," I said into a screen comprised of depthless pale gray dots too small for the naked eye. "Where *is* it?"

Frustrated, I aimlessly fed the data on Deirdre Eckels into the program. There was nothing else left and it was just something to do before giving up and going to bed. An anal exercise in pointless tidiness, I thought. Perhaps obsessive. Deirdre was connected to Misha, not to three crones and a dead man in a freezer. Even if there were some brief overlap between her life and theirs, it would be nothing but coincidence.

Oddly, there was an overlap. Deirdre Eckels had also lived in Newton, although ten years later than Helen and Nanna. It was meaningless, I assumed as the invisible gray dots shimmered hypnotically and my left eyelid continued to twitch. Still, three hits are hard to ignore even if one of them is clearly attributable to chance. Doggedly I exited the marketing program and pushed the mouse to my Internet icon.

I'm fond of the Internet even though a truly Spartan discipline is necessary to avoid getting lost forever in its maze of corridors. I have no discipline and have spent whole nights reading foreign university course offerings and waiting for snapshots of puppies from exotic kennels to load. But not that night. That night I was resolved to remain firm, goal-oriented.

Newton, Massachusetts, its Web site told me, was eight miles from Boston at latitude 42' 20" north and longitude 71' 12" west. Useful if you wanted to *sail* there, I thought as I forced myself not to click on the town's trash collection schedule. Newton had seven colleges, I learned, but no listing of private secondary schools where Helen and Nanna might have been students. Undaunted, I pressed on to find a controversy raging over the Massachusetts governor's signing of a bill making the tollhouse the state's official chocolate chip cookie. My kind of state. The citizens of Newton, of course, were lobbying frenziedly for a similar bill recognizing the Fig Newton, created there in 1891. Less than thirty seconds and already I was off track.

Fig Newtons were the first food item I gave up for Lent as a child. The choice had been obvious to me until dad explained that you were supposed to give up something you didn't already loathe. David, in a similar spirit, had elected to give up spiced beets. This train of thought wasn't getting me anywhere, I realized. The link between Muffin, Nanna, and Helen continued to evade me. It was late. I turned off the computer and swiveled in my desk chair, only to find BB standing in the bedroom door.

"How did you know I was ready to quit?" I asked him.

"Guess I heard you, heard the machine go down, who know? Sleep in a cage with a few hundred rapos and gone-off killers, you hear every soun' even when you asleep. Never know when you gonna need to *move.*"

He padded to the door in his socks, but didn't open it.

"They out there, Blue," he said quietly. "Not too close, but they there."

"How can you tell?" I asked, suddenly jittery in the stuffy room.

"Don' know, but they out there. It's like I can *feel* 'em, y'know?"

"So what do you feel them doing?"

"Nuthin'. Waitin'."

"Waiting for what, BB?" I yelled. I was losing it. "For me to go outside alone? Take Brontë for a little two A.M. hike so they can shoot us? You know, I used to do that. I used to walk around half the night out there if I wanted to. It's a desert, full of cactus and collapsed mine tunnels and venomous snakes, but it was safe! If I got hurt it was my own fault, my own stupidity, but this . . ."

My yelling had disturbed Brontë, who stood stiffly and walked to the door as if to solve the problem so she could go back to sleep. I felt like a prisoner in my own living room.

"Go on to bed," BB told both of us. "They ain't gonna do nuthin'. Not yet."

"Why not? What are they waiting for?" I grumbled. "I hate this! I hate even more not knowing *why!*"

"So, you find out anything from all that?" he asked, tossing his hair in the direction of the faxes on my desk.

"Yeah. Chocolate chip is the state cookie of Massachusetts."

"For real?"

"Yes," I answered and went to bed.

In my dream Saint Sebastian, still full of arrows, pruned a rose bush growing atop a coffee table Misha and I had bought for our beach apartment and then hated because its drawers stuck if we left the balcony doors open. I'd given the coffee table to a friend when I moved. Groggily I acknowledged that the jammed drawers pretty much embodied the night's frustration, my inability to find a pattern in a pile of data. But why a saint and roses?

"Catholics and thorns?" I mumbled to Brontë, who merely stretched beside me and huffed irritably. But as I drifted back to sleep it came to me. Nun, Catholic. Deirdre Eckels. And then the Sacred Heart icon with its thorn-wrapped coronary muscle. Perhaps I'd been too hasty in dismissing the connection between Nanna, Helen, and Deirdre, I thought. Just because I'd heard her name in the context of Misha didn't mean Deirdre hadn't known Nanna, Muffin, and Helen as well.

Lurching back into my living room, I booted the computer up again and got on the Internet.

"I may have overlooked something," I told BB as I typed "Sacred Heart" into the search box. It was going to be a bunch of religious stuff, I assumed. It was going to be the entire rosary printed over thorn-and-heart watermarks followed by an appeal for contributions. It wasn't going to . . .

But there it was. Or there something was. I zoomed around the Society of the Sacred Heart's very competent Web site, noting its mission. Schools. Nineteen of them in nineteen U.S. cities including Newton, Massachusetts. Private prep schools, until recently most of them girls' schools. This, I thought, was where Helen and Nanna had met as teenagers, and where ten years later Deirdre Eckels was probably a teaching nun. Not much to go on, but once a pattern is generated it expands. I printed the phone numbers for all the schools and a U.S. map showing the location of each school. San Francisco, Chicago, St. Louis, Houston, and fifteen other cities. It would be easy to document the movements of Muffin and her cohorts through these cities. It suddenly occurred to me that it would also be easy to cross-reference for unsolved pimp-murders in these cities during the times one or more of the three were in residence.

"Nah," I sighed. Real life is never that literary.

"Find something?" BB inquired from the floor where he was doing an endless series of sit-ups.

"Hard to say. Look at this, BB," I said, handing him the map I'd just printed. "Two of the women—"

"I don' read too good," he said, handing the map back. "Look like a map."

For the second time that day I was compelled to recognize the considerable gap between what I knew and what I was able to see directly in front of me.

"How old are you, BB?" I asked, mentally surfing the well-known data on illiteracy among young male criminal offenders. Especially minority young male criminal offenders whose less-than-ideal childhoods often included lousy schools. The hatching grounds for unsocialized primate predators. Except BB was talented and sociable, not predatory.

"Twenty-four."

"How did you wind up in prison?"

"Dealin'," he answered. "Didn't *use,* understand? Just deal."

"Right, BB. So can you read at all?"

I threw myself on the floor beside him and pointed to the map.

"Try this," I said, indicating the eastern edge, the northernmost city name printed far enough from the others to be legible.

"Al . . . Al-bay-nie, New . . . New York. That right?"

"That's great, BB! You got it. Albany, New York. You can read, you just need to practice, get in a literacy program. You know, your design business is taking off. You're going to need to improve those reading skills in order to—"

"I know, I know," he said, grinning. "Dr. Rox be sayin' the same thing. So that Albany, huh?"

"Yes, see, it's way east near the Canadian border and we're way down here in the Southwest near the Mexican border."

His facial expression suggested the same desperate disinterest felt when somebody insists on telling you the plot of a movie.

"Never mind Albany," I backtracked, framing in my mind an

impassioned lecture on the value of reading, when it hit me. Albany, New York. Frankie Lopez's postcard to Bugsy Sneller had been mailed from Albany. I began to see threads, the framework of a pattern.

Frankie, an orphaned street kid doing time for prostitution, had been kidnapped from a juvenile detention center by a white-haired woman whose impersonation of a social worker was polished enough to convince two clerks, a guard, and an attorney, all of whom saw social workers every day. A white-haired woman attuned to nuances of presentation, costume, props. A white-haired woman who knew her way around a proscenium arch.

And while the obvious fear about such a woman in such a situation would be that her job entailed returning the girl to organized sexual slavery, I didn't think that was the case. Frankie Lopez had already been on the streets. She was anything but naive. And she went with the woman willingly. Glenda Martin believed Frankie had known what was going to happen and had confided in her pal Bugsy, who had then tried to convey the information to somebody else. If the bogus social worker had been an old-fashioned white slaver, I thought, Frankie wouldn't have been so eager for her few significant human contacts to know.

I remembered white-haired Helen Tewalt playing a sweet old lady with that fairy-tale basket of cookies in the lobby of Las Colinas. The blue-checked napkin and trailing ribbon. A grandma prop straight from the image pool beneath American advertising art. In that pool each woman at her fiftieth birthday is magically returned to a nineteenth-century Currier and Ives kitchen where she wears high-button shoes and tirelessly kneads dough near a wood-burning stove. It is always snowing outside the window of this kitchen, even in Southern California. Helen Tewalt had pulled it off in a prison lobby in ninety-degree September heat. Could she have played the role of a social worker five years earlier? Hey.

But did she? I still knew of no connection between Deirdre Eckels and the three crones, yet Deirdre was clearly the link. Deirdre the ex-nun from a religious order that ran schools, one of them in Albany, New York. Albany, from where Frankie Lopez had mailed a postcard. I decided to call the Albany Sacred Heart school in the morning and find out if Francesca Maria Elena Lopez had been a student there. If so, it would only be a matter of time until the rest of the pattern unfolded, I thought with a certain arrogance. After all, I was good at this.

As it turned out I overslept and barely had enough time to drop Brontë for boarding at the vet's in Palm Springs before packing and heading to the airport for my flight to St. Louis.

"I would've kept dog except I'm goin' with Rox an' the dance team to Phoenix this weekend," BB mentioned sadly after I'd left Brontë in an immaculate run with an indoor area from which she and the other animals could watch a TV placed there expressly for them. The vet explained that since many homes keep a TV on twelve to fourteen hours a day, domestic animals find it a comfort when they're away from home. I asked her to tune it to PBS for Brontë, where there might be an occasional opera.

"Jus' don' like to see her in a cage," BB went on, breaking my heart. I'd never had to board Brontë before.

"Oh, is this the big line-dance competition they've been practicing for?" I asked in a frantic attempt at changing the subject before I burst into tears.

"Yeah. I'm goin' along, take care of the costumes, general manager, you know. We leave Saturday morning early, Roxie say. Get back Sunday night."

"Well, have a great time, and tell Rox I said break a leg," I told him.

"Break a leg?"

"It means 'good luck' in show business," I said, thinking about three women and a community theater in Rancho Almas.

Back at home I left a cryptic message on the machine, just in case Misha called.

"David's getting married!" I chirped. "Wouldn't have expected it in a month of Sundays! So please leave your best wishes and we'll get back to you when the owl flies." The Sunday reference was intended to alert Misha to the day of my return, and the owl was supposed to let her know I'd be back at night. It occurred to me that Misha probably had no idea when owls flew, and would merely think I'd gotten into animal rights. Still, there wasn't time to record another message. Quickly I packed BB's masterpiece and all the Internet paperwork, drove into San Diego, and dropped him at the shop after giving him dad's phone number in St. Louis. Then I dashed to the airport, left the truck in long-term parking, and had just enough time to call Rox from a pay phone and leave a synopsis of the previous night's research on her answering machine.

"I miss you," I said before hanging up and before remembering that I'd promised not to say things like "I miss you" to Roxie Bouchie.

"Sorry," I concluded. "A slip. Won't happen again."

It wasn't until I'd found my window seat on the plane that I remembered BB's injunction about little gold earrings. In the previous night's data-busting I'd forgotten to scrounge through the storage room for my mother's solid gold disks. I hoped Carty would have a pair I could borrow.

Chapter Eighteen

I saw my father and Carter Upchurch before they saw me. Dad looked a little older but quite fit in the Auntie's T-shirt I'd sent him. His blue eyes beneath a gray buzz-cut were as bright as ever. Carty was trim in Levi's under a natural linen jacket that looked handwoven. Her hair was now strawberry blond, I noticed, skillfully highlighted. They both craned to see over the deplaning crowd, but Carty saw me first.

"Betsy Blue!" she called. "We're here!"

Something happens at these moments that is both deeply affirming and nearly intolerable. It catches me off guard every time. There's no way to prepare for it. The chemistry of childhood still in the air, a world now gone returning in odd little sensory bites. Dad's aftershave, still Old Spice because my mother loved its scent. Carty's smooth voice narrating details of the moment as usual, a Greek chorus of one.

"Your father insisted on parking in *this* terminal's lot even though it's under construction," she said while hugging me. "So of course the car's at the far edge of nowhere between a forklift and a large hole. One of us is bound to fall in, and I just love your hair, Blue, except what's this white patch on top? And that tan! You look wonderful. Now you must tell us all about everything!"

That conflict. For a moment I yearned for a vanished past in which all hurts were buffered by my mother and these two people. It had been so good, so safe, or at least I remembered it that way. Then I felt myself swimming up to a present moment in which we were all just adults and nobody could really protect anybody from anything. The safety of childhood is a necessary lie. And there are these fleeting intersections with that lie which arouse an odd resentment. Okay, it was a lie, but why couldn't it last forever, dammit?

"I decided to get David and Lonni some of those Christmas plates," I babbled. "The red ones with the white Christmas trees around the border like we had at home, but I didn't have time to look in San Diego so do you think we could go shopping sometime before the wedding?"

Dad had stopped dead in his tracks when I mentioned the plates, and turned to wrap his sturdy arms around me a second time in five minutes.

"You're more like your mother every time I see you," he said as I cried into the witch wearing ruby-red cowboy boots on his chest. "Remember how David loved Christmas, how your mother always made such a ritual for him of getting those dishes out every year? It's a wonderful idea, Blue. Nothing could be more appropriate."

Carty was crying, too, and dabbed at her mascara with an index-finger knuckle.

"You know," she sniffled, her arm tight around my waist, "I never thought David was going to pull out of this mess despite Jake's blind faith, and your mother . . . well, she'd be *so* thrilled now that there's real hope, and I just think your gift is perfect, Blue. By next Christmas David will be free, and there'll be a baby and a fresh start, and new red plates!"

It occurred to me that what passes for social order is probably nothing but agreement on a string of familiar symbols link-ing us through time. Scarcely an original notion. Dad, I realized, had known it all along.

After dinner in one of St. Louis's countless memorable restaurants I'd gained five pounds and felt sleepily content as I helped Carty make up the hide-a-bed in dad's little home office. I like to think of myself as tough, but it was hypnotically pleasant knowing I didn't have to sleep with a gun. Not that there weren't plenty around. I'd noticed the rack in the living room displaying dad's favorite rifles plus a couple of new, high-powered models. Should marauders select this gentle clergyman's door for foul play, they would face enough firepower to make Swiss cheese out of a boxcar *and* have a priest right there for the inevitable moment-of-death confessions.

"I'm staying in a hotel so you and Jake can have some time alone," Carty explained brightly. "Besides, three people with only one bathroom is a guarantee for disaster. But I'll sleep over Friday night, since we have to get up before dawn on Saturday to get to the prison by nine. We'll have some time then for girl-talk, just the two of us."

There was something different about Carter. A warmth and shyness.

"I can't wait to hear about *him*," I said, smiling suggestively. "Must be something special from the way you're not talking. Is another wedding on the agenda? Let me see, you were dating a Texan the last I heard. An oilman, wasn't it?"

"Don't be trite, Blue," she answered, shaking a pillow into its case as if it were trying to escape. "He was a restaurateur. Seafood. But that was years ago and no, dear, I have no intention of getting married again. I can't remember all my surnames as it is."

"Not ever?" I gasped dramatically. Carty's *hobby* is getting married.

"No. So what about you?" she said, changing the subject. "It's been two years since Misha left, Blue. Surely you've met some interesting people?"

"Actually, I've met a lot of interesting people, Carty. A woman who confessed to a bizarre murder and then was poisoned in prison even though she was terminally ill and would only have lived a few more weeks anyway. She was interesting. And her friends, one of whom also died of a stroke when thugs broke into her condo, and another woman who's currently missing. Then there's a black woman psychiatrist who coaches country and western line-dancing, and an ex-con named BB the Punk who really *can* turn a sow's ear into a silk purse but reads at a second-grade level because—"

"You know what I meant, Blue," she interrupted, tying off a broken thread in the cotton thermal blanket. "You can't live alone out there on the prairie forever."

"It's not a prairie, it's a desert, and I don't live alone," I pointed out. It seemed strange that Carty hadn't shown any interest in the events I'd just outlined. "I live with a dog."

"Yes," she said thoughtfully, heading for the door. "We'll talk later, Blue. Tomorrow night we'll do some shopping, and Friday I've planned a little luncheon for Lonni, and then Friday night I want to hear all about everything. But right now you and Jake need some time. G'night, Betsy Blue. I'll see you tomorrow."

When she was gone I wandered out to dad's living room and sat in his overstuffed chair beneath an etching of St. Paul's Cathedral in London and five gleaming rifles in a maple rack. Something was up, I could tell.

"I thought," my father began without preamble after he'd provided us both with double shots of Kentucky bourbon over cracked ice, "that it would be good for you to see your brother before the wedding, just the two of you. I've made arrangements for a special visit tomorrow afternoon. Of course you don't have to go if you don't want to."

I swallowed a tablespoon of the smoky liquid in my glass and felt my eyes water from the kick. A traditionalist, dad stocks an excellent liquor cabinet and isn't afraid to use it.

"You know I don't want to go, I know I don't have to go, and we both know I'll go," I said, wheezing. "But don't expect *The Bobbsey Twins at Alcatraz,* dad. I'm here. That may have to be enough."

"It's more than enough," he said, smiling. "Now, tell me all about this exciting case you've been involved in!"

We sat up half the night talking, but I felt a lot better by the next afternoon when he drove me to the prison, escorted me through a metal detector, and left me in a room full of empty tables and chairs. The room smelled like Pine-Sol and its walls were hung with really awful acrylic paintings of wildcats, grizzlies, and timber wolves howling at full moons. The prison art therapist, I assumed, was trying to increase awareness about endangered species.

In a few minutes Henry David McCarron was escorted through a metal door which was then locked by a young woman guard who immediately sat at a table and began to do paperwork. She never looked at me. My brother did.

"Long time, Blue," he said. "How have you been?"

It was David, I thought, disguised as a convict. The tattoos, the weight lifter's arms, the prison denims like those Muffin Crandall had worn, were just props. He still looked like dad. I could see the beginnings of gray at his temples.

"Umm," I mumbled, at a loss.

We were still standing awkwardly in a sea of empty tables and chairs.

"Why don't we sit down, David?" I finally said, gesturing vaguely at the entire dim and depressing room. "This is, uh, very nice."

"Thanks. I wasn't sure about the placement of the Picassos. Look, Blue, I know you hate my guts, but—"

"Don't be silly," I snarled at the person with whom I once lay curled beneath our mother's heart. "Why should I hate you? Hey, you turned into some character named Hammer from a D movie about thieves who don't shave, and you damn near killed dad. Now suddenly you've seen the light and everything's just grand. God, I can hear the angels singing, can't you? The Hallelujah Chorus. Should we stand?"

"Count!" the guard yelled from her table, and David did stand. Quickly he walked over to the guard and stood in front of her. Then he walked back to our table and sat down.

"What was that about?" I asked.

"Count."

"What's to count?"

"Prisoners, Blue. Everyone has to be accounted for at intervals, all day, every day."

"But there are no other prisoners in here except you," I pointed out. "There are only three people in this room. Surely the guard noticed that."

"Doesn't matter. You line up for count even if there's nobody else in the line. That's the way it's done, always has been."

"This is unbelievable, David, you're like one of Pavlov's dogs!" I said, appalled. "You're operantly conditioned. What will you do when you get out of here and there's no one to count you?"

"Lonni has agreed to do a count every once in a while just to help me over the transition," he said, a trace of his old grin showing. "She drew the line on razor wire around the backyard, though. Said she'd have to spend all her time whittling skinny little wooden legs for the neighborhood birds."

The grin was bigger.

"David, gross!" I yelled as I had thousands of times in the

past. And suddenly something was different. Nothing dramatic, just a shift, a barrier down. I had to laugh.

"So what are you doing now, Blue?" he asked. "Still writing books about 'training your inner gorilla'? I read it, you know. Dad donated five copies to the prison library."

I wrapped a foot around my chair leg and leaned on the table.

"I was trying to figure out why you went to total hell for no apparent reason," I explained. "While you could have cared less, it bothered me, David. You have no idea what it's like having to tell people your twin brother can't even rob a bank without breaking things."

The grin was full-blown now.

"I hated that vase, Blue. I knew I was busted, but I was gonna take the damn thing down with me no matter what. Shooting that monstrosity is the one thing I don't regret. Hope you and Carty aren't getting us any big, cheap vases for wedding presents. God knows what might happen."

We'd fallen into our old pattern, one-upping each other, saying things without having to say them. I still wanted to strangle him, but at least my usual need to wash something every time I heard his name had abated.

"So just tell me," I said, "why you chose a life of crime."

"You wrote the book, Baby Blue," he said, stretching his arms behind his head. "I'm an unsocialized male primate."

"Wrong, you were socialized. You played the French horn," I countered. "The problem with my book is that it doesn't apply to you. All that work and I still don't know why you're here instead of out rescuing rain forests or something else worthwhile, *anything* worthwhile. So why?"

"I don't know," he said, turning his palms up. "I was full of this *rage.* Who knows where it came from? I thought I was better than everybody, only underneath I felt like a nothing. The world owed me a living, or if it didn't I was going to steal it anyway. Then when I wound up in this sewer it was stand up or live on your knees, you know? It wasn't until Lonni that I saw it any different."

The reference to knees hit a nerve.

"I have a friend named BB the Punk," I began.

"You *what?*"

"I've been working on this case, I'll tell you about it in a minute. But David, nobody ever . . . I mean you were experienced enough by the time you went to prison that you could defend yourself, right?"

My brother's eyes looked old then, older than dad's. Much older.

"Blue, you aren't supposed to know about that shit. You're my sister for Christ's sake . . ."

"You weren't supposed to know about it either," I reminded him. "You're my brother for Christ's sake. So have you been . . . all right?"

It's hard asking your brother if he's been raped. Even worse asking if he's raped anybody.

"I was old enough, big enough," he said quietly. "These pusballs don't bother you if they know you'll fight, especially if you have the right friends. I've been okay, but I've seen things, Blue. Shit that would make you puke."

The look in his eyes was that one you see in the eyes of baby hookers. That sad, cold look of someone who's been trapped in the same room with human atrocity. It had never occurred to me that a grown man could have that look.

"So tell me about this case you're working on," he suggested.

So I did. The whole thing. At the end my brother was pale.

"Stay out of this thing, Blue," he urged, his fists knotted on the table. "You don't know what you've gotten into."

"You're right there," I agreed. "But how do I stay out when I was never in to begin with? It's some kind of vendetta against

Muffin Crandall, Helen Tewalt, and Nanna Foy. The three of them. Like I said, I think they pissed somebody off royally by killing Victor Camacho, and—"

"You've got it wrong," David explained urgently, his blue eyes narrow. "You think you understand all this because you wrote a book about bad guys, but I've been living with it, Blue. You're right that Camacho was just a delta male as you call them, but jerks like that are a dime a dozen. They work for somebody for peanuts, do anything, *anything* they're told, just like BB said. But the guy behind it all, he never even sees the assholes he hires. He's not going to give a shit if three old ladies take out one of his pawns. The pawns don't matter. There are a million more where Camacho came from."

"What, then?" I asked. The time for our visit was almost up. I wouldn't get to talk to David alone again, and this was scarcely an appropriate conversation for his wedding day on Saturday.

"It was *the girl*, stupid. That's what fried this guy's balls."

"What girl?"

"This Frankie Lopez. Didn't you say she was hooking? Hooking for whom, Blue? Clean little girls are worth a fortune. It's a million-dollar business. Somebody owned her, was waiting for her to pop out of this kiddy jail so he could put her back out there. Except somebody else, looks like it was your old ladies, snatched the kid. Bye-bye, business. And my guess is it wasn't the first time. This is what pissed off the man. Somebody grabbing his property."

"So it was Camacho," I thought aloud. "He was pimping for Frankie's mother . . ."

"Those two, Camacho and Anna Lopez, two dead rats," David said, shaking his head. "Bottom-feeders on their way out. Neither of them was worth anything to anybody, but the kid was. Camacho may have handed this kid to his boss on a plate after he hooked up with the mother, but he wouldn't have managed the kid. He wouldn't even have tried. He was just a link at the bottom of the chain and he knew his place. He'd pimp a half-dead cokehead for enough to feed both their habits, but he'd turn the kid straight over to the boss, maybe get a pat on the head. This alpha male as you'd have it probably runs a stable of kids and gets as much as a thousand, maybe two, each time he sends one out. Then he pays somebody like Camacho a hundred bucks to pick the kid up and drive her to some upstanding citizen waiting in a motel with three porn videos and a cheap stuffed toy, and Camacho's thrilled. Time's up, Blue. Thanks for coming. We've got a way to go, patching things up, but it'll never happen if you're dead. Stay with dad for a month or so, okay? Let this thing die down."

"I didn't get to ask about the baby," I said. "How did you—"

"One condom, two bathrooms, contact!" He laughed. "Dad's gonna baby-sit junior for a couple of weeks when I get out so Lonni and I can have a honeymoon, practice the old-fashioned method."

" 'Since you left Plumtree down in Tennessee,' " I paraphrased from dad's favorite poem.

"It'll be the first time I've been warm," David amended the last line as I knew he would.

When the guard took him away and then let me out of the empty room, I was smiling.

"Aaah," dad said proudly, meeting me in the prison lobby. "I knew you'd do well with this, Betsy Blue. I knew you'd come through!"

"Don't overdo it," I told my father. "And let me tell you David's theory about the Crandall case. See, he thinks . . ."

Dad and I talked about it all the way home, where Carter Upchurch was waiting.

"I've made a thousand calls and found a Christmas shop in

West County that has the plates in stock," she greeted me. "I didn't know if you wanted to get the mugs and the serving pieces, but—"

"I want everything," I told her. "But first I need to check on Brontë and a couple of other things, okay?"

"Blue, I'm afraid this place closes at five and it's already three-thirty. We really do need to dash."

"Not until I check on Brontë," I insisted. "I guess the rest of it can wait."

One of the vet's assistants answered and assured me that my dog wasn't wasting away. She'd had a long run with two goldens and a basenji, was eating well, and seemed to have enjoyed a PBS concert featuring highlights from Puccini, I was told.

"*Madame Butterfly* is one of her favorites," I informed the assistant, who merely answered, "Of course."

There were no messages at dad's from Rox or BB, which meant, I assumed, that nothing had happened. They'd be at Auntie's later, rehearsing the line-dance team one last time before the competition in Phoenix over the weekend. BB had said the team would wear their costumes for the rehearsal. Auntie's would be packed. I wished I could be there. I really wished I could talk to Roxie about David. In the cool quiet of dad's office/den I saw myself reflected blurrily in the polished cherrywood of his desk.

"Stop making excuses," I told the pinkish blur in the wood. "You and David did just fine, and you don't need a psychiatrist to tell you how much easier it was when he was merely despicable. It's not David you need to tell Roxie about, it's you."

I stood back and watched my reflection slide off the desk and down its side like one of Dali's clocks.

"But I can't," I reminded myself. "She asked me not to seduce her into something she doesn't want, and I agreed." I felt oddly lonely as I walked back into my father's living room to meet my godmother. This was my family, but it wasn't my home, I thought. They were very different things.

On the way to the Christmas shop I tried to tell Carty about David's interpretation of the mess I was in, but she seemed distracted.

"You need to get back to teaching or marketing or whatever it is you've been doing and stay out of criminal investigations," she said as we zoomed west on Highway 40 at well over the speed limit. "You have no training for these things and they're obviously dangerous. I just don't want you hurt, Blue. All these years with David's problems, well, it's quite enough."

The traditional guilt trip. I remembered why people often dread family gatherings.

"You've never talked to me like this in my life," I told Carter Upchurch. "Never. What's going on, Carty?"

"I'm sorry, Blue. I just can't cope with you getting into trouble just when David seems to be getting out."

I waited until she'd negotiated the off-ramp before answering.

"I haven't committed a crime, for crying out loud, Carty! A man showed up one day and hired me to do a job. It turned out to be a nest of snakes, but that's not my fault. Now I have to keep working on it because my life seems to be in danger and that's all I know to do."

"I could kill Dan Crandall," she said fiercely as we pulled into a shopping mall. "I can't believe this has happened."

"How did you remember his name?" I asked.

"Jake brought me up to date on the whole story this morning before you were awake," she answered too quickly. "It's horrifying."

"It'll be over soon," I tried to reassure her. "Whatever it's about will happen soon, it'll end. I'm sorry you're so upset, Carty. I won't talk about it anymore."

She pulled into a parking space, jerked the emergency brake on, and grabbed her purse.

"Maybe I'm just getting old, Blue," she said.

But she didn't look old as she locked the car and strode toward a sparsely populated shop with twinkling lights in its windows. She looked angry. And she looked scared.

"Santa's Secret," the shop's sign announced. In the muggy St. Louis heat its proprietor was overjoyed to see us coming. And he should have been. I bought an entire service for eight as well as serving bowls, a cream-and-sugar set, and a platter big enough for a roast ostrich. Then I picked red, white, and green plaid napkins and had started on napkin rings when Carty suggested that I might save something for next year. The shop had no wedding paper, so we settled on glossy white with sparkly ribbons and a big star on each box. Mission accomplished.

Next we made a run through a lingerie shop where Carty bought a stunning silk peignoir set for Lonnie in an unusual pumpkin color.

"Just a little surprise for our lunch tomorrow," she explained. "Lonni has no family, and although I asked her if I could invite some of her friends from this church group for a little shower tomorrow, she said no. She said she just wants the time to get to know you, since David has talked about you so much."

I caved in and bought a forest green sleep sack, sort of a zippered bag constructed of blanket fabric with arm and foot holes, meant for cold nights.

"She's going to be alone and pregnant for a long time before David's around," I told Carty. "This thing's not sexy, but it'll keep her warm until then."

"You're the best, Betsy Blue," my godmother said over my shoulder as I dug out my credit card again. "I couldn't bear it if anything happened to you."

"Nothing's going to happen, Carty," I said, draping an arm

over her shoulders, which were ropy and muscular from a lifelong devotion to working out with free weights. "Now what do you say we investigate that interesting little pasta place I saw across from Santa's Secret? I'm starving, aren't you?"

Over seashell pasta in a spicy spinach-walnut sauce Carty brought up Misha again.

"I don't mean to pry or tell you what to do," she began, "but it can't be good for you, pining away for someone who's gone, Blue. We . . . I knew how difficult it was for you when Misha left. So when your dad told me about this, this *unusual* place in the middle of nowhere, I thought it might be acceptable for a while, but . . ."

"I haven't been pining," I told her, shrugging. "Until recently I haven't really thought about Misha at all. I've been happy out there in the desert, Carty. It suits me. But you may be right about needing to come to terms with Misha. She called me the other day."

"*Misha* called you? That can't be!"

Carter's dropped fork made a pinging sound on the restaurant's tile floor.

"Here, use my salad fork," I said. "She mentioned being in San Diego soon, maybe even now, and wanted to get together. She didn't leave a number, so I couldn't call her back to say I'd be gone this weekend, but maybe when I get back, well—"

"Blue, no!" Carty breathed, her eyes wide. The reaction was a bit extreme, I thought. As if I'd mentioned meeting with Evil Incarnate.

"Why not? I need to see her. There's something still there, Carty, something important. I've always known . . . oh, hell, I don't know what I've always known about Misha. I never really knew anything about her except that . . . that I'm supposed to fight for her somehow. I know this doesn't make any sense."

Carter Upchurch sighed angrily at her half-empty wine glass.

"No, it doesn't, Blue. It's just more of your headstrong, romantic nonsense and I want you to stop it. We all have hurtful relationships, they're just part of life. God knows I could write a book on that subject. But for her to walk out on you and then just pick up the phone two years later is outrageous. Why don't you stay here for another week and avoid everything that's going on back there, Blue? The danger to you is even worse with her around. Or you could fly back to Boston with me. We'll tour the Cape. September's the perfect time, the season's over but it's still warm and even the galleries have some great sales! We could—"

"Thanks, Carty," I said softly. "But no. I need to go home."

It was the wrong thing to say. For the rest of the meal she merely chattered politely as I'd heard her do a thousand times with complete strangers. During the ride back to dad's she was silent, and when we got there she didn't come in.

"Let's leave the gifts in my trunk until Saturday," she said. "The hotel garage is secured, they'll be safe. Good night, Blue."

"Carter has been put off balance by the events surrounding David," my father said thoughtfully when I told him about the evening. "She feels overwhelmed by so many changes and may need to regain a sense of control by protecting you, or trying to. And, she's at an age when women, well, they sometimes become fearful. She's even learned to shoot, Blue. She went with me to the range the day after her arrival. I couldn't believe it! She said she'd felt a need to protect herself. That's what I meant when I said she'd become fearful. It does happen, you know, that older women begin to feel particularly vulnerable."

"Dad, that's sexist garbage and you know it! Nothing's ever gotten Carter down. I don't believe you said that."

"You asked. I do hasten to add that for my part I agree with Carter. Your staying here for a time or traveling with her to Boston simply makes sense. You've fallen into a dangerous and exhausting situation in California, your emotional resources are depleted, and a visit from Misha at this time cannot be in your best interests. But if I've learned anything at all, it's that real life does not make sense. I just hope you'll be careful. Promise?"

"I do," I said, "and dad, I'm not sitting on the sidelines anymore."

"I knew that," he said proudly. "I could tell."

Chapter Nineteen

By the following morning it seemed clear that I could safely return to my desert fortress and everybody could quit worrying. Rox called before nine with an update. She and BB had been very busy.

"Girl, you're gonna love this!" she began after I turned on dad's computer to take notes. "I did the Las Colinas thing and BB did the streets. We put it all together last night after rehearsal. We got a match, Blue. One dude whose name keeps turning up everywhere this case has been. I think we've got the man!"

Dad uses a different word-processing program than I do, and I couldn't figure out how to set the automatic outlining form, not that it mattered. I didn't know what Rox was talking about, so I had nothing to outline.

"Rox, start at the beginning," I said. "What did you and BB do? And what man have we got?"

She'd categorized our areas of expertise, she said happily. I'd plowed through the data on the three crones and pretty much established what they had done, but that still left us in the dark about who was behind it all. The investigation required somebody with access to criminal justice data and somebody who could get information on the street without arousing suspicion.

"A prison psychiatrist and an ex-con, right?" I filled in the blanks.

"I figured the best place for me to start was at Las Colinas with Muffin's death," she went on. "So I pulled the jackets of every prisoner in the infirmary with Muffin on the day she was poisoned, both the other patients and the inmate trusties who ran the infirmary on weekends."

"And?"

"And I got nothing. Diddly. Didn't know any more than we knew before, which is that somehow Muffin Crandall wound up drinking a Dr Pepper-and-strychnine cocktail in a room with fourteen other adults, one of whom handed it to her. There were no fingerprints but Muffin's on the Styrofoam cup containing the strychnine, remember?"

"Yeah. You said at the time that unless somebody talked there was no way to identify the killer."

"And we still can't prove it, never will. But let me run this down for you. Styrofoam cups have a smooth surface that *should* pick up latent prints, right? So how could anybody hand Muffin that cup without leaving prints?"

"They're wearing gloves?"

"Okay," Roxie continued with a hound's enthusiasm for tracking, "it's early September in a hot desert community, ninety degrees in the shade and no air conditioning in the infirmary. Wouldn't you notice if somebody was standing around in *gloves?*"

"Not the nurses, the staff. I wouldn't notice if they did. They'd wear those thin, disposable gloves for any contact with a patient, especially in a prison where the incidence of AIDS is likely to be higher because of drug use . . ."

"Exactly! And the nurses were the four inmate trusties. Like I said, there was nothing significant in any of their files, so I checked docket dates. There wasn't any particular reason to, but the information was accessible. And guess what?"

"What's a docket date?" I asked.

"The court calendar. Days when prisoners have to be transported to court for arraignments, hearings, trials. Trusties are prisoners who've been around long enough to have worked their way into positions of trust within the system. Being a trusty is a privilege. It carries certain benefits and it takes a while to earn. Most prisoners are way past their initial sequence of court appearances, have been sentenced, and done some respectable time before they make it to trusty status. What I'm saying is, you wouldn't usually expect to see the name of a trusty on a docket calendar."

"But there was one?"

I could have lived without the rather thorough detail Rox was providing, but it was so good to hear her voice I would have let her ramble on until Christmas.

"Yes, there was," she practically sang. "One trusty of the four who were in that room with Muffin, all of them pulling disposable gloves on and off a thousand times. One trusty with a new court date set up by her new attorney!"

"So?"

"So it doesn't mean anything yet, but wait until you hear this. BB heads out yesterday afternoon and hits every coffeehouse and diner on the strip where the hookers hang out, spreads it around that he's got a rich, out-of-town client looking for some clean, underage action and willing to pay for it. Everybody's interested, but nobody's got the right combination until one of the gals tells him she sometimes holds for a driver she's seen moving kids."

"You're losing me, Rox," I said. "Holds? A driver moving kids?"

"Holds money, hon. Somebody brings her the cash, she gets a little off the top or takes it out in drugs, and turns it over to the driver who picks up and transports children to rendez-vous with baby-rapers. In this country child prostitution is not conducted in public as the adult version is. Sometimes it all goes down at once, with the driver bringing her cash from the john after dropping the kid off. She already knows what his take is, and hers. The balance she holds until it's picked up by the number two man in the operation. Only get this. Number two man in this setup isn't a man. It's a woman."

"You're telling me a woman would work for a child-prostitution ring?"

I knew it, of course. I'd been warned about nice old ladies at bus stations from the time my friends and I started going into St. Louis for shopping or movies by ourselves when we were in the fourth grade. No old ladies had offered me cookies to come meet their dear, crippled little grandson in a car outside, but I knew what to do if they did.

"It is unusual," Rox agreed, "which is what makes it interesting. What's even more interesting is the description this working gal gave BB. The woman only dropped or picked up the cash in daylight, always in popular, heavy-traffic areas like food courts at shopping centers. She's described as young and pretty. Apparently she once told BB's contact she was learning the business the old-fashioned way by doing all the jobs involved. Doesn't that sound strange to you?"

"Yeah," I answered. "It sounds like some forties movie with Jimmy Stewart. Black and white. Stewart rescues a freckle-faced boy from the S/M Orphanage and teaches the kid how to run a quaint-but-honest hardware store in a small town where everyone regards hardware as a form of therapy. First the kid sweeps the floor, then he counts tenpenny nails, then—"

"Then he murders Stewart and takes over the store," Rox finished with a laugh. "You got the idea. Except in this movie the kid's a girl and the store's a diversified and very legitimate corporation that just happens to get its investment capital from some very un-legitimate activities. So guess who the benevolent father figure is!"

"Don't get Freudian, Rox. I don't know. Who?"

"Here's a clue. The new lawyer for the trusty at Las Colinas, the lawyer who's filing motions like popcorn trying to get her a new trial in which she may well be acquitted because the original witnesses aren't around anymore? As it happens this lawyer, this *very expensive* lawyer, works for the same law firm that represents Wrenner Enterprises. This dude is gold. I don't have to tell you how often one of the top criminal attorneys with one of the top law firms in town represents a drugged-out, semiliterate, indigent female felon at Las Colinas, but it's spelled N-E-V-E-R."

"Wrenner Enterprises? Cameron Wrenner?" I said, puzzled. "Cameron Wrenner's one of the wealthiest men in Southern California. Cars from here to Nevada, government contracts providing fleets for the military, lots of side investments. Are you saying you think Wrenner made a deal with this trusty? She hands Muffin the strychnine and he provides a lawyer to get her out? And who's this young woman BB's informant described?"

"This is where it gets nasty," Rox said with an edge to her voice.

"Rox, it's already nasty."

"Gets worse. I had my client run Wrenner's personal stats. It took two minutes. Married twice, divorced twice, only one child from the first marriage. A daughter who's now twenty-four. It wasn't hard to pull a photo of her from the paper. She does a lot of charity organizing. BB ID'd the photo. It's the same young woman you saw with Wrenner at Muffin's funeral."

"The guard from Las Colinas," I said as my breakfast coffee began to taste funny. "Rox, this is sickening! We thought she was his wife, but she was his daughter? Cameron Wrenner's daughter, right? Who took a guard job at Las Colinas just so she could—"

"Slip the rat poison to the right person," Rox finished. "She's no longer working there, by the way. In fact, my info-gathering client discovered that on the day after Muffin's funeral our young lady flew to Puerto Rico with friends. She's untouchable, Blue. Unless the trusty talks, of course. But don't hold your breath."

"I can't believe Wrenner would involve his own daughter in this filth, Rox. The whole thing is sick."

"Depends," she answered, chuckling, "on how you look at things. Wrenner could also be hyped as an exemplary postfeminist father."

"What?"

"Sure. He's raised his daughter as he would have raised a son. He's training her to manage a financial empire, and from all appearances she's relishing the challenge. Wrenner has taught his daughter a big lesson—that the one who controls both exploiter and exploited controls the game and gets the goodies. Few women understand that, and fewer are positioned to act on it. Wrenner's daughter is."

"Wrenner's daughter is an apprentice pimp of little girls and murderer of dying old women," I yelled through nearly two thousand miles of fiber-optic phone lines. "That's scarcely feminist, post- or otherwise. That's a woman who's so co-opted she's turned into an alpha male!"

"Or worse," Rox agreed, "but it's an interesting new kink in criminal personality profiling, isn't it? Anyway, speaking of alphas, BB's come up with a plan to distract Wrenner from his chest-pounding displays at Nanna and, for whatever reason, you. That's the goal. We aren't going to be able to punish the evildoers here, Blue. That only happens on TV. The idea is to get the gorillas out of your yard and out of your life, that's all."

I didn't like the idea of Wrenners *père et fille* continuing business as usual. Still, even I could see no merit in going to the criminal authorities with nothing but speculation and highly circumstantial evidence which would in the end hurt only the remaining conspirator—Nanna Foy. Assuming she was still alive.

"Okay, what's the plan?" I conceded.

"Simple. Wrenner's posturing is all about a bunch of old ladies killing one of his lackeys and snatching the kids he was prostituting. He's enraged because they made a fool of him, duped him, or almost did. If a tremor hadn't messed up the wiring at that public freezer—"

"Camacho's body wouldn't have been found until after Muffin's death," I continued her train of thought. "Nanna and Helen were ready with a story about Muffin's mental decline after her husband died. They would have given an Academy Award performance when the body was found after a month or so when the rent wasn't paid on the locker. They would gradually have remembered little details about one of those nights when poor, demented Muffin was missing again, only to return the next day with something unpleasant caked in her fingernails. The play awaited only Muffin's death for its performance. They'd been rehearsing for a long time."

"Much longer than they expected," Rox went on. "Muffin outlived her doctors' predictions by years. She had a bad relapse two years ago. I'm sure they thought it was curtains then. But Muffin underwent treatment again, and survived. The woman was incredible."

"So what's BB's plan?" I reminded her.

"Competition from other males. A guaranteed attention-grabber. If Wrenner thinks somebody's cutting into one of his businesses—I mean his underbelly businesses—he's gonna forget harassing you-all and go after the real threat. BB has introduced a rumor in significant quarters that a certain Los Angeles operator intends to derail one of Wrenner's drug shipments. Of course we have no information about such a shipment, but

Wrenner seems to handle a little coke traffic so there would have to be shipments. It's safe to assume there *will be* one, sometime, somewhere. Wrenner's rage will be diverted toward this phantom intrusion on his territory, and he'll pull his dogs off Nanna and you, whom he seems to see as a major player even though you weren't."

"Okay," I said. "Sounds good. Sounds like my book, in fact. Using male primate territoriality to manipulate a male primate. I like it."

"That's where BB got the idea, from your book."

"Rox, BB couldn't read that thing," I said.

"We've sort of been reading it together," she laughed. "I haven't been able to interest him in reading anything until this, but he's really into it, even looked up 'hegemony' in the dictionary. I didn't know what it meant, either."

"It's like 'fungible,' " I explained. "Nobody can remember what either of them means ten seconds after looking them up."

We chatted for a few minutes, I told her about my meeting with David and about Carter's odd behavior. "You and BB have done terrific work, Rox, thanks. Knock 'em dead in Phoenix!" I said in closing and then hung up. After five seconds I picked up the phone again. "And by the way you're smart and funny and I love the sound of your voice," I told the dial tone. "When can I see you again?" I hadn't promised not to say this sort of thing, I reasoned. Merely not to say it where she could hear it.

After printing the info on Wrenner Rox had provided, I dug my own file on the case out of my luggage and phoned the Newton County Day School of the Sacred Heart.

"Yes, Francesca Maria Elena Lopez was a student here," a secretary informed me. "She graduated last year. No, I'm afraid we cannot provide current addresses for our alumnae."

It was enough. I sat at dad's desk and stared through the window at a hazy sky. So they'd pulled it off, I thought. They'd kidnapped a minor child and transported that child across state lines. Lots of state lines. Then they'd committed a homicide and frozen the corpse against the imminent day when one of them would die and posthumously take the fall for the crime. When an unforeseen event upset the plan, they acted their parts anyway, improvising as they went. Muffin's monologue had been brilliant, I remembered, omitting nothing from the archetypal female narrative of fear except the one thing responsible for their behavior—rape. They had stopped a rapist and rescued a victim. Crimes only in a society created by male primates, I acknowledged. Not crimes in a society created by wise women. And not crimes in my mind.

Frankie Lopez, already nothing more than a distasteful statistic, had been stolen from sexual slavery and sent to a sheltered prep school on the other side of the continent. Frankie had known of this plan and had wanted to go. Frankie had *graduated.* The story was inspiring. But why Frankie?

"Bugsy, of course!" I said aloud. Bugsy Sneller, Helen Tewalt's granddaughter, was Frankie's friend. Probably Bugsy had phoned home and told Helen about Frankie immediately, begging to stay in juvy that one last week in order to be near Frankie. And Helen, unlike any other parent or guardian in the civilized world, had recognized the importance of the girls' bond and allowed Bugsy to stay. To account for what would seem a gross breach of duty on Helen's part, Bugsy had refused to give authorities her real name.

Meanwhile, the crones were planning Frankie Lopez's escape from a miserable future and early, brutal death. They were honoring the bond between one of their own young and another. The elegance of their thinking and subsequent action was breathtaking. A different social code, a different reality. Irresponsible and criminal here, but then they didn't really live here, I realized. The crones lived somewhere else. Another latitude.

The phone rang and I could tell dad was talking to Carty, enmeshed as usual in complex detail planning.

"Carter has run afoul of her real estate agent and wants to know if I can drive you to meet her," he explained a few minutes later. "She's arranging the sale of that duplex on the South Side she bought after your mother's death, when she moved back to be near you kids. Apparently the neighborhood's gentrifying and she stands to make a very nice profit. The prospective buyer showed up, but the agent was late. Anyway, she's now behind schedule and fears you'll be late for Lonni unless I drive you to meet her."

"It's fine, dad. I'll get dressed."

On the drive across town I relaxed in dad's car and watched scenery. The Mississippi, the Arch, the Old Courthouse reflected in a glass office building. I'd had good times here as a child, riding the paddlewheelers, watching fireworks over the water on the Fourth of July. As we headed into the South Side I was balmy, awash in reminiscence. The feeling stayed with me as dad parked the car and waved at Carty, who was standing on the steps fronting a stone house, a duplex. With her were a young couple and a woman in four-inch heels and a red suit. The realtor, I thought lazily.

From the street I could see the duplex's two front doors. The one on the right was an old, corroded aluminum storm door with a peacock etched in its glass. The doorknob looked lumpy under a black patina of oxidation.

"Dad," I asked as we waited for Carty to finish her conversation, "isn't that a peacock etched in the right-hand door?"

"Hideous, isn't it?" he answered. "Why?"

"I think I saw this house in a dream. A dream about Misha."

"Who knows, Blue? After your mother died and Carter moved here to help out with you and David, she spent most of her time with you at our place in Waterloo. But maybe you came here a time or two. Dreams can grab imagery from forgotten memories, you know."

"I guess," I said as Carter pointed to her watch and gestured for me to get in her car.

A half hour later we were settled around a pink tablecloth and fresh flowers at a restaurant devoted to Victoriana. It was apparently patronized at lunch exclusively by very well-dressed women. Lonni Briscoe's mane of auburn hair clashed with the tablecloth, but it was obvious that she could have cared less.

"Blue," she said in the first breath after our introduction, "I know you must think I'm either nuts or a real loser to have fallen in love with David, but I'm not. It just happened, and I finally said, 'Oh, hell, quit fighting it.' So here I am, and I intend to be your friend if you'll let me."

It's hard to argue with true grit. I liked her.

"Deal," I told my brother's salvation.

Carter beamed and didn't say much as Lonni and I got acquainted. From time to time Carter got up to make phone calls, she said. Something about the realtor. Lonni asked a million questions about my work and how I liked living in the desert. And she told me about a disastrous early marriage, her struggle to get on her feet after the divorce, going to school at night, her job as a sales rep for a greeting card company.

"I have a company car and I get to drive all over restocking cards in drugstores and groceries," she explained, enthusiasm animating a squarish face softened by a good haircut and an artist's touch with makeup. She didn't look anything like my mother, but I could see why dad thought so and why David had been drawn to her. She had that same bedrock goodwill, that ability to make each person feel interesting.

"But a baby," I mentioned. "How will you be able to travel with this sales job once the baby comes?"

"I'm thirty-three," she said, her hazel eyes full of warmth. "I deeply want children and there isn't much time. The company offices have on-site day care and my boss has already said I can take a managerial position as soon as I want to. I can manage, Blue, even if David runs off with a stripper the day he gets out of prison."

"He won't," I said with conviction. "He loves you."

"And I love him with my whole heart. It's amazing, isn't it?"

"Yeah, it is."

After the gift opening Lonni went to the ladies' room and I dabbled in my crème brûlée with a cookie so thin I was reminded of Holy Communion.

"Carty, I don't remember ever going to your place in the old days," I said. "Did I?"

"I don't think so, Blue. There were a couple of gentlemen friends, to put it delicately, who were often there during those years. I distinctly remember telling Jake *not* to bring you kids over, that I'd be at your place whenever needed. Why?"

"I dreamed about Misha and that peacock door."

"Ugly thing," Carter noted dismissively and then changed the subject: "Isn't Lonni an absolute godsend, Blue? I still can't believe this has happened!"

"She's great," I agreed thoughtfully, although my thoughts were not about my new sister-in-law.

"Blue, it means a great deal to me that you're here," Lonni said when she returned. "I want this but I'm scared to death, and having you around makes me feel, well, comfortable."

"I'll be around, Lonni," I told her. "And I admire your guts. This isn't going to be easy."

"For women," she replied, carefully covering her gifts with tissue paper in their boxes, "it's not supposed to be easy, is it? That's why we're so much stronger."

"Traditionalist," I teased her as we left. But she was more than that. She was a woman who had actually chosen this path and knew what it was about. A brave soldier. In the parking lot I gave her a sharp salute that made her laugh. Already we were friends, and Carty was beside herself with joy.

And also with exhaustion. That night we ordered a pizza and dad went to bed after the last bite. I could tell he was nervous about the upcoming ceremony, but then who wasn't? Carty had curled up on the couch in the living room and was already asleep by the time I'd carried the pizza box down to the Dumpster.

"I'd planned this evening for us, Blue," she said groggily as I tucked a pillow under her head and folded a light blanket over her feet. "Thought we'd talk . . ."

"Yeah, what about the new man in your life? When do I get to hear—?"

"There is somebody, Blue," she said, smiling with her eyes closed. Then she was lost in sleep.

I turned the lights out and lay in bed feeling disloyal. I loved my family, I thought, but this event was taking forever and I wanted to go home. Home, where Brontë was and Misha might be trying to reach me. Where another woman I had sworn not to love was probably selecting eye shadow to match her dance costume at that very moment. I hated missing that. It's the little things that get you.

Chapter Twenty

The following morning was a flurry of activity as we stumbled around in the moist dawn, trying not to step on each other. Dad had selected his formal clerical collar, the starched white one that buttons to a special black shirt with pleats down the front. Usually he just wears those little white plastic tabs that fit into collar-slots on the regular clerical shirts. I knew he was going to be hot, but I didn't say anything.

"Jake, you're going to suffocate in that starched collar," Carty said anyway.

"Nonsense," dad answered, already sweating.

Carter was wearing a gauzy flowered dress in beige and off-white. She completed the ensemble with a beige picture hat and gloves. The gloves made me think of Muffin Crandall and a Styrofoam cup, but I put it out of my mind.

BB's creation received the accolades I had known it would.

"Blue, where did you *find* this?" Carter asked, wide-eyed. "It looks as if it had been designed just for you!"

"It was," I said. "A friend of mine made it out of some old drapes."

"Old drapes? Blue, this is antique watered silk. And the detail! You must introduce me to your friend. I have a length of the most exquisite Irish tweed, but I haven't found anybody who could do just what I wanted with it. A walking suit look, only not so *dowdy*, you know? Do you think your friend—?"

"BB doesn't do dowdy," I assured her. "But shouldn't we get going?"

Only then did I remember his instructions regarding earrings.

"Rats!" I hissed as dad headed for the door, his robes and stole in a garment bag over his shoulder. "I was supposed to bring mom's earrings. Those little gold disks. But I forgot, and I forgot to buy some when we were shopping."

"My jewelry case is on the coffee table," Carty said, following dad into the cloud of warm air pouring through the door. "There are some nice gold teardrops on posts. They'll go perfectly with your suit, Blue. Grab them and let's get your brother married."

I found the teardrops quickly, their posts fastened through a strip of plastic mesh Carty uses to keep her earrings in tidy pairs. The mesh was caught in the clasp of a gold chain. As I tugged the mesh loose I noticed that the links of the chain were axes. The double-bladed axes called labryses, once the symbol of radical feminist idealism. I had seen an identical necklace at the throat of Nanny Foy. It seemed weird.

"Carty, I had no idea you were interested in feminism," I said as I got into the back seat of dad's car next to his garment bag, a boom box, three cameras, and a box of paper napkins embossed with wedding bells. "That sort of puts you about twenty-five years behind the cutting edge, doesn't it? I'm surprised."

"What do you mean, dear?" she asked without turning to look at the necklace I held in my hand.

"This."

When she did turn around her reaction was, uncharacteristically, one of anger.

"Blue, it's a necklace I found at a street fair this summer in

Boston. Why *must* you persist with these silly, juvenile questions? Give it to me and stop acting like a child."

"I can't stop, Carty. Remember? I'm a new soul. You said it a long time ago and I believed you. One of the women I told you about, one of Muffin Crandall's friends, wears a chain of labryses just like that one."

"Which means she probably went to a street fair someplace and bought it. I'm sure they're about as rare as those braided Guatemalan yarn bracelets you see everywhere by the thousands. Really, Blue, your nonsense can be so tiring. Especially now, when we're all nervous about—"

"Come on, you two," dad interrupted. "Not now, please." With that he pushed a button on the car's CD player and turned the volume up. Mozart's Concerto for Horn and Orchestra. I immediately sank into a reverie involving a single canoe on a glassy lake, as he had known I would. Carty said something nobody could hear and we drove the rest of the way to David's prison wrapped in music and our private thoughts. Mine involved putting some distance between myself and Carter Upchurch before I had to face the fact that she'd changed. That she was no longer a charming mentor, but an aging, irritable stranger. It hurt too much to face it.

Lonni was already in the visiting room when we arrived, gorgeous in an acorn-colored shot-silk dress with Basque sleeves and about seventy buttons down the back. David was there, too. His jeans and blue chambray shirt were starched and ironed to a crackle finish, and I could see that he'd cut himself more than once trying to get the closest shave of his life. He looked scrubbed and boyish and I realized I was probably going to cry through the whole thing. Carter, of course, had brought Kleenex.

We weren't allowed to take anything into the visiting room behind its barred door, but a number of guards were hanging around in the lobby. They'd be happy to operate the boom box, they said. The speakers could be placed right next to the door of bars. In the visiting room a simple wooden lectern had been placed on a table. Dad stood behind it and put on his priestly garb, the linen alb, the rope cincture, and scapular. Then the elaborately worked white brocade stole our mother had hand-sewn for him, with its gold-embroidered bands and jeweled crosses. Dad almost never wore that stole. The last time had been at mom's funeral. Carty handed me a Kleenex as Lonni walked toward dad and David to the music of *Lohengrin* playing from the other side of a barred door.

"Dearly beloved," dad began in his best voice, and Carty handed me another Kleenex.

When it was over and David had kissed his bride, they proceeded as far as the door where the guards gleefully threw at least a pound of rice all over them and snapped pictures with Carty's camera.

From the exercise yard beyond the administration building a sudden roar of male voices could be heard. A guard had made the announcement. David's buddies were shouting bawdy congratulations. Then more photos including several of us all taken by one of the guards. Refreshments included chocolate ice cream, Cokes, and potato chips David brought from the canteen, which was apparently out of Twinkies.

The gifts could not be taken into the visiting room, so everybody but David adjourned to the lobby, where dad had stacked the packages on a bench. David watched, his face pressed to the barred door and his big arms hanging through, as Lonni opened them. When she took the first of the red Christmas plates from its nest of tissue paper, my brother merely said, "Shit, Blue," and held out his arms to me. I hugged him tight despite the bars between us and said, "Shit, yourself." Carty shoved the whole box of Kleenex between the bars for us and glanced at the sky outside the prison lobby.

"We're halfway there, Betsy," she whispered.

I knew whom she was talking to. Her best friend. My mother. What I didn't know was what she meant by "halfway." Things seemed pretty complete to me.

By noon our time was up. David had to relinquish the visiting room to other prisoners and the queue of visitors already lined up in the parking lot outside. Lonni thanked us profusely and said she wanted to spend the rest of the day alone, savoring the experience. Dad mentioned that he felt like writing a new sermon for his visiting preacher gig the next day, and would welcome a quiet evening in which to do some research. Carty didn't say anything.

But when we got back to dad's she cheerily packed her bags and phoned for a cab.

"Something's come up," she explained brightly. "I'm afraid I'm going to have to leave a day early, but wasn't it *wonderful?* And Jake, don't even think of driving me to the airport. You've done more than enough driving for one day. Blue, Betsy Blue," she said, hugging me, "don't stop being a new soul. And I *have* to have the number of your friend the designer!"

With that she was out the door, beige ribbons trailing her picture hat into a cab.

"Carter needs some space after all this," dad said in his pastoral counseling voice. "It's been overwhelming for her."

"Of course," I agreed. Then I changed into shorts, borrowed dad's car, and drove to the little country cemetery outside Waterloo where my mother is buried. I'd stashed a Coke and a bag of chips from the reception in my purse. These I tucked next to her gravestone.

"Mom, David's going to be all right, but something's wrong

with Carty," I said into thin air. "If you're, you know, around, maybe you could look into it?"

After that I drove back into St. Louis and ate buttered popcorn at a movie about cute swamp animals who save the children of a forgotten offshore island from industrial pollution. When I got home dad was asleep and there was a note on my door.

"I am enormously proud of you," it said. "There's a sandwich waiting in the refrigerator. Love, Dad."

On Sunday I accompanied him to St. Something-or-Other's to hear his sermon. Then we went to a smorgasbord brunch at one of the hotels near the airport.

"So what made you decide to hop back on the great, spinning wheel?" he asked conversationally as I wolfed a spinach-feta omelette. I'd selected the omelette merely to kill time while waiting for my individually prepared Belgian waffle with fresh strawberries.

"I'm not sure," I answered between bites. "Dan Crandall knew who wrote 'The Cremation of Sam McGee.' All of a sudden it was time to start living again, and I found myself involved in this bizarre murder case. And by the way, it feels more like a grid than a wheel to me, so I just think of it as the grid now."

"Ah," my father said, nodding. "I remember when you called it Snoopy. But your grid concept is interesting. I see right angles, though. Surely there wouldn't be right angles, would there?"

"It's all *curved,* dad."

"Ahhh! A sphere, not a wheel."

We'd been talking about the nature of God since I was three.

"Not exactly. Too few dimensions. Wow. Look at that waffle!"

On his fork dad held a slice of kiwifruit to the light and regarded it pensively.

"Have you given any thought to what Misha's visit may mean to you after all this time?" he asked.

"No. I just need to see her, hope she's still in San Diego when I get back tonight. There's something I'm supposed to do, fight for her or something. It's always felt like that. It's never gone away."

"Do you still love her, Blue?"

"Yes," I said without hesitation. "Not loving her would be like not having bones. I wouldn't be me, but some other creature entirely. I can't imagine that."

"Life presents only one impossibility," he told the kiwifruit gravely. "And that is going back in time. The attempt to do so may define not only cowardice and futility, but blasphemy as well."

Then he smiled and ate the kiwifruit.

"Time is flexible," I countered, enjoying the debate. "Parts of the past vanish in its folds, but other parts remain. I'll always love Misha, dad. Something happened that night in the beginning, with the balalaikas. I was, I don't know, *rewired* in that experience. It's permanent, no matter what. But that doesn't mean my life stopped then. I don't want to go back. What I want to do is my part in whatever it is. Does that make sense?"

"I have no idea," he said amiably. "My experience and yours have been too similar for objective assessment, and we both know that if sense must be made it's a lie. You know what I'm trying to say. I will never marry again, but I have loved other women since your mother died, and will again. It's time you loved someone, Blue. Someone to whom you weren't necessarily wed by the universe for reasons beyond comprehension. Our lives may be insignificant to your grid when we aren't serving its purposes, but they're meant to be lived fully."

The waiter refilled our coffees as I thought about Roxie Bouchie.

"I do love someone," I admitted. "The psychiatrist I told you about. But she doesn't want anything to interfere with her work and I respect that."

"Ahhh," he said happily and then kissed my cheek. "I think we have just enough time to get you to your plane. And remember, you've promised not to stay out there in the desert without your friend BB until you're certain it's safe. You'll stay somewhere else tonight?"

"Roger," I agreed.

At the airport I bought a paperback on the psychology of dogs and settled contentedly into my window seat on the plane. I had to drive over to Palm Springs to pick up Brontë anyway, so I'd decided to enjoy an elegant dinner alone at La Fève before stopping by the vet's. I'd wear the silk suit, maybe turn a few heads before getting Brontë and selecting a motel. It would be fun. But first I'd run by my place to check the answering machine. I had to know if Misha had called, and the remote retrieval feature on my antique machine hadn't worked in years. I wouldn't stay, I told myself. I'd just run in for a second. Surely Misha would have called again and left a number. Maybe she'd like to have dinner with me at La Fève as she explained where she'd been for two years. The idea was appealing.

My enthusiasm for it grew as I hurried through the weekend airport crowd after deplaning in San Diego. Outside the terminal a woman with wild gray hair strode through a cluster of Japanese tourists in name tags, and for a moment I thought she was Eden Snow. A delusion, I told myself as I easily found my truck in the long-term lot and began the drive home. The possibility of seeing Misha was bringing back memories I was projecting on the present. The sky was still a fading blue as I rolled the windows down to enjoy a sea breeze blowing in from the bay. It was going to be a pretty night, I thought. I was glad to be home.

It was dark well over an hour later when I hit the high beams to illuminate my gate. Dark and dry with a cool, sagey wind blowing from the mountains across the desert floor. In my rush to get to the airport I'd forgotten to lock the gate, I noticed. It was closed but unlocked. Anybody could have driven on to my property while I was gone. The thought made me uneasy as I climbed from the truck to push the gate open and then left it that way. After all, I wasn't staying.

Bumping along the narrow road to my motel I watched smoke trees, ocotillos, and paloverdes moving in the wind. For a moment the spindly plants seemed to be gesturing, their movements frantic. But then the wind subsided and they were just fixtures of the landscape, strange desert forms evolved in heat and silence for a thousand centuries.

The motel was dark, too, as I pulled up, but there were flashes of moonlight on the rippling surface of the pool and fresh tire marks in the sand fronting my door. From BB coming out to check on things, I rationalized as my earlier unease became a chilly film at the back of my neck. The marks were fresh, and BB had been in Phoenix for two days with the dance team. So who had been there? And was somebody *still* there?

Instinctively I had reached to unlock the metal box welded to the truck's floor when I remembered the Glock wasn't in it. In my mad rush to leave on Wednesday I'd left it inside, in my desk.

"Shit," I whispered, scanning the motel's facade, now eerily lit by my headlights. A tumbleweed rolled in front of the truck, its long, distorted shadow ghoulish against the stucco wall. I watched as the tumbleweed blew into the pool's chain link fence and stopped, shuddering in the wind. Something was wrong. I could feel it, taste it in the darkness behind the motel windows.

"Get out of here!" I told myself.

But I didn't put the truck in reverse. I'd come this far, I reasoned. And I'd come this far because of Misha Deland. Maybe I was just spooked, and maybe "they" were in there waiting for me, but I wasn't going to run. I had to know if she'd called. I had to. But I also had to stay alive.

After locking myself in the truck I slid below the steering wheel, found first gear, and drove straight toward the office of Wren's Gulch Inn. I was probably going about fifteen when the left front fender hit the door, which splintered and flew inward, taking the door frame with it. I was already in reverse and ready to back out under a barrage of gunfire within two seconds, but there was no gunfire. I could see nothing but blowing dust in my living room, lit by the bulb of one shattered headlamp. There was nobody there. But there had been.

From the truck cab I saw my overturned desk chair across the room, my computer monitor on the floor in a pool of sparkling glass. The desk lamp lay beside it amid fallen books and papers, a plastic water bottle, a box of floppy disks. Something had happened at my desk, I thought numbly. Somebody had been sitting at my desk and something had happened. Across the desk's surface I noticed the light reflecting off a spray of wetness. A spray of dark, tiny beads on the smooth pine. The answering machine lay against the far wall, smashed.

And I might have left then, gunned the truck backward, spun it around, and beat all hell into Borrego, called the sheriff, been rational. But I'd seen something else in the high-beam light. A rumpled pale brown lump, almost invisible against the carpet by my desk. Backing up the truck enough to open the door, I got out, walked to the thing on quivering legs, and picked it up. One nylon knee-high stocking, the ankle and foot in shreds.

"Misha!" I breathed in the glare and sifting dust. She always wore them. Nobody else did. I didn't own any.

Dropping to my knees, I pawed through the mess on the floor. And there it was in Misha's scrawl, a note begun on a sheaf of typing paper.

"I knew your extra key would be in the same place we always

kept it," she'd written. "So I came in for a while, but I can't wait . . ."

"Much longer," I finished the sentence for her. My eyes felt strange, tight and wide at the same time as I stood and looked at the spray of red across the surface of my desk. It was cool and sticky when I touched it, already congealed. I didn't have to taste it to know it was blood, but I did anyway. Salt, iron, a sweetish alkaline aftertaste.

Misha had been sitting at my desk, I thought, and turned when somebody approached her from the right. She'd jammed a foot at her attacker and he'd grabbed it, tearing off her stocking. There was a struggle. Then he'd hit her, probably slapping her first with his right hand and then with his left. The second blow had sent blood from already-broken vessels in her nose in a violent arc against the desktop.

"Misha," I said again, my voice ragged in the stillness. And then I felt the cold. It grew in liquid wires from my scalp down my arms and into my hands, swam through my chest. Ice. The sound of Brontë's screams when a bullet tore through her. An echo of balalaikas. I don't remember feeling much of anything after that. I only remember moving.

The Glock wasn't in the desk drawer where I'd left it, but the old .22 was still in the storage room. I slipped a shell into the chamber and snapped the bolt home, dropping a handful of extra shells into my waist pack. Then I went outside. The tracks were clear. Two men and a woman, heading into the desert toward the Lower Willows bypass near Coyote Creek. Back inside, I quickly changed into jeans and a black sweatshirt. Then I smeared black shoe polish over my white tennis shoes, the backs of my hands and my face. The excess I wiped on the oiled barrel of the .22 before slinging it over my shoulder. The ground was patched in moving shadows, but I didn't have any trouble following their tracks. I could have followed them without eyes.

They had headed toward the Lower Willows bypass for a reason, I thought. Probably because the intruders had left a vehicle there rather than risk getting stuck attempting to navigate the bypass. That suggested a familiarity with the terrain. I was sure the men were the same deltas I'd called Paunch and Tattoo. But why had they taken Misha? Did they think Misha was me? I'm two inches taller and ten years younger.

I was half running, keeping to the shadows and listening for sounds ahead, when it hit me. What if they hadn't been waiting for me at all, but for Misha? What if I was just a place where they knew she'd come because they'd heard her message on my answering machine? The theory explained why they'd been lurking around, but not much else. Misha had even less to do with the Muffin Crandall case than I did. Yet they had taken her, *were* taking her, somewhere.

I couldn't tell from the tracks how long ago they'd left, only that it had been that day. But they would have waited for dark, I thought. By nightfall on Sunday the weekend campers along Coyote Creek have left. They've gone back to the city to sleep in beds and flock to office jobs on Monday. By nightfall on Sunday the desert is empty of human presence. There's no one to see whatever you might choose to do there. I picked up my pace and covered over two miles in less than twenty minutes.

For some reason they'd opted to climb a dry wash in the side of a low mesa about two and a half miles out from my motel. It was easier to go around the mesa and involved no more travel time en route to Lower Willows, but they had obviously thought this was a shortcut. I went where they had gone, trying not to dislodge rocks as I climbed. About two hundred yards ahead near the top of the wash I noticed a dark shape with white parts pearlized in the moonlight. The form wasn't moving.

I stood in the shadow of a split granite boulder and watched for thirty seconds, then tossed a pebble at it. No response. With the rifle held in both hands I moved closer, then waited again. The pearlized white objects were the undersides of arms, a face. Or at least half a face. The other half reflected no light. Crouching now and scanning the lip of the mesa for movement, I moved close.

"Oh, God!" I breathed as I recognized Tattoo.

He was sprawled on his back, a Western diamondback rattler limp in his right hand. The snake's body lay over his motionless chest like a smooth cable, its rattles silent. Both man and snake were dead. But what made me gasp was his face. Its right side was hideously swollen and blue-black from neck to cheekbone, the skin split open like a rotten melon. Turning away, I noticed that the palm of his outflung left hand was cut and embedded with dirt and pebbles.

He'd fallen, I reasoned as I measured the depth of the wash where he lay. Paunch with his injured leg would have followed behind as Tattoo pulled Misha up the wash with his right hand. But Tattoo had stumbled and thrown out his left hand to catch himself as he fell facedown in the sort of protected, rocky terrain preferred by resting snakes. And a snake had been there. From the appearance of things he'd fallen directly on it. But what had obviously happened next didn't scan.

When I moved to the desert I took a course given by the rangers at the Anza-Borrego park headquarters. A course entitled Pit Vipers of the Desert. My concern was for Brontë, who would run every day in an area frequented by venomous reptiles with no legs. I wanted to understand both the threat and the treatment. It was for Brontë that I carried antivenin and a syringe in my pack, although I'd never had to use them.

But I had learned a great deal about rattlers in the class, including the fact that few people actually die from rattlesnake bites. Because venom is used to kill prey, the snake is reluctant to waste an entire supply on something it can't eat. Snakes swallow their food whole. Anything bigger than a kangaroo rat is not appetizing. Thus, when the snake bit Tattoo, it should not have injected its whole cache of venom. And yet it had, and apparently into his neck as he fell on top of it. At least one fang had probably hit the right carotid artery. He had died quickly.

But the rattler should have felt the vibration caused by feet stomping up the wash and moved away, I thought and then dismissed it. Tattoo was dead, and that gave greater credibility to my single-shot rifle. Nothing else mattered. Until I heard the sound.

A muffled, buzzing sound, it was coming from Tattoo. A sort of muted sizzle. The fine shafts of hair all over my body stood erect as my skin tightened in a reaction best observed in worms. Skin as an organ is profoundly old. It knows things from a time long before there were words. I stopped breathing for several seconds as Tattoo's corpse buzzed in the arid darkness, stopped, buzzed again. Corpses do not buzz. I couldn't make sense of the sound and was hypnotized by it, paralyzed.

And then something moved at the neck of his T-shirt. A small, triangular head emerged and bobbed delicately above his right cheek as the snake inhaled. Then it moved down his neck and onto the ground, its rattles vibrating too fast to see but painting the air in sound. Sizzle. Buzz. Death.

It was a little rattler, only about ten inches long. It had crawled under Tattoo's shirt to absorb his fading body heat, I reasoned. Which made sense. The rattler was a baby, a newborn. Western diamondback rattlers do not lay eggs but give birth to live young. Tattoo had fallen on a female rattler who was in the process of giving birth. That's why she hadn't moved away. She couldn't. And that's why she'd shot her entire load of bright yellow, cucumber-scented venom into his neck.

He'd grabbed her then, killed her with his bare hands just before her venom stopped his heart. But one of her young had crept onto his belly and absorbed the last of his warmth. I watched as the baby snake vanished beneath a rock. Then I wondered where the rest of them were. There would be eight or nine more, I remembered. I was standing in a desert wash full of hungry, inexperienced newborn rattlers.

"Misha," I whispered as I prodded at every rock with the gun barrel while climbing up and out, "what in the hell are we doing out here?"

The answer that came brought cold filaments again to my hands, my teeth. It was a shout, angry and brutal in the stillness. It had come from the low hill ahead, the last one before the land slid crookedly to Coyote Creek. I couldn't understand what was said, but the spirit had come through. Violence. It had to be Paunch, I thought, and the only person he could be yelling at was Misha.

Ignoring the shadows, I scrambled down the side of the mesa, across a moonlit field of broken boulders and up the low hill whose northern side sloped toward Lower Willows bypass. At the top I slowed and dropped to my knees. Then I crept to a creosote bush growing between two iron-stained rocks. Through the cough-medicine smell of creosote leaves I looked down at a man with a beer gut and dull, stringy hair. He was kicking the leg of a woman lying on the ground. She curled away in pain but then flung a handful of gravel in his face, hard.

It was Misha, and for a split second I just looked at her. A scrawny little woman with whose fate my own had been woven by balalaikas in a potting shed. Misha, my partner in some scheme dancing forever beyond comprehension. But then I noticed her left arm. It hung stiffly from her shoulder, and the skin was discolored by two dark splotches. One on the back of her hand and one above her elbow. She was wearing a polo shirt and I couldn't see how far the stain had spread toward her shoulder beneath its sleeve. But I knew that stain couldn't be allowed to reach her chest cavity. It couldn't reach her heart. I couldn't let it. Because if it did, Misha would die.

Tattoo had pulled her with him when he fell, I conjectured. And two of the just-born baby rattlers had sunk their well-supplied fangs into her left arm. They hadn't learned yet about conserving venom. They would have injected all they had.

Paunch was trying to drag Misha upright by her shirt as I moved through shadows to within fifteen yards of them, stood and braced the .22 against a rock. I had earned the right to do this, I told myself. I had been willing to give life if necessary. Now I was going to take it. The trade seemed fair. I had been shooting targets with this gun since I was nine. I wouldn't miss.

"Misha, get away!" I bellowed. "I'm going to shoot him!"

Paunch turned in my direction, a pistol in his hand. Misha rolled, I sighted down the barrel at his fat chest and fired. He was hit. I could tell that. I actually *felt* the bullet hit bone. But he was running. In the moonlight I saw him running, downhill, toward Coyote Creek and the Lower Willows bypass. A .22 at fifteen yards is not an Uzi. I had done my best. From my pack I took another shell and reloaded, but I knew he wouldn't be back. I had forgotten about cowardice. He'd shot Brontë for no reason, simply because he could. And a man who shoots animals is a coward.

"Misha," I cried, scrabbling to reach her, hold her.

"Blue," she answered, wrapping a skinny right arm around my neck. "Hey, Blue."

Chapter Twenty-one

Her khakis were torn and bloody at the knees, both arms were scratched and one discolored by a spreading reaction to snake venom. Dried blood was caked in her nose, and the wispy hair she always tried to style like Geraldine Ferraro's was matted with sweat. But it was Misha, alive and still percolating, if weakly, with that peculiar energy she generated. It was as if she had to power an illusion in all circumstances, I realized. Even these circumstances. An illusion into which everything around her must be drawn or the fragmented soul behind it would perish.

"I will not let you die," I said, holding her tight. "Where have you been, Misha? Why did you leave? These men, they've been after me, I don't know why. But I'm sorry they got you. It was supposed to be me."

From Lower Willows I heard the sharp crack of a handgun discharge.

"He killed him," she said, shaking violently. "He just killed the fat bastard. You smell like shoe polish. I miss you, Blue. And it's me he wants. I killed that man, Blue. My lips feel funny."

One of the symptoms of pit viper bites, I remembered, was a tingling numbness of the lips. So were the sweat and nonsensical giddiness. It meant the little rattlers had injected venom, but then I knew that from the discolorations on her arms. I had to care for her. I'd always known that. What I didn't know was exactly what to do next.

There was antivenin in my pack, but I had learned the procedure for injecting it into an animal, not a human. Humans can have a reaction to the horse serum in which snake antivenin is processed. A reaction as fatal as the poison it was meant to neutralize. The rangers had stressed that point in my viper class, insisting that only skilled medical personnel in a clinical setting could safely administer antivenin. If you were bitten by a poisonous snake you were supposed to move as little as possible while walking miles to a vehicle in which you would drive yourself to a clinical setting. Right.

"Misha," I urged as I pulled her arm from my neck and eased her to the ground, "try to be calm and don't move. Tell me how long ago those snakes bit you. Can you tell me that?"

"I don't know, not too long, but it hurts. My arm hurts. So do you die from these snakes? Why did you move out here in the middle of nowhere, Blue? Why didn't you stay in our place? I had to leave, you know. We thought Muffin was dying and I had to be gone when they found the body. I killed him, Blue. You weren't supposed to know."

I pulled up her shirt sleeve and stared at the swollen, purplish stain spreading over her shoulder and into her armpit. The vascular system breaking down, capillaries and veins swelling and bursting beneath her skin as the venom progressed toward her heart. She raised herself on an elbow and vomited. Another symptom. I could feel my own heart pounding violently as if for both of us.

"This is important," I told her. "Listen to me and answer me. Have you ever been bitten by a snake before?"

"Yeah, down in Louisiana. That's where I grew up, Blue. Did you know that? I never told you about it, about my uncle, what he made me do after my mother died. I went to live with him.

We had two trailers held up on boards by this nasty old creek, and one of them was mine so when his friends came they could . . . come in there. They paid him, Blue, paid my uncle money to use me. It started when I was only fifteen."

Her gray eyes were pure pain in the diffuse light. That mean, manipulative pain I'd seen so many times and then seen it alter like quicksilver as she reached to help anything hurt. Alter and become the light I had seen in her hands as she touched Brontë that night at the emergency animal clinic.

"What kind of snake, Misha?" I asked softly, trying to stay removed from what she'd just told me because I needed to focus on keeping her alive. "What kind of snake bit you in Louisiana?"

"Cottonmouths, mostly." Her eyes were dark again, looking nowhere. "One night I wouldn't do it, Blue. I was seventeen then. My uncle sent a man to my trailer and I told the man he could kill me but I wouldn't let him touch me. The man was drunk. So was my uncle. The man wanted his money back and my uncle wouldn't give it to him, told him to just go on and whomp me a few times if he had to. They started fighting and the man knocked my uncle into the creek. His face was in the water, Blue. He didn't move. The man left then, and I just watched my uncle with his face in the water for a long time. After a while his body kind of twitched, but that's all. I knew where he hid his money under a bait bucket out in the woods. I took it and ran, Blue. Down there, people think I did it. They think I killed my uncle. There's still a warrant for my arrest. That's why . . ."

"It's okay, Misha," I said, tasting blood from my own lip bitten in rage at her story. "You didn't kill anybody, but I understand. Right now we have to worry about these snakebites. Did you go to a doctor and get shots when the cottonmouths bit you?"

"Once," she said, her Southern accent deep now. No more

pretending. "Once I had to, only it wasn't shots, Blue. It was, you know, a drip thing from a bottle into my arm. It doesn't matter, does it? And I *did* kill somebody, Blue. I heard about you getting involved with Muffin, her brother coming and finding you. That wasn't supposed to happen. So I came because . . ."

She pointed toward Lower Willows bypass and then retched again.

I could feel gravel cutting into my knees, the wind evaporating sweat on my scalp. I could feel being alive. But if I screwed this up, Misha wouldn't feel being alive anymore. If Misha didn't die from rattlesnake venom I might kill her with horse serum. She was already delirious. Still, she said she'd been treated for a cottonmouth bite before. Cottonmouths are pit vipers. The antivenin would have been the same. I unzipped my pack and took out the syringe and needle and two of the four little vials. Antivenin powder and sterile water. They had been intended for a Doberman pinscher. By moonlight I followed a procedure memorized in case I needed to save the life of a dog. Now I hoped it would save Misha.

With the needle I drew the sterile water into the syringe and then injected it into the vial of powdery antivenin. You couldn't shake it or it would foam, I remembered, forcing my hands to stop trembling. You were just supposed to swirl it around gently until it dissolved.

"Blue, he's coming for me," Misha said as I swirled. "You need to go. They were taking me to him, those men. He's not far away. You have to go now or he'll kill you, too."

I thought it was just shock, that she was confused, maybe remembering the unspeakable horrors of her past.

"It's okay, Misha. Just hold still."

I had drawn the liquid back into the barrel of the syringe and held her good arm down with my knee as I injected a minuscule amount of it under her skin. Then I clamped the syringe in my teeth as I tore one of my shoelaces out of my sneaker. The ranger who'd taught me how to do this had mentioned testing for horse serum allergy by injecting a tiny amount under my skin if I ever had to use the antivenin on myself. Although, he'd said, the results weren't conclusive. From the gulch below our low hill I heard the sound of loose gravel rattling as it fell.

"Blue, that's him!" Misha whispered, frantic. "You've got to *go!*"

I heard another scrabble of falling rock. There was somebody down there.

"Who?" I asked, leaning close to inspect the patch of skin where I'd injected Misha. It was clear. No little red ring or puffiness.

"Cam . . . Cameron Wrenner," she answered as ice crystals flowered again inside my muscles.

"Wrenner? How do you know about him, Misha? None of this has anything to do with you, and now it's important that—"

"Blue, the man in the freezer, the man Muffin Crandall said she killed. I killed him, Blue. You've got to understand. It was before you came to San Diego. I was working with a kids' shelter downtown, raising money. I went there, it was dinnertime, to get some paperwork, and the shelter was closed but there was this girl, I saw her when I parked my car. I saw her walk around the side of the building, trying to get into the place."

"Bugsy Sneller," I said as I pulled her left arm down flat against the ground and looped my shoelace around it above the elbow joint. "She was raped and killed in an alley behind that shelter. Misha, help me with this. Make a fist. I need a vein."

"What are you doing, Blue?" she said, watching not me but the hill's surface below us. Her eyes were glassy from fear, but she kept talking. "When the girl didn't come back I went looking, went into the alley. This man—I knew he hung around the center but I didn't know his name—was on top of her on the ground, raping her. She was so quiet, Blue, so limp. And there was something wrong . . . blood on the ground. There was stuff back there, pieces of wood left over from repairs at the center. I grabbed a board and smashed it into his head, Blue. I hit him so hard I felt his skull smash. Then I hit him again. I couldn't stop. I killed him. The girl was already dead.

"I knew Muffin Crandall because she'd helped one of the girls at the center. I knew she and these other women did . . . things, secret things to save the girls. I called her. I didn't know what else to do. I couldn't call the police because they'd want my name, I'd be a witness and they'd find out who I really was. They'd find out about the warrant and make me go back to Louisiana. I was so scared.

"And they came, Blue. I waited in my car on the street, trying not to think about what was in that alley. I hid on the floor of the car so nobody could see me. When those women came I told them everything. Then they took the man's body away and I left. Nobody saw me. But Blue, they didn't know until they got there that the dead girl was the granddaughter of one of them, Helen's granddaughter. And they had to leave her there, for the police. God, Blue, it was horrible! And Wrenner knew. I think he figured it out, but not the whole thing. Not until they found that bastard's body in the freezer and then Muffin . . ."

I thought about Helen Tewalt walking into that alley and suddenly the less-than-polite treatment of Victor Camacho's body made perfect, crystalline sense. But I didn't have time to dwell on it.

"Be quiet and hold absolutely still," I demanded as I tightened the shoelace around her arm. "I'm going to inject you with a dose of antivenin." In the moonlight I could see the distended vein at the bend of her elbow. I had watched technicians draw blood from this vein in my own arm more than once, I remembered, forcing myself to remain calm. I could do it.

"Make a fist. Don't move, don't move," I whispered as I pushed the needle against her skin. I could feel the pointed tip break through and into the vein. It was like that feeling you get jabbing a finger through the shrink-wrap over a carton of mushrooms, only tiny. Very slowly I pushed the plunger down and then withdrew the needle.

"There," I said, finally allowing my hands to shake, and I leaned over to kiss her cheek. "God, I hope I did that right."

"Blue, I'm sorry," she whispered. "It's my fault. I knew I couldn't stay here forever. I knew I'd have to leave when Muffin died. That's the way they planned it, those women. They did it to protect me. Muffin didn't have long to live. They said they'd hide the body somehow until Muffin died and then say they found a diary in her computer describing how she killed him. The diary would make it seem like she was crazy. I had to be gone by then.

"It looked like it was going to happen two years ago, that Muffin wasn't going to make it. Helen called and said they'd set it up for me to go to St. Louis, that I had to leave immediately. I couldn't be here after Muffin's death when the body would be found and they'd tell their story. I had to just vanish. Except Muffin didn't die. I wanted to tell you, Blue. I wanted to call you and tell you everything, but I couldn't. They saved my life. And there are more of them, all over the country. They do things, illegal things, to save girls. That comes first. It has to. But I should never have . . . that night at Eden Snow's party . . . I should never have dragged you into this."

I hadn't noticed it before, but beyond the hazy velvet scrim of moonlight, deep in the blackness beyond, the grid was roaring. I could feel it, the uncountable black-silver intersections of intent unimaginably alive. That smell of ozone. It seemed to pull me effortlessly to my feet as another scrabbling footfall approached, closer now. Very close.

"I loved you, Misha," I said as I reached for the .22, leaning on a rock beside us. "I still do and I always will. It's part of who I am. Don't apologize for that."

"Blue, run!" she insisted. "He's almost here. I love you, too. I don't want you to die!"

I couldn't see the man climbing the surface of the hill. And we were hidden from his view by the scattered rubble of a huge boulder fallen to fragments in a time of winged lizards. But he would see us soon. I had one chance to stop him with a single-shot rifle. Only one. There would be no time to reload.

He was so close now I could hear the rasp of his breath as he climbed. I moved away from Misha, and in the thin shadow of a broken rock I raised the rifle and sighted on a ruddy face less than a hundred feet down the slope. A face I'd seen beneath a white cowboy hat, smiling down from a hundred billboards. His right hand held a revolver. In seconds he would see me, but I had to wait until he was close enough for the .22. There was only one chance.

Then a pebble dislodged from somewhere above me skittered downhill, its sound sharp in the silence. Cameron Wrenner looked up, and saw me. No time left. I began the exquisitely careful trigger pull as a familiar voice screamed, "No, Betsy Blue!" and the report of a high-powered rifle split the silence. Over the barrel sights I saw Wrenner fall, a gaping hole directly over his heart. From his mouth a gush of blood looked black in the moonlight. Against my finger the trigger held firm, halfway to firing position. The shell still lay in its chamber beneath the locked bolt. I hadn't fired. I hadn't killed Cameron Wrenner. But somebody had.

Turning, I looked up the hill behind me. Three figures stood against the sky, bathed in silver. Three women, none a stranger to me. The one holding a rifle was my godmother.

"Carty?" I said, although no sound came from my throat.

And then she was down the hill and next to me, holding me, saying, "Blue, Baby Blue, I promised your mother when you and David were born that if anything happened to her I'd look after both of you. God, this was close!"

"Carty!" I managed to say aloud. "What . . . how did you . . . ?"

It was then that I noticed the chain of labryses at her neck. And an identical chain gleaming from the neck of the woman who now stood beside her. A woman with tendrils of salt-and-pepper hair and dramatic, maple-sugar-colored eyes.

"Blue," Nanna Foy croaked, her rich voice hoarse with fear. "Thank God! But I should have known, shouldn't I? That this was inevitable. After all, you told me you were determined to find Misha, except she found you first."

"Misha," I said, immediacy flooding my mind despite the confusion I felt. "She's got to have medical care. She was bitten by rattlers and I—"

"And you seem to have saved her life," a third voice announced gruffly from the clump of rocks where Misha now sat up, her gray eyes somewhat clearer than before. The third woman waited with a bemused expression as I walked toward her. In the wind her long gray hair, now shot through with white, blew and danced. Her huge, lashless eyes seemed to hold the sky.

"Eden Snow?" I said. "I thought I saw you at the airport. I don't understand."

"You did, and no, you don't," she agreed and held out her arms to me. She smelled like cat fur and felt like a goal post in my embrace.

"Eden is here because we feared that this would be necessary," Carty said, gesturing toward Cameron Wrenner's body. "Wrenner was responsible for the horror which led to Bugsy's death and that of countless others. He could not be allowed to murder you or Misha."

"This has been *discussed*," Eden Snow said as though someone had suggested otherwise. "And while only one woman in all the world might grieve the death of this man, in her honor we also must grieve. We assume the sorrow of this man's mother at his death. The idea of her sorrow becomes your particular burden, Carter, whether or not she's still alive."

"I accept it," Carter answered somberly, standing apart from Nanna in the wind.

"Then it's done," Snow pronounced. "Now let's get the hell out of here."

I shivered as Nanna took the rifle from my godmother's gloved hands in her own, also gloved, and scrambled downhill with it. She passed Wrenner's body without a glance and continued to the gulch where Paunch lay dead, shot by Wrenner's revolver after my .22 had failed to kill him. I saw her grasp the lifeless hands, press the fingers to stock, barrel, trigger. When she was through it would appear that Paunch had shot Wrenner.

"Your gun must be left in a similar manner beside the other man, the one with the snake," Carter said behind me. "It must look as though the tattooed man fired the .22 at the fat one, but only injured him."

"Carty, my fingerprints are all over the .22," I said. "There's no way to get them all off, especially out here."

"It's your gun, Blue. Of course you've handled it," she replied. "But then it was stolen, remember? Your home was broken into tonight. You came home to find—"

"Both my guns missing, my place wrecked," I continued the scenario. "Lately there have been people out here, I'm not sure why. Gunshots one night. I thought maybe it was an old boyfriend harassing me, but I didn't know for sure. I alerted the sheriff's department to the situation. Then tonight after I got home from a long trip and found my place had been broken into, I decided to collect a few valuables and get out. I couldn't call the sheriff right then because my phone was smashed. In a little while I thought I heard shots out near Coyote Creek, but it might have been a truck backfiring. How's that?"

"Excellent. As soon as we leave you'll drive into town, call the sheriff, and say exactly that. You'll have to handle this alone, Blue. Misha, Eden, Nanna, and I aren't here, were never here. Can you do it?"

"Yes, but where are you going?"

Nanna had returned from placing Carty's rifle in Paunch's hands, and wrapped an arm around my godmother's waist.

"I'll be going back to Boston with Carter for a while," she said, her eyes sparkling. "We've never really had any time together."

If I'd had any question about what she meant, it was answered when Carty turned and buried her face against Nanna's neck. The gesture of a woman who has performed a task bravely and alone, now resting in the arms of her lover.

"Carty, I knew there was somebody, but you didn't tell me," I began. "I just thought it was another man. And the chain of labryses. You didn't want me to see it because you knew I'd seen Nanna's. That's why you were so angry on the way to the prison for David's wedding. But how do you two know each other?"

In Nanna Foy's spectacular eyes I saw a twinkle that suggested perpetual discretion in describing our afternoon together by my pool. I grinned and shook my head. Hell would freeze before I told my godmother I'd tried to seduce her girlfriend.

"We have to go," Eden Snow bellowed from the clump of rocks where she was helping Misha to her feet. "Blue, can she walk?"

I looked under Misha's sleeve. The swelling was no worse, and the bloom of leaking blood vessels had stopped. Still, one dose of antivenin for two bites on the arm was probably not enough, and I couldn't risk another.

"No," I said.

Snow clamped her right hand over her left wrist and held out her hands to me.

"Then we'll carry her. We came out here in a rented Jeep, followed your tracks in it to where you climbed up that wash. We only need to go that far, then one of us can take the Jeep and get her to a hospital while the other two drive her car back to the airport in San Diego. Let's go."

I clamped one hand around Eden's wrist and one around my own. The old fireman's carry. I'd learned it in Girl Scouts. Misha's head lolled against my shoulder as Snow and I lurched down the hill, Nanna and Carty following with Carty carrying the .22.

"Eden, what do you have to do with all this, what's your role?" I asked.

"I don't know," she said and grinned, gnawing thoughtfully on the upturned collar of her shirt. "I just write books, and all this weird stuff happens."

"Eden feigns eccentricity as a defense against the mundane," Nanna explained. "There's this network, Blue. It grew out of Eden's following when it became clear that women were again being trampled. All the legal decisions, a famous wife-beater allowed to go free after murdering his wife and another person. The powerful backlash against women. Something had to be done. It just grew, this web of older women mostly, who help girls. Nothing official. In fact, the network doesn't exist to all outward appearances. There is no network, and nothing it does is known. But when possible, girls are removed from prostitution, from enslavement to systems which sell children to adult men for their use as sexual toilets. Money is provided for the girls' education in boarding schools, all-girl schools, preferably.

Some of these young women, we hope, will later band with others to continue the fight."

"Sacred Heart schools," I said as Eden stumbled over a dried catclaw limb, throwing Misha heavily against me. "You're sending these kids to Sacred Heart schools. Must be some pretty radical nuns! But let me get this straight. Helen Tewalt impersonated a social worker and grabbed Frankie Lopez right out of juvy, and then Frankie wound up in Albany, New York, where she graduated from one of these schools. They're all over the place. But I don't get the connection. What does this network have to do with nuns? Is it Deirdre Eckels? I found out she used to be in that religious order. What does she have to do with all this?"

Carty and Nanna took over carrying Misha at the bottom of the hill.

"I wanted to tell you all this," Misha said over Nanna's shoulder, "but I couldn't, Blue. Technically these girls are kidnapped, you know, not that anybody wants them. I know how that feels. But they're minors. The women involved could go to prison. They're risking their lives. You understand?"

I thought of Muffin Crandall's complete devotion to dying in prison, perceived as a demented old woman who'd gone off one night and packed a man into a freezer. It was good theater, and the purpose behind it was impressive. To protect Misha, but more to guard the secrecy surrounding a web of women who did the best that could be done in occupied territory. They saved doomed girls, stole them away from slavery and death, gave them a chance. Muffin had undoubtedly given Helen Tewalt her paperweight as a farewell gift before going to prison and her final performance. A farewell gift to remind Helen that despite her loss, other lives depended on her. I was awestruck.

"Deirdre does the logistics, manages the details," Snow told me, glaring at Nanna Foy in irritation at Nanna's earlier remark.

"Her contacts among the teaching sisters are very useful. She also writes a newsletter we use to keep everybody informed. There. I have proven my tolerance for the mundane."

"I hope your newsletter's readable," I said, falling into a banter that made the bizarre scene feel less bizarre. "When she was here she published this awful thing about feminist analyses of banking. It put everybody to sleep."

Misha was smiling. They all were.

"That *is* the newsletter, Blue," Nanna said. "There's a code Deirdre worked out. You have to know which lines to read. But it tells everybody in the network what's going on, where to send money for the girls' scholarships, how to participate in a planned rescue. It's how I met Carty. She's one of the contact people in Boston."

We were at the base of the mesa where Tattoo lay dead in a wash.

"There's no reason to climb over this again," I told them. "It's no farther to walk around the base and your Jeep's right there."

The moon was past its zenith in the sky already, lengthening the shadows around us. Nearby I heard the tinkling sound of wind in a smoke tree. I felt light-headed for a moment. The desert would never feel the same to me, I realized. Its ancient quiet was now riddled with complexity. And there had been no time to understand any of it.

"Blue, we'll leave you and Misha here for a few minutes while we get the Jeep," Carty said. "Then we'll drive back to get her. Nanna will take Misha in the Jeep after dropping Eden and me at your place to get Misha's rental car.

"I'll call from the road on the way back and arrange for a pilot to fly us to L.A. in my plane," she continued to think aloud. "It's best if there are no medical records for Misha here, no record that she was here at all. You used false I.D. when you rented the car, didn't you?" she asked Misha.

"Of course," Misha answered.

"There wasn't any car at my place," I said. "Misha's car isn't there."

"I parked in back," Misha said quietly. "I wanted to surprise you."

There was nothing to say to that. Just nothing. As we sat in the dark I saw Carter light a cigarette and smelled Marlboro smoke drifting on the air as the three of them hurried around the edge of the mesa. It smelled like the past.

"It was Helen who called me, who told me about you getting involved in this," Misha said. "Nobody could believe Muffin's brother had hired you. It seemed impossible. But Helen understood I'd need to know. She told me they were after you. And it was me they wanted, Blue. I didn't tell anybody, I just came so they wouldn't hurt you, so they'd get me. I want you to know that."

In the dark I couldn't see her eyes, but when she kissed me I could feel tears on her face. And mine. A strange kiss full of bottomless desire and terrible distance. Afterward we clung to each other in silence, every bone, every curve of flesh familiar and longed for, yet lost in the desert wind. Lost in time.

"I don't know what to do now," she cried against me.

"I think I do," I answered, wiping my face on my sleeve and then touching her hair. I had learned what to do from Roxie Bouchie, for whom the option of pretending that life is easy had never existed.

"What's important is that you came here, willing to sacrifice your life in order to save mine. That's what you do, what you all do. You save women, Misha. I love you for that and for the magic that's in you. And it's enough. What to do is say good-bye and get on with our lives."

Those last words were an inky, flat slab of anguish crashing through me. They were intolerable, but they were true. Misha and I could not go back in time. Nobody can. And the attempt to do so, as my father had said to a kiwifruit only that morning, is blasphemy.

"I hate this, Blue," she said angrily. "If things had been different, if I hadn't killed that piece of hog shit in that alley, if Muffin Crandall had died when she was supposed to, then maybe it would have worked out."

"It has worked out, Mish," I said, nodding deeply to an invisible pattern still humming between us, but fading now, finished. "We're just too close to see it. Here comes the Jeep. You have to go. But where do you live? I don't even know where you live."

"I've been in St. Louis," she said. "When this mess hit the fan we thought I'd better move again, but if this works out I'll probably stay, just at a different address. There's somebody there I want to be with, Blue. But I had to do this, you know, first."

"Misha, were you staying at Carty's old place? That duplex with a peacock etched on the glass door with a rose doorknob?"

"Yeah. Why?" she asked.

"Nothing. I dreamed you were there, that's all."

When they were gone I brushed away the tire tracks with the limb of a creosote bush, following their route around the mesa. When I reached the wash I used the limb to brush the ground ahead of me as I climbed, but there were no toneless buzzings. The snakes were gone. Tattoo lay as he had been, his hand now stiffening around the dead rattler. I shook as I pried his index finger loose and pressed it to the trigger of my gun, then rolled the fingers of both hands on the stock and bolt. As an afterthought I took the shell from the chamber, polished it, and pressed his fingers to it before reloading it with the cuff of my sweatshirt.

I felt disconnected, as if I were watching myself in a play. I couldn't seem to stop shaking even though I wasn't cold. It didn't really seem strange, touching the icy fingers of a dead man in the dark of a desert wash. What seemed strange was that I was alone.

On the way back I swept at our tracks and those of the Jeep. I couldn't obliterate them all, but enough to render the evidence inconclusive if anybody bothered to look. My living room felt like a museum when I got back. A moon-washed exhibit of some event already historical, already impossible to reconstruct with perfect accuracy.

I scrubbed the spray of Misha's blood from my desktop, then wadded her unfinished note into one of my blackened tennis shoes. After washing the shoe polish from my face and hands I locked both shoes in the metal case welded to the floor of my truck. I'd dispose of them later, bury them far out in the desert with the empty vials of antivenin and syringe I also stashed with the shoes. There could be no evidence that any of the night's events had happened, except for the three dead men now turning to stone in a sage-scented wind.

When I was ready I drove into Borrego and called the sheriff's office from a pay phone in a gas station parking lot. "You've, you've got to send somebody out right now!" I sobbed hysterically, remembering Muffin Crandall in a dirty Shirley Temple wig. The performance I was about to stage, I decided, would be dedicated to her memory.

Chapter Twenty-two

And Muffin would have been proud, I think. When the first of the sheriff's deputies arrived I wept and after great hesitation admitted that I'd once made a terrible mistake. A few drinks, a stranger in a bar. A biker, I thought. He had these tattoos.

"The French have a term for it, when women are attracted to brutes," I sniffled. "*Nostalgie de la boue.* A yearning for mud. It was just a one-night thing, of course, but then he kept calling, even came out here once or twice but I wouldn't let him in. He knew I lived here alone. It was scary. I'm pretty sure he was involved in drugs somehow. I kept thinking he'd just go away. Then when I came home tonight—I've been in St. Louis since Wednesday for my brother's wedding—I found my place torn apart. I don't know if it was him. My guns are missing. Whoever broke in here took my guns, a Glock and an old .22 rifle. And then a while ago I thought I heard shots way out in the desert. That's when I got so scared I had to drive into town and call. Do you think it's him? What could he be doing out there?"

An hour later no fewer than five vehicles had driven across park property to Lower Willows bypass from the back of my place. My creosote-limb sweeping had been a farce compared to the obliteration of our tracks performed by various employees of San Diego County and the California Parks Department. I made coffee and looked frazzled. The frazzled part wasn't hard.

I was so exhausted even the fainting spell came across pretty realistically, I thought.

The county medical examiner's van had been summoned and was heading into the desert when I saw the deputies stop an unofficial vehicle speeding up my road. Two people dressed in malachite green and sequined vests got out. A man in dreadlocks and a woman whose distress at being denied entrance was evident even from fifty yards away. Finally she showed the deputies something from her wallet and they backed off, shaking their heads.

"As I have already *explained,* I am Dr. McCarron's *physician,*" she told another deputy at the ragged hole which used to be my front door. "Her health is fragile. It is imperative that I see her *now.*"

"Sure. And who's this?" the deputy said, nodding to BB. "Rumpelstiltskin?" He seemed pleased with his joke.

"Mr. Berryman is my driver," Rox said in a voice that could dissolve rust. "And if you continue to prevent Dr. McCarron from receiving medical care I assure you there will be legal repercussions. Now get out of my way!"

Both sets of brown eyes swept my ruined living room as BB and Rox stepped inside, but neither said anything. Both looked straight to me, waiting for a cue.

"Dr. Bouchie!" I said weakly, my head buried in my hands. "That man I told you about, the one with the tattoos I picked up in the bar? I think he came back tonight and trashed my place. My guns are gone, and there were shots . . ."

"I assume that my patient has given an official statement regarding these events?" Rox said to the deputy.

"Well, yeah, but . . ."

"Then there is no reason for your continued presence on her property. This woman's condition is such that any further interrogation constitutes a threat to her health. I'm afraid I'll have to ask you to leave."

"Wait a minute," the deputy said, scowling. "What kind of doctor are you?"

Rox inhaled and rose to her full height, the sequins on her vest blazing.

"I am a psychiatrist," she pronounced.

BB had assumed a chauffeur's attitude, standing deferentially near the door with his hands clasped behind his back. I could see the muscles of his neck straining as he controlled an impulse to grin. The deputy eyed me suspiciously.

"Let me check with the head of the investigation," he said. "I don't think it'll be a problem."

And it wasn't. Some pretty serious business had gone down out there, the chief investigator told Rox and me, but it was under control now. They wouldn't need me again until later. Just a few details. I'd stay in town, right?

"Of course," I sighed shakily. "But what 'serious business'?"

"We're handling it," he answered sternly. "It doesn't involve you."

The park service rangers insisted that all further vehicle traffic from Lower Willows bypass use the dirt Jeep trail down through Ocotillo Flat and the Desert Gardens, and into Borrego via the paved Di Giorgio Road. Immeasurable damage had already been done to the desert habitat, they said. All subsequent official travel across park property would have to go the long way on permissible routes. There was no reason for anybody to be on my property or the park's property behind it. They'd lock my gate on the way out, they said. So sorry about all this. Get your phone fixed so we can reach you. Thank you for your help.

Roxie looked strange in the dim light of my remaining unbroken lamp, but I couldn't identify what it was. An ashen cast to her mocha-colored skin. Something veiled in her eyes. BB scrounged through the storage room for tools, and made temporary repairs to the door as Rox heated canned soup in the kitchen.

"Eat," she told me, shoving a bowl in front of me as I sat on a kitchen stool. "You probably haven't eaten."

"I had a big breakfast," I said, wishing I could just throw myself into her arms as Carter had done with Nanna. But we weren't Carter and Nanna, I reminded myself. The night's events, my exhaustion and shredded nerves, didn't matter. They didn't give me the right to take advantage of Roxie's strength and kindness, to pretend I'd forgotten my promise. I would get through this alone.

"So okay," BB said from the door, "when do we hear what *really* went down out here, Blue? Somebody dead, that obvious. Medical examiner be here, that van. Whole worl' know what that van mean. So what—?"

Rox raised a hand as if stopping traffic.

"Not now, BB," she said.

"It was Paunch and Tattoo, and Cameron Wrenner," I told him. "They're all dead. And I didn't say that and you didn't hear it. For the record, I have no idea what happened out there tonight. Some ape I picked up in a bar one night, whose name I never knew, has been harassing me. I think he came here when I was gone. Something happened. That's all I know."

"Wrenner?" BB's eyes had grown wide. "*Big* trouble. Good thing you don' know nuthin' about it. I sure as shit don' know, don' wanna know. Me and Rox, we just drivin' home from Phoenix all that time. Couldn't raise you on the cell phone and Roxie worried, she bein' your *physician* and all." He stopped and looked around. "Say, where your dog?"

"She's still at the vet in Palm Springs," I answered. "I don't think I can handle driving over there to get her tonight. She'll be okay. I'll get her tomorrow."

It would be nice to have Brontë, I thought. Less alone.

"No way," BB said. "I'll take Rox's car and go get her. You call from the cell phone, tell 'em I'll be there."

"Good idea," Roxie said nervously, not looking at me.

So I walked with BB to the car and made the call.

"Here's the key to the gate," I said. "Rox seems, well, upset or something. Did the dance team lose?"

"No, dildo, the team walk away with five trophies," he said, letting his wild hair hang over his face and regarding me closely. "You think Rox give a fuck about dancin' with all this shit here? You so dumb, need a map to find which way is up."

"Thanks loads," I said as he drove away and I went inside to find Rox vacuuming the broken glass from my carpet.

"Brontë's paws," she explained beneath her veil of beaded braids. "I thought . . . you know, she'd step in it." Her knuckles around the vacuum's handle were pale.

And despite everything that had happened, despite my exhaustion and despite my deepest resolve, I loved her. Loved her with a certainty that made my breath shallow in my dimly lit living room as she turned off the vacuum. In the sudden quiet I could hear my heart straining to be near her, to be home.

"Rox, it was a mess out there," I began the long narrative I assumed she was waiting to hear, my voice too husky. "A rattler got Tattoo, but—"

"Blue," she interrupted, fidgeting with the vacuum cord, "the whole time in Phoenix I just wanted you to get back. I couldn't wait for you to get back, Blue. And then when you were supposed to be back and your phone was out of order, I was crazy. This mess . . ." She gestured to the expanse of desert rubble beyond my window. "You could've been killed."

"I'm okay," I whispered, willing myself to stay where I was, not reach for her, not touch her.

"Did you see Misha?"

"Yes, for a little while," I answered. I could never tell Rox what Misha had told me, that she had killed Victor Camacho in that alley. I might want to, but I never would. That secret would remain forever apart from whatever relationship Rox and I might have.

"And?"

"And I said good-bye to her, Rox," I answered. "That's all. But I want to tell you about the rest of it, about what happened with Wrenner."

"Later," she whispered, walking toward me. "Blue, when I thought you might be . . . I need you in my life, Blue. I love you."

She was against me then, her body trembling with the same desire that pulled my arms around her, my mouth desperate to find hers. I couldn't stop, couldn't feel enough of her, touch enough of her.

"Oh, honey," she breathed as I pulled her hips to mine, our legs pressing instinctively inward, "I want you so, I love you, Blue."

I couldn't stop moving against her, tasting her. Couldn't hold her tight enough, couldn't stand up.

"Roxie," I managed to say, dragging her onto the couch. "I promised you I wouldn't do this, but I *have* to. I love you, Rox. Hold me, please just hold me!"

"Girl," she said fiercely as her braids fell around my face and we were lost in it, wild with need, gone.

Later, swimming up from the depths, we cried in each other's arms, then laughed.

"If we start toward the bedroom now," she said while pulling at my tangled sweatshirt, "do you think we can get these clothes off before next time?"

"I don't know," I said, rising passion making my hands shake as I fumbled with the buttons on her peasant blouse. "We can try."

Much later I awoke wrapped close to Roxie's warm, cocoa-colored skin when something cold and wet began nuzzling my face.

"Brontë!" I greeted her, letting go of Rox long enough to wrap my arms around a sleek, furry neck. In the doorway BB exuded pure joy.

"Yesss!" he whispered into the darkness. "You take care of that lady, you hear me, Blue?"

"I will," I answered as a coyote howled far out in the desert and was answered by another. "I will, BB."

In the morning I cooked everything I could find in the kitchen for breakfast before Rox and BB had to leave for their respective jobs. Rox and I would meet in the city for dinner, we decided. There was a lot to talk over.

When they were gone I drove into Borrego to get a newspaper and my mail. The paper's headline was particularly interesting.

"Prominent Local Businessman Found Shot," it defined Cameron Wrenner's demise succinctly. There was no mention of Paunch and Tattoo. The article, while sketchy, suggested that an ongoing and highly confidential sheriff's department investigation would reveal unwholesome connections between Wrenner Enterprises and drug trafficking. Wrenner's daughter, it went on to say, was in Puerto Rico and unavailable for comment. It was ironic, I thought, that Helen Tewalt's obituary appeared in the same edition. She would have been pleased with the tidiness of it all.

In my mail was an envelope containing two Polaroid snapshots. Dan Crandall beside the cairn of rocks he'd built in the desert, and another of his wife in the same pose. They were both smiling.

"I'm doing better," his note said. "Thanks for everything."

The other piece of mail bore a New Jersey postmark and

contained an appeal for contributions. A tax-deductible scholarship fund for girls wishing to attend one of the nineteen prestigious schools run by the Society of the Sacred Heart. The signature at the bottom of the letter was familiar. "Deirdre Eckels."

I phoned the social worker, Glenda Martin, and told her that Frankie Lopez was alive and probably in college somewhere, having graduated from a private high school in Albany, New York. Martin asked no questions, merely sighed with relief.

"Let me know if there's anything I can do to help with whatever this program is," she told me.

"I will," I said, and made a note to include Martin's address with my check to Deirdre Eckels. The network was expanding.

Later I walked Brontë far up Coyote Creek. It was still hot, but I sensed the slow drumming of autumn in the distance. Change. I could feel it in my bones.